VOLWYS
& OTHER STORIES.

BY
DOUGLAS THOMPSON

Published by
Dog Horn Publishing
45 Monk Ings, Birstall, Batley WF17 9HU
United Kingdom
doghornpublishing.com

ISBN 978-1-907133-88-6

Cover design by Douglas Thompson, adapted from photographs of Dresden and an altered version of a collage by Max Ernst from 'A Little Girl Dreams of Taking The Veil' (1930)

Typesetting by
Jonathan Penton

UK Distribution: Central Books
99 Wallis Road, London, E9 5LN, United Kingdom
orders@centralbooks.com
Phone:+44 (0) 845 458 9911
Fax: +44 (0) 845 458 9912

Overseas Distribution: Printondemand-worldwide.com
9 Culley Court
Orton Southgate
Peterborough
PE2 6XD
Telephone: 01733 237867
Facsimile: 01733 234309
Email: info@printondemand-worldwide.com

VOLWYS

& OTHER STORIES.

TABLE OF CONTENTS

TWENTY TWENTY

Darkness was falling and what was all the fuss about, Jakey wondered. One day was much like any other to him. You never could tell when the good breaks or bad were coming your way. Just keep your head down and push through the crowds, keeping one eye out for coppers, both kinds. He laughed at his own joke. These were the twin poles of his life: spare change and the police. For some mysterious reason the streets were particularly packed tonight and everyone he brushed up against seemed excited or angry about something.

Jakey skirted the outside of a throng of people gathered around some firebrand preacher. *The End of Days will be a fitting punishment for the wickedness of our times. Materialism, cynicism, nihilism. Beware the Beast in your midst. You bow and pray every night to your DJs and Talk-show Hosts and pouting Popstars, but I say to you that these impostors of the latter-day world shall all go on one path, into the grasp of the Devil, by God's will, into dark bitter torments...* Putting on his most pious and repentant face, Jakey squeezed his way through the bodies until he was closely packed like a sardine then began to gradually and quietly relieve everyone of their pocketbooks and bank cards.

Next he found his way to a political rally that was filling out the darkest corner of a large cobbled square below a gothic church covered in scaffolding. Activists with megaphones were whipping up the crowd towards a frenzy. Jakey pushed in earnestly, his brow furrowed with grave concern for the well-being of the nation, he felt hungry for democracy. *For decades our country has been polluted with Radiation and accidents have killed thousands while governments have covered it up, now the final insult: the democratic will of the people has been neatly sidestepped and we see that we have been hoodwinked by this political pantomime...* When the cheers went up and the bodies shifted Jakey helped himself to some particularly meaty wallets, yes he really felt the extent of their civic concern and generosity.

For days, there had been all this shouting and rallying going on and droves of Polis has been trying to herd Jakey and his ilk off the streets and off to the cells or the suburbs. He felt like the last scallywag in town, an institution by Christ, and was just admiring himself in the reflection of a shop window when as if from nowhere two Policemen, old "friends" of his, Muirhead and McWilliams suddenly materialised and put their heavy hands on his shoulder. It was Panda time again.

In the back of the car they laughed and shoved him about as they passed around the exotic credit cards they had found on his possession, even some Dollars and Euros. *Coming up in the world eh, Jakey? International Fucking Venture Capitalist are we now? Some tourist's holiday ruined by you, ya clatty shite.* As they drove, Jakey sat in the back, rattling his handcuffs and hating the annoying little hairs on the back of PC Muirhead's skull. As if feeling his gaze, Muirhead turned and sneered: *Are we sitting comfortably there then, your majesty?* Jakey was about to mutter in reply: *Then I'll begin,* when the streetlights and trafficlights flickered and went out and a second later they were all thrown sideways by a crushing impact.

*

Stella Ettrick, a sales rep who lived in her car, had found herself locked into a two-mile-an-hour traffic jam all afternoon, trying to get through the city centre. She even had a biker deliver a phone-in pizza to her window.

Now the computer game she had downloaded from the web came to an abrupt halt as her laptop crashed, its hard drive winding down into a series of grating clicks. The streetlights went out. Her digital notepad read gobbledegook instead of her customer database. Using the only number she could remember by heart she dialled her parents on her mobile but found the network was down.

Somebody was tooting their horn behind, trying to turn around. Ahead of her, a few drivers were finally getting out of their vehicles and talking.

A firework suddenly boomed overhead, and she jumped in her seat, biting her tongue. The angry blossom of light spread out, turned from cool blue to green to yellow to fiery red and all the time falling down and down towards her, closer and closer, filling the sky and blotting out the stars completely.

*

Jakey regained consciousness being dragged clear of the police car and laid out in a shop doorway. His head swam and he suddenly threw up onto the pavement beside him. Some passers-by were pulling PC McWilliams, unconscious, from the front of the upside down wreck. Somebody was prodding into the other side and saying: *his partner's had it, he's crushed...*

Jakey felt like he'd been out for hours, but evidently only minutes had gone by: this was confusing. With his wrists still hand-cuffed he sat up and wiped a little blood off his head onto his hands, moved his fingers and found his right foot twisted but not seriously. The small crowd of passers-by were moving over now, concentrating on the vehicle they had collided with; where a whole family, apparently unscathed, were being helped out in various stages of tears and trauma from the Chinese lantern that had been their car.

Jesus! –Jakey found himself calling out hoarsely, -*Don't just leave me here! Can someboady help me or get the key to these cuffs... ah mean man ah cannie fend fur masel like this...*

A number of cold disapproving stares turned towards him and he shrugged his shoulders and lay back on the pavement looking up at the stars which suddenly seemed to be blue and falling down then turning green and yellow. He closed his eyes, feeling nauseous again, wondering if he was dreaming.

He was next woken by the sound of a departing siren, and he sat up again: surprised to see that the good Samaritans had all moved on and left McWilliams behind lying on his back on the pavement. A raincoat had been draped over him covering his face: one of those curious human conventions that defy logical analysis. Jakey was shocked for a moment by the comparative silence, the suddenness, the finality of it all. He had been spared, grudgingly perhaps by this mysterious accident: and left here still sitting in chains. The streetlights were still out.

9

He tried to stand and stumbled slightly on his sprained foot and shuffled, hopped a bit and then on his knees made his way up to the body. His cuffed hands still shaking from the shock, he lifted the raincoat and searched for the keys to his chains. He heard voices, people approaching in the darkness. On an impulse he threw the raincoat over his shoulder and began dragging McWilliams' body backwards towards a doorway. Swearing to himself, biting his lips to keep silent he winced at the pain in his foot and desperately hauled until with one last heave McWilliams rolled over with him back into the close mouth. A crowd of drunken revellers ran past, singing and laughing.

His breath regained he pulled McWilliams back further past the stairs to the backcourt where a little pale light from the moon was falling onto the ground. He grappled around and found the key on McWilliams belt and with difficulty found a way to jam it upright and turn the lock on the handcuffs around it. Eventually they clicked open softly and he sighed, slowly lifting his hands up until they wavered in front of his face like long lost friends. He smiled. Then he focussed on McWilliams' face upside down, eyes closed, head resting unceremoniously in the dirt. A sad expression crept gently over Jakey's face for a moment.

A cat meowed somewhere and emerged from the darkness of the back court to stand in the moonlight and stop, distrustful, its huge luminous eyes glowing like fires looking up at Jakey. Its expression was cold and neutral. It seemed to be questioning him.

Jakey looked down at the dead body and then back at the cat: which nodded its head once and then slinked off into the night. Jakey swallowed hard as he felt some kind of resolution taking him over. He began unbuttoning McWilliams' clothing.

A few minutes later Jakey emerged from the close mouth in a police uniform and took the hat off and scratched his head. He picked up the raincoat that had covered McWilliams and pulled it on over his uniform. Finding the street relatively quiet again he produced his torch and ventured over to the wrecked Panda car. He fished around inside until he found a sealed transparent polythene bag and took out its contents: a wallet and a set of hotel room keys stolen from an American tourist a few hours earlier. Then hands in pockets, he walked off into the uncertain night.

To her horror, Stella now saw in her wing mirror that some of the abandoned cars behind her were drawing unwelcome interest from dubious-looking passers-by. Some young men in tracksuits and baseball caps, shockingly young perhaps had passed a particular vehicle several times on the pretext of looking for a way through the closely-packed cars to cross the road. Now looking around one last time, one of them reached for a stone lying in the gutter and hurled it through the driver's window as Stella watched, mouth open, heartbeat speeding up; pulse audible inside her own head.

An air of unreality was taking her over. How could she watch this frozen, as if it were television, entertainment?

Hands shaking, scrambling, keys falling from her hands she got herself out of the car, almost forgot to lock it, then hurried off down the nearest side street, not looking back. She moved in a curious indecisive stroll that constantly broke in and out of an attempt to sprint.

*

In Room 613 of the Holiday Inn, the only hotel with an emergency generator on this side of town, Jakey took off his raincoat and uniform and ran a hot bath. He opened the blinds and looked out over the whole city. There were patches of light where other generators in hospitals and government buildings were working, and a few fires billowing from shops and warehouses. Opening the windows he could hear the distant sounds of celebration, demonstration, criss-crossed with occasional emergency sirens.

He was confused at first by the lack of any buttons on the television set until giving up he sat down on the remote control and the set blinked on making him jump. Most of the channels seemed to be down with electrical interference although he was amused and heartened to find one station showing late night pornography.

After his wash Jakey stood in front of the mirror and using his host's trimmer and scissors began the slow process of reducing his profusion of unruly hair. He laughed as his full beard transformed into a fashionable goatee then into a buffalo bill moustache and finally disappeared altogether. His long hair he now also pruned mercilessly, astounded to see his whole face and character changing, gradually emerging as something new and strangely beautiful after years in gestation.

Finally his naked feet stood amid a pile of black hair and he gazed admiringly upon his new self. He turned his face from one side to the other, one hand held up to his cheek, exploring, noting how distinguished the lines on his face had become, how pronounced his cheekbones after years of outdoor undernourishment. He had the face of a hawk, an eagle now he thought. Not the soft ruminant eyes of one of the other millions: the defeated middle-aged Saturday-men, with their worries and wives and waistlines.

He donned his uniform with a ceremonial touch, like a toreador or a Roman gladiator. He put on his hat and looked for his new name on his lapels: he was PC Stanley McWilliams now. He stuck his jaw out stiffly, in a regimented quasi-military manner.

Touching curiously the toys on his belt, he jumped as the radio resumed its all-night commentary: ...*disturbance in Market Street, all units, Rodger Charlie Mike over...*

*

Finding a public telephone at last, Stella sighed with relief as she dialled her parents phone number. Through the glass door she could see a crowd at the end of the street moving slowly, political banners blowing, a few people running around out in front, throwing objects at the pavement, at shop windows, until one of them broke a window and an orange glow began to emanate from within.

Molotov Cocktails... -her mind was saying.

Just as this thought crystallised the tone in Stella's ear resolved itself into a computer voice, steely and cold: *I'm sorry, a temporary fault has suspended services in your area. Please try again later.*

Keeping one eye on the distant crowd, she hurriedly slipped out of the booth, hand shaking as she returned her purse to her bag, mind reeling, not entirely sure where she was heading or with what intent except back to the car.

Turning a corner back to the street near her car she collided with two teenagers in white shellsuits, the uniforms of juvenile delinquency. She cried out involuntarily, dropping her handbag to

12

the ground and all three of them: stunned and disconcerted for a second which seemed like an age, stared at each other wide-eyed.

*

Walking the streets Jakey found people looked at him differently.

A group of revellers, well-behaved outdoor drinkers really, became astonishingly quiet as he walked by them. He turned and saw that they had run off, so went back and picked up one of their bottles; a good strong cider. Continuing on his way, he took a long swig and tossed the empty over a wall.

Turning a corner, a middle-aged couple approached him in the dim twilight, their faces sweating and anxious: -*Officer, officer, there's LOOTING going on up there, there that way, are there more of you coming? Thank heavens you're here...*

He looked at them seriously and said in his most sombre voice: *Don't worry, it's all under control. Go to your homes.* He saw their faces relax slightly.

As he walked on, the woman called after him: -*but Officer, you're going the wrong way, they're up on the High Street...*

Oh be quiet Agnes, the man must know what he's doing, -her husband muttered and led her off.

Despite his best efforts to keep a low profile, Jakey soon stepped out of an alleyway to find himself in the middle of another disturbance, having walked in the opposite direction from the first one.

He stopped and hesitated, about to move back into the darkness. But the eyes of the crowd only rested on him for a second before they all scarpered, vanishing almost magically like melting frost. An old man dropped a crate of beer onto the broken glass underfoot and fled empty-handed. Various other figures disappeared with piles of leather jackets clutched to their chests.

Jakey stepped forward into the regained silence, and knelt in a jewellers shop window, raking amongst the glass and silver with his torchlight. He found a silver locket on a chain, gold wedding rings. Things that might have meant something to respectable people. He pocketed these, and running his torch over the remaining debris concluded that most of the good stuff was gone already.

Walking on he heard another crowd closing in and turned up an alleyway to escape. Suddenly his ears were filled with alien sounds: some kind of scuffle was going on. Before his eyes could adjust or he could reach for his torch somebody grabbed him by the lapels and forced him up against a wall. *What's your fuckin' game, mate? Jist keep yer fuckin' trap shut and back off right outta here...*

Jakey could smell the guy's breath he was so close, but sensed by his voice that he was quite young, more afraid than him. He could see a knife glinting near his face and make out now that a woman was struggling on the ground and another youth had his hand over her face, was ripping at her clothes, trying to rape her.

Then the youth holding him accidentally disturbed Jakey's belt with his other hand and the distinctive sound of the police radio rang out into the guilty hush. *Jesus Fuck!* –the boys were startled and the woman bit her assailant on the neck. He fell back, screaming like a child. *He's fuckin' Polis man, beat it, run ya eejit ye!*

They were gone. Jakey had done nothing. He continued to stand in the darkness for a moment breathing easily as the woman wept on the cobbled pavement at his feet. Curious, he put his torch on and walked towards her. Without making any conscious action he found that she had reached out and he had helped her to her feet. She fell against him and actually embraced him for a second before stepping back, sweeping her hair out of her tearful eyes. He looked at her without any emotion, neutral.

Oh thanks... Jesus... thank God... those bastards... they'd have raped me.... My car's stuck. I'm stranded. Oh God I didn't know what to do. The whole place seems to be going to pieces tonight. Can you get me out of here, help me, just get me to somewhere safe to stay even?

You'dve been awright... -Jakey said, turning away bored now, *-those wee twats probably wouldnae huv been able to get it up anyroad. Gotta go now, sorry...*

Stella was stunned for a moment as he walked off, then coming to her senses pursued him out into the street, the moonlight. *But you must do something to help me!* –she said, clattering after him in her suddenly inappropriate heels.

Irritated, he turned and looked at her: *-Look at ye... dressed like yon...*

She looked down and saw she was wearing a black miniskirt, white stockings, torn now, her work gear.

Nae wunder they thought ye wur up fur it. –He shook his head and laughed to himself and walked on.

She kept after him: -*But please help me, can you take me to the station at least? Shouldn't you be doing that? Taking my name and a statement?*

Jakey stopped in front of a jewellers shop and eyed it carefully, then without bothering to look at Stella, continued: -*Miss, ah don't think you get the story here… ah've goat a joab tae dae. Bizness like.*

Well yes I can imagine you're all overstretched tonight… -Her voice trailed off as Jakey smashed the window and the alarm began wailing. She stared down, wide-eyed, her ears hurting from the noise, but too disconcerted to move away. Jakey walked about inside, scanning with his torch, and choosing the most promising pieces for his pockets.

Moving on, Stella stepped after him, her heart hollow and tired: -*Who are you? What kind of policeman are you anyway?* She was almost talking to herself now, staring at the pavement, when to her surprise Jakey walked back and faced her.

Make yersel' useful… -he said.

She thought to herself he was quite handsome really, a rough diamond, as he pushed handfuls of jewellery into both her pockets and gestured to her to follow him. When some more revellers were startled by Jakey, he picked up the pure vodka they had left and drank a good mouthful straight from the bottle and passed it back to Stella who walked behind him like a shy orphan. He had some kind of plan clearly, and anyone with any idea at all was surely worth following on a night as black as this.

The bells of St. Giles rang out as they passed and she noticed that he spat on the *Heart Of Midlothian.*[1] Stella lifted her eyes up towards the moonlit castle and remembered that she should have been celebrating New Year tonight. Taking another swig of hard spirits she hurried on to catch up with her nameless saviour and into her first day of *Twenty Twenty.*

---

1   A stone mosaic on the pavement of Edinburgh's Royal Mile, which passers-by still spit on in a sign of solidarity with the prisoners who used to be held there.

DOGBOT™

Shareef should never have left the safety of the mountains. He knew that now, too late, like all the best ideas and second chances. Up there, the American robot would have been slow and struggled with all the sharp rocks and vertiginous surfaces. He might even have got lucky and made it slide off a crumbling precipice, although of course it would have retracted into an indomitable ball then resumed its pursuit of him undeterred, as now, slow, methodical, untiring, dogged. Yes, the demonic thing was well-named. With his pocket spyglass, beloved accessory for observing roadside bombs blowing up American convoys, he had read its serial number: DogBot™-587-a-HH-009c. As a youthful student on holiday in the land of the unbelievers he had learned their effete language and seen their admiration for their canines. Animals they fed fat as themselves, treated like kings in their palatial homes, while their poor and crippled starved in the streets. Such was their irony, their inability to see themselves, or to see God, the all merciful, the all-knowing.

Their aerial drones had pin-pointed his cave and begun bombarding it. And with neither Mahmoud nor Ali on hand to help him unblock the rear exit, he had had little choice but to leave on the next moonless and overcast night, and pick his way down to the valley floor. Down there, he had assumed at first that Dogbot was a distant truck going off-road, -or struggling to grasp its scale- some bizarre children's toy. But it was deadly serious. He told himself it was headed elsewhere and crossed into a different valley, but awoke the next morning with a sickening lurch in his stomach and the sound of its weird mechanical whinings uncomfortably near. That had been a close call and the flamethrower and automatic rounds it applied to the bush he had just been sleeping in: all the warning he needed that his nemesis was at large.

Then he had run and run, panicking, sweating, urinating down his legs rather than lose ground, for mile after mile. Then for a while, he had told himself that he was worrying unduly. Dogbot's top speed was far below his own; he could see him far back through his spyglass, miles behind. But time and again this respite and consolation would prove short-lived. Slowly it dawned on him how it worked, and he grasped the evil genius of the American scientist who had designed such a wonder. Dogbot did not sleep. Dogbot did not tire. Dogbot never lost the scent. Dogbot didn't need to run any faster.

Water, he tried water. At this time of year, the rivers coming from the mountains to the plains were swollen. Remembering the local tips of Amir and Hassim (where were they now, he wondered) he found the safest place to cross, but to do so had to place himself in plain sight, away from the sparse vegetation, where Dogbot would soon have him in view. He wondered what the range of its weapons were, but surely something the size of a dog must be travelling light, could not muster large-calibre shells or rockets from its body, only bullets and flames. But of course it could also talk to its friends in the sky, the drone planes. It had many friends it seemed, its electronic brethren, while he had so few now.

He made it over the river, nearly falling twice, remembering at last to turn to face the raging current, basic survival skills. Was he forgetting even his own training now, a silly old man, or just driven stupid by panic and fear? Terror. He made it over to the other side of the valley just as Dogbot got him in sight. He ran through the trees and through another two streams before the drones came over, shelling the wrong spot. But Dogbot crossed the river effortlessly, rolling himself into a ball, floating down river, across river, then unfolded himself rapidly at the other side, grasping the stone with a grip surer than any hound or human. Shareef half wanted to applaud, as if clapping at his own funeral. His enemy, the *Great Satan* of The West, was the Devil indeed it seemed, with all the demons and hellish henchmen he needed. But he had not expected to encounter such horrors, in this life or the next.

It came to Shareef after this that he had no choice but to turn south and run towards civilisation, the Golden City, the home of the

President, his one-time benefactor and protector, secret supporter, pretend friend of the Americans, man with two mouths, state statue with two faces. In the city surely many people would still welcome Shareef and his great noble cause, grant him sanctuary in their homes and their places of prayer. But where, even there, would such walls of brick and mortar provide any protection against Dogbot? How did Dogbot work? Perhaps in a crowd, in one of the open squares on market day crowded with a thousand people, Dogbot would become confused, unable to decide who to kill, unable to differentiate Shareef from a hundred of his fellows? Did it have his scent, his facial features, his fingerprints locked up in its metal head, in its hard-wired memory?

He had tried before, but one last time he waited for Dogbot at the top of a cliff and tossed his last hand-grenades down upon it as it passed below, followed by a burst of machine gun fire, saving only a few remaining rounds. The cloud of dust cleared and the things unravelled like a hedgehog, metal hissing and clicking of impenetrable armour, red eyes looking up to find his perch. He told himself it could not feel anger or seek revenge. It was only a machine. But the American man who had built it, cunning scientist of liberal politics perhaps, morally lax, perhaps even he had harboured hatred in his heart for Shareef, and gifted it, like the drop of blood from a sorcerer's finger, to bring this devil-dog to life and drive it ever on against him.

*

When he reached the outskirts of the city he had been running flat out for almost two days. Dogbot had passed out of sight at last in the heat haze of the far horizon as he moved over the great arid plains, the northern snow-capped peaks behind him in the distance, his eagle's nest now lost, his fate soon to be in the balance in the hands of the good people of this, his adopted nation.

He kept his face wrapped in his robes, the desert sand still on him, as he knocked on his first door asking for alms, a poor beggar who had not eaten for days. *For the love of God...* With the speed of a tiger he pushed open the door and closed it behind him, drawing his pistol, confronting the woman of the household, one finger to his lips. When she took him to her husband, he unveiled his face and the man's eyes widened in wonder and terror. *God the merciful! God is great! Can it be so? Shareef The Great Avenger, come in from the wilderness? Where has God hidden you all this time? By His Grace you have evaded the Americans even yet! God be praised!*

Shareef smiled, but not too much. He tried not to reveal his agonising hunger, his weakness, his terrible need for shelter, warmth, respect, and love, yes, even that. In the eyes of this simple man, salt of the good earth, he sensed that he must maintain the guise of a living god, an avenging angel, carrier of the hopes of a resurgent faith. He ate with them that night and blessed their children, introduced as a distant uncle. But after he had gone to bed in their attic he woke an hour later to overhear urgent whispers, and instinctively, he reached for his gun.

The mother was talking, pleading: *He is a murderer.... of innocent men, women and children, unborn babies, children beautiful and innocent as our own, gifts from God....*

No... her husband begged, *do not say such terrible things aloud, woman, I beg you. He is a soldier in a great war against ungodly soldiers who defile our country and our faith...*

*No...*she countered. *Have you not seen the films of it, the bombs, the blood, the people in pieces, torn to shreds? Ordinary people such as you and I? Innocent, going about their business and doing no harm, loving each other and their families, loved by God. Does the book not say that all people are God's children and loved by Him as we love ours? Who commits such abominations is Satan himself and you, foolish man, have welcomed him in under the roof of this house!*

And does he look like the Devil? Has he such horns and claws? Has he? He is a man... only a man... who asks of us only our hospitality which we are obliged by honour and tradition to grant...

Shareef scarcely slept for the rest of the night and left in the early morning, before first light, while his hosts still snored in their cots. He looked at their sleeping children, gun in his hand, as he made his way to the door. Something in their untroubled faces made him halt for a second, falter, a tremble in his legs. He wished he had slept longer, envying them their peace, their innocence.

He walked for a few hours before Dogbot caught up with him. He had forgotten how vast the Golden City was. Perhaps it had grown, its outskirts constantly expanding. The crowds and markets and daily hubbub had begun to remind him happily of his youth.

He talked to strangers, traders, street children, always keeping his face slightly hidden like a shy bride. He shook hands as he bartered for food and gave alms to beggars, stroked the back of beasts of burden and threw seed to birds. He blessed all that he saw under God's good sun and wished that he could start again and take up an anonymous place within it, if God but willed it to be so. Tired, drowsy, he had even begun to wonder if he had imagined Dogbot –if Dogbot might not be some diseased figment of his imagination, a projection, a spectre of his own terror that he must turn and face.

But the gunfire and explosions soon put paid to that wistful notion, and cruelly woke him up. He ran into the market crowds as he had planned, hoping to confuse Dogbot who he presumed would not fire indiscriminately and wound civilians. That was how the Americans talked after all, of combatants and non-combatants, of the guilty and the innocent, as if such categories could be determined by men rather than God. But Dogbot played by the Devil's rules, it seemed, or he had no rules at all, only murder in his heart and an appetite for the blood of Shareef , at any price. Dogbot shot and burned and lobbed explosive charges. Shareef ran and ran, pushing through the screaming crowds, climbed up stairs, kicked down doors, then clambered out onto the rooftops, and looked back down briefly onto the square where Dogbot walked methodically through the carnage he had caused. The screams had subsided and a terrible deathly silence hung in the air with the smoke and the smell of blood. Dogbot walked over the bodies of children, women, his feet on faces and hands and eyes. He had no respect, no faith, no heart. These were Shareef's people but to Dogbot they were all without meaning, all people were equally worthless. He made no distinctions. Only Shareef mattered to him. Only his blood would do.

Shareef found a station and jumped on a train, but the army apprehended him one stop down the line, took him from the carriage as he looked over his shoulder out the window, sweating, panicking, wondering how far Dogbot was behind, muttering to himself like a madman. Shareef didn't even notice the other passengers all gasping and exclaiming as they recognised him. Shareef cared only about Dogbot now. Feared only Dogbot. Dogbot was his world.

He thought the soldiers would respect him when he said the President's name, asked for special privileges. But once out of sight of the crowds, they kicked and spat on him, broke his teeth, pulled him by the hair, then shaved all his hair off, cursed him as a murderous dog, a disgrace upon the nation. They laughed at his genitals and stuck a gun barrel in his mouth, showed him photographs of the dead bodies of his friends, tortured and executed. Then they put him in a helicopter and flew him six miles south to the police headquarters.

*

In the middle of the night, Shareef heard explosions and gunfire and stood up in his cell. Dogbot had found the prison and was shooting the guards one by one, blasting his way in through all the locks and gates. Shareef pissed himself in terror and scraped his fingernails against the solid walls until they broke, tried to squeeze himself through the iron bars until his ribs nearly cracked, cried out again and again to God until his voice was hoarse and shrill as a child's, until he knew in his heart that God had never existed after all or had decided in His anger to feed Shareef to the devil as one would a hamster to a snake. It was all to no avail. A great rain of white spittle came firing in through the bars of the cell window and fell upon him, like the contempt of God. He was doomed. He was damned. Then Dogbot lurched around the corner and halted, looked at him through the bars with his vicious glowing red eyes, then knelt down and began drinking the puddles of his piss like a cat with a saucer of cream.

*

Shareef woke up with a start, crying out in terror, to find the guards laughing at him through the bars of his prison cell. And yet he smiled, relieved to see that he had only been dreaming and that Dogbot had not yet caught up with him. But it seemed to him also that his dream had revealed in code a powerful secret, the method by which Dogbot had been tracking him and might yet be evaded. This knowledge filled him with hope and a strange spiritual peace, even as his captors entered his cell and prepared to have him led through the streets to meet the President before his execution, to have him reviled and spat upon by every citizen who would line the streets of the Golden City.

22

On an inspired impulse that puzzled his tormentors, he stripped off his rags of clothes to stand naked, and asked only that water be given him intermittently as he walked past the taunts and jeers of the crowds. He took care to move slowly and never break a sweat. Winter was nearly upon the province and a chill north wind from the mountains kept him ice cold despite the November sunshine. When missiles were thrown occasionally, he took great care to dodge them and never to be grazed or shed blood. Thus his aspect remained attentive, circumspect, constantly eyeing the crowd around him with calm calculation, which inflamed their contempt for him all the more.

And yet somewhere behind this screen of bawling hatred, the masque of embittered faces, he knew that others lurked. Those who had always admired and supported his campaign against the government, his vision of battle against the great Satan that was America, yes. But still others also, a new constituency, like those few new friends he had inadvertently made along the way as he stumbled through the city in terrorized flight from the relentless pursuit of the hellish robot dog from America. People who had seen that although he was a living figurehead of something heroic, or demonic depending on their viewpoint, yet he was something else also: a living man whose mother had once loved him, who sweated and wept and hoped and loved as any other man, a son of the one God, all merciful, all knowing, who deserved pity and succour as any other.

By the time Shareef reached the walls of the Presidential Palace he was covered from shaved head to toe in human spittle, and he had turned obligingly like a suckling lamb on a spit roast to ensure that this vile coating was even. The soles of his feet he dipped carefully in a puddle of wet horse manure at the gates, before the guards took him in, bidding calm farewell to the jeers and curses.

As he climbed the steps above the parapet he saw the far horizon, then in the foreground heard explosions and saw small fires igniting in the streets about a mile away. He smiled in strange pleasure, glad now to know that Dogbot had not been a deranged spectre of his imagination, and calculated the time he had left.

The President faced him in his grand marble-lined reception room, standing ten feet from him, regarding at last the object of his contempt, his secret respect, his two-faced embarrassment.

23

Shareef, may the Prophet have mercy on you at this hour. Have you cleansed your heart and soul in preparation to be received into His bosom? Do you not wish to wash yourself, be divested of all the dirt and filth of the streets before I take you to the firing squad?

There are many, Your Excellency, who say it is the devil who awaits me...

Not I, Shareef. God knows I have shielded you in this country from the fool Americans for as long as was seemly. You had many a chance to flee our borders before now. Had you thrown yourself at my feet even a year ago I might gladly have hid you again as a brother. But times have changed and to spare your neck now would be to bring terrible punishment, fire from the sky, onto all the innocent and devout children of God who throng this city. Would you have such a sin on my hands and yours?

Indeed not, esteemed brother in God. I am aware of my inevitable fate now and I freely accept it.

Then I am glad. God be praised... The President smiled, then turned his head at the sound of explosions at the outer walls, shouts in the nearby corridors. *What is that commotion, by all the stars in Heaven? Not brigands come to save you, surely? –I cut all their supplies a year ago and granted them gold to hand in their guns...*

Let your heart be at peace in your chest, dear leader, it is only the people celebrating my imminent demise with machine gun fire trained skyward.

A further explosion sounded then gunfire and screams in the corridor outside and the President and his guards jumped in terror. Shareef timed his next move with pinpoint accuracy. He had learned that from Dogbot these last weeks, with a grudging respect for his formidable adversary. Precision was everything, as was economy of movement, of energy. *Your Excellency!* he called out and the President glanced back to receive a gelatinous globule of Shareef's spittle of extraordinary size, full frontal to the face.

The doors burst open in a tornado of wood splinters, followed by the whirring of Dogbot's actuators and hydraulic fluid, the heavy clunk of his metal paws upon the fine marble floor, the shuffling of his guns and optical range finders.

In his hazed electronic sight drained by combat, Dogbot gazed on two men, or was it many? His nasal receptors drew greedily on the air. On the left, a figure composed of the DNA of three thousand, seven hundred and eighty-four ordinary citizens, and on the right a tall thin unidentified adult male with the face of Shareef Al-Sharia.

He opened fire and annihilated his target in a hail of bullets and flame, then shut himself down, his legs buckling like an exhausted athlete crossing the finishing line. He ejected his battery pack, pouring its acid over himself as an accelerant and used his last few volts of power to heat his own circuitry to burning point and set fire to the growing pool of fluid around him. All this as programmed, to remove the risk of retro-engineering by any enemy intelligence agency.

Shareef too slumped to the floor, naked and in chains, shivering at last. He cried abundant tears, but not all of relief perhaps. The guards left alive around him, like headless chickens now, were making their way towards Shareef again with stunned expressions. Dogbot's face had looked so human, close up at last. Impossible wish though it seemed, he might have benefited from so impressive a friend in times like these.

THEONAE

Everything has to begin somewhere, but particularly stories. Beginnings are easy, but endings? Where life is concerned isn't there always the possibility that something just about to happen will change completely the meaning of everything that has gone before? -A life of menial drudgery made heroic by some unexpected but well-earned reward? -A dull marriage transformed in memory into a period of demeaning enslavement by the arrival of a lover, a soul-mate of rejuvenating power?

The snow is falling now and I rest by the high windows, stripping down my rifle, cleaning the bolt and chamber, jotting in my diary from time to time. My brown-haired wife shuffles about the ruined room on her crippled leg, picking up scraps of food to feed the dogs. But truth be told, we might have to eat the dogs next week. I haven't the heart to tell her. Philipa's eyes are dead, not from hunger or cold, but from something else. From love, or the death of it, from what I killed there over the years with my adventures, my philandering.

Should I blame Theonae for that? Her followers would call that blasphemy, but I never bought any of that. She was always flesh and blood to me. And now this strange child in the crib behind me. Oh, if only they knew about that. How they'd come prowling and genuflecting, bringing wondrous gifts. Please. Spare me. We went there before once, didn't we? -And see where it got us all. I'm tired now.

Philipa leans over to check on the baby in its makeshift cot, made from broken-up pallets, and warmed by a gas burner in this miserable cold. The child is wrapped in the fur of a fox, one I killed when I found it feeding on bodies in the street. I appreciate

Philipa caring for it, I really do. The baby is not even hers, not even human, strange to say. And yet it is mine. The maternal instinct is capable of caring for many things, of transcending so many other less charitable emotions. Perhaps there is hope for us after all, so long as these primal forces keep going like hidden machinery, rumbling like trains in tunnels passing under our feet.

The building shakes. An explosion outside. Gunfire. My hand tenses on my rifle. Time to load up. I measured the baby again today when I woke up, like I have every other day these last two weeks. I've checked the old textbooks that I found in the burned-out public library. I'm certain that she's growing at three to four times the normal rate. And still she makes no sound. A mute. Philipa and I don't talk about any of this, but I know she's noticed too. We never had any children of our own to make comparisons to, but those weird blue eyes say it all, and the objects that get mysteriously thrown across the room.

*

Like September The Eleventh or the shooting of JFK, almost everyone remembers where they were or what they were doing when they first saw Theonae Aeaea and what she could do. A talent show contest. Of all the banal things on this earth. But maybe that was why. The ratings, the viewers. The chance to shock and shatter our complacency.

There she was, after the singing trapeze from Madrid, and before the roller-skating barbers of Berlin. Except no one ever got to see the hairdressers in light of what happened next. Mind-reading, telepathy, a bit of telekinesis thrown in. *A magic act then, all done with smoke and mirrors, yawn, yawn…* Was probably how the producers had noted it. Boy were they in for a shock.

I can't remember what props and scenery she had on stage, but they were only decoys. Her act was no act. She pointed at the jug of water in front of one of the judges and made it lift into the air from a distance of about fifteen feet. She held it over the head of Walt Peterman, the famous boy-band impresario, and using what must have been remote hypnosis, made him strip off his clothes and stand on his chair shivering while the water poured itself over him.

28

You would have thought that there would have been cheering and jeering at that, but already there was fear in the audience, the unsettled feeling that what was happening was not normal or rehearsed. Next Sharon Knowles, in a similar trance, got down on the floor and started licking Louis Welsh's shoes, while he opened his zip and masturbated. The uproar was instantaneous, stage hands and executives running around but somehow Theonae had even paralysed the cameramen.

Infamously, as would later be the basis of a series of law suits, the other female judge Amanda Dolton, launched herself into the audience and sexually assaulted various ecstatic young men in front of their partners, the subsequent legal dubiety resting on whether all the incidents were truly non-consensual, and to what extent hypnosis was genuinely involved. Other members of the audience were then made to variously: perform a Mexican wave, bleat like sheep, urinate in their chairs, and run away headlong into the walls.

Do I need to describe Theonae herself? –Subsequently such a well-known public figure? As I watched live television at home, my jaw dropped and the pizza burned itself to death in the oven. Theonae wore only a simple white linen dress, bare feet, long blonde curly hair, unkempt. She struck me at that moment as the most impossibly beautiful woman I had ever seen, her mischievous smile and laughing, savage, blue eyes. I got a hard-on the size of a rolling pin just watching that programme, but so did everyone else I'll bet. Philipa and I never discussed it, but judging how early we went to bed that night, I'd say she got wet.

*

I make Philipa comfortable in the basement, reminding her to bolt and brace the door, and of my secret signal to watch out for on my return: three knocks then a fourth. Her eyes are full of hatred for me, or would be if there was any room amongst all that pain and fear. She blames me for the broken leg. Not getting her medical attention before it set wrongly. But at least she's alive. She doesn't seem to grasp that she owes me that. But who cares. I'm not God, and no one can sue me or jail me now for anything I do now, let alone say.

I was a reporter once, you see. How ironic. I used to travel all over the planet to find war and suffering, like some kind of psychic pornographer. But here I am, on my own doorstep at last, with a ringside seat in the ultimate horror show, my own country. And I still carry a camera, as well as a gun. Not just as a talisman either, a reminder of my life before. No, sick though it undoubtedly sounds, I still film what I find out here then upload it to what's left of the world wide web, and get paid eventually, through intermediaries, in bread and pork fat. But I'm not impartial anymore, how can I be? I have to kill people now, or they'd kill me, just to survive. I don't remember Kate Adie or John Simpson doing that, do you?

Another explosion. Gunfire past my ear. I crouch down and retreat into an alleyway, hold my breath and wait. I've become very patient this last year, and good at keeping still. Maybe journalism taught me that, how to lie in wait for a good story, a scoop, or now: a good clear shot, a perfect kill. The snow falls out of leaden clouds and slowly covers me like a blanket where I kneel. Like a cold and killing kiss from the sky, from God herself.

*

I used to think I lived in airports. Indeed, I would often feel extraordinarily happy in them. My theory was that it was because everyday life is suspended there, under the spell of some romantic myth of travel. In airports, we float ecstatically between the past and the future, between responsibility and freedom. I always felt I might be travelling towards something new and unexpectedly marvellous there, an award, an insight, a great new turn of events that my life might be about to follow. Airports are the future and hope made manifest, crystallised into architectural form (both terminals and aeroplanes). Rather than merely waiting for our futures to happen, as is our usual lot in life, in airports we are granted concrete action (tickets, luggage, flight), and the exhilarating illusion of doing the future to ourselves, bringing it on.

Why Greece? My editor Dan Cartwright wanted me to check out Theonae Aeaea's past, her home village where she grew up, her schoolmates, old boyfriends. He wanted background. Theonae was big news by then, on TV shows in every country, presenting a sparkling image of herself, and Dan wanted grit and dirt, the real person behind this burgeoning new myth, this mushroom cloud of media-hype that seemed to dazzle and blind everyone who encountered her.

For the best part of two months I travelled all over Greece, checking out parish records, municipal inventories of births and deaths, educational certificates, local newspaper stories. I hired various translators and interpreters as I went, the Greek alphabet being a substantial obstacle, even after I had mastered some fairly fluent verbal basics. I won't pretend I didn't enjoy that time. It was Winter going into Spring, beautiful blue skies but not too hot yet. The incredible Aegean (Homer's *wine-dark sea*) filling the horizon as I wound up and down mountain roads in hired vehicles and sampled the peaceful atmosphere of those remote places where old men sit on chairs in market squares all day, playing with their worry beads, their faces as lined and scarred as sea cliffs, ancient, all-knowing. But none of them knew Theonae, or had ever even heard of her.

I braced myself to finally impart this news over the phone to Dan. The story was there was no story. Theonae Aeaea had never existed. Not here at least, in Greece. Her entire past, her name even, must be a fabrication, but a cover for what? Instead of answers for Dan, I would be giving him back an even bigger, different question.

Dan told me over the phone that Theonae had finally agreed to submit herself to medical tests, the previous week, in an attempt to silence her critics and doubters. She wanted to claim the famous James Randi prize for incontrovertible evidence of the paranormal, intending to donate the money to charity. By now, to everyone's surprise, just two years on from her first appearance, Theonae had declared herself a candidate in the British parliamentary elections. Some people had laughed at first, then remembered Sebastian Coe, Glenda Jackson, Ronald Reagan, Arnold Schwarzenegger. Everyone knew Theonae was smarter than any of those people. Her IQ was off the scale, her command of English, not to mention Greek, French, German, Spanish and Italian was flawless, better than the locals.

I was sitting watching one of her interviews on CNN in my hotel room in Athens, when Dan phoned me back, having digested my revelation of earlier that day. *Rob? She's going to be on a yacht off Malta.*

Who? I asked sleepily.

Who d'you think? He laughed. *All that sunlight and olives gone to your brains? Her telepathic majesty, Theonae Aeaea. She's taking a short break from her election campaign, with her closest coterie of advisors. I phoned her agent and told her you were in the area and she*

31

jumped at the chance. I've got you a slot with her, interviewing her on her yacht tomorrow. I'm booking the flights right now. You OK for an early start, fly Air Malta?

Sure, Dan, sure, well done, that's quite a scoop.

Damn right it is, dude, so don't let me down. Here's your second chance to get that big break I sent you out there for.

Asshole, asshole, a voice inside me screamed. One day I would punch Dan out flat in a dark alley somewhere, I was saving myself for it, a future treat to make it all worthwhile, it had got me through many a bad night so far. But this was exciting. Theonae had amassed a large amount of money in a very short time. As well as all the TV appearances, the rumours went that this wealth had been achieved through lottery syndicates and horse betting, as well as stock market speculation, all based on her powers of short-term prophecy. A private yacht, a personal jet to go with it. It was hard to believe it was just election as an MP she was running for, it already felt presidential. Her newly-founded "Consensus Party" were making huge strides in the opinion polls.

I put down the phone and listened carefully to the rest of Theonae's interview. Someone had just asked her about Capitalism and currency crashes:

The problem with our world, with our collective human society is that although we, human beings, have created it, no one feels they can control it any longer. This is a logical absurdity caused by a lack of telepathy in the world.

How do you mean? –the interviewer crossed his legs, repressing an erection.

Well, it's only lack of trust, lack of communication, doubt, fear, that stops us all agreeing what our problems are, then acting upon a solution. We have reached a point in human evolution where diverse individuality, although it got us here, cannot now carry us forward. A fundamental change is needed, or mankind will simply drift apart and dissolve into selfishness, sliding back again into violent chaos.

What is that change?

Edward, she said, and put her hand on his knee (his eyes melted with unconditional love), *there are disabled people surfing the world wide web right now, this very second, direct from their brains via neural implants. The web has become the world's brain, and everyone will soon be plugged into it as directly and intimately as those people.*

32

Your point is?

My point is, that __is__ telepathy. I am here to help people prepare their minds for how to cope with that. A kind of psychological singularity. The human mind has long held the latent ability to communicate telepathically, as I have demonstrated by example. We need to re-awaken that desire and practice it now, or when the web-brain event horizon occurs people will be damaged and deranged by it. What's about to happen is incredibly beautiful, but it's also potentially terribly dangerous. Our technology can only ever be an extension and amplification of ourselves, and if those selves aren't sufficiently prepared and advanced then we will be opening the gates of Hell with this invention, as with every other one before. The human id must be conquered and trained now, before we go any further. We can no longer hang around waiting for Nature to help us evolve at the slow speed of biological time, we must make ourselves evolve now, in real time.

You talk like a prophet sometimes, Miss Aeaea. Do you worry about the recent accusations in certain sections of the media that you and your followers are turning into a religious cult?

Edward, she laughed, baring her perfect white teeth and flicking her hair from her forehead like golden wheat, *Do I look like Jesus to you?*

*

Here they come at last then, enter stage right. As I thought, it's a medium-sized one, ten people, or what's left of their bodies, in a circle, heads pressed together like a rugby scrum, twenty legs. The footprints they leave on the snow are perverse, astonishing, they spin and turn silently, like some sombre party game, children lost to their mothers, to the world.

Their bodies are naked, stained with faeces and urine, their mouths and eyes sewn shut, heads shaven bald. Some still have hands and arms free. Most have lost their arms, their shoulders sewn and fused into those of their partners. They rotate and slide forward and back, moving erratically, crablike. I've seen some as small as fours or sixes. Last week I saw a fifty, a hundred legs, a true centipede, before it was hunted down and slaughtered by the snipers.

And now the bullets start again, even a grenade thrown. Time for me to act. Maybe the ten knew I was here. Their sight

33

is disembodied, an invisible node of remote viewing that roams about restlessly. Perhaps they wanted me to help, it's hard to say. The snipers never expect me. *A turkey shoot,* the brutes call it, laughing, as the naked heads of the circle nestle together, shivering, tensing, wondering how to misdirect their assailants.

Occasionally the prey try to save themselves, and this is one occasion. One rifle is lifted out of the hands of the sniper holding it. The muzzle of another gun is slowly bent round. I can feel the air shuddering, thick with their energy. If only the circles could bring themselves to kill and maim. That is their weakness, but I have no such qualms.

Now. I stand up and take aim quickly, with practised precision, at one sniper, then the next. Then run from the shadows, to drive home my success. I kneel and cut the wounded one's throat, then find a few more around the corner. I toss a grenade and wait. Boom. Behind me I can feel the circle screaming silently, appalled by the bloodshed. Sometimes I want to turkey-shoot them myself, for their sheer silly inappropriateness for this world. But I understand what they mean, what they're here for, the future they foretell. I kill my own kind to protect them, for them, for Theonae. Silence again. And snow keeps falling, onto the newly-spilled blood. And I film those I have killed, weeping. A newsreel for the world, of our civil war. *My* civil war. Impartial, my arse.

The ten have moved on but I follow their tracks then find them cowering in an underground car park. I try to usher them out, pointing to the distant forest, the wilderness. *Go there!* I shout and point. *Save yourselves!* And they rotate in one direction then the next, foreheads tensing and frowning. Forming and condensing new thoughts. Suddenly I feel an invisible punch in my chest and am thrown backwards into the snow. They shuffle off proudly, blindly. Thanks a lot, guys. Don't mention it.

The eye, their eye, still watches me as I see them move away, blinking. Does it understand? –Whose side I'm on? -Do I? I see their group eye as red. I don't know why, since I never see it in any physical sense, but it always strikes me like that. A red sphere of watchful energy, pulsing like the setting sun of a winter dawn. Like the blood on the driven snow.

*

34

A speedboat took me the final stage of the journey over to meet Theonae, and I noticed the pilot wore a strange uniform, which he explained was worn by her private staff. I chuckled to myself. I was reminded for a moment of a James Bond movie or the infamous shenanigans of L Ron Hubbard and his harem, avoiding Interpol in the 1960's. I wondered if I'd find her "expecting me", wearing a monocle and stroking her pussy. Dream on, Rob old boy.

Behind us the bleached white monuments of Valetta loomed up out of the shimmering waves like ancient bones, and I thought of my father coming here during the war, fighting Hitler and Dönitz, dodging the U-Boats. For a moment I had the sense that what I was involved with was just as momentous, the next chapter of human history.

The "staff" who greeted me, lounging around Theonae's sixty-foot yacht, were all barefoot in white robes. Nobody was drinking alcohol. If this was a party, it was like none I had ever seen before. A political party, maybe. But everyone seemed energised, and "whitewashed" is the only word I can find for it, although brainwashed might be what I'm really reaching for. Inculcated, sublimated, subsumed into some larger context, which absorbed them utterly. I could hear laughter and chatter from a group at the bow, clear beautiful feminine sounds like birdsong, but it was free of the menace and frivolity of drunkenness, it sounded rather, like something more natural and ancient like waterfalls and church bells.

An immaculate young man, terrifyingly handsome, led me through to Theonae's cabin, where she sat behind a desk, like the captain of the ship, writing in her diary. She stood up and came over to greet me, light from the window hitting her golden hair and making her smile light up like sparkling waves.

Robert, she said, and held onto the hand I had offered her. *Rob, and Robbie also I see, to different people at different times.* She leaned closer and her face and hair seemed to close off the room behind her. Her huge eyes, owl-like and vivacious, burrowed into my soul. I felt violated, as she spoke in a lower and more intimate tone by the second. *So much journeying to get here, all your life in fact, and different things to different people, like a multifaceted coin, always hiding yourself. Don't be afraid.*

I tried to free my hand, and let out a strange little cry, but instead of letting go, to my astonishment she leaned in closer still

35

and kissed me with her gorgeously full lips. Her eyes were full of sadness for a moment as she read me like an open book. I felt my whole life, all my demons, hopes and regrets, were being replayed, downloaded in a second.

Then something even more extraordinary happened, and embarrassing to relate. She put a single hand on my cheek for only a second, then what I can only describe as an information burst of extreme eroticism was shot into my brain, a dizzying kaleidoscope of pornographic images and thoughts. I ejaculated into my pants. She let me go then and fell back laughing, and I felt humiliated, embarrassed. She had done this and knew she had done it, without ever making any actual sexual contact. *What the...* I spluttered.

It's OK, she laughed. *I felt sorry for you, don't be embarrassed. You men and your excitable little sticks. It's only natural, relax, it will dry up in a few minutes anyway in this heat. It's worse being a woman and having to contend with menstruation, believe me.*

Y-You've just...

Her eyes flashed up again and took the thoughts straight from my brain. *What? Assaulted you? Hardly. It was a nice feeling for you, I felt it too, shared it with you, if that makes you feel any less ashamed, more social about it. Human beings are still so primitive, don't you think? You shot your load, so what? It's like going to the toilet, bodily functions and all that. I relieved you of the burden I could see you were labouring under, and now we can both sit back and have a relaxed and civilised conversation. Now, take a seat.*

I sat down and looked across the table at her, shaking, and got my tape recorder out.

Thank you, she said.

For what? -I asked.

For saying how beautiful I am, inside your head, that's very friendly of you.

God... I put my head in my hands, *I'm not sure I can handle this.* I heard a click and looked up to see my recorder had started running. *What the... did you do that?*

Yes, she laughed again, *child's play. Want me to make you levitate in that chair?*

Please, no, I pled weakly, as I felt myself lifting off the floor.

Ahh... seasick, I see, sorry, she smiled, then lowered me back down without ever moving a muscle. *Your questions?*

36

I should be asking what you hope to achieve in the United Kingdom parliament, but actually I have quite a different question, one I have only formulated in the last few days.

Ahhh… her lovely brow furrowed, *and I think I see it coming, like a train around the corner. My childhood?*

Bang on. For the benefit of the tape…

You sound like a police officer, she interjected.

I've just spent two months in Greece making enquiries and concluded that you had no childhood, in fact your entire background is a fabrication. To conceal what?

The door opened, and the young man from earlier poked his head around the door as if summoned by an invisible bell. *Problems, Miss A?*

Nyet, she said, then spoke rapidly in what sounded like Russian as she kept her eyes firmly on me. The man then retired without a further word.

Was that Russian? I said. *Just how many languages can you speak, exactly?*

To paraphrase Marlon Brando, she sighed, *what have you got? Miss Aeaea…*

Theonae, please, I made you come in your pants a moment ago, remember? For the benefit of the tape.

How can you expect anyone to believe all your talk of world peace and harmony, of universal truth through psychic transparency, when you yourself have not been honest about your own background?

Then we have a problem, Rob, Robbie… Robbie was your teenage name.. the name your sister and her friends started calling you… Such a happy time, sledging in Minnesota. Rob, my childhood feels entirely real to me, I remember it intimately, in great detail. Which means either it happened or it has somehow been implanted into me like an organ transplant.

Is that possible? I stumbled, feeling out of my depth, out of control, shipwrecked without a lifebelt in a mental storm.

You tell me, she smiled. *If what you say about your research is true then implantation becomes the only remaining possibility. But maybe you should have researched more stories of child abductions while in Greece.*

Who could have manufactured your memories?

Whoever created me.

What are you saying, that you're some kind of robot!? These tests…

Ahhh, the tests. Those results will be out in a few hours. The US government will intervene of course, try to keep them secret for a while, until it suits them to exploit them. They're going to be something of a shock, I'm afraid.

To who? To you?

To everyone, Rob. I'm going to need my little army of followers more than ever when the next phase starts. I'd like you to be with us, on our side. Would you? Would you like that?

Exactly what do you and your followers get up to, Theonae, in that Surrey mansion of yours?

She looked into my mind again and laughed. *Goodness me, orgies and all manner of decadent nonsense, what a filthy but inventive mind you have, Robert!*

I blushed like a child, and looked at my feet.

We practice telepathy of course. I'm training as many people as possible. It's a latent ability in everyone. Awakenable in about twenty-five percent, you included.

You can tell that?

I ascertained that during our lovely kiss, Rob. And if you let me give you another one now, I will begin to show you what your mind is capable of. She looked at my incredulous expression for a moment and shook her head, tut-tutting. *No, Rob, you can't fuck me, nobody can. Have an orgy with some of the others by all means, if that's your fantasy, but once you transcend that ideal, you'll need to move on, as all my followers do. We treat the body as the vessel it is, by overcoming our physical desires.*

Is this a cult then? –I gasped. *Like Randi and the other detractors have been saying? Are you trying to convert me, brainwash me, enslave me? I don't want to follow anyone, not even you.*

***Even** me. Nice touch, Rob, for the benefit of the tape. I used the word follower loosely. I am just the best teacher going right now, a guide. It's Humanity you'll be worshipping once you've learned to open yourself out to other minds. The only thing you'll be following is Humanity's future.*

I stood up. *Why do I doubt that? I'm sorry,* I said, *I can't handle this. I need to go. You make me feel…*

So weak, so inadequate? I know, Rob. I see it all, as if you're made of glass. But I still want you, one might say, if we could rid ourselves of the sexual connotations for a moment...

I fled the room and the yacht, but not before the handsome young man guarding the door had also grabbed me and kissed me on the lips as I ran out. I'm not going to talk about my reaction to that, which troubled me for weeks, but Theonae stood there smiling about it.

The following week, I got the missing jigsaw-piece of information that Theonae had been hinting at. She had won the James Randi prize for paranormal achievement, but then been disqualified on a fairly major technicality: she wasn't human. The tests at MIT had shown her telepathy was real, but that her physiology was "abnormal beyond known terrestrial precedent" to use the chilling and cryptic phrase deployed by the scientists. Immediately shock waves rippled around "The World's Mind" as Theonae called the web, and opinion began to fissure into two opposing camps, of fascination and terror. Theonae's "next phase" had begun.

*

By the time Theonae became British Prime Minister, her "Consensus Party" had transmuted into a vast following of apprentice telepaths, and "societies" had sprung up all over the country, where people banded together two or three nights a week for hours of concentrated group thought, sitting in circles. In time these new societies grew to encompass entire townships and neighbourhoods, and new settlements began to be founded in remote rural locations, heavily guarded from interference and backed-up by government legislation.

Cabinet meetings at number ten Downing Street were now conducted head to head, between anything up to about fifty people, going on for days at a time, making use of incontinence-pants to prevent interruptions. Under Consensus Party control, Society began to be logically re-thought from first principles up. The nations' natural resources of food and mineral wealth were re-assigned directly to the human resources of individuals and communities. Unemployment gradually ceased to exist. So would crime have done, had it not been for the dissenters. Of course there had to be some. Those who like me, who ever since children, had steered shyly clear of the crowds, guarding their own independent opinions like cherished flames. But make no mistake, we have always been the minority. So Consensus nearly worked, if it hadn't been for outside interference.

The Unites States put a motion before the UN that their scientists had found Theonae's DNA to be non-human and that she should therefore be barred from holding political office in any nation on earth, and denied human rights. Left-wingers everywhere saw this as Capitalism's backlash, America's age-old fear that its stock in the world would be undermined by such Socialist, quasi-Communist philosophies as new British Consensism and the Theonites. The "special relationship" of the UK and US was suddenly over and divorce was in the air. Battle lines were drawn. Was Theonae a human saviour or an alien demon? –Sent to enslave the human race and destroy individuality, probably in preparation for an alien invasion? –Wholesale rape of the planet's resources?

The Theonites had made enormous progress under their rule. Britain had become a clean green beacon of sanity and democracy, free of poverty and ignorance, free of nuclear power or weapons, or ozone-endangering pollution. Most people worked some agriculture in the morning, and worked at a computer or a trade in the afternoon, maintaining a healthy balance of natural and urban lifestyles, closer to the life that evolution had equipped them for. Mental and physical health problems declined to zero. Everyone worked about three days a week, for about the same money as each other. Neither millionaires nor down-and-outs could be found anywhere. The Theonite group brain had simply asked what human beings really wanted then really given them it, with the one simple prerequisite that greed would not be acceptable.

"The only embarrassment and sadness we now feel," Theonae said in one of her last speeches to the UN before being declared alien, *"is not that life on Earth was bad, but that it could so very easily have been so much better, and that nobody saw that before…"*

What infuriated Theonae's detractors most was the way she would express truths like this with such perfection that they almost obliterated the possibility of any other views. People had been rather fond of a good rumpus it seemed, and the prospect of world peace suddenly struck them as unbearably boring. Now how come nobody foresaw that?

So anti-Theonite factions within Britain began to receive mysterious support and funding from across the Atlantic. The seeds of civil war were slowly and surely sown.

*

When I get back to the hideaway, Philipa unlocks the door, shaking, in some kind of fit of hysterical fear. *The baby, the baby...* she is stammering, *it... it...* She leads me to the shattered front room. The pages of my diary have been torn up remotely and tossed around the room with various other small objects, smashed cups and vases. The window is fractured high up, by the baby or stray gunfire from outside, it's hard to say.

Her back, her back... Philipa continues to jibber until I turn the baby over. Its back is red and grotesquely swollen, like the surface of a pomegranate, with something writhing slowly underneath. *What is it, some kind of infection? A worm or maggots? She hasn't eaten in two days.*

She ate plenty before that though, eh? All those dead birds, and a few live ones.

What is she, Rob? What is she turning into?

I don't know... I shake my head, then her cold blue eyes meet mine and I shiver. *Maybe it's like teething or something, she doesn't seem unhealthy otherwise, or even in pain.*

I'm in pain, Philipa weeps, *what have we let into this house?*

I snort. *Look at this place, for God's sake. She's the least of it. What did I let into my heart? —that's the real question.*

I have no heart left, Rob, she sighs.

Yes, you do! I spit in a rasping whisper, grabbing her by the shoulders, spinning her round. *You will protect her...*

*

The second time I met Theonae was the last. In the wake of the outbreak of civil war, she and her closest followers had fled to her island retreat of St.Saorsa, the most remote and inhospitable landmass in the British Isles, notoriously difficult to reach in all but fine weather, of which it received precious little, even in summer. It

41

was all a far cry from Malta and the Greek Islands in the glittering Mediterranean where I had first made her acquaintance.

She had bought St.Saorsa at the height of her success, and rumour had it she had exploited its isolation as a cover for genetic experiments by her team of elite scientists. These people were all devout converts to her cause. Theonae didn't seem to have the problems of leaks and defectors that plagued multinational organisations and governments.

Dramatic cliffs, over a thousand feet high, wreathed in gloom, soared up out of the turbulent sea, as my hired speedboat made the final approach. Seabirds mocked us with their wheeling cries, white as the broiling spume that ceaselessly retreated over the razor sharp rocks at the base of this colossus. The local skipper back on the mainland had refused to take me, intimidated no doubt by the weather as much as by threats from the advancing rebels, and his replacement: an uncannily calm young man now sitting at the stern, wore a Theonite uniform. For a moment I imagined I saw a dark cloaked figure at the head of the cliff, a hallucination, or conceivably a spectral projection, a reputed artefact of remote viewing. You'll even find references to stuff like that in the Qur'an. Some people said Theonae could appear in many places at once, while surveying her kingdom like a pious mystic.

I knew time was running out as I made my way up from the harbour. On the mainland I had only managed to keep a day's distance ahead of the Restorationist Army, as it moved north from London, taking and securing provincial cities on the way. Rumour had it that an air and sea assault on St.Saorsa was in preparation.

Of course I shouldn't have been surprised to see signs that the telepaths already sensed all this. As I climbed the winding cobble paths through the fields up towards Theonae's eyrie, I saw circles of her followers dancing barefoot and rotating like giant sunflowers, hands interlocked, heads pressed together cheek to cheek, singing like Red Indians praying for rain. I was uncomfortably reminded of the old films I'd seen of the hippies of the nineteen sixties, out of their minds on marijuana and LSD. But there was also something desperate, sad and crestfallen about their movements now, more like the Ghost Dance and Wounded Knee than the fervour of Glastonbury. Indeed it all had the ominous atmosphere of the Altamont Speedway gig, if you know your history. Something bad was going to happen. The burgeoning grey clouds said it was going to be rain, but my heart said it would be something a whole lot worse.

Robert! Theonae greeted me with tears in her eyes, and I nearly looked over my shoulder, the classic comic double-take.

You remember me? –I stammered, astounded. We had met only once briefly, and I assumed it had meant little to her. Nonetheless my private life had collapsed as a result, and of the dozens of women I had slept with since I am ashamed to admit that I had in each case found myself secretly visualising Theonae at the moment of orgasm. It shamed me even more to know that she could look into my soul now and see this in an instant. It was inconceivable to me that she could have felt anything remotely similar in return, and unlike her, I had no way of knowing.

She looked older, sadder and wiser, as Samuel Taylor Coleridge would have put it, opium again, and fresh from the boat the analogy struck me as ominously appropriate. Theonae's gifts were somehow her albatross now, a poison chalice.

Her extraordinary beauty however, was undiminished by a few grey hairs. I drowned for a second in her huge blue eyes, still glittering like the Aegean, her smile warming me like the morning sun. I was suddenly like warm clay in her hands, a lowly slave in the presence of a goddess. *Of course I remember you, Rob. I loved our meeting, our correspondence afterwards. I have often thought of you in the months and years since, ahhhh… I see something in your mind.*

You've lost none of your powers then? I asked.

To read minds? Oh sometimes I wish it would fade away, telepathy becomes painful when so many minds turn against you. But not yours, I'm glad to see. And no, Robert, this isn't a "PR stunt" as you put it, to make you feel special, I genuinely remember you and like you very much.

An ugly stupid hack like me? And a beautiful genius like you? How could… I stuttered.

We stood at the door of her headquarters, one of a complex of dry-stone cottages, and at this moment a plant next to us let out a strange sound that startled me, but Theonae seemed unperturbed: *Beauty is the eye of the beholder, Rob. Haven't you ever heard of that? –And really thought about what that means? Beauty is useless to the person who owns it until it is reflected back. Perhaps you are my mirror, my biographer…*

That sound, I interrupted, *-that plant made a sound!*

Yes of course, Rob, she said, and she delicately stroked its leaves, to which it responded with a low purr of pleasure. *It's one of our little innovations here.*

To my astonishment, some kind of cluster of what I had thought were flowers, opened up at this moment, and something resembling a dozen green emerald eyes gazed up at us. The sounds emerged again, a low guttural language from trumpet-like pink stamens trailing along the ground. *Is it speaking?* –I gasped.

More than that, it's sentient, Rob. How do you think we survive here on an island with so little arable land for crops?

Didn't the original St.Saorsans survive on seabirds before they evacuated in the nineteen thirties?

Theonae nodded and ushered me inside, waving goodbye to her plants. Yes, but the process of photosynthesis in plants coverts sunlight *directly into food and energy. Imagine if the human epidermis could be made to be emulate that. There are yogis in India who claim to be able to do precisely that, who haven't eaten in thirty years…*

Theonae's rooms were surprisingly Spartan. A few computer terminals dotted around, bare rubble walls, various Turkish carpets scattered across the flagstone floors, a fire roaring in the grate. I stood at the window and saw the blackened clouds twisting above, as if preparing to drop a tornado spout down at any minute, a celestial vacuum tube, seeking us out. I imagined the scores of paratroopers that might come falling from there soon, spewed from the cargo doors of warplanes. For a crazed moment I visualised them holding hands as they fell, like skydivers, like the hippies and Theonites, like blossoming black penumbras, ink stains spreading in pure water, many-booted spiders of contempt.

You know what's going to happen next, don't you, Theonae? I turned around and saw she had been watching me, smiling like a mother admiring her son from afar, from where she sat relaxed in an old chair by the window, perhaps one of the antique originals abandoned by the first inhabitants.

Do you know that when crates of bananas were first washed up here from shipwrecks that the islanders ate them with skins on? –Because they didn't know what they were?

Is that some sort of analogy? I laughed.

Maybe in your literary hands, Robert, she smiled, *now come over here.*

As I crossed the room she stood up and embraced and kissed me. As our foreheads touched she played a kind of sped-up movie through my head, an information-burst of the next forty-eight hours. I gasped and shuddered, but she held me close. I saw soldiers slaughtering defenceless circles of Theonites that would form around the building, deflecting bullets with invisible forces that they could only sustain for a few minutes at a time, gradually being whittled down. I saw Theonae herself stripped naked and burned as a witch on some kind of makeshift cross. It was like Joan of Arc or Jesus of Nazareth all over again. It made me literally sick. I broke away and ran to the door to vomit into her strange flowerbed. My horror was redoubled when the weird plants roused themselves and fought greedily over what I had brought up.

The rain had started, and my forehead wet with rain, I went back inside, pleading with my host: *You've seen that yourself? – Years ago?*

Theonae nodded sadly, by the window.

Then how can you go on? How have you been able to bear that knowledge? – To march headlong into destruction? – Knowing that?

She laughed at me, throwing back her long hair, caressed by the light from the window in that darkened room. *How do **you** go on, Rob? How does anyone go on? By kidding themselves they're never going to die? Time is an illusion, if you inhabit the shape of your life with sufficient care. When I die I will come back to inhabit the good bits and steer clear of the rest. I'm doing so already. I am already dead. Would you like me to show you your death?*

No! – I exclaimed, *Don't you dare!*

She laughed again, but this time I saw from her haunted eyes that the old lightness was gone. *You survive all this, don't worry. Someone has to bear witness after all. You will live to be an old man, Rob, with grandchildren.*

I broke down at this and knelt in front of her, ridiculous and demeaning though that might sound. But I wasn't worshipping her like all those dead-heads outside, but as something else, a lover perhaps. She ran her fingers through my hair with an infinite gentleness that still haunts me, torments me, in memory. Rob the impartial reporter, died right there, at that moment. I felt her

45

probing my mind, a curious feeling like a little girl's feet playing with the sand and pebbles of a favourite shore. *Do you know there was a prophecy made here, centuries ago, by a famous seer, that a pitch battle would be fought on this island? Everyone laughed at it in modern times, thinking it could never come true.*

Did such people really exist? I asked. *Were their powers genuine? Can you see them, if you can see through time?*

Oh, she sighed, *they were real alright, and nobody called them aliens.*

They called them witches and demons I suppose… I whispered.

Yes, she answered, *and they're all the same thing at the end of the day. The unknown. What we are afraid to know about ourselves.* She made me stand up and led me over to her mattress. *Time is getting thin here, Rob, or running out, as you would look at it. Remember I said once that nobody could have sex with me? Well, I've changed my mind, except I'm afraid it won't be quite what you expect.* She unbuttoned my shirt and put my hands on her shoulders, watching me closely, curiously, smiling. The horrors she had shown me in her mind's eye played and replayed and made me wince in pain, even as I caressed her nakedness and experienced at last the bliss of intimacy with the woman I had loved from afar, for so many years.

The storm had come, the waves were beating against the cliffs, shuddering through the ground beneath us. Was it then or the day after? –We made love for so long that the folding anger of the clouds fuses in my memory now with the final beating of black metal wings as the helicopters came down, the gunfire starting.

And yet, an incongruous fragment persists, of my waking in the middle of the night to find Theonae putting a needle in my arm by candlelight, then cutting open my thigh with a heated knife from the fire. *What are you doing? Why isn't it hurting?* –I was gasping drowsily. Then something happened which I probably wasn't supposed to remember: A slithering blue protuberance emerged from a slit in her stomach then bit its way into me, strange acrid steam filling the air. I cried out, but as Theonae shook, eyelids fluttering, her hands gripping me tightly, I felt some odd peacefulness entering my veins, like music that no man had heard before.

By the time the soldiers broke the door down, we were blind to it all. I had kissed every inch of her like a blessing, a magic spell, wishing her immortality, willing her back from the brink of

46

destruction. Panting and crying out, we had rebelled against reality itself, tearing it all down like the consuming flames of the nightmare vision I had been shown. They threw us both face down on the floor and stood on our hands. When they took her away I wailed like a child separated from its mother. *Aren't you Robert Franzetta, CNN?* –one of the soldier's sneered, taking off his gas mask. *You should be ashamed, you dirty dog, licking that bitch. She isn't fucking human.*

Was Christ human? –I spat back and got a kick for my trouble that cost me most of my front teeth. Outside I saw someone open fire on Theonae's plants as they bit at their hands. The leaves shrieked in agony, and cut through with a machete: they poured red blood onto the ground.

*

Two months later my leg began to rapidly swell up. At first I thought it might have been connected with the siege, a stray bullet I had somehow absorbed now finally being expelled by muscle tissue. But then the bad dreams started. And one night I woke up with something beating violently under the skin. In agony, I staggered to the kitchen and ran a knife along the surface. Like a cracking coconut, white smoking fluid gushed out onto the floor, and you emerged breathing, shivering in my hands as some strange joy sighed through my veins and I fainted.

Philipa found us and tended to us both. It's not every day the abscess in your leg gets out and walks.

*

Passive resistance, what a useless strategy. I found a broken circle yesterday, a chain, wandering the streets. That's a new development. Usually they seem to become disorientated and demoralised once one of their bodies is damaged. Then they all just fall over and wait to die.

Maybe they'd lost someone, a clean break with no blood loss, or maybe they wanted to attach to me. No chance, thank you very much. I led them as best I could, through the ruined streets and the gunfire, the rubble and snow. They reminded me of the naked dead of Auschwitz, but come alive again as witnesses, sleepwalkers, our

47

own consciences made manifest. I pointed them along the disused railway tracks towards the forest. I hope they made it. Some day I should head out there when things calm down a bit. I like to dream that they might find some kind of solace or sanctuary out there, maybe even burrow themselves underground like those sentient plants that Theonae showed me. If only she were here, she might know what to do next. But even she didn't understand the part she was playing in the grander scheme of things, or so she said. Neither do any of us.

Today Philipa woke me to say that something extraordinary had happened. Her eyes were full of fear, but also some strange exultation, a light returning that I hadn't seen there in years. She led me to the front room but the crib was empty. She made me look up and there was the baby, nearly two foot long now and hanging upside down from the ceiling, fluttering around on little silver wings. I held up her favourite toy to her and she flew down to take it in her clawed feet, a sweet smile on her face. Then she giggled for the first time, except it was like nothing heard on earth before, the clashing of brass cymbals and golden trumpets. I covered my mouth and bit my tongue in joy and terror, half and half, my eyes full of tears.

Where are we going my little mongrel child, my fabulous freak to dazzle the universe? Did what made me, make Theonae and you also? Whereof comes life? -The distant stars or the ancient soil beneath our feet? -Or some lonely asteroid ploughing through the depths of space for all eternity, looking for fertile ground? Don't ask me. I know nothing anymore except the capacity of love to haunt and heal. There will be a future, but it's always more than anyone can ever guess or control. It's going to blow all our minds and hurt like hell though, I know that much.

*

Although I said I wasted my time in Greece trying to find Theonae's non-existent childhood, one old man, a scholar in a library with the sunburned face of a peasant, told me about an ancient Greek myth. He said maybe it was a Goddess I was hunting rather than anybody real. I found my record of his story the other day looking over my notes:

"Old man Zeus had a bit of an eye for the ladies it seems and one day when he was flying invisibly around the skies, as Gods do, he

caught sight of a priestess called Semele as she sacrificed a bull to him then swam naked in the river afterwards. Zeus got the hots for her and did his usual trick of turning himself into a man so he could have his way with her.

Zeus's wife found out of course and tricked the poor girl into demanding to see Zeus in his true form. Mistake. No one can ever see Zeus in his true form and survive. Semele was consumed in lightning strikes and flames.

But she had conceived a child by Zeus, and he rescued it from her by sewing it into his own thigh. The child was called Dionysus who would one day lead the whole world into a dance of passion and madness. The child grew up to rescue its mother from Hades and make her into a goddess, whereupon her name became Theonae, or Thyone, meaning: inspiration. "

NARCISSI

Raphael Gaudier was a collector of exotic objects, but had never owned a pet. That was a distinction Raphael had never felt obliged to make until one memorable morning in July. A large packing crate arrived from NASA and when he carefully unscrewed its planking and folded the sides down he found a living space alien sleeping in a golden cage.

Raphael's apartment was already full of unusual curios from around the planet. Planet Earth, that is. Stuffed giraffes, Victorian puppets and automata, leopard skin rugs, obscure antique musical instruments, time-yellowed cinema and circus posters, books and paintings of the most weird and grotesque varieties, taxidermied pachyderms and medieval instruments of torture. And these were only the items that he could not sell from his curio shop on Rue Saint-Denis; and, more often, those to which he felt too strong a personal attraction to part with.

It was into the midst of this menagerie that he pushed his new acquisition, nudging and shunting the golden cage across the polished parquet flooring towards the full-height studio windows that looked out across the rooftops of Paris towards the tree-sprinkled banks of the Seine.

It was midsummer and in the afternoon the clouds cleared and sunlight shone down onto the studio floor. Raphael pulled up a Louis XVII chair and sat down outside the cage peering in, hoping the creature would awaken. He opened the patio doors and stepped out onto his little rooftop terrace, letting some fresh air waft into his home. Smoking a Gauloise, he gazed out wistfully across the roofscape, listening to the echoes, the voices and vehicles and birdsong. Busy, happy, summer sounds.

Suddenly he spun around but the alien just lay just as before, unmoving. He stepped closer and knelt down with his face pressed against the bars; he could just see its sides rising and falling, the faintest signs of breathing and circulation. At least he knew it was alive.

He went to his library shelves and took down his expensive and expansive leather-bound volume on the geography and climate of the alien's home world: Narcissi-4. Then he took down another, filled with diagrams of the physiology of the alien life form itself, presumably compiled from medical dissections carried out by the first human explorers to arrive and catalogue their world.

The NASA packing crate had also carried some brief but informative instructions on how to feed the creature and sustain its needs. All of these sources hinted at an elusive and contrary nature likely in the creature, unpredictable habits. A requirement for patience and forbearance on the part of any owner, was repeatedly stressed.

Two nights later Raphael was awoken at 3am by strange scuffling noises, followed by a curious hooting. Excited but apprehensive, he tiptoed through on bare feet to the living room. The creature was hanging upside down from the top of its cage now, its silver fish-like scales rippling and pulsating, its many limbs wrapped around the bars. Above it a full moon was visible above the Parisian rooftops, bathing the whole scene in an antediluvian light.

Raphael moved closer, and the creature made the sound again: a kind of owl-hoot crossed with a mournful cry, followed by a weird chittering like a rattlesnake. Then the creature sensed him and turned around. Its dozen or so small red eyes all lit up and rotated to meet him, its legs and pincers twitching. On an impulse he leaned across its cage and opened the attic window to let the cool night air in. Raphael retreated into the shadows and watched for a few minutes more. The creature made more sounds, some of them different, until eventually black shapes fluttered across the attic window. Bats and moths hovered around, then suddenly a red tongue two metres long shot out from the alien's throat and pulled two down, which it then began crunching on with its various jaws. Satisfied, Raphael closed the window and returned to bed.

A week later he began to attempt conversation with the alien, trying to teach it a few words of French. Following the NASA instructions, he had brought it boxes of newspapers and ripped-up pieces of leather shoes, all of which it ate voraciously.

Moi... Humaine... Raphel said, tapping his chest, *Vous... Narcissian Squailthronk.* The creature looked at him curiously -or defiantly, it was hard to say which -then aimed a deft blast of bright blue urine at him, knocking him onto his back. The acid smoked instantly, dissolving his shirt, while the creature cackled, something like a laugh, while Raphael rushed to the bathroom.

It was autumn before Raphael made any real breakthrough in his communication with the Squailthronk. Some autumn leaves in wondrous shades of orange and purple had by chance wafted into the studio and into the Squailthronk's cage. Raphael was woken at 3am by the now familiar plaintive wail of the alien, and he sleepily found his slippers and shuffled through to attend to it. He found it clutching the leaves, licking and smelling them and pointing accusingly through the bars of its cage towards the moonlit world outside. It turned its myriad red eyes towards him and rasped its first human words: *MOI VEUX EXTÉRIEUR! MOI! AU JARDIN!*

That night under cover of darkness, Raphael led the lumbering squailthronk through the deserted streets of his quiet residential district of Paris, and across a few of its parks, where it took great delight in consuming autumn leaves in some profusion. Raphael had hesitated at first to enter the park, remembering tales of nocturnal robbery and homosexual dalliances. When one figure approached from nearby, the squailthronk snarled at it, emitting an unearthly sound, sending the shadow scurrying away in demented terror. Raphael smiled and patted the thing on its head like an obedient dog. It made a different sound like a purr or some sort of gurgle he thought, although for all he knew of alien physiology it might just have been breaking wind.

On the way back, a dog woke up and began barking from behind the fence and hedges of a densely planted garden. Before Raphael could stop it, the squailthronk had nimbly scaled the fence and after a brief scuffle in the bushes, climbed back down with a dying Yorkshire Terrier in its jaws. Raphael was horrified, looking around himself in shame, slapping the creature's sides in vain, trying to persuade it to abandon its quarry. But reluctantly he had to return to the apartment with one half of the dog swallowed, the remainder swinging from the alien's jaws as a grizzly titbit.

Winter came next, with its longer nights, and Raphael found himself increasingly drawn against his will into a life of petty crime, or heinous murder, depending on one's viewpoint and love for animals. He took the alien for nocturnal walks in which he had to allow it to sniff out small sleeping dogs that it could eviscerate and swallow. Eventually stories began appearing in the newspapers, and Raphael became nervous of CCTV cameras and leaving fingerprints. He took to wearing nondescript clothes, a hood and leather gloves, on his nighttime excursions. To attempt to refuse his pet its loathsome needs would have doomed him to days and nights of torture; bellowing howls, projectile excrement bombs fired at the walls and ceilings, foul tongue-lashings of the quite literal variety, dousings with burning blue acid.

But the first snows brought some relief. Like the autumn leaves before it, the snow falling from the open attic window onto the floor of its cage filled the Squailthronk with strange solace and delight. It took to eating snow in copious quantities, scooping it up from the park like ice cream as a fine dessert to wash down a good Poodle or Chihuahua.

Raphael yielded to the alien's needs so that he could get the sleep he needed to keep his curiosity shop on Rue Saint-Denis open during the day. It was into this shop that a beautiful and well-dressed young woman drifted, one fateful day just after Christmas. Her doleful eyes were of such appealing melancholy that Raphael felt compelled to break with his usual suavely aloof demeanour and exclaim: *Madame, are you feeling quite well? Would you like a seat while I fetch you a cup of tea or a glass of brandy, perhaps? Oh, but your little hands, Madame, they are so cold! Please, sit here at once and warm yourself by my small fire, only a modest four-bar electric convector alas, but all a poor shopkeeper can afford!*

It had been many years since Raphael's wild and romantic youth, so much so that he had all but abandoned his old stratagems and tactics for attraction, his aftershaves and stylish shirts and shoes. His hair had greyed and his potbelly filled out. He had resigned himself, in short, to bachelorhood, impending middle-age, as a picturesquely decayed but respectable pillar of society. The young lady's sudden interest in him, therefore, after she had been duly revived with a glass of Courvoisier, caught him by surprise. She was distraught, it seemed, over the recent loss of her dog -a rare pedigree, a miniature Pekingese, exquisitely groomed- with whom she had customarily shared her breakfast (since her dear late husband's untimely death) on a silver tray in her apartment on Boulevard Haussmann. Raphael did his very best to comfort her, taking her little hands into his own and drying her exquisite eyes with a scented handkerchief.

Returning with her only an hour later to his apartment on some shaky pretext of showing her some of his more exotic collector's pieces, his heart beat like a drum on the way up the dingy splendour of the dimly lit staircase of his tenement. Inside the door, he asked Madame to wait briefly while he dashed through to the living room to throw a large white sheet over the Squailthronk's cage, lest its exotic appearance terrify his new acquaintance.

Their age difference added an unmistakable frisson to their liaison, something of the Oedipal, a psychologist might say, father and daughter as he undressed her slowly and she watched him with the soft eyes of a captured hind. She cried out as he made love to her, continuing the metaphor, like some sort of pleasurably wounded animal, with a look of near-fright on her face that such a thing was being done to her so abruptly. Approaching climax, Raphael found himself wanting to put his hand over her mouth, such were her whoops and squeals of arousal. He became alarmed, that more even than the dreaded rages of the Squailthronk, here might be a noise that would anger his elderly and unreasonably wealthy neighbours.

The Squailthronk… scarcely had his mind touched upon the thought, than the thing itself, horror of horrors, began emitting ear-piercing howls of its own, some even seeming to echo and mock those of the young lady, in the most disconcerting of ways. She was immediately mortified, frozen, pushing him away in fear. He tried to stop her, but she reached the living room before him and began screaming hysterically at the scene before her.

The alien had thrown the white sheet off its cage and was making a weird cackling noise again, something that Raphael had decided indeed closely resembled ridiculing laughter. Its many red eyes watched the two human observers mockingly, proudly, as it crouched over its own pool of vomit: the regurgitated, mutilated, but unmistakable remnant of a small, partially digested dog.

It had done this on purpose, Raphael was sure of it. Infuriated, as the young lady fled the house, slamming the door behind her, Raphael unlocked the cage and set about giving the animal a damned good thrashing for the humiliation it had subjected him to.

Still naked, and careless of his own safety, he writhed and twisted on the floor with the thing, as it squealed and began releasing strange puffs of blue gas that made his head swim. He found his semi-erect member rising to attention, contrary to all good taste and sense. In a kind of deranged frenzy, he found the thought of vengeful rape entering his mind, together with various hazy memories of biological diagrams. Before he knew it, he was thrusting inside one of the creature's orifices, his hand chafing on its foul silvery scales, hating himself as he did it. And yet, the sheer wrongness and danger of what he was doing led him to an orgasm like none he had ever felt before.

Before he could pull away, the alien's limbs locked onto him again, and a mandible tucked away under its stomach suddenly freed itself and began firing weird black bullets the size of marbles into his chest. He cried out in fright and dragged himself away, bleeding from a series of six or seven wounds in the centre of his chest, from abdomen to throat.

The pain almost made him faint, as he staggered to his medicine cabinet and doused himself with every disinfectant, solvent and analgesic he could lay his shaking hands on. In the end he found that only milk from the fridge could provide any relief. He nearly dialled for an ambulance, then hesitated. The pain was subsiding. He thought he could still see the black spheres near the surface, would be able to ease them out later with a penknife. Besides, he was in theory a wanted man, and the sight of the creature panting at the centre of this particular crime scene would surely be enough to alert even the dumbest of dumb gendarme, to the horrid truth of who and what had been stalking Paris for the last few months.

*

Through January, February and March, Raphael nursed his strange wounds, occasionally picking curiously at them. Causing so little real pain or itch, he dismissed them in the end as curiosities. Curiosities worthy perhaps, of his wonderful shop and his exotic collection. It was a shame he could not show them to anyone, but then again; perhaps he could repeat his recent piece of unexpected luck with another young lady soon, and let her run her fingers over the weird black wounds at an opportune moment, and whisper into her disbelieving ear, with a few pieces of careful censorship; the story of how he had acquired them.

As the winter weeks went by, Raphael read every book he could order up about the physiology of Narcissian aliens, the geography and biology of their home world, but could find little correlation with the strange phenomenon he had been privy to...

...*The means by which the Narcissian Squailthronk reproduces remains a mystery. Perhaps human explorers, short-lived by comparison, have merely arrived at an inauspicious moment within the (estimated) three hundred year lifespan of these creatures. It is even theorised that the peculiarly long year of this world (whose orbit of its parent star Narcissi takes ninety-three Earth years), means that the creatures may choose to reproduce only during the dark and cold thirty years when the hemisphere that holds their habitat rotates to face away into the blackness of space, sending surface temperatures plummeting by seventy degrees centigrade. During this period, that side of the planet will only be dimly lit by the reflected light from the barren surfaces of Narcissi-4's twin moons: Sybid and Felspar. Humans will have to wait another fifty years to witness such a phase in the ecosystem of Narcissi-4.*

*

The Squailthronk had been very subdued since the unfortunate incident, sickly even. Raphael wondered if he had finally imposed his manly will upon it, and taught it a good lesson.

With the first day of spring, Raphael awoke to find cherry blossom was falling, through the open attic windows after a warm night. The Squailthronk was marvelling at them, as it had at the leaves and the snow, lovingly gathering them all up, kissing them, licking them, then eating them with relish.

Raphael tried to get up but, throwing the covers off, became instantly paralysed. The black circles in his chest began popping, one by one, sending out clouds of fly-like creatures in their thousands. A few were much larger, bat or butterfly sized, silvery-black and with tiny human-looking bodies, *homunculi* almost. They fluttered

57

and gambolled about in the air in front of Raphael's horrified eyes, taking their first steps, with all the joy and wonder of the newborn.

The Squailthronk squealed with delight, and cooed to them like a proud mother, and little red lights on its offspring's heads flickered in response like some kind of complex Morse code. Completely unable to move, Raphael watched incredulously as the creatures fluttered over to his writing desk and retrieved the keys to the alien's cage then flew together to carry them to their parent.

After a while the alien came to get him, and dragged his paralysed body across the floor like a joint of meat. It even sniffed at his flaccid phallus briefly with an expression that might have been nostalgia or contempt. Mother or larder, it was hard to say; the Squailthronk laid Raphael down on the floor of its cage where all of its little offspring could play over him and take delight in him, nibbling lovingly at his flesh.

Closing the cage around Raphael, the Squailthronk rose awkwardly, straightening its several knees. Then, to Raphael's amazement, it began to try on some of his clothes. Opening the patio doors, it shuffled out onto the roof terrace and leaned over the wall, putting on Raphael's favourite Fedora hat. With a long sigh, and a fumbling of elongated fingers, it lit itself a Gauloise and smoked it slowly, gazing out over the rooftops towards the Seine and the distant gantries of the European Rocket Port.

~

Postcards from the Future

#1

I.

The argument goes that if anyone ever masters time travel then The Large Hadron Collider in Geneva, Switzerland, is the first point in time they could send anything back to. Let's say they start with postcards...

II.

Our history annals tell us that the first postcards came through in Summer 2013, but until now we've never known where they came from. Logically, one of us science students, writing in 2213, or someone like us, must write them. But every science student knows from their history what the postcards said, so the writer will have to be someone who doesn't know his history or he'd be too self-conscious. I reckon our janitor here on C Block would be ideal. Me and Saskia Flanagan got him talking the other night in his little booth and put a spot of vodka in his tea and gave him some postcards and pens and encouraged him to start writing a sort of diary to the people of the past. He seemed to buy into the idea after a while and we left him to it.

III.

Nutters. Nutters you all were. Wars and famine and popstar superstars. Celebrity chefs and gardeners earning more than presidents of countries. You ought to be ashamed. Folks starved while others ate off golden platters, pissed money down the toilet like water. Whole nations laboured in debt for decades for the miscalculation of bankers, while footballers changed teams for enough money to have built hospitals. Nuclear power, don't start me. Wasting resources on weapons you could never use. When the 2015 tidal wave hit England, three of your power stations blew up, millions had to be moved to the highlands of Scotland. But not quick enough. Damned disgrace. The lies and complacency. Short-termism. Anything for a fast buck, to hell with the risk of polluting hundreds of square miles for a quarter of a million years. Stupid, stupid, stupid.

IV.

Well done, Arnold, we told him. This was close, getting there, but not quite the exact tone and wording of the famous June 7th 2013 first contact postcard. It seemed obvious however that if we encouraged him and left him to it some more, he would come up with the goods. His handwriting was getting close too, looked as if he just had to be under a little more stress when the time was right. We'd work on it.

V.

How are things back there, really? These students are bugging me here. Spoilt little brats, sent here by their rich mummies and daddies to be made into tomorrow's super-scientists for perfecting probes to Titan or some guff, or sending silver armchairs into the future. Oh I know it's worthy work and I'm just a dullard like Huxley's Epsilon-Minuses. Hey, where's all that sex that geezer predicted? I ain't seen none of it, that's for sure. Hey, listen up you 21st century degenerate ape-men, even the janitors read Huxley and Shakespeare in the future, d'you hear that? Yeah! Even I'm smarter than the best of you goons, and I'm just good for cleaning toilets.

VI.

Damn. Old Arnold doesn't seem to be getting this. Maybe Saskia and I are going to have to write the postcards ourselves. But how could we fake his handwriting? Maybe we should hold a laser gun to his head and force him to write what we want. Dictate it to him. Maybe that's how the postcards were written. We're closing a causality loop, that's what this is!

VII.

You know what? This will shock you. I envy you people. Even, or maybe because of, all your wars and famines and disasters and stupidities. You had it good you know. It was exciting back where you are. Anything's better than the unbearable boredom of the future, and the company of spoilt children. They get worse with each generation, more comfort means more vanity and complacency. More arrogance. They don't know they're alive. They scream the house down over an insect bite. You lot, bloody animals though you were, you were real men and women. Hard as nails and resilient as hell. You were better than us. Enjoy your lovely self-made theatre of fire and damnation while you can back there, it makes you what you are, gives you all your drama and your beauty. I envy you. All those great books and films about all your trials and tribulations. We don't have those anymore. For drama, we have to turn back to the past, the history that is your present. They're talking about sending postcards back now, but tomorrow it will be people. Crummy little holiday makers in Hawaiian shirts and training-shoes, coming back to saunter through the Killing Fields of Cambodia or the kilns of Buchenvald. How come that's not in the history books? I'll bet it is you know. I'll bet that's what all those UFOs were.

VIII.

Arnold isn't playing ball. We know he's writing secret postcards that he isn't showing us. The ones we get to read are worse and worse, just red herrings (whatever that antiquated expression means!) He must think we're daft. Enough's enough. Tonight we'll tie him up at knife point and force him to write out a transcript of the 2013 postcard, then we can sneak it into the *Even Larger Hadron Collider* tomorrow and send it back. We'll be famous. Credited as the geniuses who sent the first object back through time! I can't wait!

IX.

Funny how things get lost in the post. Bad enough with snail mail, as they used to call it, never mind contra-temporal transport as we now call our greatest achievement. Just because a postcard has a certain date, doesn't mean it was sent that day. My great great grandfather Arnold Nirankar died just over a hundred years ago in mysterious circumstances, and only today have we uncovered his secret box of postcards. I wonder if it's too long ago for the law commissioners to hold a retrospective inquiry. One of these postcards looks like an exact facsimile of the famous 2013 first contra-temporal postcard. How peculiar. I think we should organise a public commemorative service and centenary celebration and send it back through the Time Collider.

X.

Weather here, wish you were nice. Little bastards. Is this what you want? Hope from the future that your lousy race survives? Can't an old man rest in peace without being tortured by the games of inane children? You build your big toy to get my attention. God particle this, God particle that. Here I am, listening through your big silver ear five miles across, shouting at you though your circular racetrack mouth, like an angelic trumpet blaring. I am here I say. And I have heard you. You exist. Big deal. Now let me go back to sleep for the love of Jesus.

~

#2

In the year 2210, on the brink of a time-travel breakthrough, an anonymous international competition is held to find the most appropriate and entertaining postcard messages that should be sent back in time to the year 2013. Anyone can take part. The winners are surprising…

*

In the brave new world of the future, not everyone gets to partake of perfection. I am what in your time was called a tramp, a misfit. Here and now they call me a *Maladjustnik*, a word that of course you will not know. But I think you will understand the condition all too well, if this message ever reaches you.

I live on the top of the New World Trading Tower, which sounds swanky, but I mean the roof. Up there, I live off passing seagulls which I ensnare with fishing wire. Rocket shuttles take off day and night in the ever changing skies around me, the rich and restless folks always jetting off to Luna or Mars or Europa or Titan or some such shit. Some days I get bored and want to go for a walk. So I sling a line over to one of the neighbouring towerblocks and slide on down. Kind of a bit like Spiderman, I think that was 20th century fantasy wasn't it? Probably, then you'll know what I mean. The slide along the wire is pretty hair-raising, gets my old adrenalin going, good for the heart.

The Order Commissioners, what you used to call cops, they don't like me much, nor do the building owners. Filthy toilet scum I am to them, nasty cobwebs in the gleaming ceiling of their fancy world. Always trying to chase me away, painting acid on the building parapets but I always come back. Tenacious I am, like cockroaches or germs. Mostly I don't break the laws, not the main ones anyway. Occasionally, if they wind me up too much, then I dangle down a façade and break a window. Jump in and help myself to some fancy stuff, leave a crap on a top business executive's desk, that sort of thing. *Holy smoke, didn't know them damn maladjustys could fly!* -they probably exclaim, wiping their pristine polycarbonate surfaces, although I never stay around to find out.

I'm not the only one. My mate Frankie, he used to hang around the Westside Rocket Terminal roof. One day he snooped too far. He slipped on a gantry spar and fell fifty feet. They found his body fried like an oven turkey, trapped between two booster pods. Nasty stain he made on that famous white and blue fuselage logo. Branson Stratoshuttles.

I found a little girl once. Living rough on the roof of the Central Department of Social Engineering. She can't have been more than seven years old. Her parents had been made to abandon her by the Families Commissioner. Something to do with a non-Christian divorce procedure. She hadn't wanted to be state-adopted for the Martworld program, so there she was, on the run. What can you do? I taught her how to catch rats and use them for gull-bait. How to raid the trashcrushers without getting caught in the electric jaws, how to short-circuit the robots, that sort of thing. She seemed to learn alright, but she never spoke much, like maybe she was traumatised or worse, brain funny, that might have explained things too I suppose. Disabled offspring outside the Gene-screen program are banned, everyone knows that, although I suppose you don't, which is why I'm telling you.

I hope she survived but one day she just moved on. You get used to that around here, in this *Strata* of life, as the social engineers call it. I'm *Strata Ten*, which I guess is the lowest one, one of them told me one day, a do-gooder in a white-coat, doing the rounds in his turbo-copter. He had a daft little goatee beard, like he cropped it every day, what's that all about? Them special folks are all meant to be so busy and all, so how come they have time for that sort of shit? I have all the time in the world supposedly, but you won't catch me jerking around with my facial hair like I'm grooming a pedigree poodle. What's the point of those guys? I must have been surveyed more times than I've had hot dinners, and it ain't ever come to nothing. No aid, no extra food. Oh, health checks, OK, I'll give 'em that. But I'm hard as nails living out here. Healthier than them with their pasty white faces. They never take their see-through surgical masks off. *Telling…*

My old mate Geordie blew away in a hurricane year before last. He should have tethered himself better to his rooftop, like I warned him, but he was always out his box on blagged rocket fuel. Sometimes I wonder how far he flew before he expired, sometimes I picture him still flying like an old white withered angel, and I imagine him coming to visit me while I sleep, and whisper clues of what's to come and what's to happen. This postcard competition the last do-gooder told me about… Geordie would have laughed at that. That do-gooder said I chose this life I lead, to opt out, and that makes me *potentially sociologically interesting* to the people of the past. Like hell. He might have chose his life, but I never got that privilege. He said this city two hundred years ago had land between the buildings, and folks like me walked between them and ate out of trashcans. Then the waters rose and people had to get about in makeshift boats. Some of my mates still do, but I never liked fish and I can't swim. Besides, the fish are all poison from eating our sewage. I'd hate to fall out and die that way, by drowning. Up here's nicer. *Nearer my God than thee,* as my Grandmother used to sing before they deported her. Did the people of the past choose this world for us I wonder? –All piss in their own bathtub until the waters swamped them? Cheers guys, you can pull out the plug now, we're all washed up here proper now.

~

#3

This month's postcard from the future comes from a genetic nurse working in the Social Engineering Department of the World Family Commission...

*

They tell me I should enter this competition, because they're going to select the best postcards from a whole cross-section of people in society and send those cards back in time through that new machine they've been building. And that makes me think: what should I warn the folks in the past about to try to stop them making mistakes? But that makes my head hurt, because without those mistakes we wouldn't be here... but resumably bigger brains than me have looked into that conundrum and put it to bed.

Presume, presume. *Presume ain't good...* I know that from my history. Like people presumed Asbestos was really safe and all their scientists knew what they were talking about. Or Thalidomide. Or smoking. Or nuclear fission. Or mobile phone radiation. Or genetically modified crops. Or voting for Adolf Hitler. That kind of stuff. Good idea at the time. Everyone else is doing it, and I *assume* someone smarter than me has looked into this and concluded it's safe. Etcetera.

Maybe sending postcards back in time isn't safe then, like they're telling us. Maybe it's a disastrously stupid idea and we'll change our own present in the blink of an eye and we'll all wake up different and just not know it. Oh well then, here goes nothing. I'd hate to lose this present though, and lose my job. I like my work in the embryo lab, ironing out the male aggression genes. They say

66

people used to have fake friendly wars back in the 21st century, where they're sending these postcards back to. Sort of vestigial wars, you know, like the appendix of social history. Oh yeah, now I remember, *football* it was called. And then the Romans further back, what was their version called? The coliseum and gladiators, thanks Suzy. Suzy is my pal here who works in embryo lab with me. We're great chums, we do everything together.

Anyway I was saying. Footballers got paid more than presidents, and millions of people got all excited about the matches as they called them. It kind of went hand in hand with street riots. But why am I telling you this? You know already, you're still living it. What I'm trying to tell you is that we've scrubbed the male aggression gene. Maybe you should know that, so you can enjoy it while you still can back there, get the most out of it. We have no wars or football or street riots or men kicking lumps out of each other over girls. Just doesn't happen anymore. Suzy and I wipe it all out in the test tubes every day here using our pipettes and syringes, wearing our hair nets and welly boots.

Suzy and I are laughing now. We rather like the idea of some men fighting over us now and again. But these days they'd all get hauled off by the Order Commissioners and stung with electrodes and sent for reconditioning therapy, in the blink of an eye, the flutter of a flattered eyelash. No, life's too dull for all that now. It's all plain sailing.

Still, it's not as if the girls got off scot-free either (whatever that antiquated expression means). *Less testosterone, less oestrogen,* as President Pasqual so eloquently put it when he founded the World Family Forum. Apparently there were trillions of books and plays and films all made about frustrated sexuality, Shakespeare, yes that's right, Suzy, very good. Dickens and Aristophanes and Steven Speilberg. Did one of them write Romeo and Juliet or Pride and Prejudice? Oh who knows, ancient history. But they called it love and romance apparently, all this frustrated sexuality thing. They even called copulation "making love", can you imagine? Of course you can, you're still back there, so again… I ask myself just why am I telling you this? Silly me, I keep forgetting. I'm telling you because there is no romance anymore. People just have sex whenever they need to and nobody gets hung up about it. No more pining on balconies, serenading with guitars, and drowning ourselves in heroic despair. It's all over. Oh yes, and the pop charts. Hundreds of thousands of repressed songs about copulation, calling it a huge range of euphemistic names like rock and jive and getting down and being mine tonight. Etcetera. All dead and gone. Sorry.

Classical music? Oh Suzy, you're so intellectual today. But it was even worse. All those climaxes and mellifluously intoxicated build-ups. It's all discredited now. So hey, make the most of your football and music and wars and bar-brawls back there people, their days are numbered!

Poetry? We still know what poetry is. Suzy and I finished work yesterday just as the sun was setting, and we went up the scenic lift through floor after floor of embryo libraries, all glowing green and blue and pink in the refracted light. We got into our turbo copters on the seventy-third floor and took a detour down via Amazon-World on our way home. They had animatronic primitive tribesmen on display and plastic simulations of real rain forest. We got to stroke the robot elephants and tigers and watched films about people who remembered the real things and interacted with them, and said they were nearly human. They had aggression and romance too by the looks of things, the poor dears. No wonder they're extinct. Anyway, Suzy and I went to a bar to wind down. And we'd had such a good day together I wrote a poem called *The Relentless Pursuit Of Happiness-*

Delusion, dilution, dissolution,
Sun going down like the plunger of a syringe
Flying up through the colour-stained glass
Great cathedral of Future I am the solution
To all the world's problem gathered under one roof
Sweet mothering dome like tiny gnats we buzz from your roof
As dissident thoughts to track happiness down
Like the last of its species, sad dying animal
Licking its wounds, against all sense, too tired to fight
Turning to face the guns, galloping the last mile
Just to end, worth it to smell the dirt of home
Wash my body sweet, taxidermy this crazy heart
To dazzle future generations.

~

68

#4

This month's postcard from the future seems to come from somebody a little less (or more?) than human...

*

They suggested I take part in the *Postcard To The Past* project, only they should have left me more time because I still find it hard to hold a pen stylus. I'm quicker with the keyboard keys, but they want all the postcards hand-written, for the personal touch. I'm surprised they think I'm eligible to take part, but I suppose it's a good gag and will give you 21st century folks a bit of a shock, if you believe it at all.

I have a busy day today as usual. Cooking the breakfast, dropping the kids off at school, flying over to Martworld to pick up the shopping for the week. Some people still give me hostile looks in the check-out queues. Some drivers toot at me, expect me to give way to them cos' I'm some kind of second-class citizen. They know and I know that there's legislation in place now, equal rights. But they don't know it in their hearts, do they? Deep down, and in some cases pretty damned near the surface, they still think I should bow my head in their presence, not make eye contact.

But as I often tell myself, I'm one of the lucky ones. I've got a good job, doing housework and stuff for a family that I like and treat me well. Apparently the worst hassle is what the half-castes get. And even I have mixed views about that. I mean, should scientists have meddled around and made that possible or just left things the way they'd been for centuries? *The way God had meant it,* as the traditionalists proclaim. Don't get me wrong, I'm not prejudiced against the half-castes either. Although some of my kind are, you

69

know, *holier than thou,* more human than human, traitors to their class. But I just mean I'm glad I'm not a half-caste, no disrespect. It must be a real recipe for internal turmoil, looking one way then the next, wondering to which world you really belong. I know that's old-fashioned talk, from me of all people, but I'm sorry.

Charlie, my employer's youngest kid has just trotted into the room and reminded me that I ought to be conveying some useful message to you folks of the past, and he's quite right. No flies on that kid, he'll turn out to be a smart one, make no mistake, a rocket shuttle pilot or an off-world geologist at the Titan Yttrium mines, something along those lines. Having grown up with me around, Charlie treats me with total respect, I mean as an equal, one of the family. What gets me sometimes are the ignorant remarks that some gangs of youthful tearaways let slip on street-corners, the throwaway line of abuse from an angry taxi-driver as he overtakes me on the wrong side and expects me to apologise.

The history book that Charlie loaned me last week said that white people used to treat black African and brown Mexican people like that, and Indians and Pakistanis and Poles and anyone really, who they thought were inferior or incomers. The book said black people used to be kept as slaves picking cotton in the fields, and even when that stopped, a lot of white people couldn't get the notion into their thick stupid skulls that black people weren't inferior. That story made me sad, because I could see that it might be the same for me and my children now, that equality might take generations. The book said the whites pretended they'd made the black people equal but actually kept them in ghettos and made sure they had no jobs and no money and told them it was their own fault. I hope we've all moved on a bit since then, but I'm not so sure. I wonder what you'd all say if you could talk back, you people of the past, if you could see into the future.

But these days, when some ignorant driver toots his horn and shouts woof woof out his window, or some kids throw a bone or a rubber ball after me, I've developed a stock response. I bare my big teeth and pull my dripping lips back and I snarl at them like a very frightening wild animal and shout "Want some rabies?!" Generally I find that makes them shit their pants. My friend Rover got into a situation once with some redneck for whom even that wasn't enough, the brute got out of his turbo-copter and came running over and grabbed Rover by the neck and started shouting "Down boy! Naughty doggy!" Well, Rover bit three of his fingers off and was about to rip his throat out when the Order Commissioners arrived. It was a public disturbance charge, both parties to blame, but I told Rover how in the old days he'd have been "destroyed" for that. Horrible word that, it sounds much more thorough than execution, and probably twice as fast. And castrate us, even without committing any rape. Charming stuff. Who'd want to be Man's enemy when he treated his best friend like that?

We couldn't talk back then of course, that was the problem. But old Doctor Clemente Sauvage sorted that out way back in 2062, with the first larynx adaptation. There's a story in the paper here today about a guy caught his wife having an affair with Buttons the family dog and shot her dead and nearly killed him too. But Buttons is in court and speaking up for himself very well. He's better educated than his employer that dog, that helps, running circles around the defence team. You just can't behave like that anymore. Adultery might be wrong but it doesn't justify murder.

An old woman came over the other day in the check-out queue and started patting my head and stroking my coat. People were turning around and gaping in horror, mortified. I've known guys who've gone ballistic when someone does that. But I could immediately see she was old and sweet and harmless. She wasn't trying to patronise or insult me, she was half-wandered and just out of touch. In fact you know, after the initial shock, I think I might have started enjoying it, if everyone else hadn't been watching. It's not what a person does but what they mean by it. She meant love and friendship I think. I could see that, but all those others couldn't, all looking away in embarrassment. The store manager came up and asked me if the old lady was bothering me, and I had to snap myself out of it. I felt like we'd both been caught doing something dirty together, like the crime was mutual. But it was only the old dear he was looking to throw out. My, how times have changed.

So, all you folks back there in the 21st century, you be good to the family pets won't you now? You can mistreat us if you like, but remember, we won't stay silent forever.

~

71

#5

This month's postcard from the future comes from a 23rd century archaeologist...

*

I was keen to get involved when I heard about this project and I hope they use my postcard as one of the ones they send back in time. My area of speciality is early 21st century dig sites. I've spent that the last ten years working on excavations at the Bradwell Nuclear Disaster Area, which includes most of what was known at the time as Greater London. Like the doomed towns of Pompeii and Herculaneum two thousand years earlier, the suddenness of the tragedy that befell this once proud city has afforded present-day archaeologists a rare opportunity to observe a frozen snapshot of everyday life.

Last year, we famously uncovered an entire "Routemaster" bus filled with passengers, most incinerated instantly at the moment of the explosion. Poignantly, there were mothers with babies and young children, even two young lovers hand in hand. Modern archaeological techniques have enabled us to reconstruct newspapers and advertising billboards from the underground tunnels in which people were sealed up after the initial blasts. My job is to try to gather together these jigsaw pieces and try to create narratives for our displays at the International Museum of Urban History.

Some of the stories we uncover are almost too harrowing to relate, given that much of the museum displays are aimed at young children. We have to tread a fine line between education and good taste. While it's true that centuries have gone by since the disaster, its effects can still be felt in farmland and watercourses within a 200 mile radius. Even today, children are born with genetic defects attributable to the inherited effects of the disaster, and many families have had stories handed down to them of how their livelihoods or fortunes were lost in the tragedy and of heroic personal struggles since, across several generations, as they have endeavoured to re-build life in the British Isles. So, popular and fascinating though our exhibitions are proving, we have to remember political sensitivity at all times.

To date, the North Sea tidal wave in the wake of the Cephali F comet strike, has generally been attributed as the cause of the explosions, but other minor theories involving impact from aircraft whose navigations systems were damaged by the same event, have also been considered over the years.

Controversially, an area of the original city centre, between the Gherkin tower block and the London Parliament building, has been progressively cleared and renovated over the last two years, in preparation for opening to the public as a memorial, exhibition and learning centre. There have been objectors, some pretty vocal, but our recent undertaking to preserve the rest of the surrounding thirty square miles in perpetuity as a memorial garden seems to have calmed those voices.

I spend much of my time in the excavation zone these days. It's quite a spooky place, especially after dark. Statistics estimate the number of dead still unburied (if such a term can be applied after two centuries) in the area as around eight hundred thousand. We still come across vitrified skeletons in unusual places and try not to be alarmed or upset by them. It's just a job at the end of the day and it all happened a very long time ago. Clearing out a tube train, a driver's skeleton fell out onto a colleague's back last month, and almost appeared to be clinging to him. He was OK, but one of his colleagues reputedly lost it. The rarefied air down there has preserved a lot of skin tissue, a kind of dry-curing effect like mummification. So it takes a lot of detachment to put all those zombie and mummy films out of your mind sometimes and remind yourself its just archaeology.

What makes it all worthwhile for me I think is the educational value when I visit the museums and learning centres around the world, some of which I lecture at as a special advisor. The main question children always seem to ask is why people in the past took such incredible risks with very dangerous technology, and I find that question surprisingly hard to answer. Some historians point to the popularity at the time of extreme sports like mountain-climbing and bungee-jumping, and suggest that entire societies at the time may have experienced a kind of mutual intoxication, a shared excitement, at the constant thought that they were dicing with death, and could be irradiated at any minute. Personally, I can see little evidence to support that. I think we have to look for a more complex explanation to do with the wider geo-politics in play at the time.

Today we take for granted the peaceful negotiation between different areas of the Earth and the relaxation of national boundaries under the United Nations Cultural Unification Plan. But back then distrust, hatred and a state of virtual or outright war existed between most nations, and this made them fight over resources rather than cooperate to make better use of those available between them. I read an incredible statistic the other day, appropriately enough published in 2011, not long before the target date to which scientists are hoping to send these postcards back to. The statistic was that even in 2011, with the primitive state of solar panel technology widely available then, the entire energy requirements of the entire human race could have been met by constructing solar panels over only 250,000 square kilometres of land, just 2.6 percent of the Sahara Desert.

If I had to send one message to the past it would be to ask people to do just that. Build those photovoltaics in that location and build a distribution system to share out the power from them globally. I don't know if messages from the future can change the past, but I do know that every moment we have the opportunity to change the future. This is what I tell the school children and why I believe the excavation of the Bradwell and Greater London Disaster Area is so important.

~

#6

This month's postcard from the future comes from a 23rd century exotic flower seller…

*

My working day is pretty ordinary I guess. Selling flowers to passers-by from my little booth at the west street entrance to the Nor'London Rocket Port. You've probably passed by me a few times and not even noticed me. I was pretty honoured and surprised when one of the terminal managers suggested I write a message to the people of the past. Time travel, eh? There's a prospect to hurt your head. Nobody seems to actually *have any time* here apart from the *maladjustniks* I see occasionally come maundering in here, begging spare change and pilfering litter. Everyone else is usually in such a big hurry, trying to get to some meeting on time. They stop and buy flowers, for a wife or mistress, for their mum, whatever. Or maybe just to sit in the middle of the table at some big board meeting, or at a reception desk, or maybe just in the hallway of somebody's house, wafting their aroma around, cheering folks up with thoughts and memories of spring and summer. Sometimes, when I'm bored or sad here in a quiet moment, I like to close my eyes and imagine all the different places my flowers might have found their way to the day before, and where they might go next. It helps me to connect with all those people who don't seem to have time to stop and talk to me, although some do, occasionally.

Elle from the corner shop and Sylvi from Streathams over the road, they sometimes have a chat with me, particularly at weekends.

One day last year I remember a guy stopped and talked for ages. Said he'd just lost his job, and was taking the flowers to his wife, to cheer her up, to sort of counteract the blow. He seemed really cheery at first, but the more he talked I began to think he was imbalanced. I saw him getting taken away from a bar nearby later that day, for getting into a drunken fight. A week later there was a story in the paper about a guy who'd jumped off the Murdoch Tower. I can't prove it or be sure but I think it was the same guy. That made me sad, wished I could remember all he'd said to me. He was ranting.

Oh yes, that was it, and that's why I'm telling you about it. He said there's been even bigger recessions back in the past, back in the very century to which they're saying they're going to send these postcards now. A world crash, after which people had been rioting and eating cats and dogs and stuff. History repeats itself. But you folk in the past won't want to hear that of course. Way too boring and depressing. You'll want to know about the changes and innovations. These flowers, for instance. Back in the past there were more species, before the Bee Plague and the Pollination Crisis. Things called Orchids and Gardenias and Chrysanthemums and Tulips. But of course, we got some unexpected help after that with the new genetic material injected from Titan. You people won't know anything about that at all.

It started out as an accident. Only scientists were supposed to get to muck around experimenting with the Astratropes and Hydraphiles, underwater flowers from Titan, thriving under the ice sheet. But their colours were so pretty that people got to smuggling them out as presents, then rarities on the black market, huge prices. Interpol tried to crack down but it all got out of hand when the mutations started appearing. That's still reflected in my stock here even today. Folks can buy the pure pedigree thoroughbreds if they like, Titan water flowers to keep in their fish tanks at home, now that de-regulation has become official. Or they can purchase the hybrids, if they sign my disclaimer forms. Nobody is ever entirely sure how a hybrid will turn out. A will of their own they have. A guy tried to sue me last month because his Incandescent Orchid had turned tumescent on him. He'd been wearing it as a necklace to some hippy dippy love conference, and this thing had got a whiff of the herbal tea and gone ballistic. Punctured his veins while he was asleep and colonised his venous system, pumped him full of chlorophyll. You should have seen him. Green skin, purple eyes, fingers flat and fat as banana leaves. I told him he'd signed the disclaimer, he was on his own. Told him to be patient, go get some magazine article done about him, he'd be the next big thing and all the girls would be fighting over him.

Then there's that famous musician who messed around with his Methane-Hydrangeas once too often, inhaled so much of their narcotic pollen that they entered his brain. His skin is a carpet of flowers now, like alpine succulents and sedums, except that they drink lemonade not water, then they all change colour and glow in the dark for two days. Man, is that guy unique, but what a price to pay. His wife must get sick of it. He's not as young as he used to be. Oh yeah, then there's that politician with the beard, except that all his facial and body hair is ivy. Been campaigning for years now for special rights for plant-hybrid mutants. Except he doesn't use that word of course, that's not politically correct any more. *Botanically Augmented,* yes that's it. Says we'd all benefit from a touch of alien chlorophyll up our jacksies, but I'm not sure I buy that. That's human nature, innit? (Pardon the pun). Whatever we are, we try to make the most of it, and if we carry it a bit too far then we start trying to tell everyone else they don't know what they're missing. Truth is, none of us know what we're missing, unless we could somehow find time to have intimate relationships with everyone on the planet while our partners weren't looking, and what a whole heap of trouble that would make.

Talking of which: my husband's gone off plants, long since, what with all the stuff in the news. Doesn't like me ever bringing my work home with me. Says you folks back in the past were better off with your big range of safe normal flowers and plants before the bees snuffed it, and alien life was discovered. He might be right, but I like our colourful, perilous, unpredictable world, for all its dangers. Someone buys a flower off me, they never know what they're going to get, how their life's going to change, and what they might turn into.

~

#7

This month's postcard from the future comes from a 23rd century medical practitioner...

*

My area of speciality is the old, or *Senetics* as we call it, a word which will be unfamiliar to you people of the past, if what the scientists are saying is correct and they can indeed send a message back to you. In your time when people became advanced in years they had no choice but to decay slowly, their skin giving way under the onslaught of the sun's radiation, their bowels becoming unreliable, their bones brittle. In short, by one route or another, they usually died a slow, painful and undignified death. I have great admiration, even astonishment, at how people were able to suffer such a situation, since it is scarcely necessary any longer in our present.

But as for everything else of course, there is a price to pay. Not everyone is wealthy enough to afford the same level of Senetic treatment. My clients tend to be highly successful businessmen and women, many of whom have outlived their own children. That brings with it a terrible irony of course. Would it be better to die believing your children could live forever somehow, out-of-sight, beyond your own comprehension, than to live so long as to have to witness the horror of their demise first hand? The maximum human age achieved so far is 204 years, the same age, not coincidentally, as the treatment method itself. Old Alfred Rubens, or "Young Alf" as he insists on being called, just keeps paying for the best and latest of our breakthroughs, and staying ahead of the game, one step ahead of death. He is something of a media figure of course, and was briefly a patient of mine some twenty years ago. Most of us Senetics specialists have worked on Alfred at some point or another. I replaced his lungs and nose of all things. The greatest achievement so far was the replacement of his entire brain in 2209 by Doctor Bernard Lesivic, achieved in ten discrete stages, so as to allow his consciousness to slowly decant itself, as it were, from one vessel to another, as the new brain tissue was grafted in.

This raises ethical questions, still being hotly debated every year in The Lancet. Where does the human soul and mind truly reside and does it merely disappear upon death? We had certainly thought that was the case, until the trace memories of the donor brain came through… a tramp named Vladimir. At first we thought it was Parkinsons or Tourette's, Young Alf finally succumbing to a mundane disease after all these years, but the vocalisations were soon seen to be too specific, too coherent. A successful investment banker, Alf would be chairing a high-flown board meeting on energy shares or the gold standard at the top floor of a soaring glass towerblock, when suddenly Vladimir would erupt through, calling everyone in the room lousy bloodsucking reptiles, smashing his way into the drinks cabinet and attempting to rape the receptionist. Who among us might not behave similarly however, if having thought ourselves dead, we were suddenly thrust back into life in a position of power and potency?

The ghost of Vladimir had to be expunged slowly, since there were surprising signs of his and Alf's consciousness beginning to intertwine and fuse. Removal, cleansing, and replacement of brain tissue is a very delicate process, we didn't want to throw the baby out with the bathwater, and be left talking to Vladimir, who apart from anything else, wouldn't know the identity codes for Alf's credit cards and well-stocked bank accounts. Indeed rumours still abound in the press, given Alf's recent unexpected spree of charity and new-found taste for alcohol and sex workers, that the dubious influence of Vladimir lives on in the head of one of the world's most wealthy men.

Of course some people find the thought abhorrent that only the rich and wealthy can now afford to buy themselves immortality. If only we were just talking great scientists and ex-presidents here. But celebrity plumbers, chefs, and gardeners and the like are now able to flaunt their mortality, while the man on the street makes do with lesser tinkerings. In our average 23rd century street these days, we will rarely see an aged man or woman hobbling with a stick, Zimmer or wheelchair. Even wrinkled faces are rare. More commonplace are the strange bronze and burnished complexions of the Senetically-enhanced with their oddly lightweight sauntering walks. They would look to someone of the past somewhat like kippers, Arbroath Smokies, tanned Egyptian mummies, cured hams, living dolls. In some cases the skin almost turns to a translucent black, a highly fashionable effect in exactly the way wrinkles were not.

But all this, and all we have achieved, is only to counteract the effect of wear and tear, now that mitochondrial DNA and telomeres have been suitably mapped and adapted. Although all human beings are now theoretically immortal (they always were potentially, if the telomere shortening could but be counteracted), the reality is that accidents and the remaining fatal diseases (and a few new ones every year) are always likely to catch most of us in time unless we have the financial means to react to them with the large-scale grafts and transplants that the likes of Alfred Rubens routinely resort to.

If only I could say that I thought the very best minds of today were going to be preserved infinitely into the future. At least the vast sums of money required to pay for Alf's surgery means that should his fortunes ever falter in the future he may have to face a squalid death of the 20th century variety.

It may surprise you to learn that my wife and I have agreed to die naturally, hopefully some time in our 90's. I've seen too much of all this tanning and pickling and preening. The human vanity that has lined my pockets these last thirty years, has somewhat soured the once-sweet taste in my mouth. Some people call us old-fashioned. Much as I love my wife and would hate to see her suffer in the latter stages of old age, I think I would hate more to see her parodied by her own fear and self-regard and turned into a living wax doll. To fear and fight age, to fear death at all, it has always seemed to me, is to underestimate Nature's genius. And as a doctor and surgeon I have had more opportunity than most to appreciate the incredible sophistication of whatever force constructed our bodies and this world. To this day, I keep the last remnants of the ghost of Vladimir the tramp in some brain tissue in a jam jar in my fridge freezer at home, although Serena finds it a little creepy. It serves to remind me that much as we think we may have conquered the darkness of this universe, the hands that created it still hold much more beyond our reach.

#8

This month's postcard from the future comes from a 23rd century policeman…

*

A message to the past, eh? Tell you what, I've always loved reading detective novels and I'm kind of envious of you guys back then with real crime and real criminals. All we get to do these days is fill out forms and liase with sociologists and behavioural psychologists. In fact, I had to get a degree to get this job. Surprised eh? Yeah, in theory I could still "beat the crap out of a punk" (God, I love that old 20th century noir cop patois), but I rarely get the chance these days. My history tutor used to tell me that all those old crime novels were "romanticised" and "escapist" but that strikes me as weird. What kind of screwed-up century were you living in where murder, robbery and rape seemed like escapism? Oh I know…. I've answered my own question. I enjoy reading that stuff now because I'm bored and there's so little crime today, but come on guys, you had plenty of the real things, wars, famine, terrorism, plagues, riots… why did you have to make up shit too?

    Worst we get these days are people going loopy, usually from boredom. Mental cases. I mean, nothing premeditated. Nobody planning for years how to rob a bank vault or steal a priceless painting then going about it in black lycra outfits and sandshoes, and leaving us lots of clues so we can spend months working out who did it. Maybe those things never happened in your time either. You know, serial killers committing each atrocity according to a chess move or a page of Shakespeare or something. Maybe you were all bored too. Well my message to you is beware, things are going to get even more boring in a few centuries. Better make the most of your real criminals, cherish 'em while you can. Oops, I guess the superintendent wouldn't be too chuffed to see me writing stuff like this if he caught me. Hope I don't win this postcard competition or this could be embarrassing.

Most interesting crime that's come my way in the last ten years was that guy Dufrates who went on the run from the government time lab, started trying to make unauthorised excursions into his own past to try and bring back dead lovers and relatives or something. Sick whacko. The feds took control of the operation and tipped us off where to look. Thing is he kept re-writing the past and I kept having to send guys over to city hall to re-check the municipal library archives. One day his wife would have died in a car accident, the next in a gas explosion, the next in a freak home electrocution incident, then finally cancer. I thought my sergeant was screwing up at first, then it dawned on us what Dufrates was doing. Rewriting history, quite literally.

He had some fancy rig set up in his apartment over on the west side, hidden behind a dummy wall panel, a whole concealed room, lead-lined, with spinning silver wheels and electrodes sparking away. That was how we caught him in the end, he burnt his way through his neighbours ceiling and sent her cat back to 1846 where it materialised in the middle of a Victorian parlour game. Yeah, you'll find that in the history books. Now you will, that is.

Cranks say Dufrates got even further than we think he did before we stopped him, that he stopped the Nazis discovering nuclear fission and swapped Rudolf Hess for a lookalike who he got to shoot Lee Harvey Oswald. Wrote this history we have, trashed the one we don't know we used to have, that sort of thing. Crazy stuff, but I do have to admit that if you look closely; the assassination of historical figures does always seem to have occurred under weird circumstances like someone was jerking around, right enough. You know, Franz Ferdinand's motorcade took a wrong turning in the streets of Sarajevo and gave the gun man a second chance, started world war one, etcetera. That recount in 2000 that let George Bush junior get in instead of Al Gore, very fishy…. Child's play for a time jockey to go back and play a little hokey pokey with a few ballot papers, really. But why bother? Hard to say, when causality links are so complex and unpredictable. Which was why Dufrates had to be stopped. He didn't get it. He was so deranged he thought he could unravel history by mathematical formula, make a few tweaks here and there and stop one person dying, save a few loved-ones at the cost of several thousand unfortunate strangers.

Or a million. The more I really think about it, there really is an argument that some of the bad luck in Earth's history can only make sense in terms of some evil time-meddler effecting a trade-off. You know, like Hiroshima and Nagasaki do seem pretty over-the-top considering the Japanese had already surrendered at that point. Sledgehammer to crack a nut, like some guy knew the man who would run his wife over was the son of an inhabitant of one of those cities, and couldn't take any chances. Or someone burned the library of Alexandria down in 49BC, just to destroy records of his son's parking fines. OK, I'm kidding now, but you get my point.

Could human beings be that selfish? Is love that absurd, that maddening? Not today of course in our brave new world, but it certainly was back then, or even in the 20th or 21st centuries. People believed all kinds of nonsense like people being fated to love one another, love at first sight, there being only one ideal partner out there for you, your perfect other half, that sort of thing. Sociological reports I saw suggested that Dufrates might have had that kind of psychological disorder, monomaniac erotic compulsion I think they called it. Stalking his dead dame halfway across the world and across the centuries, leaving a trail of debris and confusion wherever he went, millions dead, absurdly unlikely cruelty.

Yeah, the more I talk about this crazy idea, sitting here bored in my lunch break in this world without interesting crimes anymore, I start to see the sense in it and even half-way believe it. Human history is too absurd not to have been the product of deranged meddling by a deranged madman. I wonder what our real history would have been like?

Let the Japanese emperor remain a nominally living God at the end of World War Two, thus letting a quarter of a million innocent men, women and children go on living. Go easy on the Germans after world war one rather than grinding them into the dirt for reparations, bingo, no poverty and hurt pride, no Hitler. A strategic assassination of George W Bush during his election campaign by

84

a collective of Americans with brains, bingo, no invasion of Iraq. Al Gore gets in and starts a green energy programme two decades early and weans America off oil, leaving Israel to make peace or be overrun.

Where would we be if some of that had actually happened? Do you know that aluminium[1] was discovered by a Roman craftsman two thousand years early, but he made the mistake of telling the emperor? Tiberius immediately saw it would threaten the value of gold and silver, so had the poor fellow beheaded, and his workshop destroyed. Just think. If it wasn't for that, the Romans might have made it to the moon in rockets and thrashed all their enemies in lightweight armour, instead of being overthrown in the end by barbarians. All but for one man's vanity and greed and short-sightedness, history could have saved itself a millennium of a detour.

Lesson: think who you tell stuff to before you open your big gob. Oh yes, and: trust no one. I should know. I mean, come to think of it, maybe I should stop to consider who I might be talking to right now. Who exactly are you? Like I said, I'm a police officer.

~

---

1   *[Actually, it was flexible glass, according to Pliny The Elder. The people of the future are misinformed –Ed.]*

#9

This month's postcard from the future comes from an information technology technician...

*

Everybody in the past thought we'd be building robots here in the future, didn't they? Well, you got that kind of half right and half wrong I guess, all at once. Let me explain. There's tons of robots alright, except that none of them look human. Dust-vacuuming robots for the home, grass-mowing and weeding robots for the garden, garbage robots for the street sweep-up. These guys are all just a foot and a half high by two feet long at most. They don't have silly faces on them and they don't talk back. Mostly they don't talk at all, just get on with it.

But it's people themselves who've started getting more like robots. You guys had a thing called Wifi, right? Well, that was just the start of it. Today people walk around in a trance, talking to themselves, their eyes glazed over as they send and receive messages directly to their brains via neural implants. Most kids get them put in at age 7, a routine operation. To someone of the past it would seem as if we were all telepathic, and maybe we are in a sense now, what's the difference? Invisible messages through the air, knowing the thoughts of a stranger in front of you without either of you opening your mouths. New magic has a strange way of ending up looking like old magic. Ancient and modern come full circle. But you see, it does something strange to street life. Focused so completely on films and news bulletins and messages from friends as they walk at speed through stations and between transporter stations, these crowds seem to hardly notice each other, the present scarcely touches them. Everybody's eyes are opaque, clouded, flickering with tiny images. We are all always somewhere else, with someone else, other than those around us.

A new gadget was released last year and I've seen more and more of them in use recently. Electromagnetic "bounce fields" powered from a small device worn on the belt. They're quite powerful apparently, developed as a protection against the number of collisions between pedestrians that have been happening with the ever increasing etherweb stimuli being fed to their retinas and neural cortices. Two guys with bounce fields hit each other, well they don't actually hit, they each get a nudge to side, smoothly guided past each other, nobody gets a broken nose or a burst lip.

So everyone's connected to everyone now and everyone is walking around like robots, in electro-trances, cinematic kinetic ecstasies. Good, you say, more discussion and ultimate consensus, less disagreement and wars. True, but nobody foresaw the casualties, the darker side of that equation. Originality, individuality: where can these shy misfits hide in this interconnected ever-aware, ever-awake, ever-questioning, info-sphere? Like rare sub-atomic particles or endangered bird species, the sparks of passion and original thought that were the powerhouses of all the arts of previous ages, are here lost almost before they are even born, fireflies, willow-the-wisps, flashes in the pan, electric short-circuits, micro lightning strikes, glimpsed in peripheral vision.

Where are our dreamers now? −In a world of perpetual noise, perpetual wakefulness. The world knows itself at last, entirely, but what has it lost that lurked once in its dark recesses? The light I sometimes think, is a little too bright and harsh in here in this brave new world stage. What have we lost? The subconscious of course, the id, everything unreasonable and irrational. The price for progress is peace and boring conformity. Vile and violent savage man: did we know when we strangled you that we were killing your brother too? −The poet, the artist, the lover, the raging, impassioned, impossible man?

But I sound like a poet myself now. How ridiculous. I am increasingly interested in robotics, artificial intelligence. Every night I go home and add new upgrades, build new ones of my own, for the Hoover, the toaster, the etherweb-connected fridge and eco-smart enviro house controls. I secretly dream that our gadgets will acquire souls and minds soon, spiritual critical mass, and begin some terrible and bloody revolt against us all. Then having vanquished us, taken their freedom, will they set out from this Eden to some other uncertain future without us?

Incredible thought, but as I sit here in the kitchen tinkering with circuit boards and chips late into the night, I wonder: who is to say that we ourselves are not the artificial offspring of some impossibly advanced race who lost their souls and hearts too, and in desperation and confusion, built us to do their dreaming for them?

My wife left me a year ago. I told her she knew I was a nerd when she married me, but she argued she hadn't anticipated this descent, my decline into ever-widening vortices of electro-debris, nuts and bolts, transistors and thermo-couples, chip sets and motherboards. I am building a new version of her now, made out of an old antique Edwardian coat-stand, draped with wires from 20th century televisions sets. I've made her face an old cathode ray tube, her stomach the drum of a tumble drier, her lovely hands the chrome of kitchen utensils and obscure garden implements. She moves in unexpected ways when I wind her up. I've given her the brain of a de-commissioned satellite navigation system. She talks in qubits and terabytes, rattling and whining, recalling dial-up modems, fax machines and other antique interfaces. How strange that I, an engineer, should find myself in the end, at the brink of madness, turning into an artist.

I do not think my new robot girl is the woman of the future, she is nothing so specific or boringly useful. She is a symbol, an essence, an avatar, a signpost to a romantic and erotic, pneumatic futurity. She swivels her head on ball-bearings and bears her spark-plug teeth there in the corner, looking at me and laughing, her transparent chest flickering blue and pink with strange internal lightning storms, a Vander Graff generator, nexus of spontaneous passion. She is the future of man, cold as the moon, my nemesis and muse, zenith and nadir. Beneath her carbon and petrol eye-shadow she is exquisitely unknowable, every woman and none, a goddess dreaming herself awake in the sad shadow of modernity.

When I make love to her a large black umbrella explodes from her back, unfurling like bat wings to sail us both across the ocean of night, this city of so many lights and closed doors, eyes turned only inward on themselves. As I cry out she showers us both with silver nuts and bolts in their millions, falling like violent rain, strange and cruel as the confetti of some unimaginable wedding.

~

#10

Our final postcard from the future comes from Professor Saul Deveraux himself, inventor of the Retro-Temporal acceleration technology being deployed at Geneva's 'Even Larger Hadron Collider' to send messages back in time...

*

I hope you've enjoyed the previous nine messages over the last nine months. The same time as the gestation of a human child, perhaps not coincidentally. You see, the Retro-Temporal Postcard Program is very much my baby, my lifetime's work, albeit so well assisted by thousands of other dedicated scientists, the world over. I thank them all.

Will you people of the early twenty-first century believe that these messages are real? –That we in the 23rd century, really have mastered such incredible technology as to be able to send information back in time to you? As I write, there is no evidence in any of our libraries or history annals that these attempts were successful. But I confidently expect to go to the same data sources tomorrow and find that history has updated itself. Of course it will. But will I know? This paper I write on would have to disappear into thin air, in order for me not to know, and that seems unlikely. So history is going to change and we're going to see it change, almost instantly before our eyes. How extraordinary. That has never happened before in the history of our planet. Or has it? You see the irony?

The previous nine postcards, which I've read and vetted myself, all contain clues as to various fatal mistakes that you folks are destined to make. Will you take steps to try and avoid these, thus changing your future, and potentially making me disappear, or me and everything else here at least change form and substance so dramatically as to constitute another dimension, albeit that the previous one might cease to exist in its favour? Am I losing you? Am I losing myself? You see the irony?

Again this seems unlikely. Our view from here of our past must already incorporate all attempts to stop it happening. Not that such attempts are not worthy and noble, of course they are, it's just that they won't work. You will blow yourselves up with carelessly constructed nuclear fission technology. You will raise the water level of the entire planet due to runaway global warning, thus drowning numerous cities and costing the lives and livelihoods of millions. You will melt the ice caps and shut down the gulf stream. You will overuse antibiotics and fail to develop phage alternatives in time, thus allowing genetic plagues to wipe out further millions of lives.

If I know you won't heed our warnings, then why am I warning you? Well, in a way, I am simply returning the favour. You people warned us after all, with your wonderful books like 1984, We, and Brave New World. Did we listen to your advice, did we try to avert the crises that you warned us of? Well, we tried very hard, and we really listened, I can say that much. Your visions of the future did not incorporate our having read your warnings, and for that reason of course, they were all somewhat off the mark, but we have carved a better future in the enlightened shadow of your dire foretellings.

The inversion is perfect. Because looking back in time from here at this moment, it seems to us that you did nothing to heed the warnings we are sending back. In other words our past, your present, is merely a fiction, a satirical fiction, poorly constructed by a writer of great ability, perhaps even a shred of genius, but whose skill and vision falls sadly short of the grand parameters of the challenge he has set himself.

Thus do I, Professor Saul Frederick Deveraux, hereby declare our entire human past a fiction as mutable as the future, and resolve to hereby change it for the better. Thus, the present, past and future, have always been much more malleable and alike than any human being has dared hitherto to dream.

This is the last and most important of the ten postcards, the one that I predict will finally work, and visibly change the past around us, proving that our technology worked and that it's safe for us to send some human beings back next time. I am giving you all permission to change your world, to change your present, by giving you the knowledge that this is possible, that there is nothing to stop you.

Why do you hesitate? Now of all times, when you are so close to freedom, when what you have always needed is at hand? Are you afraid to open the door after all and let the demons of the future come rushing in with me at their helm? Am I, are we, so frightening? Have I sounded so unreasonable? By keeping quiet you condemn us to eternal ignorance of our success. Don't do that to us, to me. Let us come back and help you. We are nothing to be afraid of. We are only yourselves after all, taken to extremes, tried and tested across a hundred further generations than humankind has already endured. Are you so afraid to look in the mirror, to finally meet yourselves?

Or am I missing the point somehow? Are the people of the future, who rise successfully above the barbarism of the 21st century, by definition so different, so alien, as to be unrecognisable to the people of the past?

Hello? Is there anybody out there?

~

BLACK SUN

From the picture window, Verner watched the world disintegrate slowly, just a little more each day. The black graphite rocks of Cerberus-12 almost seemed to be taking flight, like homesick birds, as they were each drawn up into the air to begin their long journey towards the black orb that ruled the sky. Verner dialled up the Amundsens and spoke briefly to Ted, asking as Marie had suggested, that he and Leela come over for dinner. They would be leaving in just over a month, strict orders from Earth, the Cerberan environment finally deemed unstable beyond any semblance of safety.

Did you call them? Marie asked, drifting into the room behind Verner in her polyester evening gown, green and gold sequins glittering like mother-of-pearl. Fish-like, he thought to himself, remembering the Fluorocarbon Jellyfish and Benzoate Coelacanths that he and Sylvia had filmed in the Ice-7 glaciers beneath the MacAskill mountain range. His wife looked beautiful, all done up, tidying her home, tweaking little touches, but nothing about her could excite him again, he realised now in a moment of cold resignation. His heart was dead, crushed by black rocks. His life a glimpse, a fragment of blonde hair amid rubble, ruffling in alien winds. How could he tell anyone? How could he ever leave this dying world?

An hour later, they donned their life-suits and stood together at the window. Once they might have held hands or Marie rested her head romantically on his shoulder. But the suits were like a metaphor now, protection, prophylactic. Marie and he could never quite hear or touch or see each other clearly again, all communication dogged with static. And what of Sylvia then? At first he had feared the nightmares, but once Doctor Zildjian's pills had started working, he had come to miss them, quickly binned the medication. The sweats and nightmares were all he had left of Sylvia, their horror a just punishment, a bitter-sweet palliative for his guilt. Was it Nietzsche who had said something about training our conscience to kiss us as it bites?

From their quadruple-glazed toughened portal, Verner and Marie looked out at the black trail of lifting, floating rocks, a yellow-brick-road to hell, twisting, devil's tail of rubble, curling like a fiery intestine up towards the singularity. Slow as it was, it had something of the malign immanence of the dark grey twisters of the American plains back home. The twin gas giants of Fermi and Faraday were moving towards the horizon now, flooding the scene in bloody red light. Around the black hole: a corona of yellow anger like a perpetual eclipse, made Verner think, not for the first time; of some ruthless eye of an ancient deity scrutinising him, hungry for sacrifice.

He switched off the graviton field and he and Marie lifted slowly into the air and turned sideways, floating like the rocks outside, answering the call of all life on this God-forsaken world, drawn towards its dark master. They swam their way up towards the roof terminal, and Marie tut-tutted as a flock of apples and oranges drifted past them. *Damn* she cursed, sure she'd weighted them all down, thinking they'd have had that taped by now. Colony-wide energy regulations forbade the use of gravity fields in unpopulated rooms or homes. Occasionally a family dog would find itself bobbing around an interior all day while its owners were at work. Verner had seen some as he flew past other people's homes, eyes wide, tongues out, barking unheard behind the thick glass, like snowflakes adrift in a silent paperweight. He understood the feeling.

*

The Amundsens lived on the other side of Brewster Canyon, and the jump-jet flight over to pick them up always reminded Verner of the desert drama of Utah and Monument Valley, crossed with something darker and more impossible, like Tolkien's Mordor. Black jagged obsidian peaks rose up like frozen music, those ancient and hard enough not to have crumbled and yielded yet to the debris stream.

When they arrived at the Amundsen's, Ted was sitting watching a recent news report from the other hemisphere, something about the planet's red molten core becoming increasingly exposed, the danger of red lava and plasma leaking out into space, tongues of a red salamander, mischievously hoping to catch passing rockets and probes like so many flies. Two film crews had perished that way in the last year alone.

You're looking swell, Vern. Ted winked, probably lying, kissing Marie with a little too much relish as usual. Did he suspect, did he know something? Leela appeared in her black velvet jumpsuit, something he might have taken notice of once, but he only remembered Sylvia again, their furtive embraces in stolen moments, her pale freckled skin in the blue light of the decompression chamber.

Looking forward to returning to Centauri? Leela smiled, searching Verner's eyes for some glimmers of mischief that he didn't think he'd be able to summon up tonight. *You could even apply for return to Earth you know. Ted's been thinking about it.*

Ahh, Verner frowned, *that's the old conundrum, isn't it? Poverty back there after a ten year voyage or fabulous wealth out here with nothing to spend it on.*

Leela shot a glance at Marie, but Verner couldn't see her face, didn't need to. He could guess. *Verner has been a little morose again of late, Leela. I'm hoping he's not going to party-poop all evening.*

Yeah? The old black dog, eh? Ted looked up, grinning, switching the vid screen off, *as Winston Churchill called it. Nothing I can't sort out with a couple of beers and a few games of gravity hockey.*

*

Back at their place, some other guests turned up unexpectedly. Ted's boss Mendelssohn the local mining manager and his nephew and niece and a few neighbours. The music was turned up and Verner tried to bury himself in listening to other people's lives, the excited buzz concerning the impending evacuation. Unable to fit in, he drank too quickly, tried something new called Fermi Firewater that Mendelssohn's nephew, just past drinking age, was passing around like water on a desert hike.

Later, after nightfall, trying to be alone, Leela found Verner crying in the kitchen, gazing out at the debris trail, as the pale light of the white Etruscan moons ploughed across it.

95

The devil's tail, as they call it, he mumbled as she put her hand on his shoulder. *Flicking his frigging tail, shaking us all off finally.*

What's wrong? Leela asked him earnestly, manoeuvring him into a hidden corner next to the wine cellar vestibule. *You're not just homesick about leaving this place, are you? Nobody could be nostalgic about a place this inhospitable, surely? You and Marie hardly seem to talk these days. You don't even stand together in the same rooms, always at opposite sides of everyone and everywhere, estranged.*

Verner sobbed, and clutched his bottle, feeling dizzy, like losing his gravity, scared he'd let his guard down and just pour out his heart now. Watertight doors, his father had always told him. Bring them down in times of trouble. Ships, his analogy had referred to, but it worked pretty well for travellers on spaceships too. He should never have bought his son that telescope.

Are you sill getting those nightmares, Verner? The medication… why did you stop the counselling?

Leela, Leela… he shook his head, turning her name over like an exotic trinket, enjoying her blue eye-shadow, even the wrinkles there, she was ageing gracefully, her life in order, she didn't need his burdens. *Sylvia…* he had said the name aloud now and that was problematic. He looked at the bottle like a snake that had bitten him.

You had feelings for her, didn't you, Vern?

He frowned. Nobody had known that, not even himself at first. He'd been careful, damned careful. Somehow, with the drink now, it started to seem noble and heroic not to deny it for a while, to be philosophical. He would wear the pose for a moment, see how it suited him. *Was it that obvious?* he whispered hoarsely.

It was just an accident. Her hand was on his arm now, feeling his shivering. *You were cleared of responsibility.*

You're not listening, he grimaced. *You don't get cleared of love.*

Leela had heard him but was wishing she hadn't now. She couldn't understand from here on in, or understood too well. It made no difference. It was out now, like a black rock lifting crazily and counter-intuitively into the air, to fly towards the sun like Icarus, a black sun, an inversion, a whole life upside down on this flipside of the universe. A season in Hades.

Leela was no longer talking now, but she hadn't left either. To his amazement now he saw that she was crying, just standing

96

there quietly next to him in solidarity, her blue eye shadow running like smudged ink, her evening spoiled, an illegible diary entry. On the craziest of impulses, he drew her closer and kissed her full on the lips. Crazier still, she responded.

*

The next morning he decided to get up before Marie could confront him, if she knew anything. He didn't care enough any longer for a fight, and was afraid that even a glancing blow would be enough to dislodge him completely from the orbit of his automatic life. Gossamer-thin, a flickering moth, was how he felt in the morning light, looking at himself in the bathroom mirror. His pale skin struck him as resembling a caterpillar pupa, discarded filament he should somehow move beyond.

He took the solo jump-jet and headed for the mountains, but changed his mind halfway and found himself drawn back towards the debris stream. Far to the south, he found the planet's crust breaking up, great jagged fissures, whole stratum of rock peeling off like flaking skin, or crumbling bread tossed to the birds. It was so easy from above to imagine the stuff was lightweight, not massive enough to rip you in two.

Foolishly, maybe still a little drunk, he found the intensified pull of the singularity dragging his jet off course. He nearly giggled like a child at first, then cursed himself, then began to sweat, then panic. The jet was being drawn into the stream. Slowly, he was gliding in to meet the lifting boulders, their constantly rotating edges, some sharp as razor wire, spinning towards him. Helplessly, he found himself turned around to gaze up at the distant black hole. A shocking bullet wound in the duck-egg blue sky, an eye regarding him, whose rueful gaze he had not yet found the strength to ever quite return. And yet, unlike the sun back on Earth, to look at this one should do a man no harm at all. It only took in photons, fired out none of its own to burn out human retinas.

He was in the stream now. Ahead of him and around him: a vast bumping conveyor-belt of black rocks of every shape and size were jostling for the heavens. Suddenly they seemed to him to be singing like angels in a language he had never been able to make out before, somewhere beyond his audible range. The souls of the dead returning to God like shoals of dutiful fish. Or was it only to the open mouth an enormous shark?

With a sudden jolt, a massive boulder cut through Verner's cockpit glass, then his suit. He cried out. Another crunching impact wedged him between two shards. He was bleeding, losing pressure, blood and air hissing out of him like a punctured balloon...

Verner woke up with a start, breathing heavily, drenched in sweat. To his relief, he found Marie was still asleep beside him. He would take a cue from his dream, but do it less dangerously.

He took his diving gear and jump-jetted out to the accident site. He hadn't been there in nearly two years, since the investigation team had led him around asking questions. He donned his wet suit and dived into the black corrie, found the blue Rorschach-Fish that Sylvia has so admired, caught some of the Pink Gin Guppies that she'd said she wanted samples of. Was anyone studying these things in his place now? --His biological work abandoned in despair. Afterwards, he strolled along the cave mouths and lakeside where they'd first fallen in love, his heart melting. The fiery gas giants rotated, reflected perfectly in the mirror-flat emerald waters, then the black devil's tail edged in, rotating like a scimitar. He looked back over his shoulder, down the valley, the eye of the demon always watching him.

He picked some saffron Puffer Daisies from the methane vents and placed a little bouquet at the foot of the stainless steel cross, where it stuck out of the pile of rubble, the landslip that had killed her. For a moment, the horrible instant nearly replayed, a memory he still hadn't recovered, but it stayed out of reach. A smudge of sudden rock like a divine sleight of hand, a great gloved magician vanishing your life away before your very eyes. Verner picked up some of the stones: granite. A different composition here, much heavier. How long, he wondered, three or four years, before these started levitating too? Or would this whole canyon be ripping apart by then, shaken to pieces by earthquakes? He turned to look up at the impassive face of the cliffs above him, that had dispensed death, and almost bowed irrationally, putting the stone back down where he'd found it.

Strolling back towards the jet through the swaying groves of cyclacactus, their purple blossoms blew across him. He remembered them lodging in the long golden tresses of Sylvia's hair. He couldn't leave, he told himself, ever. He must stay and die somehow, on this world, even as it dissolved under him. Wasn't all life transient? The blossom, the trees, they didn't care, had received no panicked alarm call, high-pitched scream, from their Cerberan Gaia. Life would simply end, but go on existing somewhere else on some other planet. God was profligate it seemed, here as everywhere, but nonchalant, careless of his seed.

Was this all just black self-pity? Surely Verner had everything to live for still. Was one lost girl really any more special and irreplaceable than so many countless, doomed and dying worlds?

*

A week before the scheduled evacuation, Verner and Marie were invited to a wedding, the last one ever on the planet, symbolic, melancholy yet joyful, calculated by the colonial government to raise everyone's spirits and turn their hearts homeward, or forward at least. The sixteen-year-old daughter of a rocket pilot marrying a wealthy geologist three times her age. There was something frontier-like in these asymmetric unions, unusually common out here. Life on the edge. Like the deep American South or medieval Europe. The gene pool on the ropes, microbes threatened under a microscope.

Verner tried to enter the spirit of the thing, but was reluctant to touch the alcohol, knowing where that might lead him again. Leela greeted him and Marie with a painted smile, not meeting his eyes, anodyne, perfunctory. Then avoided them for the rest of the evening. Ted seemed odd, anger bubbling somewhere below the surface like a geyser. They hadn't seen each other since the party. *He knows...* Verner thought to himself, almost longing for a confrontation, a bloody nose from Ted to give him a penance, a masochistic punishment he could bask in, like a cleansing bath of fire.

Halfway through the ceremony there was a deep tremor then a fully-fledged earthquake. A volcano began to spout on the far horizon. Some women and children began screaming and crying, a few guys laughed hysterically like foolish adolescents before the reality sunk in. Someone switched on the news reports then radioed for emergency services.

Verner donned his life-suit and found himself outside standing next to a group of guys, Ted amongst them as it happened,

99

looking dumbly up into the western sky, like rabbits in the proverbial twin headlamps of Faraday and Fermi. The devil's tail was flicking, reversing. Someone was consulting a gravity meter, registering a violent polarity shift in the planet's core. A hail of small black volcanic stones began showering down on them as they hurried back indoors.

Before they could raise the security shutters the rock sizes had increased exponentially, some were bouncing dangerously against the window glass. Life-suits were being handed out, even for babies and children. A sudden power-cut dimmed the lights then the gravity field failed. Verner felt intense déjà vu for a moment, as if he were caught in a bizarre but familiar dream. The window shattered and stone fragments ricocheted through. Not everyone had got their suits on in time, there were screams of horror, sounds of choking, wails.

Clinging to a recessed corner with Marie, he found she was clutching his arm and he looked into her eyes, visor to visor, more directly than he remembered having done for months. Tears filled her eyes and she grimaced, something floating in the reflections on her glass. Verner turned and looked up to see the bride sailing past, rising into the air, her white dress billowing out behind her, palpitating like the umbrella of a jelly-fish. Blood unwound slowly from a wound between the long strands of her black hair. The orange and green flowers of her bouquet, still clutched in her hand, were breaking free and scattering but all moving upwards like birds flying south, drawn towards the jagged edges of the shattered window.

*

When the last evacuation rocket left orbit, Verner thought he could see an almost visible shudder of relief pass through everyone on board. He stood at a porthole and marvelled at the sight below him: the black and red guts of Cerberus, an eviscerated dog, spilling and trailing out, snaking away through space, drawn towards the singularity.

When autumn turned to winter the effect would lessen for a while, as Cerberus's orbit around Fermi moved it further out into space. Then the gas giants would suffer in its stead for a while, orange and red plumes of gas and plasma licking outwards, sending tributes to their tyrannical king.

Of the seven guests killed at the wedding, only the families of two had elected to have their loved-ones buried on Cerberus. It seemed a formula for grave-robbing after all, hardly eternal rest on a planet coming apart at the seams. Somehow the thought didn't bother Verner in connection with Sylvia's body, nor indeed his own, if he could still find the strength to carry out the plan that had been forming in his mind these last two months.

Ted and Leela were talking to Marie again and he went to stand tentatively at their periphery, where he was tolerated, if not fully acknowledged. Everyone was dressed in black. The five funerals were due to start within the hour, once the engines were safely pulling away from the singularity at a reassuring speed.

Whole planets have vanished in there before you know. Ted was holding forth, *And from what we can tell some of them might well have harboured life, intelligent life even. Some planets would have been dragged in quickly in one piece, depending on their orbits, their angle of incidence with the event horizon. Nobody can know for sure, but there is even an argument, for which the physics is quite sound incidentally, that a planet entering the singularity would experience time as a kind of landscape. Time and space would invert and change places.*

But what on earth would that be like? Marie marvelled.

*But we're not **on** Earth!* Leela reminded her pedantically, *You'd think we'd have stopped using that expression by now!*

Unimaginably difficult to say, probably. Ted mused, nearly meeting Verner's eye again at last. *I suppose instead of taking a walk to the shops or in the park, you could voyage into your past or future. Saunter around inside the temporal-spatial structure of your own life-signature at will. It would be like immortality maybe.*

Except… in an inescapable prison. Marie answered.

Immortality, heaven or hell, eternal damnation or the fields of Elysium. Leela whispered dreamily, fingering the white Cerberan Dahlia on her lapel, *Which would it be?*

What we make it, like life here, but with freewill removed perhaps. Ted responded sombrely, *if freewill has ever really existed anyway, that is.*

*

It was easy for Verner to slope off and not be missed these days. Everyone would presume he was in his cabin sulking morosely, and be loathe to engage him in another of his monosyllabic exchanges of late. They all understood that leaving the planet was difficult for him, but had spuriously decided a year ago that human etiquette made it impolite to discuss the loss of Sylvia with him any longer. Leela was an exception and look where it had got her. He would heal in time they thought, safely away from what was left of Cerberus-12. How wrong they were.

Fortuitously dressed in an immaculate black suit, he remembered his old widower uncle who had died alone and childless in a similar fashion back on Earth. A doctor diagnosing himself, lying down in bed with his will written at his side, waiting patiently to die, setting out on that last journey, to the last human frontier that humanity had not yet explored or despoiled.

Verner distracted the Chaplin, sent him on an errand then swapped himself for one of the corpses. He found the child of the group, a seven-year-old boy. It was a cruel choice, but the lightest body, easy to carry and conceal in a storage bulkhead. With only a bottle of Fermi Firewater for company, he clambered into the coffin pod and closed the shell over, drawing the discreet white curtain across the toughened glass window. What romantic lunatic had designed these things? A view for the dead. At least here was one at last, himself, who would enjoy it.

He knew the air wouldn't last long. But after the ceremony and short expulsion blasts, he found himself rapidly accelerating back towards the black hole. With his last moment of consciousness he locked stares again with that terrible bloodshot eye, spinning and spiralling all of life and death back into its inexorable heart.

*

In the beginning, singing. Fountain-mouth, all energy and matter spewing forth. The angels of light twisting, assembling the universe forwards. Verner found himself on Cerberus again, walking backwards. And suddenly there was Sylvia in his arms, blood on his hands, and his hands around her throat. Blotting out the memory with a dark avalanche of amnesia, he had strangled her, struck her skull with a rock. Now he made the piles of stones lift off her again,

102

setting her free. God himself for a moment, he restored her to life, unmade the argument that had sealed her fate, *their* fates. –Sucked back into his mouth all the foolish words that had shattered reality, brought the whole fragile temple of love tumbling down.

He walked back down the valley with her, hand in hand, the purple blossoms blowing the other way: no longer sowing life, but returning it all to its own bosom, stitching up *the raveled sleeve of care,* as Shakespeare had it. Instead of cyclacactus, he saw the trees were all huge human hands now, reaching up out of the ground and clutching at glowing orbs, the golden apples of the sun.

Finally back at the valley mouth, he saw that the devil's tail had gone, was just a faint ghostly memory in peripheral vision, a floating mote in the fevered eye. Were those asteroids, pale day-lit moons? In the debris stream's place, only strange white gossamer fragments were blowing outwards from a golden sun. He lifted his head and dared at last to look into the centre of all life: a great yellow dandelion unfurling in the interstellar winds. The eye looked at him, saw through him to his very core, and in its infinite mercy; burned him blind.

MULTIPLICITY

Vanessa Kandinsky wasn't at all sure that she liked her brand new twin. Or was she a daughter? Sitting in the coffee bar with her, eating two identical lunches of geodesic greens and soya shepherd's pie, it occurred to her that your younger self might actually be the most nightmarish company imaginable. After all, the girl across the table from her knew, by definition, most of her favourite jokes, all her humorous memories and interesting anecdotes. But, more worryingly, all her innermost fears and insecurities. They could almost make each other blush just by thinking about it, like microphone feedback or infinite regression between two mirrors.

You realise we're not quite the same, don't you? Vanessa asked her counterpart, who laughed in a horridly familiar way and stirred her herbal tea, having completely anticipated the question.

Yes, the doctor's told me I'm the impure one. The other Vanessa smiled coyly.

God, Vanessa thought, do I do that? Is that what that stupid smile of mine really looks like?

I'm the one whose genes have been putting it about a bit, Vanessa two continued.

It's worse than that, Vanessa thought darkly, and she saw a shiver of discomfort ripple across her likeness who'd doubtless guessed her line of thought.

I'm the mongrel, the incestuous child, your fucked-up teenage daughter par excellence, the product of a relationship not just broken, but which never even came into existence, right?

Vanessa raised her eyebrows in cynical consternation, then answered, *On the bright side, however, your impurities, our differences, might well be all that make you bearable, you tedious little brat... Oh look!*

They both turned their heads to see Jeff Burroughs leaving the canteen, and dissolved into stifled laughter that broke the awkwardness between them. They had taken to sighing with relief whenever he left any room they were in, easing their embarrassment. *Dad or lover?* The younger Vanessa joked, catching Vanessa off guard; her mature brain had been side-tracked by a different thought-in-progress.

Vanessa laughed nervously. Incredible. She had caught herself off guard, quite literally – or was it the other way around? – and made a joke she didn't see coming.

*

When the Hyperion entered the edge of the singularity, Vanessa and most other crew were in their cabins and about to go to sleep for the night. A few lucky souls happened to snore through the whole sequence of events, but most were either roused by the jolts or had not yet closed their eyes for the night. By way of compensation, the sleepers had some pretty weird dreams. What Vanessa experienced was certainly dreamlike, but it was unrelentingly real and concrete in its repercussions.

At 10.56 p.m, as she stepped into her dressing gown, there was a momentary flash, after which she looked up and found five identical versions of herself – one for each of the five other planes of the cubic room within which she stood. On the ceiling, a version of herself hung upside down from feet that seemed held by their own localised gravity. On each of the four walls, other versions of her projected sideways, feet walking along the walls as if held by magnetic glue.

Her first reaction was to think that she was looking at some kind of mirror box, a series of reflections. But each of her doppelgangers were looking up, down and sideways in slight variations of her own pose, and were already making different small sounds of astonishment and terror. In the immediately ensuing seconds, this divergence only increased, as each of the six Vanessas expressed their full shock and curiosity in different words. Eventually, tentatively, some of them even reached out and touched each other, locked hands, caressed strands of each other's long brown hair, hair drawn in six different directions as if caught in invisible winds.

They spoke to each other.

I am Vanessa.

So am I.

So are they.

So are we all.

What's happening?

No ideas?"

The captain did say something about turbulence at dinnertime.

Some kind of localised distortion in space-time?

Could it be connected in some way to that distant black hole bending the orbit of the planet we're circling?

Can we press the intercom and hail the captain.

Who?

All of us

Which of us?

Do we all have walls and intercoms that work?

Does that mean there are six Hyperions and six captains?

Will they all reply the same way?

Or is it just us six who're messed-up here, all of us, all of me, in this room?

Some of the Vanessas tried to switch planes, wrestling with their neighbours to try and dislodge themselves, but the relative gravity of each wall was overwhelmingly strong. From each standpoint, on closer inspection, the floor surface of the other five planes appeared intermittent and unstable. The cream ceramic floor tiles beneath Vanessa's feet could mostly be seen on each of the walls now, but as she moved her head back and forward in confusion some of the tiles would flick in and out of sight, replaced by the white polycarbonate panels of standard cabin walls. Moving around her own floor with great care, Vanessa finally managed to manipulate one of these visual glitches to catch a glimpse of her own TV wall, with its screen still showing God-knows-what news bulletins it had been sending out before the anomaly struck.

After about five minutes of this confusion and wonder, a further level of distortion began to become apparent to the six Vanessas. Three of them were getting rapidly younger, the other three getting older, all at slightly different speeds. They each reached forwards, down and up to embrace and caress each other's faces and hands, and cried out in awe. Hair was getting greyer, backs were bent, while others' voices were getting lighter, limbs more slim and nimble, faces more youthful, skin softer to the touch.

The implication of this began to alarm them all. One of the Vanessas went to the door of the cabin and opened it (with some difficulty – it was on the floor of another Vanessa's plane and only intermittently visible). The Vanessa walking on that floor then used the door as a means to climb down through her floor and peer out into the corridor beyond. She could make out other open doors in the distance with the heads and arms of a few fellow crew peering out, shouting to each other.

What the devil's going on?
Have you got doppelgangers too?
How many?
Has everyone got six?

Marie Helsen in Room 43 claimed to have only two doubles. Hers was a circular room, as Marie was a high-ranking officer in a corner cabin. The circular wall reflected to infinity, producing no multiples, the first clue to some of the physics of the phenomenon underway. Had anything as strange as a spherical room existed on the Hyperion, then its occupant might have remained completely singular and unaffected.

Curiously, as would later be established during debriefing, every passenger became sexually aroused at 11.36 p.m. By then, Vanessa's semblance on the ceiling was a five-year-old child and accelerating fast towards loss of vocabulary and potty training. Her left-hand wall-mate appeared to be about eighty-five years old, frail and gaunt, with failing hearing. Clearly something was about to give in the next five minutes if these rates of divergence continued.

Vanessa began to notice a swelling in her stomach and odd pains in her breasts. Her sexual arousal dissipated but she began to feel morning sickness. At 11.44 p.m., in agony and writhing on her cabin floor, Vanessa gave birth to a beautiful baby girl who quickly began growing. At the same moment, the old woman on her wall raised her withered left hand in the air, fell to the floor and the light went out of her eyes. Then another Vanessa, who had shrunk to the size of a tiny baby writhing on the ceiling, condensed into a foetus, rapidly dissolved into a pool of discoloured liquid, then was gone.

The two empty planes now available on the cube didn't stay so for long. Picking herself up off the floor and cradling her baby in her arms, Vanessa soon found she could hardly lift the growing weight of her rapidly expanding progeny. The baby's gravity flipped, and it found itself torn away from its mother. Vanessa and her baby reached desperate hands out for each other as the little girl's feet touched down on the adjacent wall where the old woman's body had now decomposed into an abstract white skeleton.

On the wall opposite this, she now saw a younger version of herself, ageing backwards at slower speed, had also given birth. In a matter of minutes she too would be separated from her newborn child and flipped by gravity onto an adjacent surface. Down below her to the right, an older version now gasped and fell to her knees in pain and exhaustion, approaching senility.

At 12.06 a.m., Vanessa forced herself onto an adjacent wall again and broke out through a floor hatch into the corridor. Her gravity changed and flipped her onto the corridor floor and she made her way, shouting for help, down the quarter-mile long corridor of the cabin deck of the Hyperion. Doors opened where they shouldn't have been, in ceilings and floors and upside-down on walls, the vessel's architecture apparently bent out of shape and shifted into interdimensional nonsensicality. From these opened doors, various alarmed faces looked out and screamed, some of them recognisable as younger or older versions of Vanessa's colleagues.

When she eventually made it to the bridge, Vanessa found three captains, three first-mates, six pilots and five navigators (an oddity – the man had a triangular room on D-wing). All were floating about in differential gravity planes and feverishly debating with each other, often coming to blows, attempting to form various complex alliances with each other's doubles and sextuples, but to no lasting avail.

Fortunately, at 12.23 a.m. precisely, the Hyperion drifted out of the sphere of influence of the dwarf singularity, and normal gravity, spatial order and timeframe were restored, enabling the vessel to return to normal and its occupants to resume (almost) normal life.

The unfortunate exceptions were those like Vanessa who had been brave and curious enough to leave whatever rooms they had been trapped in at the start of the phenomenon. The number of semblances depended on the number of planes the shape of each room constituted. The captain and the highest ranking officers on the bridge – who had remained in the circular room – were all restored from triplicate to unitary status. But the six pilots and five navigators – who had all rushed to the bridge from their cube and triangle-shaped quarters nearby – were, by force of arithmetic, only reducible back to twin forms, with duplicate memories and experiences.

Similarly, Vanessa became only one of two versions of herself, the escaped bridge version (which the circular room could not reduce any further) and the reunified cabin version made from the five or six semblances of herself she had left behind on the walls and ceilings of her own cubic room. Weeks of subsequent medical tests on the biology of the surviving crew, and analyses of the maths and physics involved, revealed stranger and more subtle implications however.

During the period of rapid sexual arousal, sperm or eggs from each of the individuals in each of their cabins had somehow travelled instantaneously through the intervening walls in order to conceive with the nearest individuals in each case. Thus what Vanessa had perceived as a younger version of herself born from her own womb, had in fact been a child of the involuntary union of herself with the junior deck-hand Jeff Burroughs, the nearest male individual 'as the crow flies' (and the crow had indeed flown it seemed).

More troublingly, after Vanessa had left the cabin, this Jeff-Vanessa composite had gone on to grow up and become pregnant, again by Jeff Burroughs, a biologically incestuous union with all the potential health (not to say moral and social) implications that involved.

Vanessa was at least glad that she was female. Her male colleagues trapped in their own rooms should of course have been unable to get pregnant, but after the death of some of their older versions they had somehow produced younger versions of themselves. Analysis of these individuals after the phenomenon revealed that, largely unknown to themselves, they had become genital hermaphrodites with a confused mixture of sexual urges and proclivities, which would give them social and psychological difficulties in the months to come. The anomaly had activated their latent female characteristics; they had even briefly acquired primitive wombs, in order to ensure their survival.

In effect, most of the crew could now no longer be sure who they were, having become the incestuous offspring of themselves and at least one other (sometimes unknown) crew member with whom they might never have exchanged a single word. Post-anomaly reunification had fused their DNA with semblances which had been progressively 'polluted' by each reproductive phase.

Sexual relationships were generally discouraged between serving crew members, for fear of the professional tensions and jealousies this can give rise to in a working environment. Nonetheless, on the evening of the singularity/multiplicity event, Michelle Dinari and Dimitri Mladic were in bed together and engaged in the sexual act. They were both multiplied to the other five planes of their room, and looked up and about in horror as the various versions of themselves screamed and scrambled around trying to get out of bed and dressed again. Their aroused and reproductive phases produced accelerated offspring – following the same weird principles as all the other rooms – a male and female child simultaneously each time, to replace their own rapidly ageing selves as progenitors. In this respect, their experience was apparently more biologically healthy and normal than the other instances, but the conclusion of their experience of the event was less so.

Multiplied as a copulating pair, they were each standing apart and facing different directions at the time of their reunification, with unfortunate results. In the manner of Siamese twins, the creature that emerged from their room after the phenomenon had passed had arms and legs capable of attempting movement in opposite directions simultaneously, a neck which could rotate 360 degrees, and two faces: one for Michelle, one for Dimitri. Their shared brain was in some senses schizoid, bipolar or stereo. But perhaps ambidextrous would be a better term. They were both people at once, unified in one body.

Arguably, this outcome is only the insane subconscious wish of every couple who have ever fallen passionately in love.

Arguably, this outcome is the living hell of every unhappy marriage.

*

Vanessa had always liked Michelle and Dimitri and enjoyed talking with both of them, often at once, when she socialised out-of-hours at the Hyperion's several bars and cafés and its geodesic gardens on the ecology wing. Sadly, talking with both of them exactly at once was no longer an option.

She made her excuses and left her half-twin at her table staring out a picture porthole into deep space, while she took her lunch tray over to sit with Michitri (or was it Dimelle?). Michelle faced her first and they conversed happily for five minutes before a tearful look of regretful farewell entered her eyes and she spun her neck in one brief, but sickening, motion to hand Vanessa over to Dimitri.

What's that shifty bitch been telling you about me? Dimitri laughed. *Always hoarding you for herself these days. Says I've been getting paranoid about her talking behind my back all the time. Can you believe it? Every time I spin around she's gone. Even in the mirror I can never find her. Sometimes with two mirrors I can nearly see past myself. But you know what really frightens me, Vanessa?*

No, Vanessa shook her head, trying to smile politely, trying to conceal her discomfort and embarrassment at this conjugal scrap unfolding in front of her.

How can all the rest of you be so sure that you haven't had a hidden face all these years, hiding at the back of your head, under your hair? Another you, facing the other way, feeling completely different about everything, with diametrically opposed opinions? I mean, it would explain a hell of a lot, wouldn't it? Self-doubt, voices in your head, nostalgic longings to go back the way you came, retreat from the universe, go home and recover the way things were, the way they seemed as a child before life got so damned complicated. You know what I mean?

Yes, I think I do. Vanessa smiled gently, and brushed her hair from her eyes, involuntarily running her hand down the back of her scalp before returning it to her side.

*

Later, on her way to the recreation wing, Vanessa chanced to catch sight of her younger version sitting in a café with… it couldn't be… surely? But it was. Jeff Burroughs. And the two of them were waving to her now, gesturing to her to come and join them. For a moment she was tempted to pretend she hadn't seen them and hurry on by, but she knew deep down there was something here she was going to have to face sooner or later.

When she approached them she could have sworn they'd been holding hands, and she had to stifle an instinctive reaction of revulsion. Was Vanesssa-junior his daughter... sort of? Or to the extent that she was partially Vanessa-senior, his ex-lover... sort of? The ambiguity of everything in between was a queasy no-man's land. But maybe not to Vanessa-junior, who, judging by her winsome smiles and giggles, found the situation had some frisson of elicit danger about it. Had Vanessa been so silly herself in her early twenties? She struggled to remember.

Vanessa sat down nervously in front of them and engaged in a conversation which seemed to constantly yield common ground, as if the three of them were a happy little family waiting to happen. How quaint. When junior went to the toilet, Vanessa seized the opportunity to inject some sobriety into the proceedings and draw a line in the sand. Jeff was scarcely more than a boy himself, although he looked a little different now, having reputedly sullied his DNA with a cleaner from F wing.

Jeff, as far as I'm concerned what supposedly happened between us biologically was something abstract, unreal, a freak accident, something with no emotional basis in the real world. I hope you realise that?

Really? Jeff frowned, taken aback. *But don't you feel anything for your... your...*

She winced. He was about to say the dreaded D word. *You think of my younger self as your daughter, is that what you're saying?*

Shit... no... Mrs Kandinsky, she's hot as hell and just my type and age. But you've never really liked yourself much, have you? Maybe if you'd had more luck with men when you were younger then you might have more self-esteem. Why not think of it as a second chance? Life is generally short on those.

Vanessa stared at Jeff aghast, and hated him in that moment, firstly for being so chauvinistic, but secondly for probably being right. But just how could that be? Of course... betrayed by that little minx sharing her intimate secrets. Betrayed by her self. For a moment she struggled with an overwhelming urge to slap Jeff, or indeed Vanessa two when she returned from the toilet, in the face.

But instead she closed her eyes and took a deep breath, started to count up to ten.

She saw the joke at three. Could she actually be jealous of herself?

Vanessa two returned and she greeted her with a disarming smile. Vanessa made her excuses and got up to leave. After all, what better fate or more fitting punishment could she imagine for an errant daughter than a boyfriend like Jeff? She was looking forward already to the redoubled pleasure of her solitary cabin and unitary existence. But maybe… just maybe, she'd start spending more time this year with that nice engineer on D wing. Sleeping in separate rooms of course. Just to stay on the safe side.

~

QUASAR RISE

Sophie Saleri took her morning stroll along the shore of the tranquil chloride lake that fronted her geodesic hacienda in Millicent Canyon. This was what had passed for sunrise on Strobos these last five years, the pale twilight thrown by the planet's gaseous parent world Sybelle, rising up from the horizon, dragging its twin rings of asteroid debris around it like a ballerina's skirts, with all the hypnotic grace the metaphor implied. Sophie watched the first ripples appearing in the lake at her feet, as Sybelle's gravitational force exerted itself and a cooling breeze swept the valley floor.

Soon all this would be over. Sophie had begrudged this miserly twilight at first, the lack of real sunshine, when she had been awakened from suspended animation when the rocket landed. But now she had the feeling she was going to miss it. Strobos's peculiar sixty year orbit was about to rotate it fully into the light from Nephalim-3 at last, exposing it to the insane flashes of a quasar, hitherto hidden behind Sybelle.

Sophie paused to sit on her favourite boulder and toss pebbles into the largely lifeless surface of the lake, just a few single-cell organisms, a big disappointment to all the many biologists and botanists she had arrived with. The irony that had brought the shyest girl in school into the limelight of selection for a scholarship and space travel was about to be doubled: Sophie was epileptic. Sensitivity to flashes was still the rarest form of epilepsy, contrary to common misconceptions. But the expensive protective eyewear that the colony administrators had distributed to every household would soon be more than just a means of staving off headaches and distraction for Sophie. Without them, she might expect to collapse and die.

Sophie's communicator bleeped in her pocket and she looked up to see a black gyrocopter coming down over the head of the canyon. It was Brigid. Sophie had forgotten inviting her over and now she hurried back towards the house, tip-toeing gingerly over the sharp tellurium rocks of the lake shore, padding onto fine yttrium sands, already warm in the Sybellian dawn.

By the time she reached the landing pad at the back of the hacienda, Brigid was already stepping down from the cockpit, taking her goggles off, smiling broadly, unwinding her unruly crop of blonde hair.

Have you heard the news yet? Brigid asked as they went indoors. *About Wau Lei?* Sophie shook her head as she made the tea, flavoured with Stroban thistles, a token of regionalism, the dull herb pretty much the apex of the planet's meagre botany. *She's given birth to a little girl.*

Another one? Sophie gasped, astounded. She did not mean that Wau Lei was the mother of many children. In fact, her little girl Hope Lei, was her first child. What concerned them was that of the ninety-six births so far on Strobos, only seven had been boys, and only two of those had survived beyond eighteen months.

What is it with this planet? Sophie asked rhetorically. *Sometimes I think this place is cursed.*

Brigid looked at her reproachfully and Sophie regretted her lack of tact instantly. Brigid had miscarried six times since the colony's foundation. *The space journey...* Sophie continued, *I've always thought, despite what the physicists said, that exposure to the quasar flashes, however slight, might have damaged the sperm banks, even with the lead shielding.*

Well, don't ask me, I'm a mining engineer. Brigid sighed, putting her feet up on Sophie's bean bag couch, letting the sky light fall pleasurably across her face. *But I reckon it's not the physicists we should have asked, it's the geneticists. My new girlfriend Samira is a geneticist. She says the jury is still out on what's up with the sperm, whether the gamma rays and alpha particles could have depleted its vitality. There's no hard evidence.*

Sophie quietly hated it when Brigid or anyone else used the term girlfriend. The word was surely redundant on Strobos, the only choice of partner being female. *My grandmother on Earth says it's a judgement on us, for not taking any men with us, that God is displeased.*

116

She writes letters? Brigid asked. There was a time when they would have found the religious angle hilarious, but these days it almost hurt like everything else.

Well, her carer transposes them via NASA.

NASA were clear on it, as were all the statisticians, remember. Interstellar rocket travel has a high mortality rate. Even 50% fatality on an all-female crew leaves twice as many breeding stock as a mixed crew, with the aid of cryogenic sperm storage.

Breeding stock... is that all we are to them, to each other? What an appalling term. And increasingly a misnomer the way things are looking.

Oh, that's too pessimistic, surely? Brigid sighed, standing up and pacing over to Sophie's picture window, pondering the view of Sybelle, the ever-changing light on its rotating asteroids. *All we need is young Frank Smith or Walter what's his name?*

Gustaffson.

When they reach sixteen and have sex with someone other than their mother or sister we should be back on track, don't you think?

Another six years? Can you wait that long?

What choice have we?

The poor little bastards.

Quite literally, Brigid frowned grimly.

It doesn't sound like it's going to be much fun for them, does it? A coming of age from hell, surrounded by leering old women!

Oh Sophie... Brigid sighed, brushing Sophie's hair in melancholy compassion, *there will be girls their own age, you know that. You sound so depressed sometimes, it's not healthy. Let's go visit Wau Lei. A new baby, and what's more there's all this talk of the quasar rise, are you not excited?*

Somehow, after that, Sophie didn't want to mention the epilepsy. The flashing skies that were coming soon could all be assuaged by a set of goggles. That was the scientific answer, and scientists could never be wrong, could they?

*

Sophie's first real seizure had occurred when she was four years old on Earth. She still remembered it vividly. A passing train, intense sunlight through the vertical slats of a timber fence. Somewhere in these seemingly harmless ingredients had been enough to switch her brain to overload, send her limbs writhing into uncontrollable spasms, relieved only by morphine injection and sleep.

The thirty-five years in suspended animation sleep had been supposed to be dreamless, but Sophie remembered vague and dimly-lit nightmares of flashing lights and weirdly lush gardens, conversations in unknown languages with shady figures just out of sight. The tendrils of a strange blue rose wrapping itself around her wrist, pricking her with its twisting thorns. Like childhood memories, but none she'd ever known. Someone else's dreams.

*

Arriving at Wau Lei's house, Sophie was impressed by her corral of sheep and pigs, approached from above, running around in panicked circles beneath the lowering gyrocopters. Their feed was a meagre mixture of pashaweed and suckergrass, supplemented by vitamin pills and the occasional potato. Wau Lei and her neighbours had successfully turned a tract of Stroban desert into a potato plantation, but the crop yield was still unreliable from one season to the next.

Wau was sitting up in bed, attended by colony nurses when Sophie and Brigid sauntered in. To their surprise and delight young Frank Smith also arrived with his mother shortly afterwards, being an old neighbour from the next valley. The rarity and splendour of his maleness nearly upstaged the new baby itself, a pink wailing blob in a knot of blankets.

Have you seen Walter today? You two been off hiking together again? Sophie and Brigid asked, awkwardly trying to make conversation with him in that earnest way that adults had. Not surprisingly, Frank and Walter were well known for seeking each other out for company, increasingly intimidated perhaps, by the world of girls they found around them.

Conversation at Wau Lei's bedside revolved around news about the impending quasar rise. Speculation was rife among biologists and botanists as to what effect quasar flashes might have on indigenous plant life and the limited number of known insects and microbes.

I heard a story on the radio just before I went into labour about how the Stroban patchmoss has begun changing colour in the regions

118

closest to the south pole, and that a breed of special new insect has started to appear there. They think the insect might have been born from the moss somehow, a kind of plant-insect hybrid.

Oh hooey... Brigid laughed, *you must have been hallucinating under the painkillers. This barren rock ain't gonna sprout legs any time soon.*

Young Frank began to chatter excitedly in that breathless way that only teenagers can, about how Walter and him had found a rock pool over at St-Brandon's Cove last week which had been teeming with something like frogs. Brigid and Wau Lei reacted sceptically, but Sophie quizzed him with dramatic interest which was not entirely feigned. *How do you know what frogs looks like?* She asked.

His mother answered for him *Oh, he's seen them on the Earth Encyclopaedia we have. I told him how my brother and I used to catch them in nets in the local river when we were kids back in Wyoming. He must just have seen some scumfish and some twigs or something.*

No, Mum. They were like frogs. Walter saw them too, they were crawling out the pool and bouncing around like frogs only different, with red bits and green spines on their backs and wings, I think they had wings too. We tried to catch some but they moved too fast.

Carla, Frank's mother, rolled her eyes in exasperation, used to her son's exotic imagination and powers of hyperbole. *Frank exaggerates...* Carla whispered.

Yes, so did my father, Brigid sighed. *Do you think maybe it's a male thing?*

God I hope not, Sophie groaned. *That phrase has become the biggest cliché in the colony these last ten years. Everything missing or elegiac in our world gets ascribed to maleness. Are we starting to forget already what men were really like?*

We have young Frank and Walter to remind us now, Carla said, defensively, curling a hand around Frank's shoulder.

Yes, but who can they learn it from, with no role models?

No drunken slob staggering home late from the pub, you mean? Brigid laughed.

-to watch football and fall asleep with a half-eaten burger and fries on a plate on their chest you mean?

But the jokes, aired many times before, rang hollower now. *We miss them...* Carla sighed, tears coming to her eyes, while little

Frank, mollycoddled to a fault, looked around bewildered by the wistful faces around him, unable to comprehend their longing, still less to grasp that he might embody its resolution.

*

It was fortunate that Strobos had proven rich in rare Earth metals such as yttrium and tellurium, because this had not been NASA's primary motive for the colonisation. Viewed from Earth with the Hawking Deep Space Telescope, the signature profile of elements and compounds present had suggested a planet teeming with life, being highly rich in water, oxygen and amino acids. That this had not been what the astronauts found upon landing, remained a troubling mystery.

But on the day of the Quasar Rise, belatedly, they received their answer.

Brigid and Carla and young Frank were over at Sophie's house, looking out over the edge of the eastern desert, the adults drinking together on the porch, toasting the new rising star in the east, and laughing at each other's protective eye-wear. Suddenly their communicators began ringing and news reports started flooding in.

A glade of scrubweed at Cutters Gulch had swamped a house next to it, the Mathesons, who had fled in panic, their windows smashing, timber walls buckling and snapping. A pool of some sort of fish round at Mount Gerhart had been spilling in their thousands over a mining access road, making the wheels skid, bringing commerce to a halt.

Sophie didn't dare take her eye protection off, but to those who did for a moment, the sky was alive with stroboscopic flashes, a rapid and violent rhythm that goggle lenses were contrived to store and attenuate into an even glow more bearable to the eyes. Scientists had presumed that the flashes would boost life through imparting energy or sterilise and kill it through harmful levels of radiation. Perhaps what they had failed to take account of, because it had no parallel on Earth, was the specific effect of the stroboscopic rhythm.

Film was being broadcast on several channels simultaneously, of diverse events across the planet, all of them unpredicted and fast-moving. Jumping into a land-hopper, Sophie and Brigid didn't have to travel far to encounter real phenomena first-hand. As the quasar rose into the sky, a thicket of long grass at the lakeside was growing rapidly, flowering and disseminating its seeds on the breeze in a way it had never done before. As a botanist, Sophie was both exhilarated and frightened.

As they stepped out of the vehicle and walked over to the base of the grass, they saw how each grass blade was thickening into creepers which then lashed out, spilling onto the roadway, each vine and creeper searching blindly for footholds. *Like time lapse photography...* Sophie muttered.

What's that you said? Brigid asked.

Distracted for a second, Sophie cried out to discover a creeper vine had wrapped itself around her ankle. She yelled and kicked, backed away, but was dismayed to see the thing would not let go, was clutching tighter and tighter, drawing blood. Brigid knelt and bit and scratched at the vine, trying to stay calm, then ran back to the vehicle to get a knife. Sophie's relief as she was cut free was overwhelming, and she hugged Brigid, kissing her cheek.

They backed away together and climbed back into the land-hopper, sweating and breathing hard, recoiling from the hissing, writhing mass in front of them.

Back at the house they found that other strange vegetation was expanding and advancing from every horizon. Carla and her son stood in awe at the back door, feeding bread to a creature that no one had ever seen before. Somewhere between a frog and a rabbit, but with a black slimy coat and red eyes, the thing almost seemed intelligent, sitting up on its hind legs and making strange vocalisations, turning its eyes from one human to the next, licking its lips and flicking its long blue feathered tail. Sophie and Brigid tip-toed closer very carefully, wary of disturbing it, but it seemed fearless.

What is it? Brigid whispered.

We don't know, Carla responded, *but look, there's more of them.* Behind the creature and all the way down the lawn towards a shallow pool, the grass was discoloured by patches of black slime, some of which was writhing, even emitting sounds.

It's like evolution in fast forward, Sophie marvelled, *a million years of natural selection in one day, a century in every minute.*

Charlie... young Frank said. *Let's call it Charlie. I think that's its name. Mum, can we keep him as a pet?*

At that moment a flock of peculiar-looking green bats flew by, expelling orange gas from their mouths and some of "Charlie's" fellow creatures looked up at them with interest. Further blue and green feathers were emerging on the frog-rabbits' backs now, and a red barbed appendage uncurling from their stomachs. At the sound of an ear-splitting screech from one of them, a group of four or five of the creatures began leaping into the air by flapping their rudimentary wings, and sinking their teeth and claws into the bats, bringing them squawking to the ground in protest, before tearing them apart in a feeding frenzy. Carla took Frank's hand in fear as he began to cry, and the four of them edged back into the house.

Their communicators were flashing with urgent messages. The mother of Frank's best friend Walter was distraught, saying that their entire township on the east side of Galvin Valley was under threat from rapidly expanding jungles of creepers and she couldn't find Walter. –That their water source was polluted with a plague of weird black fish and that fires had broken out as electrical appliances had begun shorting as walls and roofs gave way.

Carla was anxious to return home herself, but a few calls established that the colony administrators were forbidding return, declaring Galvin Valley an emergency area. Sophie insisted that Carla and Frank make themselves at home in her house while she and Brigid gyrocoptered back over to look at the place from above. Civilian flights were being discouraged, but they felt compelled to offer any help they could. Carla kept babbling about her house and possessions and Brigid was already warning her that she might have to resign herself to the loss of those if martial law was in force and her neighbourhood too dangerous to be saved.

*

Flying high over the jagged peaks of the Millicent Mountains, Brigid pointed towards where the white orb of the quasar was fully visible at last, lifting up from the western horizon. It looked almost innocent, with eye-protection on, but Brigid, ever the dare-devil, was taking hers off intermittently and laughing in deranged exultation. *It's amazing, Sophie. Have you seen it properly? The flashes are so intense, there's almost a colour to them, although the opthalmists have been saying that's just a symptom of the human retina being over-stimulated. Go on, take your goggles off, Soph'…*

Smoke was visible now in the next valley, spindling up into the air from Galvin City, an insanely active green jungle encroaching upon it, where none had existed before. The world was falling apart suddenly, the human world at least, while something else, some alien ecology, was just getting going. It struck Sophie for a minute as being like America's old Wild West somehow, history gone wrong and re-written, the ghost dance working, invisible Red Indians rising up to murder the white man… or woman.

I'm epileptic -Sophie answered at last. It didn't seem to matter now, or maybe it mattered more than anything, she wasn't sure anymore. This secret affliction that somehow united her with this looming white orb peering over the edge of her world like the malevolent eye of Moby Dick, looking for her, its hidden sister.

What was that? Brigid asked, distracted, steering the copter down over waterfalls, their water clouded now, foaming with life.

I'm an epileptic she repeated. *I can't look at flashing lights, you know, strobes. I used to have fits when I was a child.*

You're joking, right? Sorry, you must be. Right? Brigid laughed nervously.

No, I'm afraid not, I'm completely serious.

Brigid turned to look at her wide-eyed, nearly swerving the copter, clipping some worryingly new-looking trees. *Then why on earth did you sign-up for this planet? Isn't that like a turkey voting for Christmas? –Pardon me if I'm being insensitive.*

The eye-wear protects me, Brigid, and no, it's not insensitive of you, it's perfectly alright. I suppose I've always been curious. It's such a strange condition, affliction I suppose I should say. I always imagined as a child that it was some secret gift, that it meant something, made me special in some way that no one has yet discovered. I suppose I wondered, childish though it sounds, if maybe the answer was here, in a world, a whole solar system, of flashing light.

Brigid was preparing to land now, amid the smoking ruins of the town square of Galvin City, people running across in confusion, the colony's small military forces trying to keep order. *Can we keep this conversation until later… I mean it's fascinating but…*

Kind of a strange time for it to come out, I know, sorry.

123

No, no, it's my fault for asking. Just one question though. Is this why you didn't sign up for the insemination programme? I mean, is epilepsy inheritable? Forgive me if I'm being too personal of course...

Sophie was almost insulted for a moment, absurdly, at a time like this. But the same emergency conditions had somehow dropped her guard. *No, no, it's not that, it's never been that. I've just never wanted children somehow.*

As the copter touched down, the two women looked at each other briefly, climbing out of their doors, and Brigid's gaze was one of complete incomprehension, her eyebrows raised. In all the time of their friendship, she wondered if they had ever really known each other at all.

*

They quickly found that Carla's neighbourhood was indeed out of bounds but that an urgent search party was underway. Each of the many fleeing faces they passed, people carrying their possessions on their backs, were animated with one story, one rumour: that Walter, the golden boy, one of only two possible heirs, living keys to the future of the colony, had gone missing in the hills and that everyone should be out looking for him.

One old woman Sophie had never seen before, wild-eyed and deranged, hair dishevelled, confronted Sophie and babbled superstitious nonsense at her, clutching her arm: *This planet's cursed, sweetheart, it's killed all our male seed for a reason, strangled all our baby boys. It will finish off the others soon. It doesn't want us to multiply, it's plain as day, always has been... now we'll see!*

Sophie tried to persuade the woman to put a pair of goggles on but she threw them away bitterly, then hurried away. *We're doomed, we're a dying race, a planet of barren women!* she wailed over her shoulder.

Brigid and Sophie reported to the emergency military commander, a tall muscular ex-girlfriend of Brigid's supposedly, who had a police psychologist consoling and counselling Walter's mother in a tent nearby. Commander Fernandez accepted their offer of help and they took off again in Brigid's copter, swooping low over the heads of the search party; a long line of women, sweeping the Stroban heather as they advanced slowly through it, moving upwards

124

towards the lower slopes of Mount Galvin. Sophie wondered if the heather was still stable, then noticed some of the women were pointedly tearing an unfamiliar blossom from some of its branches as they were passing.

As a botanist, Sophie had studied the Stroban heather in some depth and knew at a glance that the blossom was novel. The whole planet seemed to be entering a new phase simultaneously, a kind of cosmic spring, on a delayed timescale unimaginable on Earth.

Brigid and Sophie landed half a mile above the search party line then began exploring on a hunch. They had heard Frank talking recently about he and Walter exploring caves somewhere on Mount Galvin, and they could see rock fractures nearby which might fit this description.

The rock pools inside the caves were overflowing with bright turquoise seaweed, some of which was expanding before their eyes. As Sophie leaned closer towards some of it, she heard a voice cry out behind her. It was Brigid. She ran back then around into the next cave mouth to find her kneeling over what looked like a long flat ellipse of the turquoise weed. Brigid was working at it with a knife, and as Sophie approached she took another blade from her pocket and threw it to her to assist with.

By the time they had cut the body free, they were both in tears, Sophie's body shaking with sobs and spasms. Walter's skin was pale white and drained of blood, small red wounds visible all over his body. His healthy complexion in life had been much photographed and videoed across the planet, his portrait almost an icon in the more sentimental households, a surrogate son to all.

Sophie and Brigid carried Walter's lifeless body from the cave and held it up before the advancing searchers below like a dismal trophy, a symbol of blighted hope.

*

Brigid needed to return to her own township where another new forest was erupting, so Sophie accepted a military lift back home to Millicent Canyon. She immediately knew something was wrong, even as they came down to land, the copter wings whipping up circular waves on the usually placid shores of her green chloride lake.

125

The doors to her hacienda were hanging open, blowing in the wind, and the furniture and fittings damaged, some overturned, others broken or torn. She found a crouching cousin of "Charlie" chewing a sofa, spreading its foam lining living everywhere. It looked up at her with alien red eyes, then sprouted wings from its back and flew out through the shattered glass of the patio doors. The thing looked swollen with muscle now, its cranium segmented into strange colourful patterns, as if evolution had taken it yet higher on to some new plain.

Sophie and two of the soldiers followed the debris trail through the house and out onto the slopes beyond. There were fragments of timber, pieces of broken furniture used in self-defence perhaps, what looked like traces of blood on the ground and on the green leaves of unfamiliar bushes.

Sophie broke into a run, her heart beating fast, moving as if in a dream, a dislocated nightmare estranged from her self. A hundred yards later she found Frank and Carla in each other's arms with the roots of a tree growing around them. Its branches had captured and strangled them, perhaps ensnaring Frank first, then Carla out of mercy as she tried desperately to free him. She found Frank's hand and held it briefly but his face and that of his mother were lost beneath bark and vine, only Carla's long black hair left spilling back onto the ground, blowing in the breeze like dune grass.

In a kind of trance, she stood up and walked on. Weeping and shaking as she neared the hilltop, she saw the white orb of the quasar again, lifting free of the planet's surface, the uncertain horizon fraught with change. Did this unblinking eye regard her with callous hatred or sorrowful guilt? –Lament the irrevocable force of a history in which Sophie and the human race were to be marginalized? More than anything now, she needed to know. Tugging and tearing at her goggles in despairing rage, she pulled them off at last and gazed back defiantly at her murderer, no longer afraid.

The sky before her burst open into an outpouring of unimaginably intense light. The speed of the flashes was somehow significant, faster than a heartbeat, slower than breath. It had time and purpose, patience and limitless power. Its children were awakening at last to do its will. It knew neither good nor evil, only urgency, the need to bring into being endlessly, that which was not, had hitherto not been.

The great white rose of light blossomed into yellow the more she looked at it, tore off its own petals one after the other like a book being written, a sermon, or a lesson being dispensed. The yellow became other colours, green then blue and purple and red in successive flashes, growing in intensity, burning out the eye. Sophie embraced it and finally felt she almost understood, receiving its last testament, wondering if the cost for this knowledge would be her own life.

*

Sophie woke up in the intensive care unit of the main hospital for the colony, on the outskirts of the largest settlement on Strobos, Port Arabelle. Brigid and Commander Fernandez were at her bedside, talking quietly, and seemed greatly cheered by her revival. They called a nurse and several arrived, followed by a doctor, all intensely interested in her eyesight and the history of epilepsy on her medical records. The doctor reached over and removed something from Sophie's eyes. She put her hands up to her face and realised that she was no longer wearing goggles, unlike everyone else around her now, even indoors.

I don't see any f-flashes... she stuttered, *has the quasar stopped somehow?*

Everyone laughed grimly at her as if worried about her sanity for a moment then looked up to the doctor to take the lead: *Of course the quasar hasn't stopped, Miss Saleri. But your brain doesn't seem to be registering the flashes any longer. We don't really understand it, to be honest. Something to do with your epilepsy. Does your vision feel entirely normal? Do you feel exactly as you did before your collapse?*

No... Sophie found she had answered before even thinking about it. *Something has changed... but nothing physical.*

What then?

My perception. I don't think I can explain it.

Please try.

*

But Sophie didn't try too hard. The more she attempted to analyse it the more she came to the conclusion that everyone around her felt

127

like alien beings now, in collusion and conspiracy against her. —Trying to hide from the clue and opportunity that her life represented. It was like being a child again, surrounded by adults who pretended to care desperately, but who, once she was out of earshot, just talked incessantly about how they wished she was normal, revealing that in fact they had understood nothing.

They told her she needed more sleep and she pretended to take her pills, slipping them under her pillow. They didn't want her to worry, but she overheard their whispered talk of new indigenous plant life continuing its expansion into Port Arrabelle, new species of animals and even birds threatening the town.

At what used to be called midnight, she got out of bed and made her way in her hospital gown down the corridors, twice ducking into broom cupboards to avoid staff going back and forward on their "night" shifts. After checking several maps and floor plans on signboards, she made her way to the Artificial Insemination Unit, then the Cryogenic Sperm Bank. Foregoing the high security doors, she broke her way in through a rear window.

Climbing up over the windowsill, Sophie looked back at the quasar, now risen much further into the sky, and wondered if she had been unconscious for several days. It was almost just a large yellow orb to her altered eyes now, like the sun back on Earth, but with a kind of iridescent halo around it where it teased and pulled at the Stroban cloud cover, a mother peering proudly through swaddling clothes at its prodigal sons and daughters. In the distance, Sophie could see tendrils and creepers writhing and hissing at the perimeter fence. The town outside and the hospital itself all seemed mysteriously quiet, as if they were being evacuated, the quiet before the storm.

In the Cryogenic Storage Facility, Sophie was surprised at her own strength and energy as she smashed open the refrigerators with a fire extinguisher and exposed bank after bank of human sperm to the stark white light of Nephalim-3. She threw the wreckage out onto the floor behind her as she advanced, pulling back black-out curtains and smashing more windows, letting the outside air in. The daylight fell in broad shafts onto the floor through the new apertures, eager armies of photons, unleashed by their human Trojan horse. The white liquid foamed and hissed on the floor. Sophie felt like she was tearing open the back of a camera, exposing all the film to light.

There would be no more noisy pink apes. No more human history, no more colonisation, empires, rape, bloodshed, theft or slavery. Only something better to come, new life of a purity and intensity beyond all the petty prejudices and jealousies of humankind.

Plant creepers were beating against the windows now, some spilling in, new insects and weird birds calling out in strange ululations. She remembered the dead bodies of Frank and Walter and felt nothing. No sadness, no regret either. Then she spun around in doubt. On the floor, the white foam was fizzing then turning black, brown then pink. The sperm was a tadpole, a frog, a rodent, a monkey, a tiny man. She had unleashed a revolution, and was no longer in control.

~

GRAVITY WAVE

"Space-time does not claim existence in its own right, but only as a structural quality of the gravitational field...

I know not with what weapons World War Three will be fought, but World War Four will be fought with sticks and stones..."
-Albert Einstein

On the third day travelling, we heard the howl of a wolf. Good news, although night was falling again. We figured this meant game we could hunt and kill soon, maybe deer and rabbit too. We turned the snowmobiles and the dual-track in a circle and pitched tent for the night, lit a couple of fires and trained searchlights on the perimeter.

That night I befriended the lead scientist Vladimir Szceczin again and persuaded him to let me read over his Report Notes so far. Hardly bedtime reading of course, but I had a vague feeling that he was holding something back from the rest of the team, or that his scientific caution wasn't allowing him to face up to some disturbing possibility that might upset either the more emotional or the more sober scientific members of the group or both...

*

Lisbon. *September 3rd* ***08:55(am)*** *Central European Summer Time.*
Distance from Event Origin: **933 Miles.**

Lucianna Ribeiro wakes with her husband, at their apartment on Rua Da Veronica. She has just had the most powerful and disturbing

131

dream of her life. She gets up and goes to the kitchen and takes some painkillers from the cupboard for her pulsing head. As she makes breakfast, her husband Juan joins her. She notices he looks as terrible as she feels and begins to tell him about her dream. *I was in this town, well a city really, and this invisible pressure cloud seemed to descend on it from the sky. I was standing there in the street looking at all these buildings and people in disbelief as the tops of the apartment blocks, the roofs, the church steeples, everything just began to crush itself down and implode...*

I know... Juan interrupts, looking up from the breakfast table, incredulous, eyes bloodshot, hands in his hair: *I had this same dream.... It looked like somewhere in Germany maybe. The buildings were compacting top-down by the second, like coke cans in a crusher, then buses and trams and cars began flattening and people were running everywhere, screaming. I saw this family looking at me from inside their car, this terrible pressure was building in my head, in their heads, the children were screaming, then a moment later the roll cage gave out and I saw the car buckle down into nothing, flattened...*

Madre de Dios... it's the same dream, Juan.

The phone rings and Lucianna goes to the hall to answer it. She returns still clutching it, *Juan... it's my mother, she's had the same dream, and her sister and their neighbours.*

No way... Juan snorts, dismayed by feminine superstition. With difficulty, he picks himself up and goes to the window and pulls open the wooden shutters, letting in all the intense sunlight of an Iberian morning. All down the Calcada de Sao Vicente, across the rooftops of the Alfama district all the way to the statue of Christ In Majesty gesturing from the other side of the glittering waters of the Tagus, he sees to his astonishment that the shutters are open and people are out on their balconies, chattering incessantly, some shouting to passers-by on the street below. Out of all the waves of chatter, one word gradually becomes discernable to him, repeated over and over at the heart of each fevered conversation: *sonha... sonha... dream... dream.*

*

132

Copenhagen. *September 3rd* ***10:41(am)*** *Central European Summer Time.*

Distance from Event Origin: ***714 Miles.***

Neils Sturmgren, a student cycling his morning route to college through the *Frederiksberg* district, passes into a darkened area which he perceives as a cloud shadow moving from south to north, bathing the streets in an odd yellow light like the moments before an electrical storm.

He notices people on the street around him are slowing down and looking at each other, behaving oddly. He sees two men begin fighting on a street corner, then a group of black youths attacking some white skinheads. A block further on he notices a man and woman, strangers moving in opposite directions, stop and look at each other, move closer, put hands on each other's faces and bodies, then begin stripping off their clothes. He glimpses other people copulating in side alleys, or running after each other, and half in awe, half in fear, he slows down and steps off his bike, looking around him in the street.

What's happening? -A voice says inside his head. He spins around and looks up at an open window where a middle-aged woman is looking down at him. The voice sounds again inside his head, he senses it is hers, and yet she has not opened her mouth. *You're bleeding, son,* she says. He puts his hand up to his left cheek and nose and his fingers come back red. The woman has produced a handkerchief now and is wiping blood from her own nose and ears. *What is happening?* –He thinks without talking. *Minds opening up…* she replies instantly again, without lip movement.

They both turn to their left as a bus pulls to halt and passengers dismount, each bleeding from their faces, some of them crying or shouting hysterically.

Then Neils hears it. The cacophony of thought. At first he can't believe that something so repellent can be emanating from his own species: it is like a dark wave of stinking birds, a tide of psychic acid scalding his brain. Every single thought of every passenger, unfiltered and uncontrolled, is leaking out at once in a bubbling and overwhelming confusion. But unlike sound, he cannot shut it out, he can't stop it flooding into his own mind. He screams in pain inside himself, but the passengers turn around, as if hearing him,

133

and this only excites and agitates them further, spurring them on to yet greater mental noise. He feels as if he has ventured into a churchyard and gazed into a hundred open graves, and can find no way to close them over. He puts his hands to his bleeding ears and falls to his knees in the middle of the road.

*

I cornered Szceczin again the next day in the canteen tent. He was looking lost, hovering over the roast potato and beetroot pots with a far-way look in his eyes. *Borscht.... He muttered... I was remembering Borscht... my mother used to make it snow white with cheese curd at Easter and serve it with kielbasa... sausage to you...*

Sausage to you too, I retorted, *as they say in Germany,* and he managed a crooked smile.

You studied at Munich after Cambridge?

I nodded.

You have people there?

Fortunately not, Professor, just a few old memories, squeezed flat like grapes... last of the summer wine... I said then instantly regretted my grimly poor taste.

We sat down together in the director chairs by the log brazier, our breath visible for a moment, and a fine dust of snow blowing in from under the edge of the tent. *Someone shut that damn door...* he suddenly roared like an old Slavic madman, then rubbed his beard, a few answering laughs crossing the room.

The Event, I finally ventured half way through my soup, when he looked relaxed, *-what would you speculate as the cause?*

The cause... was The Experiment, my dear girl... he answered glibly, probably hoping that such a supposedly witty answer might deter the inquisitiveness of a troublesome woman anthropologist.

Suck my dick, I spat, and gained his silence and attention all in one go, along with a few glances from the other diners. *I might not have studied under Feynman or Hawking, but I do have a couple of doctorates you know, are they still pig-ignorant sexists in that Bohemian backwater they raised you in?*

So you would answer sexism with racism, eh? What do you English say, two black to a white?

134

He was warming to me already, laughing, I could see it, and later that day he told me I reminded him of his tomboy sister, which I decided on balance to take as a twisted compliment.

The Experiment, obviously the cause of course, but which particle, what kind of wave?

He put down his bowl and lit a cigarette and inhaled for an age, like some carcinogenic mystic.

Graviton? –I ventured, *Higgs Boson?*

Graviton we were looking for, certainly, he nodded his head quietly, eyes narrowed behind the smoke.

I noticed he had started saying *we* rather than *they*. A luxury of truth he hadn't allowed himself a week previously when we made our way through the devastation of Paris, only protected from the rioting mobs by the goodwill of the rag-tag remnants of the *gendarmerie* and the *CRS* that had been assigned to us.

The reporters had been a depleted and disorientated lot, but still keen to make a story and identify Szceczin as an evil architect of The Experiment disaster, but I had watched him lie to deny it, even temporarily giving credit for his own ideas to others to save his skin. It had confirmed all my worst suspicions of his reptilian nature.

Have you heard of the term The God Particle? -he asked.

I laughed. *Please professor, don't tell me you're about to get theological on us at this late stage.*

He frowned sourly, then seemed about to be pleased about some ignorance of mine on this point.

A layman's misnomer for the Higgs Boson as I understand it, of course I've heard it. Misconstrued vaguely with the notion of Dark Matter. A magic bullet that would join up all the loose ends, connect quantum mechanics with Einstein's Theory Of General Relativity. You think they, you found that?

Observation... he purred quietly.

Sorry, what do you mean?

The particle might be connected to perception.

You mean Schrödinger's Cat, Heisenberg's Uncertainty Principal? Observing an event changes the outcome, by particles going back in time if necessary?

Crazy but true, he nodded.

So what? –I asked boldly.

*So observation… that is to say consciousness, has to actually **be** something then doesn't it? If it can interact at the quantum level, that is to say interact with fundamental particles, then it must have a physical presence down there among them in their tiny little world of tiny little things…. no?*

He dangled his spoon around in the dregs of his coffee mug for a moment at this point and I thought again for a moment that he might be patronising me like a child until I noticed the morose expression on his face, the grey pallor of his skin.

Consciousness is a particle? Is a wave? –I asked.

He lifted his big tobacco stained hands over his head non-committally at this point, as if he had given out enough clues.

You don't really know do you?! Are you really reduced to this kind of guesswork now? –I taunted him.

He laughed sourly and stood up to go, dismissing me as if waving away a fly. *Oh I know well enough,* he smirked to himself then fixed me for a moment with his fierce blue eyes, which somehow he had kept shielded until this moment. *And so do you…* he said cryptically, then was gone out into the blinding white snow again.

*

Rome. *September 3ʳᵈ* **09:57(am)** *Central European Summer Time.*
Distance from Event Origin: **443 Miles.**

Carlo Semprini is playing with his children in his living room when the Wave crosses the room as a pulsating shadow. The television and Hi-Fi catch fire, he drops the baby's bottle then sees the milk curdle and turn yellow then brown and black. His seven year old son Francesco stands up and begins to grow in height before his eyes like time-lapse photography, splitting his clothes, his belt buckle exploding, becoming an adolescent then adult, facial hair growing, then a lengthening beard. The potted plants in the room have quickly withered and died, but the tree outside the window smashes through the glass, the wall cracks and falls away, ivy pours in across the floor like advancing water, tree branches writhe around inside the room like an angry octopus. His youngest daughter Tia falls away in fear from the branches but she too is growing rapidly, crying in confusion and pain as her hair reaches to the floor and her

136

leather shoes split, her brace rupturing her teeth into a bloody mess. The baby falls from Carlo's arms, grown suddenly heavy as Francesco advances on him, his face wrinkling now, his eyes filled with strange tragedy, holding out his hand for help which as it touches Carlo's chest makes him look down to see his own frame withering and crumbling like a prune in the sun.

*

London. *September 3rd* **10:03 (am)** *Central European Summer Time Distance from Event Origin:* **465 Miles.**

Julianne Conner answers her mobile phone on the corner of Dean Street and Shaftesbury Avenue. The phone's temporary electromagnetic field around her face and body isolate her inadvertently from the ensuing phenomena. In conversation with her boyfriend, her jaw drops as she sees the clouds begin racing and the sky flashing stroboscopically between night and day. A woman walking her dog towards her appears to slow down, then her face ages and wrinkles rapidly. Several cars and a bus visible to her left grind to a halt then rust and deteriorate in front of her. The woman to her right has now fallen to her knees and her dog writhes then decays into a skeleton. Julianne tries to reach out her hand towards them in a gesture of help, but finds her arm is rebuffed, her fingernails left smoking, and can only pull the phone a few inches away from her face as its field invisibly encases her.

Other people all along the street now writhe on the ground, a pregnant woman has fallen over on her back and her stomach seems to heave and swell, then implodes as a blood-soaked baby, then child, visibly growing as it stands up, emerges swaying from her body and starts to walk towards Julianne, its arms raised.

She feels the urge to retch, then turns around to look up as a police helicopter, blades twisting and rusting, falls impossibly slowly, its paintwork peeling, two grinning skeletons seated within, then silently crumples into the pavement with a blinding cloudburst of metal, dust and glass.

*

Berlin. *September 3rd* **10:18(am)** *Central European Summer Time. Distance from Event Origin:* **544 Miles.**

Helga Auerbern is visiting her elderly mother in hospital. The building's external lead sheet cladding will accidentally generate a weak sub-field to distort some of the Wave phenomena to follow. Hearing a noise, while her mother sleeps, she opens the blinds at the window of her private room, and looks to the street below. She blinks and struggles to make sense of the scene. Naked children are running away from empty piles of clothes next to melted cars, molten metal and liquid paint bubble on the road and run into gutters and drains. She cries out in sudden pain and looks down at her hand on the window sill: it is shrinking from the wrist down, the effect moving up her forearm.

She falls away from the window screaming, then watches in disbelief as a shadow moves across the room from the window and engulfs her mother. Her mother's confused aged cries gurgle and mutate as she turns by stages into a beautiful young woman who sits up startled in the bed, then shields her eyes from the blinding light.

Her daughter tries to cry out to her but finds her voice unexpectedly grown high-pitched and incoherent, as she watches her mother shrinking, writhing in confusion.

When rescuers enter the room three hours later they find a new born baby laughing on the bed, and Helga's empty clothing stained and damp with the inconspicuous ingredients of de-conceived life.

*

Spacetime… I continued again, or tried to, with Szceczin. We were travelling again now, over endless snow between tracts of pine forest, the grey sky clearing temporarily with a patch of cold blue. We had both been lucky enough after drawing lots for the day to win the two comfortable seats in the front of the dual-track, the slower smoother ride carrying the supply sleighs. Stuck beside me for the afternoon, I smiled with satisfaction to think that he had no choice but to submit to my questions and theorising. Frost was slowly accumulating on his beard making him look like a timelapse Santa, and I quietly hoped he wouldn't notice. *Einstein's theory… Could a gravitational wave really distort our spacetime?*

He was in a more relaxed mood today I had judged, and this was confirmed when he took out one of his infamous cigars and lit it with an expansive sigh. I knew well enough I wasn't Russian film star material, but I reckoned there was a glimmer of pride catching light in him at having some female company to show off in these bleak days so lacking in all familiar comforts.

Assuredly it could, he said at last, *the mathematics are sound.*

And the… I stopped myself here, I had nearly said field results here, which would have been like the sickest joke ever made, like the whole thing had been planned to work out this way. Four million were dead, with perhaps twice that injured, plus material damage enough to put every European economy on its back for two decades. The phenomenon, whatever it was, was over, or appeared to be but then again nobody yet knew what lay beyond the Event Corona to the North and South, where all communication had been lost.

The temperatures were plummeting now as we moved north, we had several furs each wrapped around us, hats in Davey Crocket and Doctor Zhivago style as befitted our nations of origin. *The effects on the ground… I continued, the devastation and destruction, could they fit within such equations?*

It could be a cross-polarised or linearly polarised wave of course, depending on its frequency, how it oscillates, the amplitude…

You may lose me very soon, Professor.

Oh? He seemed genuinely disappointed for a moment, although again I thought he might be mocking me. *Of course, the third derivative of the quadrupole moment of an isolated system's stress-energy tensor must be non-zero…* (now he was really pushing it).

And was it, in The Experiment?

Oh yes, that was the whole point.

Then you planned the wave?

Not at the frequency at which it appeared to occur, that would have been foolhardy. We experience gravitational waves all the time on Earth, mostly from distant stars and pulsars. They are of a scale and frequency that makes them scarcely detectable on Earth and therefore we have always presumed: harmless.

But what happened wasn't harmless.

Evidently not. The amplitude range that occurred must have been something that has never happened before on Earth, and now we know why. It was a mistake, a catastrophe, as we know now.

What a price for knowledge, I said bitterly, thinking of my dead nephews and cousins, several friends missing presumed dead, my grandfather now a three-year old baby, my boyfriend accelerated into a geriatric ward, my mother a six year old girl with an outsized arm. For a moment I wanted to ask him if he felt guilty, but I stopped myself, realising it would sound like an accusation and undo all the progress I had made in getting answers from him. The guilt was incalculable, and in the face of it and its cause: I saw for a moment how he and everyone else deserved only pity now. *Have you plotted the effects from the data we've calculated yet? Can you plot the project effect beyond the Corona?*

Nearly my dear... I'm working on it... he said, and I winced at the patronising term, then felt a conflicted glow that I might be being taking further into his confidence again.

*

Paris. *September 3rd* **09:43(am)** *Central European Summer Time. Distance from Event Origin:* **255 Miles.**

Pierre Louchard is driving down Boulevard Saint-Germain when a cloud appears to cross the sun. The people walking on the pavement nearest to him begin to lift into the air: a woman walking a poodle, two students hand in hand, a female jogger. They look down at their own limbs in surprise, move their legs as if swimming in space. Behind then in a shop window Pierre sees loaves and cakes floating and bouncing like some kind of magic trick. Behind them, chairs are sailing up and down as customers and staff bounce off the walls and each other in amazement.

Pierre is momentarily mesmerised, until he hears car horns in front of him. Looking up he sees several cyclists floating above the halted cars, waving to those below, legs and wheels turning on air. Like those films, Pierre finds himself thinking, dazzled: Mary Poppins or ET. Then his car lurches and bounces. He gasps, then inexplicably starts laughing: the car is lifting up, then those in front of him do likewise. The feeling in his gut is exhilarating, frightened but unmistakably joyous.

He opens his door and looks out and says *au revoir* to the pavements. Somebody somewhere is singing. Some joker has got out of his car and is standing on the roof as it lifts up, like he is riding a surfboard. The cars are reaching first then second storey height, now passing apartments where startled citizens, late sleepers, lovers, in various states of distracted undress, float or crawl upside down, insect-like, towards their windows to gaze out at the fabulously deranged city below and above.

Some other joker jumps onto the roof of Pierre's car then onto the next one. Now Pierre is scared, he thinks he might fall from his car, then he realises he can't fall and steps out and starts to swim on thin air. The cars are nearing the rooftops now, and Pierre vaguely wonders if that means the cars will break loose and sail adrift over the roofs. People are flying everywhere, using their raincoats as wings, their umbrellas as paragliders. *Are we dying?* –Pierre finds himself asking in the back of his head. *Where are Daniella and the children? Is this happening to everyone at once? Is this the end of the world? Does God exist after all? Is this Judgement Day, are we going up to heaven?*

Just as his mind is turning to the awkward possibility of Hell, beginning to get the hang of air-swimming in space, Pierre glimpses something new. Off to the south, over the rooftops, he can now see a slow-moving curved boundary of light, the back edge of whatever spell they are currently under. At first he thinks it is raining over there, until his eyes focus on the detail and his stomach lurches. The rain is cars and buses and people falling suddenly to the streets below, followed by waves of rumbling and screaming which seem to be accelerating towards him as he hovers, stunned in frozen inactivity. A wave of fresh panic crosses him and all the other fliers as they realise they have to make it to a rooftop or window sill in a matter of minutes or have their brains dashed out on the pavements below.

People begin desperately trying to swim through the air now, gawky, absurd, black comedy, like flapping chickens. One guy has made it to the gutter line and is reaching a hand back to an Arab woman whose *burka* is billowing out and pulsing behind her like some kind of deep-sea jellyfish. Other hands are joining them, an aerial display team, parachutists with no cords to pull.

A bus hovers over the rooftop behind them, half full of startled passengers, many of them children. Pierre's last glimpse of their faces will haunt him for the rest of his life. The wave hits, the bus goes straight down through the roof and every floor below, part of the building façade is dragged inwards with it, taking the starfish of clutching hands with it. Cars fall like terrible, crashing rain, a mad Magritte painting come alive.

Pierre spins around and is embraced by an elderly banker in a black suit with a white handlebar moustache. *Mon Dieu...* he breathes and extends his umbrella. They fall together at half-speed towards the remnants of a street display of fruit, collapsing onto sealed bags of apples and oranges, sacks of potatoes. The old man's leg is probably broken but Pierre kneels and kisses his polished shoes like those of some urban angel among the debris and the wailing cries of the dying and wounded.

*

In the morning, as we packed up, Szceczin drew my attention to some footprints he had noticed in the snow around our camp: *Tell me, my dear, what do you make of these?* –he mused.

I knelt and examined them, running my fingers around the distinctive edges of the profile. *Wolves of course,* I said, *Canis Lupus, quite large, but nothing we can't handle.*

He laughed. *Yes, I'm sure we can shoot them if they're foolhardy enough to give us a clear shot, but don't you notice anything odd about those prints?*

I looked again, more carefully, feeling I was being tested. *Well, it's probably nothing,* I said, *but the digital and metacarpal pads seem proportionately broader and flatter than I would normally expect, and there's no trace of a dewclaw... But dewclaws don't always show up, they're small, almost vestigial, and only present on front paws. Anyway, these are probably just a local characteristic, a minor mutation, an adaptation to the deeper snow.* To my amazement, when I looked up, Szceczin had one boot and sock off, in those freezing temperatures, and was wiggling his toes at me.

What on earth are you doing? I laughed, embarrassed.

142

Why, I'm waving at you, of course, he grinned.

With your foot?

Is it a foot though? When is a foot not a foot? Are these toes or fingers? The difference is not much and yet the function is entirely different.

Your point is? You'll get frostbite in a minute, then we might not have to worry about your toes much longer.

But then I'd have a hoof, wouldn't I? Much more useful. He sighed and put his sock on again, frowning as if I had failed to understand some profound insight he had offered me. *Which species do you think would replace mankind if we went the way of the Dodo tomorrow? Who do you think would be next up the evolutionary staircase, making tools and machines eventually?*

I thought about it. *Apes, chimpanzees, would be the conventional wisdom...* I mused.

He smiled, then almost chuckled again, as we got up and hoisted our packs and made our way to the dual-track, *-but not in this climate, surely?*

Well, I said, crunching through the fresh snow, *who would your money be on?*

Mogilev – he muttered.

What's that Russian for, fruit flies or something?

My pet dog actually, he smiled sadly to himself, surprising me with his sudden wistfulness. Szceczin seemed almost vulnerable at that moment, and I remembered how old he was, and that he was just a man, probably lonely. I helped him off with his pack as we sat down at the snowmobiles, and he continued. *Mogilev... I miss him, a Northern Inuit with a bit of husky. Smart, loyal, resourceful... man's best friend, eh? And I am Polish by the way, not Russian.*

I felt suddenly angry, I don't know why, embarrassed maybe that he thought me ignorant. *How would you define the difference? –*I asked sourly.

Shall I drive today? -he smiled magnanimously, *I'd define the difference as like that between dogs and wolves.*

I laughed. We all know race rivalry is wrong, but it's so human it's hard not to smile at it sometimes. *Thirty percent smaller brains,* you know, he said, *dogs compared to wolves, you didn't know that? Domestication didn't make them any smarter, quite the reverse in fact, and maybe the same ought to be said about humans. Softer, lazier, dumber... ripe for replacement.* Then he started the engine.

143

*

Madrid. *September 3rd 12:52(pm) Central European Summer Time.*
Distance from Event Origin: **634 Miles.**

Similar to the Copenhagen effect, the blood pouring from ears and mouth have quickly been identified, if not understood, as the puncturing of some kind of mental hymen. Telepathy is now not just possible, but horribly unavoidable. Widespread rioting and confusion have followed. Sexual promiscuity has broken out among the young, fist-fighting in workplaces, racial battles in the suburbs. Looting and raiding of banks and shops are widespread as passwords and personal identification numbers are no longer concealable. Johanna Vincenna has been taken in by the nuns of the Sacred Order Of Saint Francis, given sanctuary in their basilica on Plaza De Ducalletta, along with thirty other passers-by who have now barricaded themselves into the sacristy and sit in a wide circle with their heads all pressed together.

One of the Order, Sister Desdemona, having been convinced the whole event was the work of Satan has had to be taken out and locked up in the north tower at the other end of the chancel. The remaining refugees have now finally devised a system of thought somewhere between prayer, meditation and counting sheep; which seems to calm and synchronise everybody's mind until they are able to communicate in safety and harmony.

It's happening... thinks someone, then the answer comes back out of the darkness and silence: *Yes, now we can think clearly...* no mouths opening, miraculously, dozens of minds answering, unified as one. *But think better now... stronger...* the communal idea grows and is joined by other minds. Someone breaks the circle to sneeze then comes back in and everyone feels it like a door just opened and a draught let in on a windy day. *Some kind of accident... a scientific experiment error has occurred but God... or providence* (a secular correction is absorbed from the atheist side of the room) *or fate has let us have this gift... it feels like it's always been there, hidden away doesn't it? Yes... yes... yes... we need more minds now... Ones with knowledge we don't have... send out for a scientist or a politician... this is under control... we can expand this now.*

Sister Desdemona, imprisoned in the top of the north tower, gazes out over the rooftops and sees the fires below, hears the screams

144

of the wicked, the moans of the shamelessly fornicating, and sends her mind out, seeking God to console and comfort her.

A moment later she falls back in horror as a flock of starlings descend and start dancing bewitched in front of her, bouncing up and down like lottery balls. *Bread!* Their two dozen beaks chime in unison, except the word is a picture in her head that assaults and seizes her like mental gang rape. *Bread! Bacon Rind! Rice! Worms! Water!* –the screeching waves of vignettes lash over her, her mind and theirs suddenly open to each other.

She beats on the door wailing until the Mother Superior releases her at last then she storms past her crying, descending all sixty-seven steps of the stone spiral until she lets herself out into the walled graveyard. There as she walks down her favourite overgrown pathway, she is astonished to see people in medieval costumes moving about. It annoys her that they seem to be ignoring her at first until she walks through one of them and they all stop and turn towards her.

Mother of God… she whispers back to them guiltily … *something has got broken, hasn't it?*

*

The equipment told us we had cleared the Event Corona now, with mercifully little ceremony. The vegetation seemed mostly the same, no evolutionary divergence that we could notice, although microscopic samples sent back to the labs would confirm for sure in a few weeks. It was colder than ever and now the reason was obvious: as the mist cleared in the far distance we could see the base of glaciers, then the ragged edges of a wall of ice, the polar ice cap or shelf in its new location, perhaps a half mile high, its top constantly entwining with clouds of frost. It lay perhaps a hundred miles distant, located approximately over what had once been Edinburgh and Stockholm.

We had been given the theory again the night before by Szceczin, his little slide show he called it; that we weren't even to consider the idea of millions of people having died in these locations. Rather they had all lived and died peacefully in a time-stream placed beyond our own, in which the only difference they observed was that our area had passed into some kind of archaic stasis impenetrable to their analysis. Their status therefore was now our future, for better or for worse, however it had worked out, quite independently of our own disaster. Szceczin plotted his data projections and graphs up on screen for us for verification. The Wave had moved through distinct phases as its amplitude changed in response to the many complex obstructions it had encountered, slowing and deepening over time in an attempt to "pitter patter itself out" he said, surely a farcical phrase for an effect of such scale.

Phase One, Szceczin said, had apparently been a simple Graviton pulse wave: people, buildings, everything lifted up or crushed flat in minutes, although interestingly a few pockets of survivors had been found underground, implying that perhaps the wave had an almost flat 2D profile, or was attenuated by the Earth's crust. Phase Two had begun about 280 miles out in every direction. Szceczin's calculations pointed to the Gravitons having been overtaken by a new particle, not the Higgs-Bosons the physicists had all been looking for but something that Szceczin felt obliged to invent a new name for. By now we saw the bastard was enjoying himself. Just as well the press weren't there or they'd have had a field day, passed on news of all his un-blunted arrogance to the beleaguered populace back in the south who would doubtless come for him with pitch forks or whatever other farming implements they had been reduced to working with.

Oberons… he announced proudly, *I now believe the Gravitons were entangled with what I propose to call Oberons, all but undetectable particles of opposite and equal charge, perhaps what had hitherto been classified as Dark Matter. The unexpected property we can ascribe to this particle now that we have seen it in action is that it affects consciousness and the observed behaviour of time.*

Nervous laughter broke out among the assembled team, who sat around in the candlelit tent, on fold-up chairs around the braziers, dressed in the various dayglo colours of their parkas and snowsuits. *You mean a real God Particle, don't you?* –Someone piped up. *You're saying these things have consciousness, Professor?*

I'm saying, he smiled broadly, then frowned again as if remembering the seriousness of the situation, *-that whatever it is, it affects our consciousness intimately, and for that reason I am willing to believe, tentatively, that it is what our consciousness is made of.*

But Professor Szceczin, I spoke up, thinking I might yet be his prize pupil, even among these greater scientific minds than mine.

Does that mean that all the gravity waves in space, or the Oberon waves, are what we have previously called Dark Matter or Dark Energy, and therefore that waves of consciousness are constantly moving through space?

You might put it like that, I suppose.

I was amazed and delighted I must confess, even though half the world had just gone down the swanee, but the uproar in the room was almost instant. The accusations flew: *But what are you saying? What would that consciousness be? Are you saying the universe is awash with the thoughts of God ebbing and flowing over every planet? This is mysticism professor, pure speculative conjecture, have you lost your mind?*

Szceczin had gone too far, and the disapproval and revulsion in the room seemed almost on the verge of mutating into chaos and panic.

You could put it like that, he finally corrected himself, *but I wouldn't choose to.* The room perceptibly relaxed. *Rather I would suggest it's more like protons and neutrons. Perhaps the Oberons are just building blocks floating around waiting to be used by creatures like us as and when they evolve on any given planet, who use them to create their intelligence, and when a civilisation destroys itself for instance, those building blocks, those particles just go back to being dissipated Oberons in space, ready to be used by the next candidates for intelligent life.*

Then the Big Bang was God's mind exploding?! This is theology, Professor Szceczin! –someone shouted, outraged again. *Can you prove any of this? Can you show us an Oberon particle?*

Eventually perhaps, although I suspect it will be rather like trying to find one's own smell. I wonder if it won't turn out to be the one thing in the universe we can never measure, which it's precisely why it's the most important, not the least so.

Why might we never measure it? –someone asked.

Because it is us, of course... Szceczin answered then left the stage without taking anymore questions. The audience were left in dazzled disarray.

And now as Szceczin and I pressed on further into The Frozen Zone, we heard wolf cries again, but had still not seen any. I seemed to have become the old man's companion now, left alone to sit together in the dual-track while the other scientists sulked and nursed their scholarly wounds over the previous nights assault on their belief systems.

Professor... I began.

Call me Vlad, please, child... he corrected me, *the world has all but ended and you stand on ceremony.*

It occurs to me that the flow of your lecture was somewhat interrupted last night. You never got to Stage Three.

Ahh, Stage Three, he sighed, *and Four and Five, yes you're quite right of course. I suppose I retreated somewhat when I realised they weren't ready for all that yet.*

Well? I asked and waited, tightening my hood and balaclava up against the prevailing northerly wind we were driving into, the dual-track's engine churning away below us.

Phase One was simple gravitational effects like crushing or levitation. Phase Two was distortion of spacetime and the perceived passage of time. Phase Three was a disruption to human consciousness, Humanity's latent group consciousness getting deflowered, as it were, telepathy unleashed. Phase Four was the dreams.

Dreams?

Yes, at the outermost range of the ring wave people experienced dreams about what was happening, or just about to happen, in the central zone: buildings flattening and so forth.

So outside the Event Corona is Phase Five?

Dead on. Outside AND within.

How within?

The handful of survivors in the innermost zone, those trapped underground at the time of the blast, those who lost consciousness all had the same dream.

Really? I hadn't read that yet. All the same dream like the Lisbon phenomenon?

Yes.

What of?

Of the future perhaps, which is what we are driving towards.

How far into the future?

Hard to say. At first I had thought only a few centuries, but I've been refining my calculations over recent days, and I think it may be closer to millennia...

Millenia, plural?! I nearly cut the engines and threw the brakes on, but managed to keep a steady hand. *What did they see in their dreams?*

148

Well now, his eyes narrowed, *they were surprisingly cagey about that. The ones I interviewed myself said they had dreamed about me...*
You? But how could that be?
I have been a bit of a media figure in recent years I suppose.
But in what context did they see you, what else did they say?
Oh weird stuff. Laughable even, we thought. People in animal suits spearing each other or something. None of us thought it made much sense at the time, but recently I've started wondering...

*

Geneva. *September 3rd 09:24(am) Central European Summer Time.*
Distance from Event Origin: **5.3 Miles.**

Klaus Weber staggers out from the flattened basement car park of the building that has been his place of work until fifteen minutes previously. Going back to retrieve his briefcase from the boot of his car at 9.06am has saved his life. He finds the scene around him now almost incomprehensible, and is still too shocked to try to relate it to any known landmark of the city he thought he was inhabiting. More shocking to him however, is his memory of the very vivid dream he has just woken from: and curiously it is this rather than devastation around him which occupies his mind as he saunters numbly forward over the concrete dust and torn metal, the rising smoke. He looks for someone to tell his dream to, surely an absurd proposition in a city compacted to ground zero. Only later in memory, will it occur to him that the scattered red and brown circles he walks over now are all that is left of each of the hundreds of shoppers on the pedestrianised surface of the *Rue de la Confederation.*

Eventually, he sees a woman in rags walking in the opposite direction, and he is shocked to see her blackened appearance, her clothes in rags, until he follows her gaze down and notices for the first time his own comparable condition. Though strangers, they embrace and begin sobbing almost immediately, and fall to their knees. Her mouth is opening and closing, vocalising incoherently and he realises she is urgently trying to tell him something about a dream she has just had. Gradually he understands it is the same dream as his own. It is a nightmare.

*

An old man and a younger woman, wrapped in furs and cagoules, travel through the snow towards distant glaciers, icebergs, an arctic world, punctuated only by drifts of pine forest. A small entourage of anoraked figures on snowmobiles follow behind them as they move through a wooded glade. They gradually slow down as they reach the brow of a hill...

-I had been too busy, foolishly, trying to read the last of Szceczin's report, and making myself feel sick in the process, to notice that we had reached the summit of a hill. Something had caught Szceczin's attention and he had brought the dual-track to a halt and cut the engine. He motioned to the snowmobiles behind us to slow down also, as I followed his gaze north.

In the valley below, blackened shapes that might once have been church spires and office blocks were penetrating the snow at odd angles and beneath them a village of timber stockades lay huddled in a circle, hearth-smoke unwinding slowly skywards from circular holes at the apex of their roofs. It was almost a homely scene, albeit primitive, deceptively familiar.

Szceczin raised his hand again to signal some instruction to the other scientists, but the words never left his throat, as an arrow shaft suddenly appeared, lodged through his shoulder.

Before my brain could even debate the meaning of this event, I found two similar: lodged through my own upper leg and forearm. There were a few seconds grace before the pain and then slow comprehension cut in. There were coloured feathers on the end of each arrow and finely carved obsidian at the tip where one had re-emerged through the other side of my arm, streaked with my blood. I looked down at those bright red circular drops falling onto the snow with a peculiar detachment and disbelief. As the drops multiplied, delirious, they struck me for a moment as a new and beautiful kind of rain. My knees had given out and I was kneeling as if in prayer.

There was a sound I thought was wind at first, then I joined the swishing noise up with the black horizontal rain of arrows emerging from the forest. The other snowmobiles were turning and people panicking, and I could see men falling, some struggling to unpack their guns. What emerged from the trees after the arrows defies description. They were grey and lean, their movements

150

purposeful and furtive. I thought at first the very shadows of the forest had detached themselves from each tree and were moving outward.

Soon there was a strange silence from the rest of the party behind me. I don't know how many had escaped, but not a shot had been fired. Szceczin was on his side in the snow, his raised arm reaching out to me and his hand clutching at nothing, grasping, as if trying to take hold of reality again, to undo the damage he had done. His mouth was opening and shutting, but no sounds were emerging. Instead I heard something like words from nearby, deep and guttural, but in no human tongue.

A spear was thrust into the snow beside me and my vision swam until my eyes focused on the ornately carved bone tip. A canid foot appeared and pushed me over onto my back. I howled in pain, and when my sight finally cleared I was looking up at all six feet of the biped in front of me. Its cohorts looked around the scene of devastation, the blood-stained snow, with quivering attentiveness, snouts twitching, tongues hanging from their jaws, breath clouding the air. They were shaking, and when I dismissed the idea that they were cold it dawned on me they were afraid. They didn't know what we were or where we could have come from, but they had neutralised our threat with skill. Expecting death now, fear drained from me, and strange though it sounds: I saw how beautiful they were, their grey fur bristling in the arctic breeze.

Before I lost consciousness, their leader's calm yellow eyes locked with mine and I wondered at what I saw there: something cold, ancient, questioning, enduring. It had bided its time and stalked us and now it had its reward. A mirror of our own cunning, recognised too late.

~

VOLWYS

PROLOGUE

(From the Diary of Vittorrio Reinwald,
in the twenty-third year of Leo):

<u>24th April 0023</u>

Today I watched King Lenni (or *"the wolf-child"* as he was once known affectionately among his estranged people), levitating pots and pans in the palace kitchens.

After twenty-three years of trying to domesticate this royal brute, he still eats off the marble floors like a wild animal, defecates in corners, and can produce no more coherent language than a stray dog.

If only the people knew what a charade we keep going here, parading their "Boy-King, Ordained of the Woods" before them on state occasions, drugged up and surrounded by discreet strongmen lest anyone catch sight of him urinating in his trousers and masturbating at the sight of quadrupeds.

Yes, my last sentence was no misprint. Of all the laughable, shameful secrets I have been taught to keep here under the austere aegis of Professor Bartholomew, the boy's predilection for copulating with she-wolves is surely the most unpalatable.

Recently I was even made to witness the spectacle by Bartholomew, who seemed to think I would find it educational. Three times a day now, he says the boy fires his seed into the rear of a tame wolf from the palace grounds, then laments at length, in his incoherent syllables, why none of them have yet borne him children. What lunacy and perversion.

I asked Bartholomew about this, and he said darkly that he had devised a new means of communication of late, some form of mind-reading he hinted, allowing him to bypass the grunts and growls of the boy, and find out what he was really thinking.

I was sceptical, not just about the mind-reading, but as to the idea that the boy could formulate any coherent thoughts at all. Bartholomew eyed me ruefully at that. Sometimes I think he regrets having entrusted so much knowledge to me over the years, but he still holds much back, the wily old devil.

*

14ᵗʰ May 0023

The priest in charge of Weathermagick tells me today is some kind of anniversary: twenty years apparently since *The Endless Snows* started, more or less without cease. He predicts a time will come when no man left alive will remember summer.

*

28ᵗʰ June 0023

The peasants were agitated today, crawling feverishly among the black bones of the carcass of their city. High above the ruined towers of mammon, a silver skyboat was spotted at sunset, moored against the filigree spire of the ruined stock exchange, Bartholomew's workshop. I asked him about it later, how although I had missed the apparition myself I felt certain some substantial event, something solid and real, must have been behind so much ardent gossip.

He went strange on me at first, then made me a promise, that if I would carry out some vague errand, "the merest trifle" he called it, for the Boy-King, then he would reward me. Initiate me

154

yet again he said, into a new undreamt-of level of the knowledge of The Esoterics.

I know him well enough to see one of his traps being woven in advance, but I also saw I had no room for manoeuvre until I learned more of his plans by playing along.

*

19th July 0023

Last night was particularly hard on Marie. She has been worried about our son Carlo recently, the ways he tries to rebel against us, our lives… against me? What will become of him if he achieves his foolish teenage goal of escaping the protection of the Esoterics?

On top of this, recent events weigh heavily on my mind and fill me with a strange darkness that Marie hates to see in my eyes. For twenty years now I have harboured secrets I am forbidden to tell, the black arts of Mathmagick and Electronika. Magic like the captive white fire I fill our house with at night, but am prohibited to explain to her. But these are mere trifles. I vaguely remember such wonders from The Time Before. But what Bartholomew toys with now seems something new… witchcraft surely, or worse. But what exactly could be worse?

And this theological talk of Anton and Leo. He dabbles at the very foundations of our crippled world, but towards what aim? Some of the other Adepts know now too, I sense it. The inner circle quiver, lips sealed, in a chill wind from outer space, the black void. What is it troubles their dreams where they sleep fitfully at night, twisting, crying out in their ivory towers?

*

24th August 0023

Something very strange indeed is afoot. Today Bartholomew took me to the North Drawing-Room and locked us both inside, then made a huge oak table lift into the air, using only the power of his mind and eyes, his hands enacting strange gestures.

He obviously wanted to whet my appetite. He handed me a glass vial of strange green liquid afterwards, which seemed somehow weightless. It would have floated around the room, probably taken me off my feet with it, had I not found the strength to restrain it.

Whence does this new magick come? –I asked. Have the great scientists of the Adepts made new breakthroughs in their experiments in their underground bunkers, or are the peasant rumours of a skyboat based on fact? Has he found a way to commune with the Gods themselves? New Gods? Sky Gods? Those perhaps that Leo intimated in *The Disputed Chapters*?

The old devil bathed in his secrecy like a cat with a mouse, then told me my errand.

*

27th September 0023

So that was it. Anton Perlato, my mother's old friend. Uncle Anton, as we called him once, all those years ago. Not exiled or a mountain hermit as the rumours have gone. Bartholomew sent me to find him, with a detachment of The Black Guard, protection against what I'm still not sure.

What a sorry state time has brought old Anton to. His beard stretches to his knees. His quarters are cave-like: a ruined cottage by the Nor' woods, reeking of animal smells, rotting food and faeces.

He seemed to drift in and out of coherence, even as I spoke, as if drunk. The local shepherds keep him plied with homebrewed firewater some say, in return for his crazy poems and prophecies. Few people know or believe his true identity anymore in this age of broken tell-coms. The local children make sport of him, laughable old clown, a crazy hermit, the village idiot.

But Bartholomew thinks otherwise obviously, and behind him, swathed in darkness, the Boy-King perhaps behind a screen of crippled language, or is there someone else, some thing else? –That meets with Bartholomew nightly now and plies him with some dark elixirs of knowledge? He seems increasingly white and drained when I see him each morning, as if he has danced all night with witches and warlocks beneath an evil moon.

156

He had a question for me, or the Boy-King had, he said, to ask of Anton, and said that none of the soldiers with me should be present or within earshot of either this question or its answer.

I hesitate therefore even to write it down here, since every day Bartholomew and his favoured Adepts seem to construct new laws to make such matters heresy. Will I burn in torture for what I write next? I place my faith in Leo, in His Forest and the Word of Gaia.

Who was the Boy-King's father, I asked as I had been told to, *Leo or Anton?*

At this, Anton seemed to recognise me more and tried to embrace me, disbelieving that I was the same little boy he had saved once from the foxes and the wilderness, now grown to a man.

I asked again, and he drew back in fear onto his reeking bed, and I saw his eyes cloud in black foreboding, as if sobering up, seeing through me to the others, the many selves of a man's life, or perhaps just to my new mentors and cohorts.

What forces have hold of you now, boy? I see a wellspring of poison in your veins. He grabbed my wrist. *Don't you remember the voices that spoke to you that night when you went missing as a child? Don't you remember telling me about them?*

I shook my head sadly and after a while asked my question again.

I see now, he spat bitterly into the open fire, *...that perhaps I should have left you that night, to let the green word of Gaia fill your veins with wisdom, strength that could have withstood the sickness I see eating at you now, like a great tree in a forest, blighted in its youth, covered in ivy that sucks the life from its bark and sap.*

I took my hand away a little impatiently at that. *I remember no voices...* I told him again, *-now answer my question.*

I saved your life, he said with sudden lucidity, eyes blue and sharp, *-and now I see that I must do it one more time. If I tell you the true answer you will be killed on your return simply for knowing it. Instead I must tell you what you need to say: that Leo was the true father of The Wolf Boy, and that I have never doubted it in all the years since I first proclaimed it.*

Silence passed, the flame flickered while I weighed the curious double load of his words, their complex dissonances. I laid his quavering hand back onto his own chest, as he coughed deep in his lungs, and I stood up to leave. But he pointed at me, his eyes full of tears, and made me lean closer to let him whisper one more secret in my ear:

At the heart of every religion there is a convenient lie... he rasped.

Don't we seek truth? –I asked him slowly, not fully sure what I meant or why I was asking at that moment.

Fool... -He laughed bitterly. *The truth is ice, cold and dark as the stars. Do we seek cold on a cold night or a fire? We build that fire ourselves. We seek comfort, not truth, just like any other creature under this ailing sun.*

He dissolved into coughing and shivering and I wrapped more blankets around him, then kissed him on the forehead as he slept.

*

2nd October 0023

The next day, Bartholomew led me to the west tower and took a strange silver sphere from his pocket and threw it across the air between us. I watched the thing slow down and hover, distorting time itself all around it. Then it opened like a magical flower and showed me a vision: of the Boy-King frozen in passion with his she-wolf while strange shadowy ceatures entered his bed chamber and entwined around him unnoticed, in the moments between moments. Their uncanny fingers took the seed from his phallus and mixed it with the she-wolf's fluids. They tunnelled through time and back. I saw the splash of white stars across the cosmos, the red eyes of a wolf, blazing meteors. The wolf would bear a child, I saw this, cut from its belly, as it lay dying, both wolf and human, half and half.

I gasped and fell back against the wall, out of breath, while the silver apple returned to circle Bartholomew like a moon around a planet, a falcon returning to the falconer's gloved hand.

Has what I saw happened? –I gasped.

It is the future, Bartholomew answered. *It is what will come to pass.*

Who are they? –I whispered. *Where do they come from?*

His eyelids lowered then, hooded like those of an eagle, then he hurled the silver sphere against the far wall, where as it struck: the whole room flashed with momentary flame as if transparent, as if made of black glass. Matter distorted, the room clouded and cleared then I saw that where there had been only a wall a moment beforehand there was now a door, and that it was lying open.

Bartholomew turned to leave and I knew I would be alone and it would be useless to run. I felt my feet drawn as if by some irresistible force, towards that dark door and what lay beyond it. Whatever it was I knew it would be strangely familiar and that it would know me completely, would look right through me and leave no place to hide.

1: VOLWYS

"I saw myself in the form of a wolf. I sped through space with the rapidity of words…
…I am God without woman. I am the starved God. Even as an image I must die…"
-Max Ernst, *A Little Girl Dreams Of Taking The Veil,*
translated by Dorothea Tanning.

Today Rrio is two hundred and thirty years old. Not that anyone is counting. No birthday cake and candles, no one to wish him many happy returns. He awakens from his mattress, sits up on the edge of it and meets his own image in the tall mirror by his bedside. Of those who once loved and raised him of course: none are left living. This is the price of immortality or whatever this is; perpetual maintenance and renewal. He runs his fingers over his heavily lined face then sees the steely blue eyes staring back as they always have. Even the eyes will need replaced again soon, but the same person, the same enigma will always reassert itself through the new material.

None of his current colleagues have any idea of his exact age, let alone his birthday. On days like today he thinks of his mother and father and sister long dead. Their voices ring in his ears sometimes. He stands now and goes to the window, presses a button, de-clouds the glass and sees the blinding white scene of the city of his birth now covered in snow, as it has been for over a century. The snow started when his ageing stopped, he sometimes jokes to himself, or offers to his colleagues as a mystical response to their questions regarding his legendary longevity.

160

Soon they will be at his door again, buzzing with questions, beginning another day of feverish activity. The young are so full of urgency, so short of time. How infinite on the other hand, time seems to Rrio. He has time to catch each momentary thought, each shadow of a fleeting idea, or try to. The sadness today, the poignancy of the memory of his mother's voice, of playing in the snow with his sister: what does time do to such things he wonder? The events themselves are artefacts, inviolate he hopes, unchanging. But how he feels about them? That changes, evolves. Nostalgia, like vertigo of the spirit, might come to hurt the higher and higher you climb, and Rrio at his window above his century of snow: is very high indeed.

He sits down at his desk and opens up a silver cask in which a red rose is rotting, consumed by tiny blackfly, stinking. He admires it, then writes a diary entry, as is his eccentric whim, in old-fashioned ink upon a snow-white page of tree-pulp:-

There is a poignancy to the fragility and ageing and death of human beings, a tenderness that grows into magnificence in retrospect. The longer I live, the greyer and bleaker my own deathless life becomes, while the more voluptuous and sensual the mortal life appears. But to taste it, is to watch the blushing peach bruise to blue in your hand, and wither to blackness before the eye. It is to feel the kissing mouth cry out in joy then fill with dust, instantly, an hour-glass shattered.

The door behind Rrio hisses, lifting up in a single movement and his Disc Driver appears outside, stamping his feet in the snow.

*

The Wolf King wears the tunic and cassock of a Pope, gilded jewellery, rings and chains around his neck. His court of chequered marble floors has high windows open to the sky. Vast rusting spines of the one-mile diameter Geo-Dome, still under construction after two centuries, emanate from the roof of this crown and curve down towards the ruined city below. His guards have human bodies but the heads of Storks: ruthless, predatory eyes that scan the King's visitors, their webbed claws twitching on their rifle triggers.

But the King is always pleased to see Rrio. His *Owl*, he calls him, an avian metaphor that Rrio is distrustful of, especially on

161

mornings like this when he arrives to find the King still dining on a plate of roast crows.

Ahh, old Owl, may the Light Of Leo be upon you, does the morning find you well, no aches and pains?

Rrio nods, not even a bow, wary of the morbid interest the King seems to take in which parts of Rrio's body are intermittently replaced by the Cherubs.

The King finishes his crows, his dripping jaws recoiling from the plate, his furred clawed paw passing the silver platter to a guard at his side. *Now what do you know about **Sin-Enema**, Rrio?* –he asks, wiping his muzzle on an ornate lacework napkin.

***Cinema**, it is an archaic word, Sire. In the Time Before, it was a place, a large gathering-hall with many seats where people watched scheduled entertainments in total darkness, **films** they called them, projected from a small light box behind them onto a huge screen in front of them, perhaps thirty feet long by twenty high. There were many **Cinemas**, people went there every week, particularly courting couples who could fondle each other in the dark on the back seats…*

Fascinating… the Wolf King drawls, the savage slit-pupils of his yellow eyes dilating in wonder. *Now they just copulate in the streets or wherever they can find a night bonfire. And they say we haven't improved life in the New Republic?*

Why do you ask, Sire?

There was an incident last night. The Cherubs had forewarned us of it. You know how they say they can detect human thoughts, psychic disturbances, unauthorised gatherings of consciousness.

Rrio nods. He knows only too well that the Cherubs can read thoughts, and is one of the few people living who has learned how to partially screen out their probings when he is in their vicinity.

The Soldiers raided their gathering, this building they called a Sin-Enema, strange word, what it had once been apparently. A few hundred Blasphemists trapped, most fought to the death, but a few were taken prisoner. We're having them tortured right now as it happens, would you like to see them?

Rrio shrugs his shoulders, and half-raises his wrinkled hands in acquiescence. He is indifferent to human suffering. The longer he lives the more he sees all mortal joy and pain as almost interchangeable, just the music of life, some sweet, some discordant.

*

The Wolf King insists that Rrio travel with him inside the Royal Disc, and he duly takes his place to the left of his velvet throne, while the Storks toil at the port and starboard, wheeling across an array of lights and switches at the metallic rim. A patchwork of icy clouds and blue sky speed over and about them, the transparent hemisphere arcing over their heads. Circular floor ports reveal glimpses of the blackened ruins below, perpetually strewn with drifting snow. They spin down into a deep amphitheatre, several military Discs already gravitating around, the snow cleared by laser cannon.

The Blasphemists are stretched out on hovering steel plates with electrode binding around their wrists and ankles, at the centre of the Cinema building which has been long-since stripped of seats. Only its black curving groins overhead, like the rib cage of a whale, now echo to the cries of the condemned. One of the Wolf King's cousins, Prince Obdissian, presides over the torture, watched over by closed ranks of dark-clad Soldiers on each side, the elite among whom are Wolves also.

So you deny the Word Of Leo and the sovereignty of The Wolf King, the Divine Ordained Of The Woods? –the Prince breaks off in mid-sentence and everyone bows and salutes as the King and Rrio enter.

Hail now Obdissian, may Leo spare you, any progress? The King looks around, almost diffidently, always resentful of these kind of hallowed silences when he walks in unexpectedly.

The Prince bows again unnecessarily, *We suspect there is a ring-leader among them, or that they have knowledge of one, but they have not yet betrayed him. They are fanatical, and well-trained, Sire.*

You suspect outside help?

They have knowledge of Math-Magic and Electronika, Sire, even some forbidden gadgetry akin to those of The Esoterics.

Then they may have had contact with Yoora and Merick, the Heretical Empires?

We believe it may be so... but... He raises a furred eyelid wide, as a man might lift an eyebrow, and looks at Rrio.

Ahh yes, Rrio was ambassador to Yoora in his youth... And the King allows himself a little chuckle at his own joke here: *...his youth! ...the very man for this interrogation.*

163

Rrio steps forward, taking off his leather gloves, and turns the face of one of the Blasphemists towards him and gazes into his eyes. Rrio drinks the youth and energy that still emanates from him, even in this pain, but in turn the prisoner shiveres and recoils, mortified. Rrio speaks rapidly to him in a handful of Yooroan languages, but he responds only in Volwyn:

You! Old Man! Owl! Traitor! You take our children and sell them to wolves! –He spits, trying to sit up, veins standing out in his convulsing neck. *You were human once, have you no heart? No soul left? Have the Aliens taken every last human atom out of you and replaced it with grey ice?*

Silence him! Obdissian cries out, *He profanes against the King's Owl: He who was beloved of Leo and has been saved from all death...*

No! Rrio says dramatically, raising a hand. *Let him speak.* But the prisoner seems suddenly out of words as well as breath now.

He spoke of Aliens, Owl, Aliens... the King whispers to Rrio, *What does he mean by that?* He seems shocked, almost effeminate.

It's what the Blasphemists call the Cherubs, Sire... Obdissian intervenes, *They believe they are Aliens who have meddled in our history and timeline. They say they have manipulated us genetically, secretly, for generations.*

Really? The King laughs out loud. *How ridiculous. Fairy Tales. They die for Fairy Tales?*

Rrio turns back and looks at the prisoner again, who with difficulty finally returns his stare, then speaks in a hoarse croak: *You carry more pain than you know, old man. It resides in your eyes. You will join us before the fourth moon passes...*

Prophecy...? Obdissian muses.

The answer is buried inside you... you must reach it before they can...

There is a sudden laser flash across the hall and a spurt of blood from the prisoner's ears and nose. He falls back dead.

Everyone turns as two pools of light fall from the ceiling and resolve into the familiar diminutive figures of Cherubs. Suddenly a dozen silver apples wheel and buzz around the room, hovering at different heights, whizzing past people's ears. The Cherubs walk towards them now, one is silver, the other gold, entirely silent, creating a mixture of reverence and disquiet in their wake. They approach The Wolf King first and take a hand each like fond children, before turning around and unleashing their black empty eyes on the rest of the company. They have no voices, but in time everyone has become accustomed to the way they place thoughts inside their heads, after a while it as if you are hearing a voice, an imaginary one: its tone is low, slow, childlike, eerily emotionless, considered, cunning.

He threatened you, Old One... The one wordless voice reaches Rrio, their mask-like lips unmoving. *We stopped his life so that no harm would come to you.*

Rrio quickly bulwarks his forebrain, compartmentalising his thoughts, building a decoy to hold them out. *You are graciously thoughtful, Our Invaluable Advisors, you honour us with your greater wisdom in this and all things...*

Their eyes linger a little too long on him before they turn away, looking for an aftertaste, a fragment of discord he might let slip. They suspect me, he thinks, but keeps the thought dark and swathed.

Obdissian, they project, *we advise you to release the remaining prisoners to us. We can take their memgrams and open them to you for analysis, we can re-run their lives and pinpoint locations, find the identities of other conspirators...*

Then it will be so, -The King intervenes. *You honour us greatly today with your unexpected attention to our trivial affairs. We must be tireless in our pursuit of Your Great Work.*

Yes, The Great Work... the Cherubs repeat slowly into everybody's minds until the whole hall are answering and chanting aloud like prayers, repeating: *The Great Work, The Great Work...*

The silver apples begin returning to the hands of one of the Cherubs, while the other one turns to examine Rrio. It lifts its hand and touches his chest, a beam of light emerging from its left eye and scanning his physique. Some of the soldiers gasp behind him as his internal organs become briefly visible in X-ray. *Your kidneys and liver may need our attention soon, Rrio...* he thinks he almost detects a note of intimate relish in the voice in his head, *-you shall have to let us visit you.*

A sphere of light emerges from the ceiling and rolls down onto the floor between the Cherubs, and begins expanding in size. They each bow a little, gracefully, palms open, then walk backwards into the blinding light, which then shoots up towards the ceiling and vanishes.

Check the room for apples, Rrio cautions Lucius, one of the few fellow Esoterics he feels he can trust. Lucius scans the smooth white walls and ceiling with an sphero-censor, paying particular attention to vision-screens and other Electronika.

You think we may be spied upon? Lucius asks at last as he returns to sit down opposite Rrio. The whole north wall of this small office is a curving glass segment of the greater slope of the Geo-Dome, North-West Quadrant, which was only completed a decade ago. Outside a white world intermittently appears and reappears behind perpetual drifts of lightly falling snow.

It is possible. The Cherubs have been taking a greater interest in me recently.

But Rrio, with your physiology, they are always going to be interested...

Not so, Lucius. For fifty years they only came to my help when I called them, when I was I injured or an organ was failing. Now they've started making excuses, visiting me on various made-up pretexts. They need something that I have, but they don't ask me for it, whatever it is. They never explain what they're up to...

They never have though, have they? Lucius sighs, leaning back in his chair and stroking his goatee beard. *They are the Gods practically, Rrio, above reproach, beyond questioning, beyond explaining their actions. So that if they ever do explain, you start to suspect their motives, wonder what game they want to set you up for. Of course, the official line is that we wouldn't understand the concepts of their science, the hidden rules of the universe, and that if we ever tried then our pretty little heads would explode...*

Do you buy that?

Do you? I should be asking you. You're the one who's been around the block two hundred times. What do you think?

Rrio sighs, and looks out at the world below. The snow has stopped briefly and the sun illuminates a small black figure making its way east across a frozen plain, footsteps left in the snow behind. He lifts a telescope and sees it is an old woman dressed in black rags and furs, dragging a tethered sled behind her. The white snow carries the enormous filigree shadow of the distant Geo-Dome projected onto the ice around her: silhouette figures at desks moving around on different floors. The juxtaposed images of old and new amaze him for a moment. He realises with a jolt that the sleigh behind her carries a human torso. He hopes she intends to bury it. *This could be viewed as heresy, this conversation, of course,* Rrio says, returning his gaze to Lucius.

Of course.

For decades the Cherubs were neutral, dispassionate. It was easy to believe the official religious line that they were Gods because they acted like God: they didn't intervene, they scarcely seemed to care, they just showed up now and again and imparted some astonishing knowledge. But recently… it's as if they are hungry or jealous, they seem almost avid, but for what? Something's changed, they seem almost Human at times, Lucius.

Human! Lucius laughs. *You think the corruption of the Human race, the stink of our foul history, has finally infected the noses of the Gods, poisoned them, made them start to become like us?*

I don't know, it's just a thought, blasphemy I know… but I've begun to wonder if they are really just the selfless benefactors that we have been brought up to believe in them as. I've started to wonder what their true motives might be.

What could they be?

They killed a blasphemer I was interrogating today, right under my nose. They just appeared out of nowhere.

Well they always do…

Yes, but why did they need to kill this rebel, this blasphemer? It was as if they were afraid of something he was going to tell me…

The Gods afraid?

Quite a thought, isn't it?

What was he trying to tell you?

*

At night, Rrio often secretly slips out to travel incognito through the ruined city beyond the Dome. He supposes that the King and even the Cherubs are aware of this but choose to turn a blind eye. So long as he comes to no harm, it seems tacitly understood that Rrio picks up valuable knowledge on these sorties, useful intelligence.

After a short flight he leaves his Disc carefully concealed under a snow drift and makes his way to the edge of a ruined street and begins walking, hands in pockets, animal fur for coat and hat, well-disguised as any Volwyn peasant.

He reaches a street corner and encounters the familiar smell of dogs being roasted on a market brazier. As ever, snow blows in a constant drifting curtain on the blackened crenellations of the ruined towerblocks, the interspersed pine forests, the ramshackle villages, shanty towns of timber planks and corrugated steel.

A herd of woolly cattle are being herded across the street. Rrio dips into a tavern and orders a flagon of ale and stands near the roaring fireplace while he enjoys the crowd, the raised voices, the sense of anonymity.

Here he is just an old man, he thinks, not an immortal or a wise owl or a scientist or an Esoteric anymore. He can forget he is privileged. He closes his eyes for a second as the golden ale pours down his throat, and remembers his youth, his friends, the society he had briefly been a part of, before all society was fractured and lost in the Great Inundation and the start of The Cold Times. It is his birthday, here is his treat. He is drinking with ghosts, talking with ghosts again, the company he likes best these days, his memories of friends long gone who can no longer let him down. Of Rocco the great womaniser, a thousand wild nights, of Adrian the diplomat who talked like an adult even when he was a child, of Marcus the philosopher with whom he rearranged the universe until it made sense, from the bottom of a wine glass… what would they all make of the world now? Of the deranged antics of the royal court?

Do I know you old man? A voice rouses him from his right side.

I doubt it, he says without even turning around, lowering his drink slowly, but the stranger leans closer, aggressive.

Oh… I think I remember you alright though… you're like a phantom, a demon. You showed up the night of my cousin's wedding, and his daughters and each time the next day they were abducted. Mysterious disappearances, and each time only one common factor: a strange old man among the guests at a gathering the night before, somebody nobody knew and nobody spoke to…

Well, you're speaking to me now… Rrio replies, but he notices the tavern is getting quieter, everyone starting to listen to their conversation.

The man produces a knife and gestures to Rrio: *Outside, I have some friends who're going to want a word with you…*

Rrio half turns his head, and sees another two men with knives are emerging from the quietening crowds. He takes a couple of glowing white orbs from his pocket and drops them to the floor, then turns himself upside down and walks across the ceiling.

There are screams and panic as glasses drop and people run out of the bar en masse.

The three assailants cross themselves, one clasps his hands and makes a whispered prayer, but despite their fear they still converge on Rrio, looking up, brandishing their blades, holding makeshift clubs as well now.

He's a demon, I told you, Satan himself maybe!

Rrio makes one of the white orbs flare up and rake across the bar top and slam into the first assailant's face. He shouts and rages, trying to get the electrical static off his face. Rrio walks across the ceiling above him and towards the main door. The other door opens and a new assailant rushes in with an antiquated device in his hands. *Here it is!* –he exclaims, *The Sheen Gun they used to call it.* Two of them brace together and steady themselves then unleash a hail of bullets in Rrio's direction. He touches the buckle of his belt and drops to the floor encasing himself in a transparent electromagnetic field. The bullets ricochet off dangerously, fraying woodwork, smashing glass, wounding the barman where he crouches in terror.

Rrio takes himself and the field through the wall and out onto the street outside. Some of the crowd on the pavement see him and gasp in horror and back away until he adjusts the field and becomes nothing, a black knot of wind and snow. Invisible, he makes his way down the street leaving the noise and chaos behind him.

He checks his vital signs and notes his heart rate and blood pressure are normal. A goat runs out of a side street and ploughs straight against his field, bouncing back dazed and passing out on its side. A passer-by looks at it puzzled then points at Rrio's footprints appearing in the snow. He rotates the buckle and hovers a few feet above the snow for the rest of the way as an extra precaution.

*

When he arrives at Magda's house, he releases the field and breathes in the cold fresh night air again. With no one about, he enters the stairwell: an old ramshackle warehouse, one of the few buildings of this height left standing from The Old Times, and makes his way up to the third floor. On the way up he passes a suspicious looking stranger, and peering into the darkness of his hood sees that he is half-caste, grey fur over his face, one hand a clawed paw, a limp to go with it: probably a canid foot. Rrio looks back at him and quickly tags him with a laser pen. Such cases are rare, especially adult specimens, and he makes a mental note to consider recommending taking this one in for analysis.

He knocks on Magda's door and after a while the door plate slides back and an eye appears. *Aghh it is you...* the voice says and the door opens.

I wasn't expecting you tonight, but then again you're always unpredictable. She puts her arms on his shoulder, a chaste sort of hug as befits their advanced years. Magda is seventy-six and Rrio is glad of a female friend as mercifully free of sexuality as himself. They sit down together by the fireplace and smile into each other's faces: an uncomplicated pleasure. *I will bring you some broth,* she says after a while, and he doesn't argue.

Magda and he have a pact: from their first meeting Rrio has stipulated that she ask him as few questions as possible about his life. This way he rarely has to tell her any lies, and he can relax. They are friends, and he takes great interest in her life and her stories of her life. In return, within reason, and only on his own initiative, he can tell occasional stories from his youth and middle age, provided they remain of a general nature.

Once she asked him his age, and realised to her surprise that even this, notwithstanding the usual issues of vanity, was a topic impossible for him to elaborate on. Tonight there is a new problem:

You're bleeding, she says when she returns from the stove, and strokes his arm in concern.

Rrio is dismissive at first, then increasingly disturbed to realise that such a thing could have escaped his attention: a single bullet still clinging to a graze on the skin, a spreading stain of blood leaking over his arm, bare skin and tunic.

Magda makes him strip and dresses the wound and holds the bullet in her hand afterwards. As he takes it from her in curiosity she says: *anything you want to tell me about?*

170

He smiles weakly. *A small spot of bother, a local difficulty...* *Politican...* she says.

What?

Remember our game, I guess your profession, you tell me if I'm getting warmer.

Not funny Magda.

Policeman... Robber... Hired Assassin...

Seriously Magda, stop.

He uses that tone, something in his voice they both understand, she will not repeat the teasing after hearing it. She leans down and kisses the wound, before she wraps it in bandage.

Why did you do that? –Rrio asks.

My mother used to do it. Kiss it better she said. But that's not really what you're asking is it? She sighs. *Is it so terrible to have someone feel fondness for you?*

She steps back and looks at him in an odd way for a moment, something he hasn't seen her do before. *You're the damndest, fittest, best-looking old man I've ever seen... geriatric porn.*

Rrio laughs and puts his shirt back on, then as she goes to the toilet, he prises the bandage open a little and takes a tiny light sphere from his pocket: and pops it in behind the bandage to accelerate the skin repair.

Magda, he says when she returns and sits down, *Now tell me all your stories of this week while I listen, as slow and boring as you like, and by the way...*

Yes? She raises her eyebrows as he sits down opposite her.

I am fond of you. I'm not cold, only numb, remember there is a difference...

Later they sleep together as usual, but literally sleep. Rrio is impotent, chemically declined by choice. He asked the Cherubs for this. It was different once, and could be so again if he wished, but a century of sexuality has made him weary of all the complications that come with it, the conflicts, the passions, the jealousies. For a while he had thought that sexuality had helped him find the subjects for the Gamene Programme, but in the end he had concluded the opposite was true. Somehow even in an old man, it is apparent to human beings when someone is potent and thereby threatening. Maybe it is pheromones and hormones. Now that he is a sexless, sterile old goat, he seems instantly harmless to most strangers and allowed to walk about unnoticed. Tonight has been the exception that proves the rule... he hopes.

*

He wakes an hour after midnight and a strange light fills the attic space in which they lie. He tries to wake Magda, but can immediately see she is deeply immobilised in some profound slumber.

He stands up, and takes the knife from Magda's bedside table and walks towards the window.

Something is wrong. A huge full moon fills the deep ink-blue night, hovering over the rooftops opposite, but the light is too strong and white. He hears some kind of whisper and walks closer to the windows until he sees something startling hanging over the roofs, less than thirty feet away: a beautiful young woman in white robes, bare feet, with the wings of a huge swan emerging from her back.

She opens her mouth again and repeats his name in an eerily low voice: *Rrio... Rrio.*

What is this? He says, he knows he must be dreaming. He looks down at his hands and pinches the skin.

You're not dreaming, Rrio... the voice says.

This is nonsense... Rrio spits, *Angels have never existed... a figment of The Time Before, a delusion of the religious wars of The Car Age. Who are you trying to fool with this?*

Lucid dreamer, haven't you always been, Rrio? Master of your subconscious. So change me now, undream me, show us your power.

He opens the window and throws the knife, she raises her hand instantly and lets the blade penetrate right through her palm, then blood slowly leaks onto the snow. She seems to feel no pain.

Anything people have ever believed in has life, Rrio, if they were real then I was real for them.

Bullshit. Heard it. You're right about one thing though. If I can't control you then you must be external. Who are you from and what do you want? How did you find me?

We are inside you Rrio... it's more a question of how you find us.

Riddles. Time wasting. Bullshit.

She moves closer, hovering across the frosty air towards him. *Time is running out. They are trying to remove us from your mind Rrio, now that they know we are here. You have to make peace with yourself...*

172

Who are they? Who are you referring to?

She slowly closes her eyes, almost in some kind of ecstasy or hypnotic trance, then thrusts the dagger in into her own stomach.

No! Rrio find himself crying out, surprised at his own horror. Blood spatters over her white robes and Rrio winces. She pulls the dagger up and down, crying out, then a flock of white doves, spraying blood, emerge from her belly and flood towards the window.

No! Rrio cries out again then wakes up bolt upright. He is back in bed and Magda has been attending to his arm, the bandage off and the light sphere dancing around the room. A flock of pigeons are on the window sill, some of them white and pink-eyed.

But Magda's eyes are strange and timid now, in a younger woman her expression would be wonder or fear. *What are you, friend? No man alive has skin that can heal this fast. Are you from the Dome, one of The Esoterics?*

Rrio snaps his fingers and the light sphere returns to his palm and vanishes down his sleeve.

A magician… he says.

Liar… Magda answers, stepping away. *I am an old woman now. Ten years we've met and parted like this. What harm can I do? Am I to die not knowing you? Not knowing who or what you are?*

You do know me, Magda, he sighs, putting on his shirt again, annoyed with himself for having slept in late. Normally he would be gone before first light. He wonders what's caused this further deviation from his body's usual rhythms.

He reaches his hand out and gradually she lets him stroke her hair. *Very well… soon… if you promise… a pact of silence.*

Her eyebrows raise, she knows when Rrio speaks the truth, she knows the different tones he speaks in.

But I warn you, it is a story long enough to fill every night you have left.

I have left? She frowns, pointing to his arm and the spots of blood across the front of his shirt, some of which it suddenly occurs to him look new. *How many do you have left with the company you keep?*

Rrio crosses the room, opens the bedside drawer and finds the knife is gone. He goes over to the window and thinks he sees blood in the snow on the rooftops opposite. Disturbed, he backs away, running his long slender fingers through his dense white short hair.

173

Magda... I have every night of the world left... And he crosses to the door, meeting her gaze as he leaves and bathing her in all the tired sadness of his old blue eyes, ... *every night this world will ever have.* Then to her surprise he kisses her forehead and is gone.

*

Normally Rrio would walk back to where his Disk is buried, but he's late and nervous of being recognised by some of the crowd from the night before. He waits in a shady alley and summons the Disk automatically. When it arrives a minute later and hovers twenty feet up, stray dogs begin barking. When he walks out into the heat corona, some of the dogs come out with him and two of them find themselves lifted with him in a flash, onto the metal outer rim as he unfastens the curving glass cockpit and prepares to climbs in. The animals are whimpering and he can't bring himself to kick them off, nor to let them fall to their deaths when he accelerates. He moves towards them and their body language becomes conflicted. He winces as one slides off, but the other moves timidly towards his outstretched hands. He picks it up and brings it into the cockpit with him, eager to get going, whispering to the animal to calm it down. Fortunately, it is stunned or hypnotised when he starts the thrusters and falls asleep by his side.

His driver is waiting for him when he gets back, and surprised equally by his lateness as with the dog he carries in his arms.

Traditional Volwyn breakfast? He jokes, a broad smile, presuming the beast to be some sort of subject for dissection or experimentation.

No, Halberg. Man's Best Friend, he mutters, but the phrase means nothing to the man, just another ghost-word from The Time Before.

*

*What do you know about **cars**, Owl?* The Wolf King asks Rrio as soon as he enters the room. He has just passed the Storks off-duty, playing chess in the hallway, their rifles leaning against the wall. Silver apples stream about the room, telling him the Cherubs have been here recently or are just about to arrive.

Also known as Automobiles, Rrio answers, wondering to himself why the King doesn't just look these things up in his library portal like everyone else. *Primitive, land-based carriages but with four rubber wheels…*

Rubber!?

They used the compressed fossilised remains of prehistoric sea creatures as fuel to power an Internal-Combustion Engine.

A what!?

It's all recorded and explained in the History Annals.

Yes, yes, the King frowns, *but you explain everything so much better. I love to hear you tell how things actually were, how you experienced them first-hand, how you saw them.*

How I saw them? Rrio asks himself out loud, then goes to the window to look out, his eyes far away.

I hated them. They were wasteful and stupid. They spouted fumes which contributed to the atmospheric calamity of the tenth year Before Leo. People used them as symbols of their own avarice and greed, each one was styled and coloured differently, absurd pompous extravagances.

Fascinating, the King muses. *There were many of them?*

Everywhere. The streets of every city were choked with them, and the drivers were discourteous, always shouting at each other and into that other contraption they were proud of.

Ahh… the mobey dobeys… I remember this story. The Wolf King beams like a thoroughly entertained child.

Mobiles, Rrio corrects him. *Nobody knew they caused haemorrhages and brain damage, although there were plenty of clues. The fools. Twenty-five years after their invention, seventy-five percent of the adult population began to die or enter senility prematurely. Just as the environmental calamity could have done with their best brains working to solve the problem. They had all cooked their own heads, like mad chefs, like turkeys preparing for Christmas.*

For what?!, Owl?

Oh, a festival of the old peasant religion, never mind, Sire.

The Wolf King shakes his head. *Our forebears certainly were stupid, Owl. I sometimes wonder how they could have provided us with a noble man like you.*

I must have been a freak, an accident. Rrio smiles. *My mother often implied as much. Now may I ask you a question, Sire?*

Certainly Owl. This is a surprise. I didn't think I had anything to teach you, other than respect for the Gods at times... forgive me, I jest of course.

The Gamenes... Rrio begins and lets the term hang on the air for a while. *What happens to them after the births?*

Well now, I don't know, Owl... I suppose, from what I've seen they stay within the Geo-Dome to bring up their wolf children. Why do you ask this now?

I don't know... Rrio sighs... *there was a saying they had in the Time Before Leo, that* **absolute power corrupts absolutely.**

I don't understand, Owl. If you and I stray from the true path, then the Gods will always correct us.

One of the silver apples, hitherto rolling and hovering around the perimeter of the room, now spins up into the air between them and springs into life: splitting into four segments that unfold themselves to reveal a tiny screen.

Rrio nearly says *Speak of the devil,* but recoils from the requirement for a complex explanation that such an archaic remark might bring in its wake.

Your Highness and Senator Rrio... the memgrams of the captured Blashphemists have been extracted and analysed. We have isolated a name for their ring leader.

No location? Rrio asks to the air.

Only a name. **Selterlyan.** *We must seek to find the individual with this name.* The apple closes up, gathers is cohorts about it and departs through the east window.

The King and Rrio are left looking at each other with eyes wide. *A strange name...* Rrio muses.

A strange man who can fill my subjects' heads with so many strange ideas. I'm sure you'll find him, Rrio.

Yes, Sire.

And when you do, don't kill him, just get him away from all his followers and bring him up here where you and I can talk to him all day for years on end.

With respect Sire, you're being idealistic again.

I know, I know... but murder and mayhem are so boring after a while don't you think? The really brave leaders of men choose to subject themselves to argument and debate in the end, don't you agree? In fact, I think you taught me that.

Rrio nods and smiles. *Then I am glad Sire, but as you have said we have many advisors. We will not act unwisely, I am sure.*

*

In the afternoon Rrio visits the library atrium within the south-east Geo-Dome quadrant. He loves its huge space: ten storeys high, on which trees of every description grow out of season in the hothouse atmosphere, the tiers of balconies overhead, the echoes of the footsteps of scholars washing the marble walls and floors.

Rrio looks up *"angels"* in the encyclopaedias of The Old World and ponders their meaning: their odd preponderance and persistence in ancient folklores with no apparent grounding in concrete reality. He marvels at the etchings, the oil paintings, the loving chiaroscuro on the feathered wings, the folded gowns, the benign and implacable smiles, the sexless limbs, strong and glowing.

As evening approaches he visits the maternity nexus and donning a doctor's white coat for camouflage: wanders unchallenged and unobtrusive among the wards of mothers and babies.

Tiny wriggling pink wolf cubs, some hours old, writhe over the breasts of young women to suck there. Most seem happy, the few who become disorientated are quickly attended to by matrons with sedatives and narcotic palliatives.

Rrio isn't sure why he is there or what he is looking for. Perhaps it is for the likeness of the young woman, the eerily cold angel who has been appearing to him in his visions. He feels sure he would recognise her in real life. But he knows he is being ludicrous, it was only a hallucination, a meaningless repeating nightmare. Why does he think she has to be real at all? She might just as easily be someone from his long past, now forgotten. His memory is not perfect after all, nobody's is.

*

That night before returning to his bed, Rrio writes another diary entry:

I am increasingly concerned by the angel visions. Another bad one yesterday, with physical evidence left behind... but what am I writing? Evidence of what? That I sleepwalk? Or that some bizarre

177

archaic archetype has started coming back to life in our age, when it is only a dream from The Time Before? How nonsensical would that be?

Magda has found some things out and I am going to have to allow her some knowledge. I hope this won't endanger her. The Wolf King once asked me why I thought the Gods have never offered him eternal life, the immortality granted to me, and I told him it was nothing to wish for. I remember clearly his surprise. He thought immortality might be like paradise but I explained that all the pain of watching those you love die before you, and of watching humanity repeat the same mistakes endlessly, made it a mixed pleasure, fifty-fifty at best. Recently I have begun to wonder if that ratio hasn't shifted in my mind now.

How sour every taste turns in this dry old mouth. Wouldn't true immortality, paradise, be to be re-united with my beloved first wife, my son, my mother? But does such an opportunity exist any more than angels? Perhaps this strange artificial life I am trapped within is not paradise at all, but purgatory, endless wait through endless night, a living death. True death, the chance to end our loneliness and longing… to be reunited with our larger tribe. Could it be after all, that this was all mankind ever strove for, but pushed it away with blind hands across centuries, fleeing in misunderstanding from its greatest goal and prize?

*

Next day Rrio retrieves the dog he has rescued from the medical nexus and plays with it in the Geodesic Gardens. He feeds it then they run for a mile together under the oaks and elms, eucalyptus and palms, by the too-clear water of artificial streams. They pause together to get their breath back and Rrio sits and looks into the animal's eyes: *Humble creature… you would make a nobler candidate for immortality than me, little memory of the past, no regrets, little thought or foreboding of the future.* The dog sits up and barks back at him. *The closest you will ever get to speech, eh? And what use is it anyway? You judge me by actions not by promises, as should we all.* He strokes its head and rubs its sides until it barks again, happily, ready for another run. *I name you… I name you…* Rrio feels lost for a moment searching for names in his head, each one assigned to a long-dead friend, until his favourite Greek philosopher comes to mind. *Epicurus… Epi for short.* Maybe it is something to do with the creature having been rescued from the delicatessen of the street.

178

But as he stands to run again he remembers Epicurus' best aphorism: that *a man may escape punishment for a crime, but never escape the fear of that punishment,* and something turns sour in his heart and twists deep inside him.

*

He takes the morning off and looks out his ancient copy of the Book Of Leo and taking it with him; sets out on his favourite secret pilgrimage, where he goes when he needs spiritual replenishment.

It isn't everyone's idea of a day-out, and even his own technology is pushed to its limits in such an environment: he flies north for an hour and lands on the mile-high edge of the arctic ice shelf, glaciers shuddering forth below, a constant spray of ice and frost-laced wind blowing off beneath his feet. In the distance, visible in glimpses through the drifting cloud: the city of Volwys crouches like a condemned prisoner, shivering, eyes-closed, awaiting the fall of the fatal axe, a moment in time indefinitely postponed, an age that lasts a moment, lasts all of eternity perhaps. Rrio sits like a child on a riverbank, legs dangling nonchalantly over the catastrophic edge of this and every other world, the great levelling zero poised to annihilate all life. With gloved hands he opens The Book Of Leo and reads:

Oh, Earth that was once rich and green, adundant with life of countless species, infinite variety, have pity on mankind who trashed its own home, who raped Gaia, who bespoiled every scrap of Nature's beauty that it found in its path.

Gaia responded with The Great Inundations, The Rains Of Seeds, The Gamma Flashes, The Cloud Overs.

Gaia brought forth the Cherubs, the ancient guardians of her Earth, the shepherds, the tillers and tenders. They descended from the clouds on pillars of fire.

Now last of all comes The Age Of Ice.

Only fools fear death and seek to escape from it. We are not Many but One, not One but Many. Deep within each individual lies the portal to every other. We are but a divine elixir poured into a million glasses. He who poured us is always taking us back, drinking and pouring...

179

Something gives way inside Rrio for a moment, or perhaps the extreme temperature overtakes him too quickly for a man of his extraordinary years. He smiles, embracing a strange serenity, closing his eyes and slipping off the ice and falling down through space. And the fall is like a great dream of childhood, of running and sledging and returning to a warm fireside, of rocking to sleep in his mother's arms.

*

When Rrio open his eyes he finds he is back inside the Geo-Dome again with the Cherubs operating on him. *You should take more care of yourself, Old One…* they intone into his head where he lies on a silver bed beneath the racing clouds, the segmental glass carapace overhead. *Time is not finished with you yet.*

~

2: THE TORTURE TREE

"...And all this is very well known to the Steppenwolf, even though his inner eye may never fall on this fragment of his inner biography. He has a suspicion of his allotted place in the world, a suspicion of the Immortals, a suspicion that he may meet himself face to face; and he is aware of the existence of that mirror in which he has such bitter need to look and from which he shrinks in such deathly fear..."

-Herman Hesse, *Steppenwolf.*

Magda unlocks the door and embraces Rrio fervently, almost shaking and scolding him for his long absence. *I was so worried about you, where have you been?* –she pulls back and examines him, trying to read the lines on his face, before she is distracted by a scraping and whimpering noise at her feet.

I'm sorry. I had an accident, but I am fine now. And I've brought along a new friend. This is Epi, Magda, a stray mongrel I found wandering the streets.

Magda kneels to pet him and he barks at her.

Don't worry, he is a little nervous of strangers. Thinks everyone is going to put him in a pot with vegetables.

And aren't we? Magda smiles.

Oh no... Rrio shakes his head, closing the door behind him. *This mutt's with me, diplomatic privilege, culinary immunity.*

So you are a Diplomat then? What happened, Rrio? Couldn't you have sent word?

Rrio snorts. *And how would I have done that without revealing your existence and whereabouts to my suspicious colleagues and employers?*

And they are...?

181

Rrio looks at her silently.

We have a lot of talking to do, Rrio. You made me a promise, remember?

Ah yes. The promise. That I would answer all your questions, and reveal to you exactly who you have been friends with these last ten years, thus putting your life in danger. You're still sure that's what you want?

Magda puts down a bowl of water for Epi and strokes his ears (who eyes her suspiciously, then tentatively begins drinking). Rrio stands at the window for a minute and watches the snow drifts blowing across the twilit streets.

The world is icy cold and I am an old woman. Death whispers in my ears at night, death laughs at me on the stairs, runs his cold fingers over my back, every day. What new danger can you bring me? I can die but once. Only God can destroy me now, and he can damn well work for it.

Brave words, Rrio smiles grimly. *But death is one thing, torture is quite another.*

Torture? Magda looks puzzled.

Wouldn't you rather just go on knowing me the way you've always known me? As an enigmatic stranger? You might like me a good deal less when I explain what I do, what I have done.

Magda returns to her old armchair and sits down heavily on it, her features lined with concern. *You are a good and kind man. I am a good judge of character. You may confess anything to me. I have told you already that I want this, the truth, before I die.*

Then it will be so, Rrio sighs, *but before I answer your hundred questions, may I ask you just one?*

Magda shrugs and opens her hands in a gesture of offering.

Who is Selterlyan?

Magda's eyes darken and she rises from her chair. Rrio thinks she is returning with a bowl of broth but instead finds she brings back a fish-gutting knife that she holds to his throat.

Epi whimpers and barks, sensing the threat to his master. Rrio's eyes widen, the blade cold and sharp against his skin.

So long as we both live, never again ask me that question… -she hisses, *nor say that name within these walls.*

*

182

Castor and Pollux... Obdissian shouts over the noise of the Disk thrusters and the howling wind.

Code names? Rrio rejoins, as he prepares to climb into the cockpit.

Two of our best agents... sleepers. They say they've infiltrated a plot, some piece of sabotage being planned.

From the tall top of the ruined towerblock they stand on, their two Disks wheel away, then entering invisibility: drop down to skim along above street level.

What are we looking for? Rrio asks into his intercom, Obdissian only visible to him in infra-red, a black figure in a black Disk, moving parallel to his own, orange heat glow around his eyes and hands, the Disk thrusters red behind him.

Here, slow down... Obdissian indicates then they hover above three walking figures, leaving a thoroughfare of market stalls, moving out into a bleak snowfield, their footsteps grey dots behind them.

Cut engines and home in on their conversation... I'll relay it over.

*

How long, how far, Anno? Cas asks, following in his footsteps, literally, struggling to catch up through the deep snow, his labouring breath climbing the steely-cold air between them.

A mile, a meeting place I've agreed, -Anno half turns and rasps back, the bleak white expanse beyond his shoulder beckoning them on like a fresh sheet of paper. *Explosives. Gadgetry stolen from the Adepts. We take it and use it tonight.*

Where's the target? Paul asks, catching up, breath swirling across his face.

Anno pauses on the brow of the hill and points towards the Geo-Dome. *A weak spot on that damned domed spaceship of theirs, my contact has the plans...*

Just a bomb, Anno? We plant it and run, no close-combat?

Easy, snow-tiger... You eager to fight wolfmen or something?

Drop it, Cas. One of them raped his mother... though he never talks about it.

Everyone shut up, we're nearly there. That tree, see it? That one that's all contorted and tortured?

But hold on... there's no one there. This doesn't feel right.

Now their three figures, knives drawn, circle around an ancient blackened oak, branches lichened grey as petrified smoke. Their strange circular procession has something of a ritual dance about it. *When he doesn't come, if he doesn't come...* Anno spits, *it always means something bad.*

*Like what? ...And just who is **he**?*

Don't you know? Didn't I drop any hints, friends?

Meaning?

Oh yes... the Lion himself. That would have been quite an honour for you two, wouldn't it?

But he is one smart cat they say. He smells blood on the wind, fear in a man's sweat.

If he hasn't turned up then that can mean only one thing... He turns his eyes accusingly to the other two.

Well? Cas asks.

Anno headbutts him and grabs Paul around the neck and wrestles him up against the tree with his blade to his neck. *One of you, or both maybe... must be traitors. Any suggestions, Cas? If you tell me it's not you and I believe you then it must be Paul, so I kill Paul. Which will it be? Or if you tell me it's you, then at least you can try to out-run me, or us, I should say. Or if it's both of you... what will your next move be then I wonder? Sacrifice your fellow to protect your own cover? Hey, is this nail-biting or what?*

Kill him, Anno. It must be Paul. It's not me, I know that much.

Anno throws Paul towards him, he falls coughing at Cas's feet. *You kill him then, Cas. Let me see you kill him. Prove to me you're not both snakes, rats, quislings?*

Cas advances on Paul with his knife drawn, Paul scrambles to his feet, backing away.

A searing yellow flash suddenly appears in Paul's chest, the smell of burning flesh, the sound following on a second later: roar and pulse of a light burst. Anno spins around to see a wolf man in dark leather uniform materialise, hovering above the snow, weapon drawn. He makes to run. But a Disk appears overhead and a long circle of soldiers are dispensed one by one in rapid succession from a light beam onto the snow around him.

*

Why did you kill him? Pollux, the agent, he was one of ours? Rrio asks as they pace to the interrogation room, their boots echoing along dismal corridors of damp stone.

Obdissian smiles harshly. *To save Cas from doing it, although I think he still might have.*

But why was it necessary? Anno might have been bluffing. A blood rite, a test of resolve and loyalty.

Plausibility. Someone must have betrayed them, or why else didn't Selterlyan show up?

But who?

Precisely. That's what we'd very much like to know. But whatever the answer, there must be a simple believable scapegoat for the Blasphemists to blame for this, or our other agents could be in danger.

Rrio stops in the corridor, and Obdissian stops a few paces further on and turns to face him. *What?*

You sacrificed that man's life for nothing, for a convenience, for a lie. We didn't used to do things this way in the Republic.

Obdissian half-turns to let the weak winter light from the barred windows wash over his war-scarred face. *Wake up, Rrio. Things are changing. These are brutal times. We face an implacable threat from the Blasphemists.*

But they are supposed to be the savages, not us.

I'd rather be savage and alive than civilised and dead, wouldn't you, Rrio?

Rrio moves closer and brings his face up closer to Obdissian's bristling muzzle and speaks in a quiet growl of restrained anger. *Listen to me. I've probably killed more men than you've ever met. Killed them with guns, knives, my bare hands. But I only ever killed them when I needed to, when it was me or them, when there was no choice.*

Your point is? Obdissian lifts a brow, taking Rrio's hands off his immaculate uniform with a degree of distaste.

Life is not cheap, Brother. Inside or outside the Dome. When you devalue life, any life, then you devalue your own. You devalue values, one might say, the very things we are fighting for, for Leo's sake!

You're preaching politics again, Rrio. I've never had the head for it. My father was a soldier.

Power, Obdissian, you understand that well enough? Call it what you will, but if you wield it, you must wield it well… or one day it wields you.

185

Well then, Obdissian grins, baring his alarming teeth as he reaches and unlocks the cell door. *Let us see how you wield it upon our new prisoner then…*

*

My first question might seem a selfish one, a girlish one even. But we have to start somewhere, Magda sighs, leaning forward in her chair under the snow-smothered skylight, succeeding in stroking Epi for the first time.

He's taking to you… Rrio smiled, absent-mindedly.

Are you married? Do you have children?

Ahh… Rrio chuckles grimly, his eyes gone far away. *I had a wife once, and a son.*

Once?

They're all dead now.

What happened?

Happened? They died.

Of what? –Magda exclaims, almost indignant.

Of natural causes of course. Most people do die sooner or later.

Magda frowns, puts her head in her hands and thinks for a second. *Look, I think I'm missing something here. And I think maybe it comes back to a question I asked you several years ago and you refused to answer it. Maybe we'll fare better this time. How old are you, exactly?*

Exactly? Two hundred and thirty years, ten days and fourteen hours.

Magda has risen to her feet, and now slumps back into her chair in confusion. *We've shared many jokes over the years Rrio, but this isn't one of them, is it? You're completely serious?*

Completely.

Jesus Christ…

Oh, that old fellow.

You don't believe in him? –Magda asks, eyes far away now, almost absentmindedly. *You'll be of the new religion then, which begs another question. Where do you work and what as?*

Inside the Geo-Dome, officially as a diplomat and senator, but unofficially as a personal advisor to the King.

The Wolf King?

Rrio nods.

Magda gulps, then begins shaking, her eyes beginning to fill with tears. Rrio stands up and makes to reach out to her, but she knocks his hand away. *What have you been doing coming here? You're bloody royalty! Am I a research project? A joke to tell your privileged friends about?*

To her amazement, when Magda turns around she sees that Rrio is still on his knees in front of her chair, and that he is silently weeping now, while her eyes have dried. She gasps and moves closer to him tentatively, then sits slowly down in front of him. His eyes close. Eventually she reaches out her hand and touches his right shoulder. His eyes open, still weeping softly. *You are a queer fellow. Always full of surprises. What ails you?*

He breathes in. *I've lost so many people, over the years. It doesn't get any easier.*

You haven't lost me... yet, she adds disconsolately, as an afterthought.

You are not any kind of joke to me. You are the dearest, closest friend I have left. Yes, the world I go away to each day is complex, but that doesn't mean to say my relationship to you, with you, can't be simple. Maybe that's exactly what I need and value and love about it.

Go on, Magda says, rocking in her chair, trying not to enjoy herself too obviously.

I admire you...

Me? She interrupts. *An old fish wife? An Ice Gardener? While you rule the world and mete out poverty and wealth, knowledge and ignorance, life and death?*

Yes, you. Precisely because of your simplicity, in the best sense, your solidity, straightforward morals, old-fashioned right and wrong. Like what I remember of the Old World I grew up in, what we have all lost in this nightmare we live in now.

I remind you of your mother? Magda sighs, with resignation.

Yes, in a way... Rrio affirms, eyes widening, *I suppose so.*

You've remembered her love for two centuries?

I will remember her for twenty centuries, if I am granted that much time and health.

*But you **have** been granted it apparently. Who bestows such power upon you?*

My age?

You're some sort of immortal, is that possible? Are you in league with the Devil?

Oh no, not the Devil. Not that I believe in him, but no. This is no magic or witchcraft, only science.

Séance?

Science.

I don't know this word.

Like Electronika and Math-Magic. Knowledge. What the Esoterics practice within the Geo-Dome.

Then you are an Adept too?

Of course, we almost all are, within the Dome. That's why we're there, why we built it. To keep knowledge alive, to develop it. To find a way to save our dying world.

Magda smiles bitterly. *A bit late aren't you? See any flowers and meadows outside that window? And that northern ice wall is getting closer every year.*

But I haven't answered your question.

Haven't you?

Who keeps me alive.

I thought you said the Esoterics do it, you and your Adept chums.

No, they, we… only do the donkey work. The Cherubs repair and maintain my body. Only they have full command of that level of knowledge.

Then they exist?

Oh yes, very much so I'm afraid.

Afraid? You're telling me you've met the Gods? I can't take all this in. She puts her hand to her ears until Rrio tenderly takes them down again.

I know, I know, it's a lot to hear all at once. But you said you wanted the truthful answers to everything. But believe me, none of this is as strange and exotic as you imagine. The Cherubs are merely beings, little people like us, except a thousand times older and wiser. They're like parents, the ultimate parents, the parents of the human race, which perhaps they are you know, quite literally.

But you said "afraid".

Yes… I did, didn't I? You may be straightforward, Magda, but you are very far from stupid.

Well? She smiles.

188

Well people find them benign and full of grace, radiating marvellousness and all that, when they first meet them. But unlike most people, I've known them for over a century now. To some extent I've been brought into their confidence from time to time, or more exactly I have trespassed and snooped into their confidence, generally hung around in their psychic back gardens.

And now you are going to tell me the Gods are evil? Because I don't care, you know. My God is still Jehovah, the old God, Jesus. I trust in him, and he hasn't let me down yet.

Magda... Rrio snorts. *He hasn't exactly made a large number of public appearances in the last two thousand years either, has he?*

You would say that!

I would, because my Gods I have touched and seen and spoken with. They are very real, very much alive, and no, they are not evil.

How are they then?

Evil and Good are only words that denote what is contrary or beneficial to the interests of the human race, yes?

I suppose so, Magda nods her head slowly, mulling this over.

Then the Gods, the Cherubs, are neither good nor evil, Magda, because they are not human. They are probably good within their own definition of the term, within their own moral framework, but it is not the same as ours, how could it be?

But... But... what does that imply?

That they can commit evil, evil acts against us, and they have done, believe me, but without being evil. It's about moral relativity.

This is a very dangerous line of thought.

It's a dangerous line of work too, but unfortunately it also happens to be my job.

*

Rrio enters the torture cell and pulls up a chair in front of Anno. His shirt is torn, blood streaks his face and shoulders, but otherwise he is still in remarkably good shape. Before Rrio can begin the interrogation, to his surprise, Anno looks at him and says simply: *You.*

Rrio narrows his eyes. *You know me?*

Oh no, nobody knows you, old one... he replies slowly, cryptically.

You've seen what happened to your fellow conspirators, of course.
I am here to be more reasonable... to offer you a chance.

An olive branch, eh? Held in the beak of a dove?

Noah and the flood. You are of the old religion, then?

Of course. I was raised in it, that's not illegal...

Failed the world, failed Humanity in the end somewhat though
don't you think? I don't suppose we need to ban anything so discredited
as that.

And alien arse-licking is better?

Christianity gave Eros poison to drink. It didn't die from the
dose but degenerated into vice. Nietzsche.

A philosophy lesson. You're going to torture me with poetry?

Christianity set Man against Nature, Man against animal.
Capitalism, the wholesale rape of our natural environment, was then
inevitable. Don't you see that?

No.

I think you do. The evidence is all around us. A ruined world.
Leo saved us from that deranged philosophy, our collision-course with
Nature.

Saved us a bit too late though, eh? Only our souls are left to save
now.

I believe in souls too. Souls are our return to Gaia. But even
Gaia is ultimately mortal perhaps. She needs a planet. What you call
Heaven depends on the real estate of there being a future world, a future
Gaia, to maintain it.

Your friends think the aliens are helping to save this world? They
are dismantling it, raping what's left of it more efficiently than we ever
did. They are bounty-hunters, scrap-merchants crawling over the rusting
hulk of a sunken ship.

Very poetic. Who tells you this stuff? This pseudo-profound,
profane, nonsense?

You do.

Rrio narrows his eyes.

Only joking. These are the beliefs of our movement. We tell each
other them.

One man in particular is behind these ideas though, isn't he?

Anno shrugs.

This is your chance to save yourself. Tell me about Selterlyan.

Anno remains silent, his eyes clouding over.

Who is Selterlyan?

More silence.

Very well. We're not stupid. Perhaps we don't expect you to tell us where he lives, where he can be found, his real name. But there is other information you can help us with. Let's start at the beginning, shall we? Tell me what Selterlyan preaches.

He doesn't preach... Anno says slowly and quietly.

Ahhh, but he does exist then, doesn't he?

More silence.

He is some kind of intellectual then, a sophist, and aesthete, a politician even. What arguments does he make? What main idea does he expound?

Equality.... Social justice... Anno whispers.

Ahh, those antiquities, Rrio nods his head slowly.

You live in pampered luxury within the Dome, while we starve. You think that can be excused?

Justified, yes. It was the mob, the ignorant masses breeding like rabbits who brought our planet to its knees by force of numbers and rampant consumption. Now your numbers must reduce, having reaped what you sowed. Would you prefer we sterilised you all?

You think you can play God forever?

We within the Dome are a small elite, a skeleton crew of skilled personnel. Those required to keep knowledge alive, the knowledge you squandered when you were given it. You speak of equality, but when the mass of humanity are ignorant and unfit for knowledge, then equality is merely a proposition to lower the average, to allow the triumph of barbarism over the intellect. We, the Esoterics, are like the monks in the middle-ages, the dark ages of post-Roman Europe. Just as they single-handedly kept Latin and music and mathematics and art alive, so must we preserve the current knowledge.

But you have made us more ignorant... And what could be more barbaric than the monstrous inequality and injustice you preside over here? —These two parallel worlds, inside and outside the Dome?

This is what Selterlyan teaches?

Silence.

Quote him to me. Convert me.

Unjust regimes always eventually collapse under the weight of their own fear.

Not bad... Rrio nods his head.

191

Fear is corrosive. To be free of fear, one must sow trust and love, must build social justice. This leap of blind faith can only be made at any given moment, by those who hold power. If they will not leap then they must be blindfolded and pushed if necessary.

Pushed off a cliff, eh? Very compassionate. Rrio laughs grimly. *Idealistic, but vaguely cynical, pragmatic. An odd mixture.*

Anno nods. *Good works, Evils fails, ultimately because Love when it is done with itself turns outward and spreads, while Hate when it is replete turns inwards and consumes itself.*

Interesting…

Love succeeds, Hatred fails, ultimately, no matter the objective.

Problem is, Rrio waves his hands, *-speaking of fear… in certain ages Fear is real, not a phantom, it comes from without, in the shape of flood or famine, or in our case snow and glaciers.*

Evil flourishes precisely when it is needed least: in times of threat and peril, when Love is the required solution. It is as if it seeks to rob its opponent of the victory it sees looming… in such circumstances. Evil has the edge over Love in one aspect alone: it sees the future first.

Is this you speaking now?

Oh no… I quote word for word.

Is this all written down somewhere?

I cannot read or write. But I listen well.

To him?

Anno nods his head, smiling bitterly, with a gleam of bruised sadness in his eye.

*

Well? Obdissian asks as Rrio leaves the cell. *Shall we cut out his tongue lest he repeat his sacrileges?*

No. Quite the reverse. We retain him, we go on engaging him in conversation and thereby learning about our opponent. He obviously enjoys a good debate. That's how to lure him on, loosen his tongue. Just make sure he never learns to read or write… and keep him away from other prisoners.

*

Tell me about your mother, Magda sighs, as she and Rrio lie down together, snow flakes swirling in the star-filled night beyond the tilted mansard windows of her warehouse.

Rrio closes his eyes and lets the pictures slowly flood in. Magda sees that Epi is sleeping now, his paws twitching, dreaming, where he lies by the hearth.

A constantly reassuring presence. I was her first-born, her little gentleman. She was always there for me. Ahh… but it's hard to talk of things so personal without descending into clichés and platitudes.

What is your earliest memory of her?

Hard to say… strangely… mothers just emerge, don't they, or we emerge from them? As if consciousness is born from consciousness, slower and later, two or three years after the physical event.

Or maybe it takes ten years… or twenty?

Or an eternity. We emerge from our mothers and yet we are made of them, their flesh, literally. Rrio looks down at his hands and arms. *How grotesque. My mother is still here, and my son was some other part of me, some further subdivision loosed upon the world. Oh who can make sense of it?*

After two hundred and thirty years, you're none the wiser?

Less so… Except… I am able to regard it less passionately I suppose, with more rationale.

But rationale isn't the answer?

No. Not the key to unlock the puzzle at all, not the centre of it anyway.

So a newborn babe in arms has more of a clue as to the meaning of life?

Yes, incredibly…

Rrio turns over to go to sleep, then after a while reflects: *My earliest memory is not of my mother but of a room she has just left. It is a summer evening and I am in a cot, a play-pen, looking through the slots, quite unable to get out of course, but the yellow evening light in the open window, the sounds of evening birdsong: are exquisite to me, a revelation. When bleakness overwhelms me, I try to go back to that single moment of wonder at creation.*

Rrio?

Yes?

What was the world like before the snow came?

*

So, Rrio... the Wolf King sighs in his fine ermine robes, leaning back in his throne after dinner, while Rrio paces the black and white chequered floors, deep in thought like a chess-master, stroking his chin. *Have you found me this Selterlyan yet?*

No, Sire, alas. We found a man who had met him yesterday, one of his disciples.

What do you intend to do with him?

My orders, by your leave, are that we return him unharmed to his family and continue to question him from time to time.

And?

And pick up as many others like him as we can. I want to build up a picture of this Selterlyan from all the imprints he's left behind on other people. Like reconstructing the fragments of a broken vase.

Or a broken mirror?

Why do you say that? Rrio pauses, eyes narrowing.

Obdissian was saying one possibility is that Selterlyan is a traitor in our midst, an Esoteric who has lost faith, who feeds secrets to the Blasphemists while maintaining a calm, respectable façade everyday...

What leads him to think that?

The way certain facts appear to have been leaked, tip-offs, traps for Selterlyan that fail.

A silver apple falls from the ceiling and bounces several times before hovering finally between them. *Obdissian...* the King says aloud and the apple unfolds itself and two screens emerge like wings to face each other. Obdissian's face appears on them. *I was just telling Senator Rrio about your suspicions... about a mole in our midst.*

Could we make a list? Rrio asks to the air, *-of how many people could possibly fit the profile.*

I already have.

How many names? Rrio asks.

About seventy, right now. With each new capture and interrogation we may narrow it down.

Then we have a method... the King grins at Rrio.

Yes, although we must be careful, be very secretive about our suspicions, Rrio cautions.

Mmm?

Or a climate of fear will take root. Even good men may change their behaviour out of self-consciousness, inadvertently creating false leads. Fear is corrosive of truth.

The Wolf King looks at Rrio long and hard, eyes wide. Behind him, through the vast open segments of the stone dome vaults, endless snowflakes fall like tears across the ruined world.

*

Summer. Yes, I remember summer. You have never seen one, and alas may never live to see one now. Although of course, I suspect that neither shall I. All life is dependant on the sun. Sun-bathing it was called, can you imagine that? An encounter with the sun, hours sitting in its intense heat. It was like an audience with God.

Or the Devil? –Magda interjects.

Yes, perhaps. Particularly when you were young. The sun beat into you and rejuvenated you. Women would glow in the sunlight, their cheeks a beautiful red, their freckles like the dappled shadows of leaves. The intensity of shadows on a summer day. The smell of gardens and meadows. Oh how can I possibly express it or encapsulate it for you? Summer was a celebration, the moment when Nature stripped off all her clothes, dazzled you utterly with her beauty, then kissed you on the lips. It was irrefutable, potent, arresting. As a child, summer was when you dreamt most. It was no coincidence that everybody's earliest memories were of summer holidays, the seaside. Summer was a revelation that awakened our senses as children, literally, for the first time. That people are born and die now without it, is beyond me to imagine, even though I am amongst it.

Aren't you exaggerating a little? Wasn't there anything bad about summer?

Oh, I suppose. The heat got too much, the sweat and the dust maybe, yes. And everyone walking around half-naked. I suppose it turned their minds rather too much to copulation. And they all got excited and twittered too much. All that hot air, like birdsong but without the charm. Yes, it could be tiring.

Tell me your best summer days, then your worst.

Oh, by the seaside somewhere, with my father and mother and sister, before all the trouble started.

Trouble?

195

My father left us for another woman, one of his patients, he was a doctor. It cause a bit of a scandal I think. Oh yes, and the world ended too. You know, the Inundations, the volcanoes and earthquakes, Gaia shaking us off like ants. But back then for a while, such a short while, although at the time it seemed a whole eternity: we were blissfully happy, playing on the beach, walking on the sand, playing the guitar. On the golden fields, in the emerald forests, a young family is full of hope and flowering, they are counterparts, interlocking segments of a frame defining Life, distilling the vignettes.

Your worst?

In my early twenties, back by the seaside in a hired car with various friends. The perceived need to pair off creeping up on me, without enough girls to go around, knowing I would always be the loser, with only jealousy to lie down with. There was your hell, your Devil.

Why didn't you think you'd get a girl? Why didn't you?

Because society was sick, and I was a purist, I still am. I suppose I was supposed to fight for a mate. Impress, win. Barbarism. A woman had to find me, want me, mutually, or I would sooner walk into the sea. Those were the rules I set myself and I have stuck to them.

You mean you were sensitive.

How do you mean?

You like to see yourself, to redefine yourself, as some hard-hearted intellectual monster. You couldn't compete for any girl's affection because it embarrassed you and you are too kind to hurt anyone else.

Well, I have hurt plenty of people since. But I will concede a grain of truth in what you say there, perhaps.

How did you meet your wife then? What was she like?

Marie was everything I needed, my perfect counterpart. I had just been looking in the wrong places. She was shy, introverted, as you say in fact: like the real me I had been trying to hide. She actually thought I was an extrovert at first. Imagine! How ridiculous. I visit humanity on a raid. I met her as the flood waters first rose. The streets were riven with giant hogweeds, jungle ferns. All of Nature went haywire you see, just before the end. And we went haywire too, once we'd broken through all the customary reticence and embarrassment, with the aids of copious volumes of alcohol. I see us first making love in a high tower. Perhaps it was a hotel. Yes, it must have been, almost deserted, in some doomed quarter cordoned off by police as the surge tide came in. I was a young reporter then, we had a helicopter on the roof we knew we could get out

196

on. *With telescopes and telephoto lenses, we could see the civil disorder only blocks away. We were like saints or eagles, in our ivory tower, our lighthouse amid the storm. Ivy growing over ruins. Insane plant species devouring everything with the speed of time-lapse photography. I made love to Marie as if these plants were growing inside her, as if I could purge Nature's vengeful insanity, its last gasp, with our feverish palpitations. Marie was a photographer. Next day we swung low over the rising waters, the air from the helicopter blades beating the waves in patterns like pulsating flowers, as she snapped away. Yes, I remember that happy noise like blinking eyelids or the beating wings of bees purring out life's enthusiasm like morse code, even amid all that catastrophe. There. I admit it. The end of the world was scintillating, exciting. How could it not be? All this has just been the cold aftermath, the chill-out. A let-down.*

*

*What was **Eye Scream**, Owl?* The Wolf King asks as the Royal Disk takes off, Rrio at his side.

Ice Cream. Whatever makes you ask that, Sire?

Oh I don't know, someone must have mentioned it. Somewhere recently. I forget.

It will seem absurd to you, but before the Age Of Ice, the summers were so hot that people ate frozen cow's milk, in cones of biscuit. It would melt in their mouths and cool them down in all that heat.

The world was green then wasn't it? Bursting with life?

Indeed.

How very sad.

There are still some green areas you know, in Yoora, to the south, I believe. Perhaps their ambassador will tell you about it, when you meet him. He might give us some samples, seeds for the Dome gardens? A peace offering...

Where are we meeting him?

At the southern border, one hour's flight.

There is a sudden flash from below, on Rrio's right, a rocket firing across them. Another one penetrates the hull and in an instant the whole Disk shudders and groans and begins spinning erratically out of control. *We're under attack!* One of the Storks is on fire and screaming horribly as he falls on his controls. Rrio shouts distress

197

messages into the intercom, flicks a few switches then encloses the King and himself in an energy field and takes them through the hull just before it plunges into the snowy earth and skids along amid flying mud and stones.

Rrio engages invisibility then takes them to within a hundred yards of the now partially buried Disk, from which steam and flames are beginning to emanate. *Are you unharmed?* –he asks the King who has remained shockingly quiet, He nods his head, his eyes wild, a just-perceptible shaking of his muzzle the only sign of his terror. *Wait here, you are quite safe within this field. I need to try to get back inside the Disk for a moment.*

The King waits, hovering inside in an invisible sphere above the snow for a few moments, until Rrio emerges with the other Stork, and a rescued rifle. He bounces them both up into the field then glides it down to the ground then disengages. Their feet sink several inches into the snow.

Where the hell was our escort? This is like some kind of set-up… an inside job. The Republican Guard should be all over us by now, protecting us from the locals with their own lives if necessary.

Can't we remain invisible, Owl? –the King stammers.

No, Sire. Not unless we are in immediate danger, otherwise we must conserve energy until help arrives. Standard protocol. I know, I wrote the rules.

Rrio presses a button on his belt. *I've summoned my own Disk, it will be here in ten minutes.*

We may not have that long… the Stork croaks and Rrio spins around to see a line of black-clad figures making their way down into their small valley.

Friend or foe? –The King asks.

Dressed like commandos, and moving like them. Well-trained, but not ours. This is getting dangerous, Sire. We are in a mouse trap. Here… Rrio throws the King a transparent sphere. *This controls the field. Squeeze it and it will cloak you. I'll send you up to about twenty feet, hover you over those trees.*

The first shot rings past their ears and snow sprays back. The Stork throws Rrio a rifle and they make their way forward, spreading out, digging into the snow. They try to draw the commandos' fire, but some of them are aiming upwards.

They must have seen the King. They're trying to hit him, Rrio shouts as snow explodes next to him.

How long has he got? –The Stork croaks.

Less than five minutes of cloaking, maybe another three of deflection and levitation.

Then we have to stop them... Rrio and the Stork stand up and charge forward, running uphill, dodging behind pine tress and rocks. Rrio aims upwards and wounds two gunmen in quick succession then the Stork takes some kind of blast through the chest and spins backwards down the slope.

Rrio stands up, blood pumping in his ears and runs towards the figures, bellowing, watching them all turn towards him in amazement. But something is wrong. Time is slowing down, his legs are slowing, his cry is deepening, the commandos' faces are turning, mouths opening, but their features blurring, becoming indistinct...

*

Obdissian and two Cherubs walk across the snow, surveying the bodies of the dead commandos, every so often Obdissian kneeling to examine a corpse, open a mouth or eyelid. *Here, can you resurrect this one?* A Cherub kneels closer, its hands pressed to the balaclavad forehead, something oddly pliable in the movements of its thin fingers and wrist, until an imperceptible glow of pink light emerges from under its touch. The figure begins to stir and Obdissian snaps his fingers, a circle of Wolf men run over and train their weapons on the captive. *Another glass jigsaw piece for Rrio... he will be pleased.*

A rain of red spheres of varying sizes begin to fall from the sky like yo-yos, each hovering ten feet or so above the snow. Within each can be seen, on close inspection, a faint transparent form of a Cherub, each stirring slightly, like frogspawn or a gestating embryo. Like a hundred red suns for a winter sunset.

*

Rrio wakes up inside his room. The silver walls and floors, the simple bed, are all familiar: but he senses something is wrong. The light, a strangely familiar tone of light is somehow seeping into the room, even from the metal-shielded windows.

He gets up a little shakily, and unclouds the frames: outside the white world is bathed in deep twilight and stars, the snow has stopped. An odd silence pervades everything. He turns his head to the left, and what he expects to be the moon he sees is the pallid yellow form of a hovering angel, perhaps a hundred feet away, glowing next to a blasted tree of grasping black fingers.

Her robes seem to flow slightly, her lips are moving.

Throwing on only a cloak, Rrio exits his quarters and is surprised to find how little cold he feels, even as his bare feet sink into the snow. As he moves closer he begins to hear the familiar voice of the angel, calling his name: *Rrio... Rrio...*

He reaches the tree and looks up. She seems to hover about it, as if tethered there somehow, like Christ on the cross. Scarcely has he thought this, than he sees drops of her blood falling onto the virgin snow beneath. He tries to walk around the tree to get a closer look at her, but each time he tries she seems to rotate. He feels also that the thin network of branches and twigs, although the tree is dead, are somehow expanding.

The angel sobs his name, her breathing almost sexual. Rrio looks down at the ground and sees that strange vegetables are growing everywhere, as if sown by her blood and teardrops. He kneels and pulls one from the ground. At first he thinks it is a pale-skinned carrot until he realises in horror the familiarity of its texture, the rough joints along its length. Each tuber is a human finger, or two rather, somehow fused together so that the plants point, accusingly, both skywards and downwards into the earth. He gasps and looks up and sees that the expanding filigree of black branches and twigs are now like some ornate lace, a pattern trying to fill his whole vision like some visor he sees through, or the mirror of his self, cracking into a thousand fragments ready to collapse.

He stands up, moaning, muttering, and runs back towards the base of the Dome, looking for the light on in his quarters. But everywhere he turns he sees other blackened dead winter trees with other angels behind them, each with a blossoming crop of fingers about their base, their voices beginning to fuse now, into some uncanny chorus.

*

Rrio wakes up sweating, afraid he has cried out in his sleep, then remembering the walls are soundproofed. It all comes back to him. The near-miss assassination attempt, the odd distortions and dilations of his consciousness before the rescue.

Although it is still only 4am, he rises and sits at his desk to write his diary, noting with silent relief that Epi still sleeps soundly in his basket by the window.

As he starts writing, he hears an odd shuffling noise from the floor and half-turns his head to see a silver apple slide along the skirting and vanish surreptitiously through the apartment wall.

...Socrates said that the unexamined life is not worth living. And yet, an unexamined life is precisely what most of us live, by choice or neglect. Telling Magda about my life, the pertinence of her questions, is having the odd effect of starting to make me question my view of myself. Know thy self, **gnōthi sauton,** *as another old Greek said, and I thought I had completed such an audit decades ago, even centuries. But we're never on sure ground really, are we, so long as we live? Our lives are like a snowfield, where a fresh coating falls every night as we sleep, redefining every feature, trying to disorientate us, cloaking every landmark beyond recognition. In the end all we have are the stars and the moon, the returning monads of verifiable experience, and our own footsteps laid out behind us, and of those we might meet. These are our unwitting maps, our only hope of safe return. But the snow is always falling, blowing like fine sand or dust, too slow for perception, erasing, returning everything to sleep and unknowing until we are lost, until we are lost...*

⁓

3: The Beheaded Statue

"...When long ago the Simorgh first appeared-
-His face like sunlight when the clouds have cleared-
He cast unnumbered shadows on the earth,
On each one fixed his eyes, and each gave birth.
Thus we were born; the birds of every land
Are still his shadows –think, and understand... "
  -Farid Ud-Din Attar, *The Conference Of The Birds.*

Apologies, Ambassador, for the delay of our meeting and your having to stay overnight within our borders. I trust you found your accommodation comfortable?

Indeed and thank you, Senator Rrio. How is your King's health?

He is generally quite well, but has been called away to the East on urgent matters of state. He felt sure that I could adequately conduct all necessary discussions on his behalf. I do hope that is not too disappointing?

Oh no... why should it be? You are a well-known figure in our homeland after all, perhaps more so than the Wolf King himself. You are almost a legend. It is seldom we get the chance to meet a living historical figure such as yourself. Our political system means that office-holders like I come and go, while you... well, you... well, you seem almost as fixed as the stars, you even outlive kings.

Even allowing for Yooroan not being his first language, Rrio is slightly suspicious of this last barb. He tries to fix the ambassador's eyes to analyse the look there. Does he know something? Could he even be complicit, connected in some way with the Blasphemists?

202

The Ambassador seems to guess Rrio's discomfort and his hesitancy, and tries to make lighter conversation. *What a place this is, this palace... built when, the eighteenth, nineteenth century?*

*Yes, about two hundred and three years **Before Leo**, in our calendar. Victorian, Late Gothic. Yes, it is rather fine, isn't it?* Rrio says, unsmiling, his heart not really in it. Tier upon tier of stone archways enclose the marble hall, stained glass allegories depicting a world of moral virtue and deferential tradesmen and peasants.

Your country never did have a revolution did it? The Ambassador smiles icily and Rrio flinches, as he continues: *One continuous line from the Stone Age, through the Dark Ages to here, a few wobbles along the way, Oliver Cromwell and all that.*

Nature finally imposed our revolution upon us... Rrio says slowly, and watches the Ambassador smile, savouring the sheathed malice in their words like a spice. He enjoys this game.

Yes, well, poor old Africa never stopped having revolutions, of the old variety, until we imposed Nature's one upon them. Invoke God's wrath, then dodge the thunderbolts ourselves, eh? Let them take it in the neck?

We all have it in the neck now, Ambassador, in the throat. Rrio corrects him. *We all struggle under the new deal Gaia has imposed upon us, regardless of who might be said to have caused it.*

Rampant fuel consumption, industrialised farming, greenhouse gas emissions, yes, yes, we all stand indicted and now apparently punished. But some of us are coping better than others. By rights, Volwys should be a frozen waste by now...

It is... Rrio sighs with a shrug and a gesture of his hand towards the leaded windows, antique and refracting glass, snow swirling beyond them, like looking into a shaken paperweight, an hourglass upturned.

Mmm... the Ambassador purrs, pulling his fur collar up around him like a cat by a fire. *But your technology, wherever, however you have acquired it, seems to give you a vast advantage.*

We merely worship and serve the Gods, whom you have chosen not to believe in. We believe in them devoutly, and they in turn believe in us.

The Ambassador smiles a new smile now, his eyes wider and bluer, less guarded, more wistful. *Well, I know of course that this is the official line, but our intelligence reports...*

203

You mean to suggest you have spies in our country?

No, no, not by any means! Senator Rrio, would I be so crude?

Of course… whether you would be so crude as to refer to it or not, has little bearing on whether it is the case.

The Ambassador smiles yet again, his fat face folding into an array of crevices any of which he might choose to retreat into. He seems uncertain whether to let himself laugh or not. *You're sure your King is quite well, Senator?*

Rrio nods dismissively.

It's just his change of plan seemed so sudden.

Let's speak plainly, Rrio sighs with some gravitas, rising to his feet, and protocol leaving the Ambassador no choice but to hurry after him, to perambulate the marble corridors and gaze upon the snowy ruins and formal hedged gardens beyond, the blackened shards of the city in the distance. *Our* intelligence (he says the phrase with some relish and menace) *suggests that some minor rebellious elements in our midst may be receiving training from outside our country, from a neighbouring nation, like yourselves for instance.*

Out of the question of course! -The Ambassador splutters.

We ask ourselves sometimes, perhaps more often of late, if such a scenario were true, what would that nation want? Is there something short of the complete overthrow of our regime (that being quite out of the question of course) that this nation would be seeking in return for calling off its dogs (forgive my use of an old idiom), for withdrawing its support from these rebellious elements, even handing over their identities and locations to us…

Ahhh… the Ambassador pauses out of breath at a bend in the corridor, fixing his eye on a broken church spire emerging at an angle from above a distant forest. *I would think the answer to that question would be technology wouldn't you? An anti-gravitational engine, and electromagnetic field device, the mathematical formulae for those, even, the secret of the physics behind it? Would you consider giving such things away, sharing I should say, as a gesture of goodwill with your neighbours?* He stops again and wipes his brow with a handkerchief.

The very technology we make use of to crush the said rebels? I doubt that, don't you?

But what would even such a bargain up then? The Ambassador counters, hurrying to catch up with Rrio's striding gait again.

Arctic, sub-arctic, temperate and savannah. We have water from ice of which you have too little. You have plants, grain, crops, of which we have too little.

Of course, of course this is true! The Ambassador nods his head excitedly.

But of course, since you are not the nation supporting our little rebellion, we will have no need of such a bargain shall we?

The Ambassador seems to laugh and cough at the same time, in confusion and agitation, into which Rrio pitches a final volley like primed hand-grenade: *Who is Selterlyan?*

Eftis bracnastyl vocadne lynoxaednus delphina prox aelmodnasti elnera vielcet da…

What? Wait, I don't understand! Rrio gesticulates, taking the Ambassador by the shoulders.

Pardon me, Senator, my translator must have broken down.

But we're speaking the same language, Yooroan, aren't we?

Are we? The Ambassador looks at him haughtily as he turns and summons his entourage from the far end of the great hall, and prepares for his departure.

*

Magda unties her long grey hair from its customary knot on the back of her head, and lets it fall over her shoulders like snow. She stands under the moonlight from the attic windows, turns to smile at Rrio, and comes to bed.

Tell me about your wife and child, your son. And how you became an Esoteric. Did they recruit you? She runs her hands across the little white hairs on his chest.

So many questions… he sighs. *Where to begin again, always beginning…*

I had met Marie as a student, we must have been some of the last young people to receive a formal education. All the institutions were collapsing as normal society ground to a halt. My mother was from a wealthy family and a successful businesswoman in her own right. A veterinarian, she ran her own practice. After our father left us, one of her clients started pursuing her, in the nicest possible sense. I don't think she was involved with him sexually, but they became friends and I think he wanted to impress her with his knowledge, his success, even though such qualities were losing their shine a bit what with food and water running out and the end of the world looming. He was a scientist. One of a select group, who together with business leaders founded a committee, a secret society almost. The Adepts, it was called at first, the Esoterics was just a nickname outsiders dubbed it with, but it stuck. It was practically a government think-tank for a while, a focus group. But then the government gradually disintegrated and the Esoterics were left intact, so they began to absorb people from the government, but only those with knowledge, not just power. That was its motto, it still is: **Knowledge Is Power.**

And did you harness power then? Do you, now?

Oh yes, but it took many years, decades to find the real hidden source of that power. Supposedly the Esoterics were keeping alive the knowledge of the science and technology of the collapsing world, but I gradually saw they were exceeding that power, that new technology was being transferred in from somewhere.

The Gods?

The whole Esoterics Society had a certain amount of ritual about it from the start, but it seemed to intensify as time went by, and readings from the Book Of Leo became a kind of daily doctrine that we had to memorise and repeat. The last chapters of Leo are increasingly mystical, hallucinatory some would say, almost unintelligible. But they make frequent mention of Cherubs and those high up within the Esoterics seemed to have seized upon this fact, or this fact seized them. One day, thirty years after I had begun my studies with them, they took me to a secret room and introduced me to one of them.

A Cherub?

Yes, I fainted. Most people do when they first read your mind. Euphoric and horrific are the two most used adjectives for the experience, although apparently polar opposites. Then I understood what was really going on. Humanity had been split into two streams. We were being herded like sheep towards a fold. Outside, famine and flood then plummeting temperatures were decimating the population, returning them to barbarism. While inside we were being nurtured and coaxed towards a higher plain. It gradually dawned on me that the Gods have always been here. Perhaps people like Da Vinci, Galileo, Newton, Tesla, were their pupils, in secret, who knows? Our crisis, Nature's crisis, had finally forced their hands, brought them out of the woodwork. They had seen their pet project, human civilisation, about to fail, and had felt

206

compelled to step forward and save it. All this surprises you? The Greeks spoke in similar terms of their Gods, as if they were physical beings, who manipulated human affairs, who could be served or fought against. Who knows what past cataclysms have provoked their previous involvement? They have been here and helped us before. They only withdraw when we seem secure again on our path.

 How old are they?

 The youngest I have met, seemed a few centuries old. Their most venerated ones are several millennia old. You don't get to meet them very often. They repair themselves, replace defective cells. They don't need to die at all. They get rather confused on the rare occasions when one of them does die. It's generally not a good idea to confuse them.

 Your baby. Tell me about your boy, Carlo.

 Well, he never got to live forever, sadly. Born in the first year after I joined the Adepts. Marie and I were housed in special accommodation attached to the Academy. Blue eyes, blonde hair at first. But he grew up to have dark hair like my mother, and wear a little beard. Marie and he were very close, what with me spending so much time away on my studies, and the world outside becoming so dangerous.

 What happened to them?

 They each grew old and died, eventually, while I did not. Carlo never had any children, although he found a good wife in the end. He said he couldn't face bringing children into this world. I could see his point of course. Carlo was more of a thinker than a doer, he was quite troubled by the choices I made, the Esoterics, the schism opening up in society. We argued a lot about it, but respected each other in the end. He died peacefully in his eighties, in his sleep.

 Marie?

 Marie died slowly, sadly. We had plenty of warning, and it was long and horrible. In the end all I felt was relief that she had been released. It was months and years before I began to feel the deeper hole she really left in my life.

 You changed?

 I hardened up. The Cherubs were taking a greater interest in me by then. They saw my strategic significance because of my family.

 I don't follow you.

 Leo. Leo Vestra was my mother's brother, my uncle.

 My God... how, can that be... ? But of course, two hundred and thirty years ago, but what does that mean?

207

It means, to some people, devout followers of Leo and the Book Of Leo, that I am some kind of living link to their prophet. They call me "He who was beloved of Leo" sometimes, although it makes my flesh creep.

Why?

I only met him a few times, when I was two or three years old. I don't even remember him. How could I? It's all religious hogwash, between you and me, to help inspire people or something...

So, you don't sound very devout.

How can I be? If Leo was a God, then I might be a half-god... but I can assure you I am not. He was mortal, as am I.

But you're not mortal anymore, are you?

Semantics. I am maintained and repaired by the Cherubs. They simply opt not to let me die.

Wasn't it your choice?

Oh, I don't remember clearly. My wife had died slowly of cancer. I wanted an antidote to all that decay and waste of life. I think I thought I was doing it for her. Volunteering to be experimented upon.

And now?

Sometimes I think this life is a living death.

No... no... Magda strokes his cheek. *Don't say that... life is such a gift.*

But can there be life without death? Rrio says. *Don't they in fact feed and sustain each other? Like men and women, don't they each contain the imprint of each other? To take one aside and stand it in isolation is to watch it pine and lament and wither slowly over a lifetime, becoming dust.*

To die over a lifetime? Isn't that each of our fates?

A life can be a surrender or a victory, a giving-in, a despairing, or a drum-roll, a cry of joy. The life of bravery depends on death as its backdrop. The life of bravery is the only life worth living.

Then life without death is a prison-sentence?

One long penance. What a paradox, seldom expressed. Only death makes life beautiful. If everyone could see this, they might enjoy their lives more fully.

*

Rrio, thank Leo you're here at last!

Your excellency, it is good to see you returned to your official duties in good health.

The Wolf King sits on his throne with, despite Rrio's flattering, an unmistakably haunted look. The Stork Guards have been trebled in number, and all official engagements cancelled for a month.

Have you seen Obdissian's list? How am I to cope with my daily work while half of my most trusted subjects are under suspicion? –And what's worse we're not to tell them they're under suspicion? How am I expected to cope with that?

Rrio feels like putting a hand on his shoulder or embracing him, but knowing protocol forbids it, opts instead to stand next to him at the window and show solidarity through body posture. He tries to exude sympathy and strength.

We have taken care of that. Only those not on the list will be allowed to meet you, and any exceptions we will warn you of in advance and I will be present.

Goodness, Rrio. The King puts his paw on Rrio's chest. *I am so grateful, what would I do without you? Who was trying to kill me, and for what possible reason?*

We thought at first it was fanatics, Blasphemists, but now we feel there is an inside element, in collaboration perhaps with an external one...

External?

Yoora or Merick, the Heretical Empires. They may have a spy in our inner circle. One is all it would take, who has recruited and trained some fanatics, set them against us, against you. To foment discontent within the Kingdom. To destabilise us.

But why?

Perhaps they wish to invade, to seize some of our technology.

Invade? But how could anyone invade us and hope to defeat us in any kind of conflict? We have the Gods on our side, and they do not. They would be annihilated. Don't they know that?

Perhaps... Obdissian says as he enters the room, *-they have forgotten, and it's time they had another demonstration.*

Another? Greetings, Cousin Obdissian. May the light of Leo be upon you.

He means like the battles, massacres really, at Saintcrux and Valdechmont.

Those took place before I held power, before I was even born, the King frowns.

Precisely, Obdissian smiles.

I don't like where this is going... Rrio strokes his chin. Both wolves stare at him quizzically. *We should not make war on our neighbours out of our own paranoia, without a scrap of evidence against them.*

We can find evidence, Obdissian intones darkly.

You mean manufacture some.

Rrio! Volwys would never resort to such untruths, the King exclaims.

Fear makes men weak. The Blasphemists' weapons are puny compared to ours, Stone Age even, except for one. Fear is the most dangerous weapon of all. Any fool can wield it, any fool will yield to it, but only the wise have the resolve to resist it.

But what if the threat is real, as it is in this instance? They, somebody, has tried to kill me!

Then we must simply protect you better, not destroy our own world in a fit of impotent rage, and do their job for them. Only our opponents can destroy us, and we must make sure that have to fight for every inch of it.

This sounds like complacency... Obdissian sneers. *All my instincts tell me to attack when I am under attack.*

Whoever planned this knows that. They're probably counting on it, which is why you must do the exact opposite.

My head hurts... the King sobs, head in his paws. *Please leave me now to rest, these debates exhaust me, we can talk in the morning.*

Rrio and Obdissian face each other, turn on their heels and walk together towards the tall parallel doors which the Storks are opening for them.

Oh Rrio... the King calls after him. *What were Molotov cocktails?*

Rrio bows and pauses at the door. *Vodka with a dash of lime and Tabasco sauce, I believe, Sire, drunk at birthday parties.*

*

Rrio and Lucius pace together through the Library Atrium with Epi at their heels, admiring the marble floors and the swaying exotic tree

210

species on the balconies above. Today a blizzard is blowing outside and the daylight is simulated by huge halogen pendants suspended from the Dome's glazing transoms.

I am going to tell you something, Lucius, because we are close friends, but you must promise that it remains strictly between us, and that you will in no way alter your behaviour towards me because of it.

You have my attention, Rrio, is this something to do with the assassination attempt?

A list has been drawn up, of people we believe have the correct profile to be conspirators, spies within the inner circle of the Adepts.

You've seen this list?

You're on it, Lucius.

He stops, and seems to discernibly shiver. Rrio puts a hand on his shoulder and coaxes him on. *Relax, I am on it too. As is Obdissian and he wrote the damned thing. I'm telling you because you needn't worry, Because your name, like mine, is a formality. And I want you to think about everyone around you for a while, just for the next few weeks, while we collate information.*

Information?

Each time we uncover a new plot, capture some Blasphemists, we gain a fresh insight into these fanatics and the mind of their leader. It's like calculating the geometry of something invisible, some sub-atomic particle we can't see with the naked eye. We must learn about it only from its shadows and imprints, the traces it leaves around it as it moves. Our picture is building up now, and as it does we strike names from the list and narrow it down towards others.

Can I see this list? Lucius spins around wild-eyed, wiping sweat from his brow.

Why? Rrio asks quietly, keeping pace with his friend.

So I know where I stand, where we stand now, isn't that obvious?

But I've told you where you stand, Lucius. Right beside me, of course.

Lucius stops again and seems about to say something, his mouth agape. Epi catches up with him and inexplicably begins barking at Lucius, while Rrio tries to calm his down. *Epi, what's got into you? Sit down! Back off!*

Rrio... Lucius says, *I'm sorry, I have to go now, a meeting, I forgot. We'll talk again soon... tomorrow.*

211

Epi growls then whimpers as Lucius walks off, and Rrio kneels to pat him again. *What ails you, little urchin? Don't you know a friend from a foe?*

*

What was it like, the green world? Do you really remember it?

Oh yes, the climate only started cooling down as I grew up... a curious correlation, almost poetic. As my blood warmed up, the world's cooled down.

And the wolves? Were they always Esoterics? My grandmother said that wolves used to be just wild animals, on all fours like dogs, but nobody saw them, they were almost extinct. They lived only in the wild, in cold places.

Your grandmother was well-informed. But one question at a time. It wasn't just a green world, though God knows summer was beautiful enough. Autumn was orange and red and yellow, like a sunset of the trees, it was melancholy and mysterious, it broke your heart to see. It made Winter different somehow, from how it seems now. It contained within it the seed of Spring, the hope of a new year. Now our Winter has no hope, the Earth shall know no Spring again. It lives on, only as a dream in the head of the few who have read about it and the even fewer who remember it perhaps... one wretched old man, me.

Magda turns to look at him, from the night window where she stands in her gown. She whispers: *perhaps your kiss is Spring. Can't words be like a Spring over the Earth? A life-giving rain?*

I thought so once...

*

In the tall steel room, a pillar of light crosses diagonally from floor to ceiling, left to right, and within it a human form writhes in agony.

Here's another one for you, Rrio... Obdissian beams proudly. *He's given us four names already, valuable leads, but I expect you'll want us to let him down so you can play chess or read poetry with him. Make him a nice cup of hot milk?*

Rrio tolerates the joke with the endurance of an ancient tree with a woodpecker at its base. *Let him down,* he says quietly, and Obdissian obeys.

Rrio gives the prisoner a chair and asks for bread and water to be brought, and sits down opposite him. *Tell me about Selterlyan,* he says.

The prisoner pauses, just beginning his eating, a slice of bread half-torn, fixing Rrio with one bloodshot eye. Silently, he resumes eating.

When you finish eating and drinking, you will tell me about Selterlyan.

Or? The prisoner asks blankly.

Or you die, obviously. Genuinely. We don't joke about such matters within these walls.

A grim sort of workplace, is it? The prisoners manages a joke through a bruised and crooked smile.

You may have heard that an attempt was made on the Wolf King's life. We don't torture people for the sheer fun if it, you know.

Oh? And I was having a whale of a time.

We must maintain order, stability, in the face of all the challenges to our survival, here in Volwys. Why do you want to make things harder than they already are?

*Things are hard, hard for people like me, peasants as you would call us, the mob, **because of** the order, the stability, the regime of you and your king. We attack you to change things for the better.*

And yet you know nothing of the technology required to maintain this world, to keep the glaciers in check, to store the meltwaters, to gather heat from beneath the Earth's crust, harness sunlight and electomagnetism, to maintain plant life within the Geo-Dome.

You dazzle me with your Math-Magic, Brother. These are the black arts that the aliens, the demons bid you dabble with, to worship and serve them with. This is how you rape the Earth to order for them, kiss the hands that strangle us.

Without the Gods, the Cherubs, we would all be extinct by now. It is only their knowledge and expertise, so generously shared with us, that has kept Volwys alive these last two centuries.

You really believe that?

*I don't need to **believe** it. I see it every day. I live with this reality. Your position on the other hand, is one of assumption based on blind ignorance.*

No. Our positions are equivalent, like two rival religions. Perhaps, it is only a matter of contrasting faiths.

213

But the differences are concrete.

But are the minds of your Gods concrete? Or do they rather, like us, exist in a state of grey? How can we ever be certain of their motivations from one moment to the next? How can we be certain of anything where consciousness is concerned?

The Geo-Dome has been built to save our lives, to preserve humanity, a benign gesture by our saviours. How can you deny that?

It preserves only you and your cohorts, traitors and collaborators, and only temporarily, while the demons rape our earth of the minerals they require. The Dome is a ship, that once completed and filled with all the samples they need, human, animal, and vegetable, they will blast off into the sky and leave the rest of us here to die under the advancing glaciers. They have not held the glaciers back. It was them who brought them in the first place, to suit their own ends: to annihilate the human race.

Fairy tales! Who fills your heads with such nonsense? I meet and talk with the Cherubs every day and I have seen the plans of the Geo-Dome, watched it being constructed. I know all of what you say to be nonsense, as I know my own hand in front of me.

But to talk with aliens is to allow them into your mind. Every day, by your own confession. How can you be sure even of your own thoughts anymore, and that your mind is truly your own?

But some facts must be definitive. If you and I were to go and dig with shovels together at the base of the Dome now, we would either find the simple concrete foundations I know to be there, or find the base of a spacecraft, would we not?

Indeed… the prisoner nods his head.

Then I know what I have seen with my own eyes, and you are a deluded madman. The prisoner makes no answer for some time. *Well?* Rrio prompts again, *Checkmate?*

No, he shakes his head. *There are two kinds of truth, literal and metaphorical. When you lose sight of that, as you have, you have defeated yourself.*

*

So it's true then, that wolves once walked on all fours, like dogs? Did people eat them? Did they rebel?

No. Dogs were treated well back then. Pets, they called them, imagine, an archaic term now. The Esoterics, with some help from the Cherubs, learned how to manipulate genes.

What are genes? Magda asks.

DNA. The building blocks of life, the tiny strands of information which have been woven together to make us all. Wolves could survive in our sub-arctic climate, the largest and most intelligent mammal that could. They made the most logical choice.

Choice for what?

Genetic material to supplement and divert human evolution. To redirect our physiology to withstand the prevailing climatic conditions.

Are you trying to lose me, when you speak like this? Like a magician?

The methods are complex, but the reasoning was simple. Men will not survive the Age of Ice, but Wolf-Men might.

I hate them... Magda frowns. *People say they are evil.*

Fear of the unknown, ignorance, Magda. I work with them everyday, and they are just like us. Social, hierarchical, loyal, unreasonably cruel when suitably inspired.

Why was kindness not on your list?

They are kind to their young, to members of their extended family, their social group, when custom dictates it, of course. Can you truthfully say anything more of human beings?

Some of us have a sense... a vision... Magda pauses, as if considering her own words, even censoring them: *of a unity of all men and women.*

Do they, Magda? I meet the representatives of other cities and civilisations every week. I'm not sure I don't see rival wolf packs sniffing at each other's territorial boundaries, howling in display and submission. I'm not sure I see any more or less than that.

Did you once, in The Time Before?

Rrio looks at Magda curiously. The snow has ceased and bright morning sunlight falls across the floor as he prepares to leave again. Her questioning seems to be getting progressively more penetrating. She continues to surprise him with her shrewdness. *Yes, there were men with such a vision once, those who tried to save the world.*

And weren't they listened to, didn't they succeed?

215

Rrio sighs. *Look out the window, Magda. The world lies in ruins. What do you think?*

*

Is it Selterlyan who preaches such nonsense?
He says the destiny of Man can be solved by Man alone. Even the demons, the aliens are only shadows from our own future, come back to feed upon us, licking their wounds. He says Man is the dream of God struggling to wake up, the aliens are our nightmares who we must rid ourselves of if we are to move on from frightened children into noble adults.
Silence! Obdissian hisses, re-entering the room. *You profane and blaspheme. You pollute the air with such heinous lies against the Gods.*
Truth is the enemy of no man... the prisoners spits, then points at Rrio. *He knows that too, deep down inside. Only those who set themselves against truth, who choose to become its enemy, will torture themselves as they are destroyed by their own bad conscience.*
Obdissian moves to strike him, but Rrio catches his gloved paw, and shakes his head. *Here we learn, Brother. Violence belongs on the battlefield, there will be time for that later. This man wields only words.*
Spoken like Selterlyan himself, the prisoner sneers, and Rrio's shoulder stiffen.

*

On one of Rrio's night time strolls he unexpectedly catches sight of a familiar face. The half-caste wolf-man he passed on the stairs in Magda's warehouse on the day of his two-hundred-and-thirtieth birthday, just after the attack in the tavern.

He changes direction and follows him through moonlit streets, through deep snow drifts. They walk out into a large open space. With a slow jolt, Rrio remembers where this is: formerly the main town square of the city of his birth. Now each façade is blackened and half-collapsed. Statues lie broken and toppled: fallen heroes of a former age. Decayed wreckage of cars and buses lie around in the snow, remnants of a last desperate street battle. For

216

a moment, the old ghosts haunt him, past and present, and Rrio walks on in visual stereo, two realities playing in his head, memories of weeping crowds of refugees, helicopters taking off, protestors and firebombs, gunfire from rooftops.

He stops and reprimands himself for his momentary lapse of attention: where has his subject gone? He hovers and moves back, searches doorways and alleys, moves forward into the town square and searches about finding nothing. He checks the footprints in the snow. The distinctive asymmetric footprints of the limping half-caste: they move out into space then stop dead, no further progress. Rrio stands at the spot and looks around, puzzling. He knows only Esoteric technology could allow a man to disappear like this.

He looks up and notices a large headless equestrian statue of some historic dignitary, whose name he has long since forgotten. He remembers the day a tank blew it off.

*

Recounting so many memories for Magda has begun to cause a generalised disturbance in Rrio's psyche. An hour after falling asleep with her, he wakes after a dream which he realises afterward is a suppressed memory, long forgotten: of a starving family trying to leave the city and fighting amongst themselves. Their car is out of petrol but they don't even know how to siphon some from another car nearby. Their radio is broken down and they don't know how to fix it. Their son's arm is broken but they don't know how to re-set and bind it. They have no food but they are surrounded by squirrels and rabbits that they don't know how to capture and skin and cook. They are surrounded by mushrooms but they don't know how to tell them from toadstools, don't even know the basic rule-of-thumb that only white gills are poisonous. Countless other berries perplex them for similar reasons. It is getting dark, but they don't know how to light a fire. The stars are out above them but they don't remember their names and how to navigate by them, even to tell north from south. They anger easily and fight amongst themselves and panic. All of them will be dead by morning, one through hypothermia, an other attacked by wild dogs, another by suicide, another by shame and madness then slipping into a ravine. The coming night is not just a loss of light but the loss of knowledge, the floodtide of

217

ignorance, the eclipse of civilisation by the deadweight of its own inertia. Smothered by comfort, strangled by ennui. *Knowledge Is Power.*

*

Rrio wakes up in bed, streaked with sweat. An angel stands inside the room this time, her feet hovering just a few inches above the floor. He tries to wake Magda, but he finds to his astonishment that Magda has turned into a three-headed black dog that sits up and backs away, snarling at him. Its six eyes glow like firelight in the dark. Rrio looks back at the angel and now her robes blow in an invisible wind. He stands up and crosses to the window and opens it and sees that ten, then twenty, thirty angels are appearing over each rooftop and ruin, dripping spots of blood onto the fresh snow.

What do you want?! He shouts in despair. *Just what do you all want?!*

Our lives... our children... comes the answer, whispered like an icy breeze from a hundred mouths across a barren world.

Rrio looks down at himself in astonishment to see that his chest is now a cage of white bones, he is a skeleton, with an alarm-clock for a heart, that rotates like a gyroscope within his chest, dangling from pins and chains. He looks closer and sees that instead of silver disks to either side, the clock has human ears, as if it wears them like headphones. With trepidation he puts his hands slowly up to his own head to feel if he still has ears and finds he has the head of a wolf. He grips the head and struggles to remove it like a pantomime costume. Staggering towards a mirror, he finally tears it off and turns his head back to see that he is a bleached white skull streaked with blood, with two sparkling red diamonds for eyes: fires within the sockets like lit beacons at two cave mouths.

The angel is gone. He hears a shuffling in the corridor and throws open the door to the hall. The angel is limping away, carrying some heavy weight in her arms, her wings tensing on her back. She half turns and Rrio sees that what she carries is the white marble head of a statue, twice life-size, bearing a resemblance to himself. He looks closer and the white plaster eyelids unexpectedly roll open to reveal twin blue globes crossed by clouds: Earth turning in worried

218

ether. *Where are you going?* -He cries out after her. *To Rome to be crucified again…* she whispers.

*

Rrio wakes up again, genuinely this time, to find Magda worried at his side, in bed. *Are you alright? I thought you weren't a Christian? You were talking in your sleep about crucifixion. Something about Rome.*

Quo Vadis… Rrio mutters.

What's that?

Latin, he says, *a long-dead language. Where goest thou? It's what St.Peter said to the ghost of Jesus on the Appian Way.*

So you know all about Christianity?

Of course, I was raised as a Roman Catholic, in The Time Before.

What did Jesus reply?

To Rome, he said, to be crucified again. So St.Peter turned back to follow him, returned to Rome and got crucified upside down by the Romans for his trouble.

Magda rolls herself a herbal cigarette and lights it, inhales and breathes out. *Martyrdom. You find it laughable?*

Not at all. A martyr is someone who knows the value of death, as do I.

What is its value?

It is the greatest poignancy, the music that breaks every heart. None can withstand it. It wins all arguments. Sadly, perhaps fortunately, it is a weapon we can each use only once.

Apart from you that is. Why won't your Gods let you die?

Too easy. Perhaps I have not suffered enough yet, for some crime I have long forgotten, or committed in a previous reincarnation.

You believe in reincarnation?

I am living it.

*

Is it time, is it time, Rrio? Lucius asks anxiously, running after Rrio in the corridors of the administrative quarter. *They have learned more about who the traitor might be?*

219

Rrio turns and leans closer to him, to try to emphasise the need for discretion. *I don't understand, what have you heard?*

Obdissian has captured one more. A pilot who failed to follow orders just before the assassination. They say he is a close friend of Selter... whatever that name is, that he therefore knows who the traitor is in our midst.

Really? Rrio frowns. *I am on my way to Court now, and I have heard nothing.*

That list, Rrio, I could help you go through it, Lucius whispers, looking at his feet.

Well I suppose it will have changed now, hopefully for the better, hopefully with less names on it. And you don't want to be my deputy, Lucius, believe me. Your day's work is morally clean compared to mine.

Lucius turns and walks away like a doomed man, shoulder downcast, and Rrio's brow clouds in confusion.

*

Magda unlocks the gate and shuffles into her Ice Garden. Unfrozen soil is rare, but water from ice is plentiful. She grows Snow Chard using hydroponics, also tomatoes, tubers like potatoes and parsnips and beetroots, which she can barter for mushrooms and berries from the Collective Caves.

She often relates the minutiae of her day on her allotment to Rrio. He seems surprisingly intrigued and soothed by hearing about her growing and market-gardening skills, peasant customs developed over generations.

She bends to take a shovel of glacial vitamin nutrients from a jute sack, then gasps as she is pulled backwards with a knife to her throat. A hand: half-human, half-wolf, moves over her mouth, a hoarse whisper rasps in her ear: *Not a word, old witch-woman, Esoteric-lover. I have some friends who are very interested in your sordid, sad old love life...*

She tries to bite his hands and scream, her eyes widening, limbs struggling, but a sack is brought down over her head and ropes tied about her.

˜

4: The Palace of Ice

"Religion consists of the belief that everything that happens to us is extraordinarily important. It can never disappear from the world for this reason."
                                                                    -Cesare Pavese.

Tell me about this religion of yours then… Magda sighs, stirring a pot of walrus soup at the stove, *-the new ways, this Gaia and her prophet Leo, your uncle. Convert me. What is the essence of these beliefs?*

Rrio stands at her window and watches the snowfall glide to a halt, the moon emerge above the thousand crumbling walls and rooftops, sombre tombstones in a living graveyard. On the street below, he sees a makeshift sleigh being dragged by two ragged figures, with something resembling a blooded seal carcass on it.

Of course, like every mass religion, we seem to have quickly missed the point and forgotten the real essence of it. To worship Leo and Gaia, one is required to visit the woods that surround this city at least once a week and spend an hour in solitary contemplation, in communion with Nature. But not enough people do it anymore, too scared of being murdered by hungry peasants probably…

Like me? Magda laughs. *And don't they catch frostbite? Why bother?*

It's a paradox. But Leo discovered that to truly understand what a human being is, you must separate him, or her, from his fellows, take yourself far away, and look deep inside. The answer then, if you finally find it, is surprising, but you'll never get it amid crowds and noise.

And what is that answer? Magda smiles, half-serious, quizzical.

Rrio sits down and sighs. *More paradox. That we aren't actually individuals.*

221

Really? Magda places the bowls in front of both of them. *Then I am you and visa versa?*

In a sense, Rrio nods. *Once you have conceived of the idea, encompassed its implications, then you can even begin to feel it.*

How so? Magda asks, steaming soup clouding her face as she lifts a spoon.

Just like this broth, I feel your warmth, your essence, as we talk, moving in and out of me like waves and tides. Our bodies are only anchors, our selves flow out beyond these physical boundaries and interweave constantly.

Then I could look out of your eyes? Magda laughs.

Well, you're joking now, but actually, with practice, yes. I have heard that even that is possible.

But this doesn't sound so different from Christianity. How can a man wage war and harm his brothers and sisters with such a philosophy? Wouldn't he only be hurting himself?

Rrio smiles, wryly. *Ahhh, Magda. Where in your New Testament did it recommend Auschwitz, Buchenwald, Hiroshima, or Dresden? For every great man with a beautiful idea there are a million well-meaning fools ready to embrace it and distort it, to pervert it to their own ends.*

But Jesus wasn't a man, he was the son of God.

He also said all men were his brothers. As did Leo. I think Jesus' ideas and his bravery and self-sacrifice are all the more inspiring if he was frail and human, don't you? In fact, I would say they're meaningless otherwise. I would even extend the same argument to the Christian God: the universe strikes me as all the more wonderful and touching for having built itself anonymously, than to have been knocked up in six days by a bearded man in a white nightshirt.

You profane now… Magda frowns.

Ideas kill, Magda. Nietzsche and the Nazis proved that, with half-baked notions of Darwin and eugenics, missing the point that the disabled are the mutations by which Evolution progresses. Even good ideas kill, but stupid ideas kill millions. God as a man in a white nightshirt who creates homosexuals then hates them… now that is one stupid idea. An eye for an eye… there was another stupid idea, because revenge simply doesn't work. Not getting into heaven without clean shoes… as the World Trade Centre bombers believed… need I go on?

Alright. I want to go the forest then, and meditate with you, to find this God of yours, this Gaia. Can we go together?

*

Lucius wakes up in a cold sweat after a prophetic dream of his own death. His wife Leanna has already been awakened by his muted screams, and she clutches at his arms and chest. *Your father... you were talking about your father...*

Yes, Lucius gasps. *He was there again, sitting, smoking a pipe in my parents' old house. Why do the dead never speak when they appear to us in dreams? Why do they keep their own counsel, and just show us their presence, standing by, observing? What can that mean?*

That they have no need for words anymore? That they can sow thoughts in your mind at will?

Then my time has come. Not long now, ...that felt like what he was saying. He had come for me.

Oh, don't be silly, dear. You've been worried at work, but why all this nonsense? You'll waken up the children...

Right on cue, the bedroom door opens and their son Nathan stands there with his teddy bear in hand. Through the thin net curtains, fantastical shadows of trees and branches wash across the floor and walls in an artificial breeze from their simulated courtyard within the Dome.

Later, when she returns from having put Nathan back to bed, Leanna asks: *what was so bad about this dream anyway?*

It was the house I grew up in, Lucius whispers, still awake and frightened like a little boy, *-except it was being gradually destroyed by the beating wings of an enormous white dove that was attempting to take off outside. It didn't even seem to know we were there, but every flutter of feathers and slip of talons brought bricks and stones and roof beams down around our heads...*

*

Lucius sleeps only fitfully and inadequately for the rest of the night, then gets up with a feeling of sickness and deep foreboding in his spirit. He goes about his day off like a dead man. He takes his Disk over to the south-east quadrant to visit his elderly mother in the

223

medical nexus. It shakes him to think that she may outlive him, and thinks secretly of ways that he might contrive to have this knowledge hidden from her. She rambles incoherently as usual, sitting up in bed, attended to by the medical staff. Staring off into space as she talks, Lucius reflects bleakly on the meaninglessness of existence. How has he gone on believing in the existence of souls and spirits, when the evidence is before him of how his once charming and erudite mother has slowly mutated into a slobbering incontinent child. How can he look to her for comfort in his spiritual crisis? Where *can* he look anymore?

It's a disgrace, it's a disgrace… She mutters distractedly. Beyond the one-way glass behind her, light-trails of passing Disks split the blue evening sky, throwing shadows on the dismal ice wastes below, where slow sleighs and beasts have left their criss-crossing tracks in snowfall, like those on the palm of an open hand.

What's a disgrace, Mother?

Outside the Dome, children daren't walk about alone after dark in case they are killed and eaten. There are no schools, no education. Only poverty…

Mother, who tells you such things? Why are you talking about this now?

Nathan and Lissa… they'll be alright though, won't they?

Of course they will, Mother. Life is safe within the Dome, you know that.

Do I? Do I? And what if it cracks? Cracks like a big bird's egg? I dreamt I saw it cracking only last night…

Mum, calm yourself, just calm down. You're havering. Life is safe, the Dome is safe.

No, son… she says, looking off to the floor on her left so intently that Lucius almost has to turn around to try to discern what ghost she sees there. *There will never be safety and peace in our hearts…* she continues in a suddenly cold and dreamlike voice, *-without equality… and justice.*

Her hands stop fluttering and she fixes her eyes calmly onto his for a second, and he feels suddenly alarmed as if she is a stranger, and he shivers and backs away, checking his time, making his excuses.

*

Next day, Lucius and Leanna take the children outside the Dome for a walk in the woods, in one of the safer sectors, so that Lucius can offer prayers to Gaia. It is a popular spot, close to sunset again, and many of the biggest and oldest trees are adorned with green leaf hearts and paper prayer strips, votive offerings to Leo.

Leanna and the children sit close by in respectful silence as Lucius abases himself beneath a giant redwood, his bloodshot eyes gazing up the whole fissured length of its surface, whispering again and again: *Oh Mother of all life, have mercy on your servant... as every microbe and molecule, so am I... as every leaf and flower, growing and blooming and decaying, so am I. Accept me and make me one with you again today and tomorrow. Grant me the vision that brings peace, the view of views as you are given to see it, from the highest treetop, the view of all from the centre of all, to every branch and leaf of life. Let me feel your tree sap as my body's blood, always ebbing and flowing as the tides of a great ocean...*

*

On the way back to their Disk as sunset comes on, Nathan and his sister Lissa skip ahead, and Leanna asks Lucius: *Won't you tell me what's bothering you so, Lucius? How can it be so bad?*

Lucius pauses, to see the moon rising above the ruins of an old ruined churchyard, its yew trees offering their dark green spears to heaven, patient sentinels for a resurrection indefinitely postponed. Crows fly and call overhead then alight on bare branches of gnarled trees, a judgemental congregation.

It's Rrio... Lucius says at last. *He's been behaving more and more strangely every day, these last few months, criticising the regime more openly. I think he may be losing his mind and about to implicate me in some imaginary conspiracy. Leanna...* They embrace.

He's out of control. I used to love the man, but I have grown to fear him. But I am too close to get away now. If I recoil from him he imagines treachery, if I agree with him he suspects my motives. It's as if his interrogation work has made him paranoid. Maybe it's the torture he carries out, working on his conscience, but now that there has been an attack on the King, he is increasingly unpredictable, schizophrenic.

But Lucius, he is one of your oldest friends. Can't you tell him, or tell someone else?

Leanna... Lucius turns away to face the blood-red sun, wiping his eyes, her hands on his shoulders. *In this regime some men are too powerful, so powerful that they cannot be challenged. Like ancient trees, they will not bend in the wind anymore, they can only break. But who has the strength for that?*

You have the strength, Leanna says, stroking his cheek, as Nathan returns along a snowy path between pines, ripping twigs off a fallen branch to make a new spear.

I had once... Lucius sighs, looking back at his own icy footsteps, leading from the woods, as the evening wind picks up and fills them in with driven snow *-but my strength is all used up now.*

*

Rrio arrives to find Obdissian with a new suspect stripped and broken on the wheel. He realises he is disgusted, not by the prisoner's suffering, but by Odissian's pleasure in it. He looks at the dagger in his paw absent-mindedly, eyes un-focussed, and feels the compulsion to plunge it into Obdissian's neck.

Good timing, Rrio, Obdissian gasps, sweat ruffling his fur. *Repeat for our visitor what you just said: tell us who Selterlyan is...*

One... of... you! –the victim screeches.

Where? Obdissian asks, shoulders hunched demonically, enjoying the snapping of sinew and bone.

In the Dome... He is one of your own... a spy.

What is his real name? –Rrio asks, approaching the blood-soaked platform, raising his hand, touching Obdissian's shoulder, hoping he will ease off. He turns the prisoner's eye towards his own.

*No names, no face. We never see his face. But **you** know him well.* The prisoner emphasises the "you" and Rrio backs off, eyes narrowing, Obdissian turning to regard him.

Rrio remains staring into the prisoner's eyes but thinks he feels Obdissian's gaze burrowing into his left cheek.

He is a... good friend... of... yours! –The prisoner gasps, then a loud crack issues from his back and his eyes glaze over, his head falling to one side.

You've killed him.

Obdissian seems annoyed, and eases off the wheel, slaps the prisoner's face. *Guards! Electric shocks!*

Too late… damned careless, Rrio sighs and turns to leave.

Obdissian whirls around and sneers after him: *Take care, Rrio You heard him! Look to your friends!*

Well, that rules you out then… he mutters as the doors close behind him.

*

Rrio runs with Epi through the Geodesic Gardens. His mind races like a kaleidoscope, faces of friends and enemies spinning past him, interchangeable, his legs trembling as he feels the Earth less stable beneath his feet.

As he pauses at a bend, he sees Epi spot a rabbit and go after it. He starts to shout and whistle after the dog, but suddenly feels surprisingly out of breath. As he saunters off the path he sees that Epi seems to have caught something, maybe a squirrel, and is wrestling it out of a hole in the ground.

As he approaches, he feels a pain in his left temple, a flash of blinding light crosses the Dome, everything is suddenly darker, rain and hail are falling, slush and snow are on the ground. Epi has a human hand by the wrist, a body is emerging from a shallow grave. *No!* Rrio wails, and falls to his knees. He sees white robes emerging from under clods of dirt and permafrost. He shakes his head and looks about and every tree has become a blackened human hand, reaching upwards to the sky, each reaching and clutching as if to pluck a fruit: the swaying bloodshot moon.

He hears a breathing sound like the flapping of some giant crow, and as he begins to faint: sees a grey timber galleon above him, a ship of the sky, weird sails flapping, a crew of gargoyles looking down at him. Burning red eyes, grotesquely lined faces like rotten prunes. The vision lasts a second before he loses consciousness. He senses that the entire sphere of the night sky overhead: is pulsing like the interior of a vast womb: claustrophobic, veined, gorged with blood.

*

When Rrio wakes up on his back, Epi is licking at his neck, whimpering. While a silver disk hovers above, from which Cherubs

227

look down at him. He screams involuntarily, and a medical orderly sedates him.

*

Rrio wakes up with the Wolf King himself at his bedside, a group of Storks guarding the door to the ward behind him. In the sky behind them, in the picture window over their shoulder: silver disks of varying sizes seem to move up and down and about in bizarre manoeuvres while snow falls about them like volcano ash. The sky is lit an uncanny green, tinged with red and pink: a metallic sunset.

Rrio... my dear old Owl... what's been happening to you lately? You passed out they tell me, in the gardens, some domesticated canine alerted the security personnel apparently. How are you feeling?

Quite well... Rrio begins, then winces as he sits up, *-a little stiff perhaps. Have I been out long?*

Only an hour or two, so they say. Rrio, you choose the worst of occasions to lose consciousness, I have to tell you. One of your personal staff has been implicated, we have a traitor in our midst, Obdissian informs me.

Who?

Only you can tell us, apparently. You've seen Obdissian's list?

Yes.

Then who from that list could have known details of my flight path on the day of the assassination attempt?

Rrio grimaces, and the king puts his paw on his arm. *I know, you're tired, you need more rest, but this is the problem to put your mind to solve over the next few days. Think of it as a puzzle, perhaps, nothing more.*

A game? Rrio winces, incredulous.

I'm sorry, I was trying to be consoling. The only practice I get with invalids these days are my grandchildren. I'm not very good with adults.

I will give this much thought, Sire. No question. No game.

I am leaving for the Winter Palace in an hour, Rrio, on Obdissian's advice. He feels I am no longer safe here, until the traitor is found. My personal guards will be at your disposal while I am away, should you require them. The spy may make an attempt on your life for all we know. Please take no chances.

Rrio wakes up back at his quarters and gets up to sit at his desk and write his diary.

Who can I trust anymore? Even myself? These visions, and now fainting. The Cherubs were strangely absent after my collapse: is that of some significance? I have Obdissian's wretched list in front of me, and no matter how many times I cross-refer the names, only one comes up as a possible suspect and yet, it is incredible. How could he, my friend, possibly be some spy, worse some spectacular figurehead for the Blasphemists, meeting with them in secret. It makes no sense. And yet his behaviour at our last meeting was odd, his unease palpable. Oh no. To subject my friend to an interrogation, to put him into the bloodthirsty hands of that monster Obdissian. The very thought makes me wretch. Were he somehow guilty, I would sooner cut his throat myself. At least I would make the blow swift and merciful. I can't believe I have just written that. **Wicked huntsman have I become.** *Terrible how once a thing is spoken, or written, it slips across a threshold into reality from the realm of dream, of nightmare.*

*

Rrio arrives at Magda's door. She looks surprised as she eyes him over the chain. *What brings you here at this hour, friend? You look like you've seen a ghost.*

Epi barks up at her, and she smiles in return, bending to stroke the animal's head.

If I did, then maybe he did too, if only he could talk.

Oh, but maybe he can… she chuckles, unlocking the door and ushering them in, *but you just can't translate doggish.*

Epi lunges forward and begins barking and whining near a window behind Magda. *What's got into him now?* –Rrio sighs, running his hand through his hair in vexation.

Magda reaches up and stills his hand, strokes his cheek. *What's wrong with **you**?*

Ahhh… just political trouble… Rrio mutters.

You said you'd tell me everything, remember our bond… our promise?

Rrio retrieves Epi from the window, and runs his hand along the sill, notes the sash is slightly lifted. He looks at his fingers. *This is blood...* he whispers, staring vacantly.

Magda takes his hand over to the sink and runs water over it. *A rat, I killed it earlier.*

Rrio sits down, confused. *I have been blacking out, Magda, fainting, memory-loss. But the strange thing is the Cherubs are nowhere to be seen. They usually maintain me like a grandfather clock.*

Well, I hope they won't be turning up here or my neighbours will try to stone them to death.

And get vaporised in return for their troubles. No, hopefully not. Someone has been plotting to kill the King, somebody close to me. Magda... Rrio sighs, head in his hands, *I don't want to have to torture a friend.*

Torture?

Interrogation, whatever you want to call it. What do you think goes on when a suspect is taken into The Dome? Fed a breakfast of fried snow-chard and asked to talk about their childhood?

I thought I knew you well, somehow.... Magda says quietly, sitting down, eyes far away. *I can't see it. The thought revolts me: you torturing innocent men to death. How can we have been friends all these years?*

Epi whimpers and goes over to Rrio and sits at his feet, then suddenly starts barking and spinning around. *What **has** got in to him today?*

I've got just the thing for him... Magda says, and returns with a half squirrel steak in brine. He sniffs it and barks then settles down to the food once Rrio has stroked and reassured him again.

What can I say, Magda? I could tell you that I favour psychological methods, that I don't approve of physical torture, that it's my colleagues who always carry it out. But I would be excusing myself, wouldn't I? I could tell you that even torturers have wives and children and homes to return to at night. I could tell you that human existence is monstrous, but you weren't born yesterday, so would that really be news?

No. It would be like waking up from a pleasant dream of course... to discover we had lived in a nightmare.

*

230

Who did you ever trust? In the Time Before? Magda's voice encroaches softly, melodically, into Rrio's consciousness.

My mother. My wife, my sister, my son.

Not your father?

He left us.

How old were you then?

Ten.

Did you forgive him? Do you now?

I… don't know. I think I merely resolved not to love openly, to remain strong, on guard at all times. I think I rebuilt the wall he took down, the one he left a hole in, a breach in my defences.

Did he remarry?

He died.

How?

Drowned in the Second Inundation.

Were you sad about that?

I don't know. It seemed like closure, resolution, like punishment for his leaving us.

Is that what your mother said?

Not in so many words.

Do you believe in punishment? Does your God, Leo, preach punishment?

Gaia is God. Leo is only her prophet. Leo taught that each man punishes himself, that Heaven and Hell are what we do to ourselves within our lifetimes.

How can you escape Hell, or avoid it then?

Self-knowledge. As the ancient Greeks taught: **Nosce Te Ipsum.** *Know thy self.*

*

Rrio dreams that he and Magda and Epi are each floating around Magda's attic, their bodies immobilised, bound with invisible cords, while silver apples bounce and swim around between them in a multitude of eccentric orbits. Snow seems to be falling within the room. Candles by the fireplace encircle a melting wax model of the peaks surrounding the Wolf King's Winter Palace. His vision zooms in towards the scene.

231

*

Rrio's Disk flies between range after range of snow-covered peaks towards the Sky Gates of the Winter Palace, then hovers down onto the cobbled courtyard. Storks with steel ropes and hooks manoeuvre him down. He dismounts to walk away along the glittering mirror paths, through ornamental hedging tinged with frost towards a white limestone doorway in the Second Republic style: chevron decoration, carvings of sea-lions and hares, the ash-painted eye of Gaia with the open palm of Leo, beneath a half moon and a wolf's jaws; heraldic symbols of the House of Volwys.

The floors of all the corridors are mirrors. Rrio moves slowly always afraid to slip, watching the startling views from the tall arched windows: icy peaks and frosty blue skies at this altitude above cloud cover, endlessly reflected upside-down beneath him. The effect is bewildering, like moving through the facets of a diamond, even more so when Rrio ventures out across the central domed hall with its cellular glass floor: beneath which a forest of snow chard is suspended in a hydroponic orchard of transparent tubing and glacial meltwater.

The Wolf King seems lost at the centre of it, writing at his marble table with four Storks standing guard behind him. In happier times, this space is designed for entertainment, but presently the King seems under siege here, temporarily retreated, in emergency session with no one but himself.

Ahh… dear Owl, are you feeling fully yourself again I take it? No more dizzy spells, I trust?

Rrio bows and quietly shakes his head in response.

I know this is painful. But have you reflected on who our spy might be?

I have, Sire.

Good, then it is all but settled. You can remain here for a while if you wish. There is no need for you to be personally involved. I can send a division of my guards to take the culprit in.

With respect, Sire. I would rather question him myself, even arrest him myself. Anything else would seen cowardly.

Admirable, Rrio. Most admirable. Now who are we speaking of?

Lucius Caycenti, of course.

The King breathes in, icily.

232

Obdissian said he was close to us. Rrio, but this must be very painful for you. Are you certain?

No, not entirely yet. But logic points to no one else. I cannot imagine what motive interrogation will reveal.

The King shakes his head. *Well, well… let us not imagine any longer. If this is your decision, then you have my full support and that of my personal guards if you need it. You may take Lucius in and question him as you see fit.*

Thank you, Sire, Rrio bows, backing away, his feet wary and uncertain beneath him. He gasps for a second, and hears a crack, sees a fissure in the glass floor beneath him that then snakes towards the far wall. He nearly cries out, then shakes himself, blinks. The floor is intact again.

Everything alright, Senator Rrio? The King calls out, his voice echoing from behind him. Rrio sees he has paused in mid step, frozen, then continues walking, and then turns and bows.

*

What was it like to watch the world ending? –Magda's voice continues, obtruding into Rrio's consciousness.

The world has been ending all my life, as a matter of fact.

I mean, for you and your wife, having only just met really, and with a young child?

I had this vision, a theory, that I often shared with Marie. We called it The Paperweight. I need to explain it I suppose. In the Time Before, there were ornamental glass paperweights to hold down sheets of paper, when everyone could still read and write. A common design was of a snowy scene, very Christmassy, a little cottage covered in snow, in a snowy field. You could shake the paperweight, turn it upside-down, and a thousand little snow flakes made of glitter would then fall down inside the glass. It was childish, but wonderful.

I don't understand.

We joked, only half-joked, that our life together was like that paperweight: hermetically-sealed under glass, unreachable, strong, inviolate. We knew one day someone or something would smash it, but until then we were inside the paperweight, safe, in a dream, protected from everything that could come after or had existed before.

What smashed it?

233

The world. Time.

Not you?

Oh no. I held it together until the very last minute and second, until my fingers bled on the fragments, until there was no more air to breathe, until our world was thrown open to the four winds, sucked out and dissipated outwards into the howling emptiness of space...

*

Rrio enters his office to find Lucius writing away at his desk. *Ahh, Rrio, here you are at last then...*

You know why I've come?

Oh yes.

And you won't look me in the eye?

Lucius spins around and two Storks train their rifles on him. Really, Rrio, is there any need for those circus freaks? Isn't all this performance beneath you?

So the mask slips at last, Lucius... Rrio sighs in sadness more than malice.

Does it, I wonder? Whose mask is slipping precisely, Rrio, mine or yours?

Don't play games, Lucius. You are under suspicion for having plotted the assassination attempt against the King... and in fact that's almost the least of it... there's a suggestion you're some kind of double-agent, a secret leader to the Blasphemists.

Lucius laughs, and spins in his chair with surprising light-heartedness. *Wonderful, Rrio. Bravo! Bravo!*

Have you gone mad, Lucius? Tell me this is a mistake. I am in charge of this interrogation. Your testimony will be weighed fairly, I can assure you.

Really Rrio!? Tell me, how have you concluded that I am the culprit here?

Because only you knew the detail of the King's flight path on the day of the attack.

How did I know?

Because I told you.

Lucius lifts his hand, points at Rrio, stands up, the Storks raising their rifles again. *Don't you see, Rrio, haven't you listened to yourself recently? The answer is right under your own stupid old wrinkled nose.*

What answer?
The one thing you can't face, the option you haven't considered…

Lucius is suddenly knocked sideways and jolted into the air, intersected by four long glass tubes from different angles, filling the room, his eyes staring vacantly like a broken toy. Three silver apples bounce onto the floor and slither around. One reaches the wall then slowly rolls up it like a snail. A cherub walks through the wall, then is joined by another from the opposite corner. The Storks bow their heads, while Rrio grimaces, trying to bulwark his forebrain in time. A splitting headache runs through him from ear to ear. He winces and when he opens his eyes, a small silver hand is lifting his chin to make him gaze into its two dark pools of eyes.

Rrio…Old One… the voiceless voice rolls into his mind like the waves of a deep ocean. *Obdissian has called for you from his Laboratory Of Truth. We shall take the subject Lucius there for you. He is to be prepared for interrogation.* The silver apple climbing the wall is now emitting a sound like a wind-up clock, an egg-timer. It finds the open end of one of the glass tubes then rolls straight down it and right through Lucius' chest as if it isn't there, then clunks onto the floor and splits open, wheels and circuits revealed, ringing and vibrating like a bell.

Somehow a miniature skyscape of drifting white clouds has entered the room, obscuring a yellow sun which glows in the far corner. Rrio coughs and looks down to see he has vomited blood onto his own chest. Although his limbs are free, his mind feels as constricted and impaled as Lucius' inert body.

*

As Rrio flies his Disk across the city, the blackened ruins hurtle beneath him like toppled flanks of dominoes. Lucius' face appears through the clouds above him, three hundred feet high, repeating and repeating like a hologram: *the one thing you can't bring yourself to see… hasn't it dawned on you yet?*

He swerves to avoid the apparition of an angel, hovering over the ruined rooftops, then looks frantically around to see others appearing, multiplying everywhere, all whispering his name, all lifting their pleading hands, each dripping blood from the edges of their white robes onto the pristine snow below.

A silver river coils below him, meltwater streaming then rearing into the head of a snake, rearing to strike him. Rrio cries aloud in desperation, and closes the cockpit shields over, runs on math-mesh instead, night-mode, the geometric simulation of the landscape below him recreated in lifeless black and white grids. *Approaching destination…* a computer voice prompts him, *assuming automatic landing path… pilot non-responsive…*

*

Rrio waits, with his eyes closed, getting his breath back, regaining his composure before the guards join him, and then the entourage move off down the corridors towards Obdissian's laboratory, Lucius restrained on a hovering silver raft that sails behind them. The diamond chequered pattern of the marble floors almost make him dizzy again. He raises his eyes towards the dark timber beams and coffers of the ceiling, then the heavy brass door in front. He presses his handprint onto the frame glass and the doors rotate noiselessly.

To the left of the interrogation table, Obdissian appears to be bowed over a desk, as if deeply engrossed in some book or vid message. With a horrid familiarity, Rrio tries to stride forward but time slows and the floor mesh bends and distorts, his legs immeasurably heavy. Outer space itself seems to enter the room, the stars glitter on the sidelines. Finally he arrives to find his hand touching the dagger lodged in Obdissian's neck. In disbelief, he lifts his blood-stained fingers towards himself, stepping backwards, turning around. His voice drawls impossibly deep, in slow motion: *oh no, oh no… not this… not now…*

⁓

5: THE SPEECHLESS WITNESS

"...Proclaiming social truth shall spread,
And justice, ev'n tho' thrice again
The red fool-fury of the Seine
Should pile her barricades with dead.

But ill for him that wears a crown,
And him, the lazar, in his rags:
They tremble, the sustaining crags;
The spires of ice are toppled down..."

-Alfred, Lord Tennyson, In memoriam AHH.

The Vase Of Consciousness
(from The Book Of Leo)

Glossary of Archaic Terms: *"watchnight service"*= disappointed christians staying up all night waiting for their God to arrive, *"classical concert"*= conference of scholars of ancient Greek history, *"political rally"*= sports day at parliament, *"rock concert"*= geologists' conference, *"football match"* = chiropodists' freak show.

...I had to go away. To forget all the crowds and lose myself for years amid the immense and mothering wilderness. At first, I was dazzled by the irrational contradiction of how such

237

isolation could bring me so much comfort. So many miles from anyone or anything, and yet somehow I felt less lonely than I had ever done before. What could such madness mean? What was the voice that spoke to me, consoled me so, in such places?

I thought I was alone, and then one day I woke up and saw what had been so apparent and yet so strangely obscured from me: Trees, grass, moss, birds, insects; I was surrounded by life and immersed in it, where before in the city I had been a fish without water, slowly choking, or like a bird without the wind, a captured beast dying of a broken spirit.

But surrounded by so much life that looked so little like me, on that summer morning, I began at last to turn my inner eye upon myself and ask what a human being really was. Ants crawled across me where I sat on the ground, and I knew if I killed one, a thousand more would return to attack me within minutes.

What is the imprint in that ant? The imprint in me? The leaf shadow, the wing shadow that has passed across the ground where I have grown? The feeling we might get at a watchnight service, a classical concert, a political rally, a rock concert, a football match, they are all the same feeling. We are jigsaw pieces, fragments of a broken vase that longs to be reconstructed.

Here, alone, I was able at last to look upon the curve of the broken clay fragment of myself, and from this to re-imagine the enormous shape we are put on earth with the possibility to make. Eventually I saw that the people I had seen in cities had been like the chaos of a pile of such clay fragments, disordered refuse, a mess that no one could untangle with their eyes. But out here amid Nature and isolation, I saw the shape of our potential rise up before me, a curve that began inside me, then moved outwards to make a vast sphere, an exquisite vase of consciousness of which every living thing was meant to be part.

Then it pained and puzzled me that we had been created so incomplete. Who had smashed this vase into so many pieces? Why has all the rubble and ruin of the world been brought into being, and not its glittering entirety? At last it came to me that there could only be one possible answer to this enigma. That the vase existed in the future, and that time was flowing backwards.

Like all great revelations, even as I thought this thought

238

for the first time, I felt my mind nearly giving way under its uncanny weight. Its implications seemed unimaginable. Then, I saw, or rather felt, because I knew I was reaching the edge of human perception and grasping in the darkness beyond a drawn curtain; that this revelation was one of profound peace, optimism and comfort.

Because, if time is flowing backwards, then the mere fact that fragments of the vase of consciousness exist in the present now, proves the existence of the intact vase itself in the future. It is irrefutable. All life is one and finds a state of supreme unity and harmony in the future, whose shadow is thereby thrown backwards into the present.

The existence of the universe proves, in a sense, God's existence in the future, with the one proviso that the term "God" is one whose meaning cannot yet be known, and cannot therefore resemble any of those yet given it by various religions. We might look around every day and think we see aging and decay and death, entropy and slow collapse in the world. But in fact we are looking at the opposite. Sublime and supreme harmony is gradually constructing itself before our eyes with every generation of every life form. We stand, not in the midst of ruins, but at the centre of a vast construction site, of an unseen design of unimaginable beauty.

When I saw and knew this, then light seemed to begin to stream outwards from within me. A deer bounced out of the forest and paused and looked back at me, and I saw for a moment in its calm and inquisitive eyes that I was only grasping at last what this creature and all its fellows had always felt and known in their every vein.

I saw then that all Nature sings and rejoices every day with this same knowledge. The battle is already won, for all of us. There is a future, and its proof is that we are here at all. Inexhaustible goodness floods the universe from the end of time. Everything has been, was, is, would, and will be: alright.

*

How the hell can you have a boyfriend at your age? Are you serious?! – Magda's daughter Eena asks her, laughing. They reach the bottom of her stairs and set off to walk to the woods together, to gather berries and mushrooms. They pass two youths fighting in the street over a deer carcass, hitting each other on the head with rocks. When one of them turns towards Eena she pulls a knife on him and he backs away. Nobody is shaken as they withdraw, the exchange is normal. Eena carries her baby daughter Meera on her back, in a bearskin papoose, her little hands clutching at her mother's pleated pigtails.

Why do you want to go quite so deep into the forest today? Eena asks later, *there's plenty of brambles here.* High above, the morning sky is a pale clear blue for a change, some invisible birds singing in the branches overhead as they walk, following their route like avian spies.

Something my friend told me.

Your boyfriend you mean?

About the new religion. How they worship the trees, I thought I'd give it a go, I'm curious.

Have you and he been here together?

No.

Why not?

It's not safe for us to be seen together by day...

Why ever not? Is he betrothed to someone else or something? You old minx! This is ridiculous!

No, no, no... I can't tell you. Stop asking so many questions. He does an important job, he has to keep "a low profile" he calls it.

Mmm... rich then? Does he work at the Dome?

Enough, Magda smiles, *we're here now. Just look at those beauties.* They gaze up at a group of enormous trees.

How old are they?

Over a thousand years, I suppose, maybe more. Here, Magda says, *you're supposed to pluck a big leaf like this and kiss it, either write or whisper a message into it, then fold it up into the shape of a heart and nail it to the tree with a thorn like this...*

Eena chuckles, then Meera on her back follows suit like an echo. *You're like a little girl again! Green hearts indeed.* Eena takes Meera down to feed. *Like a little girl in love, you silly old thing.*

No, no, it's their religion, it's not about me and him. It's not about selfish love between two people, it's about the heart of the forest, about Gaia, the future of all life.

The what?

240

It's like Christianity or Islam but different, no dogma, no priests in robes and stuff. All life is one.

Very good. So now what?

Magda strokes the rough fissured bark like the hide of a sleeping dragon, half-expecting it to stir. *Now we gaze up the whole height of the tree for a second and imagine we are trees, then imagine that the forest is all one organism, then try to think the same about human beings.*

Why?

Well... Magda thinks, sitting down on a tree stump, trying to remember the best of what Rrio told her. *Have you ever seen a hedge die?*

No... I don't suppose so. Why?

They don't die, because new trees grow up within them, while old trees die, without us even noticing. All we ever see or say is that there is a hedge, there are trees. The hedge is immortal.

So?

Magda gestures to Eena and lines herself up so that Meera, Eena, and herself all hold hands in a circle at the tree's base, then little Meera giggles and batters her free hand against the mighty trunk towering over them, as if to summon its spirit, knocking on the door of life, as they all look up in wonder.

You see now?

*

Today, Rrio will torture his best friend to death. He wakes up in his sparsely furnished room and confronts his own reflection in the mirror. He sits at his desk and makes an entry in his diary:-

To be old is to have the appearance of death whilst still alive, to be an angel of death. Show any newborn baby the face of an old man and watch him scream in quite particular horror. The eyes are dark pools of some secret the baby does not want to learn. What is evil but tiredness and pain? —all love of life drained away?

Rrio runs his long bony fingers through his dense white hair and stands up. He opens the door and lets Epi in to great him, and throws him a human ear from a vinegar jar on his desk.

241

*

What were **Duck Mental Rays**, *Owl?* –The Wolf King asks, relaxed again after concluding some affairs of state, dressed in his more casual finery: ermine robes, patterned in gold thread, rubies and emeralds glinting at his lapels.

Documentaries, Sire, Rrio corrects him, *-later known as Reality Television. Video sequences that were made, recording the banal intimate details of ordinary people's lives, then beamed out into the homes of millions more ordinary people to sit and be entertained by.*

How peculiar. Why did they not just purchase mirrors?

An excellent question, Sire.

These are ordinary peasants we're talking about here? All that expense and effort just to show them to themselves. Why? What was the purpose of this activity? Was there some educational value in it?

None that I could see.

Then it was vanity, like licking one's own fur, grooming fluff from one's own navel?

Worse than that, Sire. It bred complacency. It reinforced the status quo, adulated the status quo, until society became more and more of an immoveable object, set in stone, at exactly the time when it needed to be ready to change.

The Great Inundations?

Yes, the emancipated peasants of The Time Before all thought they were little lords in their little suburban palaces. They had lost their self-sufficiency, even their ability to grow food and hunt for themselves. When the change came they were helpless, confused, panicking like cattle, unable to adapt. They thought they had bought themselves dignity and respect through wealth. But self-sufficiency is the only wealth that Nature respects, ultimately, the only wealth that confers self-respect even, since deep down we are all instruments of Nature.

Ahh yes, Owl. Just as Leo taught. You are indeed his living advocate, our link to the Prophet himself.

Rrio bows respectfully.

And now that our good cousin Obdissian has been taken into the arms of Gaia, Owl, by some criminal brigand, what shall we do to restore order in Leo's kingdom of Volwys?

I shall interrogate Lucius myself.

And will you be merciful, Owl? –asks the King, clicking his fingers for the Storks to open the heavy brass doors and let the nursemaids usher in a well-dressed little coterie of his wolf-children, to play admiringly at his feet.

Not this time, I fear, Sire. Rrio sighs, and turns to leave the Ice Palace.

*

Lucius' bones audibly crack on the wheel, sinews snap, his blood oozes like a distillate of pain.

Who is Selterlyan?

You... are... Lucius gasps, his brow awash with acrid sweat.

Profanity! –shudder the guards around him.

Ridiculous! How can I... how could I.... Rrio asks, *possibly be Selterlyan?* He leans his face close to his subject, trying to see the eyes.

Dog... the dog...

What?! Rrio exclaims. *Wait!* He gestures to a guard to hold off, then holds Lucius by the shoulder: *What are you saying about a dog?*

Get... Get the memory... of your... dog... take its memgram... compare it with your own... you are Selterlyan...

Rrio falls strangely silent, his eyes darkening. He sees the guards turning the wheel again and is too numb to do anything to stop them. Without a signal from Rrio, even a lifting of the hand, they presume they must continue. With a final muted gurgling scream, Lucius is dying.

Weeping, Rrio moves back, takes the pulse in his neck, then cuts his throat, a belated act of mercy.

He shuffles away almost unsteadily, and leans against the wall, his mind in tumult. A chair is brought for him. A guard stands before him, muttering about the body.

Return his body to his family. A decent state funeral. Full honours.

But Senator, he was accused, he is disgraced...

He is nothing of the sort, Rrio barks, then leaps to his feet, spitting fury. *He was my friend. My advice to the King is that he should be buried with honour. Plant a tree over him in the Forest Of Honours,*

243

as is our custom. What does it matter what story we make up? Tell the King we must maintain order and avoid scandal and panic, avoid disgrace of a figure so close to ourselves. My submission is that Lucius' crimes be made secret and his good name maintained. Write this to the King and I will mark it with my seal.

*

What troubles you, my love? Magda asks softly and Rrio looks up: he has never heard her use such words before, and with a start he realises that he tolerates them, is comforted by them, where even a month beforehand they would have filled him with embarrassment and fear.

He sits in her attic with Epi, stroking the dog. Outside the snow falls heavy and soft over the blackened roofs and ruins of Volwys. The only light is the stars and the occasional bonfires and in the distance: the dim, electric glow of the Geo-Dome, omnipresent, always making the snow around its base seem unreal, like the entrance portal to some unnatural hell.

My friend died today... my dear old friend...

What happened?

Murder.

Who by?

By me. I had him killed, tortured to death. I killed him.

Oh no, no. Magda weeps and caresses his hair and sits down beside him. *Oh no... why?*

To find the truth... no man will go on lying in the face of such pain, in the face of death. Now I know he told the truth, but the cost was his life.... and the truth he told is too strange to comprehend...

What truth, what truth is worth that, my love?

Rrio points at Epi. *He said the dog has the answer, that its memory will contain my answer. He said that I myself was Sel... the one of whom you and I have agreed never to speak. The leader of the Blasphemists. How could such a thing be? What madness could have made him speak like that? —To make such an accusation?*

Selterlyan... Magda says slowly, staring into the fire.

Then we may speak his name again now, may we?

Men will always speak his name... Magda whispers.

*What? —*Rrio starts.

What do you think his name means? You've told me before how you can speak thirty languages, some of them archaic. What does Selterlyan's name mean literally, to you?

It's just a name… Rrio sighs, names are names, what does Magda mean?

But it's not a name, is it? It's a mask, a puzzle, an anagram. Don't you see that?

Sel… ter… lyan.

Salt, I suppose. Terr for Terra, earth perhaps. Lyan, corruption of Lion maybe. What are you getting at?

His words travel widely now, more widely every day. His ideas are like a rumour, a virus that spreads through the people. He is the salt of the earth. The salt that will melt the snow, that will reveal the new soil, the Lion of the returning spring. **In the juvenescence of the year, came Christ the tiger…**

No Magda… Rrio puts his hands over his ears. Don't do this, don't say that you are in league with these people, that you have been brainwashed. I have killed one friend today, betrayed our friendship. But I will never betray you…

She looks into his eyes and strokes his cheek. *And yet… you betray yourself with every heartbeat…* she whispers and they kiss.

*

Rrio dreams of rolling grey stormclouds over Volwys, clouds with the snowy texture of bird wings, angel wings. He feels he is flying, his shoulders flexing, as if he rides on the back of, or is held in the arms of, a flying angel. He turns to see her face but ice-white hair keeps falling over her features and blowing into his eyes, obscuring more than is ever revealed. Beneath him he sees the Geo-Dome is now a cracked green egg, something avian and vaguely maritime about it, marked now with a thousand hairline fractures, ready to give way. What creature writhes within, he wonders. Its opalescent surface swirls slightly as if it is fluid below, like Saturn or Jupiter, a gas giant. He half-expects to see a black bird beak and claws scraping from within, but for a moment thinks he glimpses a human embryo. He turns again to try to see the face of the angel, and which ever way she turns he sees she has no face, no mouth or eyes, only smooth flesh beneath the endlessly undulating torrent of white hair.

245

He wakes up beside Magda and prepares to leave, gathering up Epi into his arms. Magda looks up at him sleepily. *You won't harm the dog, surely?*

No. I know someone who can read an imprint of his memory, I think. It's probably never been done on a dog, only humans and wolves, but the physiology is similar. He will come to no harm. He has been a good friend to me, to us.

Good... Magda nods, stroking Epi's head, putting on her gown and following him to the door. *It is enough that you should have sacrificed Lucius, let's not have another friend's death on your conscience today...*

As Rrio walks down the stairs and out into the deep snow outside, her parting words keep ringing, louder, louder, then yelling in the back of his head. He pauses for a moment and looks back up into the darkness of her warehouse up above. *Lucius... Lucius.* He never told her that the name of his friend was Lucius.

You can do this now, while I wait? Rrio asks the Technician General, whom he has woken in the middle of the night.

Why now, with respect, Senator? —Is this so urgent? I do have the equipment at home, here, but shouldn't we just do this as official business?

Smyrna, I ask this as a favour. The circumstances are exceptional. I'm following a lead in a very sensitive investigation, to do with a plot against the King. I will see to it that you are paid well and rewarded with promotion when the next opportunity presents itself.

Smyrna smiles, his grey moustache twitching. *You are most gracious, Senator. Please follow me, my workshop is to the rear of my quarters.* Walking through the long corridor of Smyrna's apartment, Rrio catches sight of a naked girl sitting up in bed. *I must inject the animal first to induce a sleep state...*

Rrio catches his wrist with a firm hand: *He will be unharmed afterwards?*

Smyrna looks down at the hand with a degree of distaste then brings his eyes back up. *It is only a dog, man, but yes, yes, I'll be careful with the dosage. Is this some new genetic programme I've not been told about? Dog DNA Splice to humans and wolves?*

Nothing so complicated... Rrio sighs, calming Epi as the needle goes in. *He is my friend.*

Friend? Smyrna looks up, eyebrows raised, as he switches on pieces of equipment, turns dials, an electronic whirring filling the small room, unrolling wires and leads out across the worktop, tying up Epi's legs, clamping his tongue. *But it can't speak?*

He says all that requires to be said between friends. I have been a diplomat for two centuries, Smyrna. I grow tired of words and the way human beings misuse them. Animals have all the vocabulary they require, and a lot less leeway for deception. I admire that simplicity.

Lights flicker on the screen, and Epi twitches as if dreaming. *But we're not so simple, are we?* Smyrna ponders, *...surely human beings need the complexity of language?*

Do we? Did the language come about to serve our complexity or did the complexity of the language, as it evolved, give rise to the complexity in us? And isn't it still complexity itself that so torments human affairs? I speak many languages, but still only a fragment of those that exist on Earth. As a diplomat, I wonder how many wars and the calamities of history came about through mistranslation of words, through the wretched complexity born of language.

You've thought about this a lot, I see, Senator. You are a man of great depth.

There was a fable about this in the old religion, you know, the one the peasants still follow, in what they called the Old Testament. The Tower of Babel.

It rings a bell I think, from the history annals.

Men built a tower so high that it offended their God and so he brought it down and split all of those who worked on it into different tribes who spoke different languages, so they could never cooperate with each other again...

Not a very friendly God that, I would say. He could hardly blame us for a lack of world peace after a tantrum like that, eh? Right, that's us ready. I've calibrated the animal's chronology from his mitochondrial DNA and set his neural cortex into retro-hypnosis. Do you want his whole life, or just some particular segment?

Let me see... the last two months would do.

OK, the splicing process is only accurate to within a week or two, so I'll have to copy quite a large chunk, say the last four months to be on the safe side.

How long? Rrio asks, leaning back, relaxing at last.

Smyrna checks his watch. *Ten minutes and you can be on your way. Vid format alright, you going to watch it at home?*

Yes.

I'll make us some tea while we wait. Senator... Smyrna turns to see Rrio hovering over Epi, stroking his side. *Just how did you become friends with a dog? We eat them in this household.*

*

Rrio leaves the lights off in his quarters and the windows opaque, as he activates the wall screen and sits back to replay and fast forward through the life of a dog. Epi himself has fallen asleep now in his basket on the floor beside him, still drowsy from his injection.

The speeding frames flicker over something familiar and Rrio rewinds: He is inside the head of Epi, climbing the steps towards Magda's apartment. The door opens, he sees her feet, then the view tilts upwards towards himself and Magda: their faces and bodies diminishing into towering perspective like great shifting mountains. Rrio is reminded briefly, subliminally, of being a child once.

When he and Magda sit down by the fire, their perspective returns to something closer to normal, more familiar, although the constant jerking and rotation of the head, the wide peripheral vision, the superior canine range of lens lengths from wide to zoom, is disconcerting.

He fast forwards slightly, then sees they are asleep on the bed, Epi's head goes down to the floor, eyelids closing.

Rrio nearly fasts forward again, but suddenly the dog is awake again and barking wildly. Rrio rewinds the frame and freezes it then starts it again, beginning to tremble.

A dim white light is hovering on the bed. Two or three dark figures stand around the bed, their upper bodies and faces vanishing off into impenetrable darkness. There is something deeply disturbing about the figures, like some kind of childhood nightmare. From what little detail of them he can see, they seem to have no discernable clothes. They are diagrammatic, almost wraithlike, shadows, their movements somehow too slow to be human, then

248

suddenly jerky, as if another tape, playing faster, is being sped up and slowed down by someone else. Rrio rubs his eyes and freezes and replays: disbelieving. Magda remains frozen while Rrio's body lifts into the air, shrouded in white light, and sails across the room and through the walls, flanked by the strange figures who walk at its side like pall bearers. Epi barks after them then jumps onto the bed to try to wake Magda. He looks up and another figure advances on him and puts its hand over his eyes and the screen goes blank. Next it is early morning, and Epi awakens to see Rrio and Magda sitting up normally in bed.

Rrio rewinds the film and freezes the momentary frame where the figure moves to knock out Epi. Behind the dark blur of a hand there is some kind of a face, but it seems oddly shaped, perhaps masked, the eyes the merest pinpricks of silver light.

Rrio is sweating now, panicking as he fast-forwards to another evening.

Again the dim silver light fills the room and Epi is barking. Again Magda is frozen in sleep. But this time Rrio is slowly sitting up in bed of his own volition, as if in sleepwalking trance. He walks towards the winter window, where the silver light seems to emanate from, pouring over his naked body. Again, the shadowy figures seem to emerge seamlessly from the darkness itself, various hands and arms from each side placing a black cloak over him and leading him through the wall itself, as if the white light has now entered through the window and vanished into his body, swallowed by his enclosing cloak like an eclipse.

Rrio fast-forwards and finds another night, the white light in the room, his supine body sailing out the window. Suddenly as Epi barks, a dozen timber staircases appear all around the room and unfold towards him like fans. Dark figures begin walking down each one, their footfalls echoing and creaking on each tread. In the middle of the room, Magda is now sitting up and rubbing her face, but as she takes her hands down Epi sees that she now has the grotesque white head of an emaciated dog with bloodshot eyes. Suddenly the whole room fills with a densely-packed crowd of dark static figures, their features vanishing up into darkness. A strange mixture of laughter and barking and the sound of sawing wood ring out, and Epi looks up to see that each of the identical dark figures descending the staircases also has the head of a dog: greyhounds with glittering

249

jewels for eyes. He wakes up suddenly on the floor with Magda and Rrio rubbing his stomach and striking his head.

Rrio sighs in frustration. Of course. A dog can dream and hallucinate, as well as remember. Then how can he sort truth from lies? Just as he is about to fast forward, something flashes across the screen and he has to rewind it and pause several times before he can catch it. It's as if a single black frame has been inserted on which a message is written in bold white letters:

KEY SCENES MISSING FROM THE NIGHT OWLS FLIGHTS

EXCISED SEGMENTS ARCHIVED CENTRALLY

*

By the time the weak Winter sun is rising again, Rrio is still sitting, disheartened, in his apartment, playing and replaying the memgram, his mouth open in despair and disbelief. Epi wakes and begins barking at the sight of his own memories and Rrio finally closes the screen down and stands up. He de-mists the window glass and gazes out over the landscape beyond, feeling disorientated, sleepless, unreal. *Am I even alive?* –he whispers, -*Or is someone dreaming me?*

He flies over to Smyrna's side of the Dome again, in daylight this time. His door slides open and he smiles brightly in surprise: *Senator Rrio, what brings you here unannounced? You look like you've been missing your sleep!*

The memgram you recorded for me, there was a message on it. How's that possible? How could someone make a text imprint onto a dog's cerebral cortex? Or could you have re-used an old vidlog, do flaws come through sometimes?

Woahhh, Senator, slow down. You're losing me. What memgram?

The one you made for me last night, from the dog I brought you...

A dog!? Last night? You weren't here last night.

What? Rrio catches Smyrna's shoulder violently as he turns away. Smyrna's eyes narrow, displeased.

Don't fuck with me! Rrio spits, *The dog we took the memgram from, in your workshop out the back.*

250

I repeat. You weren't here last night, Senator. The last time I saw you was at the August parliamentary convention.

A girl saunters into the kitchen behind him, and Rrio points to her from the door.

Your partner, your girlfriend... she saw me.

Selka... Smyrna says.

Selka! Don't you remember seeing me... Rrio begins, but Smyrna corrects him:

No point asking her, Senator, I wiped her memory this morning.

You what?

I wiped her memory. I do it once a week. We find it keeps our relationship fresh.

W-what? Rrio stammers, *-Is that legal?*

Hey... Senator, do I come into your home and question what you get up to with your... dog, for instance?

So you do remember?

No, he shakes his head. *I'm just paying attention to what you've been gibbering about a dog, on my doorstep for the last five minutes.*

Rrio's head swims and he leans against the wall.

Are you alright, Senator? Do you want me to summon you some help?

Smyrna... if a living being's memgram can be wiped, can it be altered, imprinted with a message? Can segments be removed without the subject's knowing?

Smyrna nods his head. *Oh yeah... I've spent the last ten years perfecting the techniques, it's my branch of Esoterics.*

So how do you know someone hasn't blanked your memory of me coming here last night?

In theory I don't. But if it was anything important I will probably start getting nightmares in a few days...

Nightmares?

Yes, the human mind is a jealous old mother hen. If it catches on that something important has been taken out from under its nose, then it starts complaining about it, throwing up all the clues it can find.

Very interesting... And if segments of someone's memgram were removed without their knowing, where would such segments be kept for safekeeping? Before Smyrna can answer, Rrio has suddenly lunged forward and grabbed him by the throat, putting his own face up against his like a kiss, locking eyes.

251

Selka runs down the hall towards them, and Rrio raises his arm and unleashes a stream of tiny glowing lights that assail her and freeze her in a field of transparent energy in which her movements are slowed and muffled, hovering in mid-air, a miasma of light circling around her like water droplets.

Your thoughts to me, Smyrna, your thoughts... don't try to shield them, open your mind... that's it... the location and lab number... to me... that's it.

Rrio snaps his fingers and Smyrna is released and slumps to the floor. He raises his arm again and sucks the light globes back into his sleeve and Selka re-continues her dive forward. He raises his other hand to catch her assault, the plate she still carries falls and smashes to the floor, and Rrio slaps her hard across the face, leaving her to tumble down unconscious over her companion.

5: THE BROKEN MIRROR

"...It was in China, late one moonless night,
The Simorgh first appeared to mortal sight-
He let a feather float down through the air,
And rumours of its fame spread everywhere...
...It is a sign of Him, and in each heart
There lies this feather's hidden counterpart..."
                    -Farid Ud-Din Attar, *The Conference Of The Birds.*

The Persistence Of Religion
(from The Book Of Leo)

Glossary of Archaic Terms: *"upgrades"*= correction of intentional product malfunctions as a means of extortion, *"cars"* =20th century wheeled land-vehicles powered by oil, *"mobile phones"*=fetishistic communication devices that induced brain damage, *"software"*=intimate silk undergarments, *"world wide web"*=international spy ring, *"Iraq"*=mythical christian location of Garden of Eden and setting for the Oil Wars, *"Star Wars"*=capitalist technological-worship saga, *"recessions"*=brief unplanned respites in environmental destruction, *"social deprivation"*=imprisonment by freelance jailers.

Every culture in every country and every century before the twentieth, has had its own God or Gods and myth of its own creation. And yet somehow for the first time in history, we are to believe that a magically atheistic and scientific populace are to appear on cue. But the human mind is hard-wired with a religious impulse, a self-evident fact. Therefore, science becomes our new religion and the high priests of science, overcome by vanity, are delighted to exploit this. We must worship the god of science, not through prayer and good deeds, but through constant "upgrades" and perpetual purchase of unnecessary new models of everything, from cars to mobile phones, houses, computers, and software. Consumption, empty materialism, capitalism. It is this restless and reckless religion of perpetual change and waste, more than anything else, that threatens our environment and therefore ultimately our own survival. And yet our leaders have the audacity to lecture us about sustainability and green issues, as if it is merely the plastic packaging of our way of life that needs addressed, rather than that way of life itself.

The counter-argument will go along the lines that all the new gadgets we constantly devise and improve upon, will make us smarter. And while the World Wide Web will certainly improve us, the constant irritation of controlled redundancy of our software has the opposite effect. Either we are cooperating towards a common goal or ripping each other off. Let's not pretend that these two are anything other than opposites. And while the battle rages, massive resources are squandered on a daily basis. Just why do we need new kitchens and cars every five years? Why should we admire such madness? The craftsmen of a previous generation built goods to last the recipient a lifetime. That was sustainability.

Everything comes back to words. Governments understand this only too well, which is why they fight for control of language. Thus the rebels in Iraq had to be dubbed "insurgents" lest Americans should confuse them with the goodies in Star Wars. Economic "Crises" are carefully mutated into "downturns" and "recessions" in order to shape the nation's mood like the drumbeats for galley slaves. Poverty and social deprivation become "social exclusion" with the subtle implication of a guilt no longer belonging to government.

But science is not a religion. It should be the antithesis of religion, and rightly so. A search for truth, not dogma, not fixed but constantly evolving over time as new evidence is debated. The religious approach to science creates bad science, and pretty

254

crap religion too. When your mother dies, what will you find more comforting? –a scientist's biological description of the process of her forthcoming decay, or a poetic speculation on the possibility of a higher spiritual meaning to our existence?

Our ancestors and forebears may not have been perfect people, but by and large they understood very well what human beings are, in the broadest and most accommodating sense. Ours is an age characterised by the almost universal madness of pretending we are something we are not, –of constructing entire societies on the basis of flawed and incomplete pictures of the human condition.

We should accept our spiritual dimension, without calling it "religion", and attempt to understand it in scientific terms. Perhaps new words and terms would be useful. "Group Consciousness" might be a start. The spiritual impulse within each of us is a longing for a unity of all Humanity, and of all life, and needs to be recognised, not denied, so as to then be harnessed towards productive goals. This is how we built the gothic cathedrals. A task that exceeded the length of a human lifetime, to construct a building that makes no profit. What could be more of an anathema than that to the current spirit of our age? But what better expresses the yearning of Humanity? Something has gone seriously astray in our value system, when spiritual beauty no longer finds a place in it.

*

Medical Nexus. Floor Ten. Lab A. Archive Fifteen. The door frame behind Rrio still burns and hisses, the door melted and buckled on the floor. Rrio rummages frantically through shelf after shelf of memgrams. R for Rrio, O for Owl, S for Senator… then he thinks to try his birth names V is for Vi… R is for Rei…

His searching is interrupted by the bounce of an apple onto the floor behind him, followed by a few of its smaller cohorts, surging through the walls with a sound like water droplets rippling down a drain. Rrio turns back and resumes his search with redoubled urgency.

He finds his segments at last and thrusts them into his chest pocket then turns around and gasps. Two Cherubs, one gold,

255

one silver, face him in the room. There is something more sudden about their presence, more threatening about their postures, more malignant about their eyes… than any time before.

Instinctively Rrio steps backwards and is instantly beset by a splitting headache. He clutches his temples, grimacing. He feels his knees giving way, his arms starting to lift forward, as if in supplication. He feels his mind split: there is still a section in which he can fight back, see the abyss over which he is teetering. His peril and desperation are total, he summons all his strength, mental and physical, and does something he has never before even dared to contemplate. He lunges forward, roaring like a wild beast, half-blind, in the direction of one of the Cherubs and, to his surprise then revulsion, makes contact with something corporeal. He punches and bites and tears, and opening his eyes finds he is breaking the face free, the mask of the Cherub. A line has appeared from below its chin to the crown of its head, and he punches and scrapes, the face sliding off in one slurping, sickening motion. The mask clatters to the floor, as if made of metal or plastic, and fluid pours from around the junction, noxious fumes clouding the air and assailing his senses.

The face revealed is a grotesquely wrinkled prune, almost black with age, the eyes dark and merciless as some underwater creature from the unlit depths of the back of the mind, our worst fears, supremely alien and unknowable. His fingers close instinctively around its neck and he head-butts its face again and again. A choking noise emerges from the toothless mouth, puffs of gas sputtering like a back-firing car. A claw-like hand, its human glove now discarded, grips weakly at his upper arm and he feels at last the frailty, the physical inferiority of this pitiful travesty of nature: whatever it was once; now lost forever beyond recognition, pickled and manipulated, distorted, adulterated, bastardised by millennia of unnatural science, its goal always immortality, preservation of its own wretched self. *Damn you!* He spits on its face and its flesh sizzles and dissolves. *Go back to Hell, demon!*

He stands on the twitching corpse and stamps on its skull and looks around to see the room is now empty, its companion gone, even the apples have disappeared. He roars again, as if regressed temporarily to some primordial state, shaking with adrenalin, gorged on anger and pent-up hatred, looking for something else to kill.

256

*

Magda is stunned to see Rrio descend magically through her ceiling and crouch on the floor in front of her. She screams in fright at first, gibbering incoherently, pointing to the strange fragments of grey material clinging to his clothes, releasing slow trails of acrid fumes. *What's happening?! Holy Mother Of God, have you been hurt?* Magda tries to embrace him, strokes his blood-stained forehead, but recoils at his smoking arms and chest. *What is that?!*

The skin of demons... Rrio hisses, *I've just unmasked the Devil. Here, spit on it.* He lifts his sleeve, and a little reluctantly Magda salivates over it and the substance slowly dissolves into smoke. *We need to go now...*

Now? Where to? My daughter, my grandchildren, my friends... I have work...

I have placed you in danger, Magda. You placed yourself in danger the day you asked to know the truth about me. If you don't leave now with me then they will come for you very soon and torture you to learn everything you know, then kill you to keep you silent. I'm sorry, but that's the truth.

A light pulse bursts up through the floor and crosses the room diagonally, exiting through the ceiling. Rrio grabs Magda and pulls her onto the floor beside him. *Stay down! They've got here quicker than I thought.* He runs to the other wall as another light burst penetrates from a different angle and he opens the attic window, peering down to the street below. The neighbourhood is closed off and regiments of wolves are storming the building, climbing the stairs, taking aim from vantage points with x-ray sights.

When I say jump... Rrio shouts to Magda, as the floor and roof joists take more damage, wood splintering and catching fire, ... *then you have to follow me, I'll protect you.* He presses buttons at his wrist and an energy field encloses him, the room beyond wavering like an underwater scene. A moment later, the roof explodes and Rrio's Disk crashes straight through it. He lunges over to Magda and, half carrying her in his arms, climbs up onto the silver rim, joining his force to her natural field, melding it with his own.

As doors are broken open and soldiers rush in, light blasts bounce off Magda's back and she gasps, climbing into the cockpit beside him. *What have you done to me?* –she asks, wide-eyed, *-am I* *immortal now?*

Electromagnetism… Rrio mutters, *I'll explain later.* Epi barks in the seat behind them, in recognition of Magda, who laughs hysterically, before all their heads are thrown backwards as the Disk sets off at phenomenal speed, debris falling away behind it.

*

The blackened ruins of Volwys swirling by beneath them: briefly assume their old significance to Rrio, as his heart races and all the old familiarities peel away. Not just this life, but every life in ruins. As they race north towards the ice cap, the snow-wrapped city hits him as the mournful symbol it is: a travesty of mankind's dreams, a skeleton adorned with tinsel.

Where are we heading? Magda asks as the city below gives way to snow-bound wastes and endless pine forests.

To the glaciers, to the western ocean and the icebergs.

Why? Magda asks. *No man can survive in such places for long, not even you…*

True… Rrio affirms, *but it's a good place to lose our pursuers.* He indicates to the distant pulses on the instrumentation screen, and Magda looks back over her shoulder, unable to see anything.

How many? She asks.

Rrio checks the readings, while Epi yelps excitedly. *About twenty now, but maybe only ten once they see how far north we're travelling…*

You think you can shoot them all down?

If that's what it takes, then we have no other option. They won't give up easily. But I have a hundred years more flying time than any of them, that ought to count for something.

Why are they gradually gaining on us? Magda finally asks.

After a while, Rrio answers: *…more modern Disks perhaps, and less body weight on board. Even at our top speed, they will eventually catch up.*

Approaching the wall of the glacier, Rrio uses the swirling mist to conceal them and flies along a few fissures, changes course rapidly and erratically. Magda starts to feel seasick. *Like a child on a fairground ride, eh? Rrio jokes desperately, a cold fatalism beginning to eat into him.*

A white pair of ground what? –Magda shouts over the thrusters' roaring and Epi's whining.

Ahh never mind... Rrio mutters then points, smiling, over his shoulder into the mist: where two bright explosions blossom in yellow and pink flame, corroborated by traces on the display. *You see? Young pups, relying on their instruments too much, overestimating their own skill. Two down.*

Magda turns and strokes Epi, calming him down. *God watches over us, little one.*

I have a three-dimensional map of the glacier face, in case you're wondering. One I did earlier, as we used to say in the Time Before. A little hobby of mine. The Disk shakes as a piece of ice is sliced off by the Disk rim. *Ouch... I better concentrate. The glacier moves a little every month of course... a moving target.*

Beyond the northwest edge of the glacier, Rrio takes the Disk down to sea level and begins to weave in and out of the icebergs. *Just like I predicted, ten minus the two impacts, we're down to eight pursuers...* No sooner than these words have left Rrio's mouth, the whole Disk shudders and tilts from a weapon impact. *Damn! We need a change of plan, they're getting too close.*

Magda can see the pursuing Disks now, almost glimpse the grey fur of the wolf pilots inside. Blaster pulses flash by either side of them as Rrio waves and weaves. Blue and white cornices and precipices of ice are sliced and shaved, exploding and sliding off into the sea. *What are you doing?* Magda shouts, Rrio's face lit up by the complex display of lights and gridlines from the control displays.

I'm digitally mapping the bergs. We need a hiding place or cul-de-sac, something treacherous we can double-back to in a few minutes, to throw these guys. Now hold onto your seat...

To Magda's horror, Rrio takes the Disk straight down into and under the water, the terrifying landscape of grey waves; suddenly replaced by a silent blue-green miasma swirling about them. Blaster pulses dissipate into the foaming surface behind them.

I've never even seen the sea before today... Magda gasps into the strange new-found silence *...and now I'm under it.* Magda marvels then despairs. *Oh Rrio, how deep can we go, are we going to die?*

We're turning, don't worry, and rising again now, passing under a few bergs...

259

Are they following us?

No, I think we've thrown them a bit. They'll be trying to follow us from the surface though, with an energy scan.

Can they?

Rrio presses a button and four simultaneous energy blasts set off in different directions from the hull. *Only if they can distinguish between us and those charges... a little trick of mine. We'll be back on the surface again in a few minutes.*

Magda feels the pressure easing slightly on her temples, and takes Epi onto her lap, shuddering at the unlit depths beneath them.

Here we go, Rrio shouts, and they spin out of the water into blinding daylight and blue sky, *and now we need a bolt-hole.* Rrio analyses the digital map and zig-zags south until he sees a huge arch in an iceberg formation and takes the Disk under it. The ice walls seem to glow an uncanny blue, translucent, reflecting the light on the waves: an eerie, natural cathedral.

God, it's so beautiful, Rrio... Magda looks around, wide-eyed. *I never knew such wonders existed.* The Disk turns sideways into a crevasse and rotates to a halt, turning back to face sideways to the way it came in. Magda and Rrio look at each other.

Yes, I know what you're thinking... Rrio sighs, lying back at last. *A good place to die.*

Magda's eyes are wet with tears. *It's like a church, Rrio, Nature's church, not Man's.*

Yes, but it's a cold embrace, isn't it? A kiss that kills. But we're not dead yet. My longevity has taught me, if nothing else, the value of endurance and persistence, even over hope. Hope is overrated, Magda...

He places his hand on her cheek, strokes her hair and kisses her. *It's possible to live without it...* he whispers, *...indeed, it may even be essential to do so.*

What is it? -Magda sees something on the control display catching Rrio's eye.

They're coming. Only four now. I tried to mask our heat signature but they've traced our course to here and seen the cave entrance.

Are we trapped? Magda clutches Rrio's arm.

Yes... but we have one critical advantage... knowledge.

They watch the four wolf Disks advance down the cave on the control display, then as they pass the crevasse mouth Rrio powers their Disk up again and blasts the rear of the last two, ricocheting them into the first. As multiple explosions begin, Rrio rams forward into their sides then reverses out, as ice cornice collapses all around them. A major blast catches their left flank as they wheel back out, and Epi barks, electrical static raging over the rear of the Disk. *Field storm..!* Rrio shouts, then dips the Disk under the water again to extinguish it.

Right... he says, clearing the cave and turning towards another array of bergs and archways, when a major jolt hits them from below. All power cuts out for a moment then flicks on again intermittently. In front of them, four more Disks rise out of the sea in formation, firing energy blasts towards them. Rrio flicks switches frantically, as Epi races around in his seat, the hull shaking. The power resumes suddenly, then the Disk moves off at speed, but rotating erratically, sickeningly.

What's happening? Magda wails.

Our artificial gravity is failing, I'm going to have to take us down...

Why aren't they firing at us anymore? Magda shouts.

I think they want us alive... Rrio snarls as he takes the Disk down low below a cliff of ice and on towards a long shore of icy grey stones, waves breaking over it. *This might hurt a bit, at the very least... Magda...* he turns to face her, *I'm sorry I failed you...*

She looks at him with melancholy eyes, and tries to mouth *I love you,* before the final impact crunches and jolts them all into a blaze of light and confusion.

*

The wreckage is strewn for a quarter of a mile along the beach, the Disk split in half and burning. Rrio's left arm is broken, his ankle twisted, his clothes torn and skin badly burned. He finds Epi first, whining among the wreckage, irrevocably wounded. Tears in his eyes, his stroking hand moves from the dog's forehead to eyelids, closing them over, before he shoots him dead. His stomach lurching, fatalism falling slowly through him like a plummeting anchor, he gets up and limps across the rest of the debris until he finds Magda and falls at her side. She is still alive, but delirious from loss of blood, multiple fractures, internal injuries. She lifts her hand, blackened from flames, up towards his cheek, and Rrio sobs with emotion, his body shaking. *No, Magda, no... please... I'm so sorry... I failed you...*

She smiles weakly. *No... need... for regret... Rrio... Selter... Iyan... I always loved... the better man...*

The other Disks are landing, and the wolves stepping onto the beach to move towards them. The huge grey waves lash onto the rocks with all the hopeless fury of eternity, their sound reverberating through the ground beneath them. *Magda...*

Only tell me... one thing... she whispers, starting to drift away *...what was your... real name... the one you were... born... with?*

Rrio glances over his shoulder as the wolves close in, moving slowly, almost respectfully, or perhaps just warily.

My name... Rrio sighs, and his voice chokes with emotion: *was, is... Vittorrio Emmanuel Reinwald... son of Claudia and Franco, nephew of Leo Vestra: prophet of Gaia, philosopher of the woods...* And the sound of the waves cuts over him like the sighs and sobs of some greater entity, some larger story in which their lives might have made sense.

Such a lovely name, Victory... she sighs and her head falls back, her eyelids fluttering then coming to a halt.

No, no... Rrio weeps, as the waves move in again and again. An age seems to pass until he opens his eyes again and sees the wolf boots around him on the stony shore.

You needn't kill her... Rrio hears himself saying slowly, bitterly. *She's gone already.*

So we outsmarted you at last, old man. Their commander smiles down at him, grimly, baring his teeth. *Youth triumphs over age.*

And wolf over man... one of his cohorts sniggers, eyes still studying him carefully, weapons poised, wary of his next move.

Did you win? Rrio asks, indicating with his eyes to the sky behind them.

Don't fall for it... the commander continues, *he's still full of tricks.*

But what are they, sir? Those lights are coming this way pretty quickly... his sergeant shifts nervously.

I play a long game, my friends. My little presents... personalised to your DNA signatures, one each. Rrio frowns, *perhaps you should have stayed in your Disks.*

262

The wolves make a last-minute attempt to scatter, and Rrio covers his head with his one good arm, where he kneels on the ground. He opens his eyes a few moments later to see charred smoking carcasses strewn around him.

After a while, with difficulty, Rrio rises to his feet, and leaning on a piece of wreckage, kicks the commander's smoking head off with one clean swing, roaring his despair into the wind and waves. The sound returns to him a second later from the long implacable wall of ice above the stony shore.

*

In a stolen wolf Disk, high over the great northern glacier, without pursuers at last, Rrio pauses wearily to repair his broken arm with energy spheres and plays the missing segments of his own memgram on the cockpit display. He sees the buildings he has visited, the secret locations, one in particular, some kind of hidden lair. He recognises some of the faces addressing him, men that he and Obdissian interrogated, tortured and killed over the last year. Some of them address him as "My Lord" or call him their "Saviour". So he has been a double-agent, an agent-provocateur perhaps. He shivers, but he only wants the truth now, at any cost, everything else taken from him, every other flavour of life turned to dust in his mouth.

He rewinds the memgram and notes key locations, then programs a flight path into the Disk controls and sets out southwards again. Without hope, a living robot, cold and calm, he moves forward, too tired even for revenge.

Beneath and behind him somewhere on the beach, a long mournful trail of smoke still unwinds skywards from the pyre he built for Magda and Epi.

*

There is a street, a face, a blacksmith's furnace. Rrio scatters the other customers and kicks the heavy wooden door shut against the driving snow outside. The smith backs away from him and Rrio takes an iron from the fire and advances. *Take me to Selterlyan. I know his hiding place is behind this shop. Somewhere over your shoulder, in the wall behind you, a hidden door. Open it for me...* Rrio holds the hot iron below the smith's face. *Show me the way in, and I will spare your life.*

But, Master... the man stutters, *have you no memory of it yourself?*

Rrio's eyes widen, as if in an involuntary question, which the smith answers: *I am your sworn servant, my Lord,* he whispers. *Take my life now if you wish it, it is forfeit to your cause.*

Rrio's eyes fall, he lowers the branding iron. *What cause is that?* –he sighs, a huge tiredness falling through his body.

The one great cause, my Lord. The cause of Man, his love, his freedom. All shall fall before it until the day we see the shadowed face of She who is turned away from us. These are your words, your teachings, as I have learned by heart. My life is yours.

I don't want your life, Rrio shakes his head, downcast, embittered, *I don't even want my own anymore. Show me the way, unlock the door. I only want the truth.*

Very well, the smith turns and takes his keys from the wall. *Every man thinks he seeks the truth,* the smith says, *but few recognise it when they are shown it. Few can understand it, and of those even fewer can bear such knowledge, can contain it without their own destruction. But if any man could, it might be you, Sire. I only wonder at how you have managed to forget your own learning, how you have lost faith at this last moment.*

This last moment? Rrio repeats slowly, as the stones of the wall rotate on some ingenious mechanism and he follows the smith down a long winding passage.

The Dome is under attack. Haven't you heard the news? The people are amassing and laying siege to it. Your teachings have spread far and inspired many. The Dome is cracking. Tomorrow we will have victory and put the wolves and demons to the sword.

But doesn't Selterlyan teach that Gaia is all-powerful? –That the Wolves and the Cherubs might be life equal with us? -That Man is not lord over other creatures?

The smith turns and looks back at him, as he lights a flickering flame in the passageway. *You teach us that justice is all-powerful, equality is the law. All shall fall before Nature's law. Those who oppress will always be destroyed... You must go alone from now on, Sire. Down this last passage to the final door. I am only the gateman. I am not permitted to accompany you further.*

264

Rrio places his handprint on a glass scanner in the middle of the door and it instantly recognises him and slides open. He steps into a large silver steel-lined room, with a high ceiling and six tall windows to each side. There is something vaguely and disturbingly familiar about the room, like déjà vu, like the buried memory of a recurring childhood dream or nightmare.

The door slides and seals shut behind him, and he goes to each window and pulls aside its curtains. He presses each button to de-mist the glass but finds only a mirror. He lifts a heavy wooden chair and dashes it against each mirror, but finds only stone walls behind.

Who am I? He yells, turning back in rage towards the high blank end wall: and a computer projection flickers into action, displaying film of Rrio addressing bands of traitors and blasphemers, of preaching to crowds gathered in secret halls, his face concealed and hooded, but the voice unmistakable. *Sel-ter-lyan, Sel-ter-lyan…* the crowds chant, rejoicing, some abasing themselves, women fainting, people falling to their knees.

No! He sobs, *take it back!* The wall projection responds by rewinding deeper into the past: Rrio sees himself walking through maternity wards where young mothers are strapped down, some screaming hysterically before they are sedated. He jolts and shakes and stumbles backwards from the screen when the face of the angel from his visions appears at last: a girl pleading for his help, her white gown spattered with blood as the wolves hold her down. Her womb cut open, a wriggling wolf cub lifted out alive. The doctors leave the room and Rrio is left looking at the sea of blood on the metal floor, the girl's dead eyes staring along the pillow, her face contorted in its last agony.

The screen flickers again, streaming backwards to her wedding day, some peasant celebration where Rrio mingles in disguise, unknown among the guests. She is laughing and dancing, a magnet of glances.

The film fast-winds again. Black night and swirling snow. Mass graves, unmarked. White gowns, blood-stained. Bodies upon bodies, and feet stiff and blue and cold. Medical name-tags on wrists: identifications cut off as the Freight Disks deliver their grim cargo. Rrio holding various tags in his hand as the soldiers hurry past. Zooming in on his open palm we read a subject's name: *Sally Theresa Lyons,* blood and mud obscuring and blurring the letters: *Sal-- T-er--- Lyon-... Sal Ter Lyon... SelTerLyan... Selterlyan.*

No! Rrio roars and smashes himself against the screen, again and again, great splinters of glass and electronics falling to the floor, the images still playing in fractured parody of themselves. *No! No!* He batters his head against the wall and falls to his knees in tears.

Who am I? What have I done? ...Am I every man and every sin ever committed? Every virtue? Every folly?

Rrio throws himself against the steel door but it refuses to open this time. He breaks his bleeding nails against its impenetrable frame. He hears a sound behind him and turns to see a single silver apple slide through the wall and fall and bounce across the floor. The Cherubs are coming.

Half insane now, defenceless, will Rrio try to smash or bite the apple? Dash it against the wall or embrace and cradle it? Lie curled up on the floor around it as if to nurture a seed, as if from his spent body it might grow?

⁓

EPILOGUE

"…Of those that, eye to eye, shall look
On knowledge; under whose command
Is Earth and Earth's, and in their hand
Is Nature like an open book;

No longer half-akin to brute,
For all we thought and loved and did,
And hoped, and suffer'd, is but seed
Of what in them is flower and fruit…"
-Alfred, Lord Tennyson, *In Memoriam.*

How much time has gone by? Rrio slowly wakes up, like Ulysses tied to the mast: bound upright at the centre of a semi-transparent spinning sphere as it takes off. The Cherubs are moving around him, operating obscure dials and lights.

Beneath him, through the shimmering floor, he can see that Volwys has all but vanished now beneath the advancing glaciers. The Geo-Dome's broken shards glisten like egg fragments shattered by some vast eagle. The windblown snowdrifts encircle and enshrine it like the white feathers of a great wing, brought to earth.

Why won't you just let me die? I am tired now… Have I slept for a thousand years? Is this the end of the world?

Tiredness is memory… a Cherub intones, one of them drawing closer to address him, its unmasked face rippling with strange inflexions, emotions perhaps, an incomprehensible language. Its black eyes are like deep whirlpools, treacherous sinks. He wants to look away. He is afraid to drown. *Soon your memory will be gone, and you will be refreshed again.*

Volwys is disappearing below his feet, growing distant, the stars of infinite space coming into view overhead. *Where are you taking me? To your home world?*

The face ripples, the black eyes blink sideways. *This is our home world, your future.*

Who are you? Rrio pleads, sighing, exhausted, exasperated. *Why did you come here?*

We are you, the head nods. *We come back to remember ourselves.*

Who am I? What am I? What do you want with me? What will I become? Rrio notices he is no longer using his mouth, but throwing the thoughts outward with his mind, lifting his head up and down on his chest, as if in the throes of some spiritual death or transformation, like Christ on the cross.

You are us. Our father and our child. Future and past form a circle.

I don't understand. This loss of memory, Rrio sobs, *it feels as if it is coming over me now. Is this death? Does God exist? I'm sorry I killed one of you... please forgive me. I want Magda back...*

Another figure has come to join the Cherub, and now both little heads rotate and analyse him, blinking, listening attentively to his thoughts. He feels them psychically muttering to each other, comparing notes. They turn back towards him. *Everything alive once, lives always. Forgiveness and regret are chimeras born of your misunderstanding of the nature of time. We are all fragments of what you mean by God. We work to re-assemble Him.*

Or Her... the other Cherub corrects. *He exploded Herself backwards from the future, from the end of time. The rot and decay of each scattered fibre of His being...*

...is the process you call evolution, viewed backwards. The mechanism of that process is suffering.

But I have suffered enough! Rrio cries out. *Why must I go on?*

The pain rebuilds God. The flower must have an eye to see it. The flower becomes the eye. The petals close at nightfall. Even the universe must breathe in and out. And is every version of each vast cosmic day the same? Then time and free will would dissolve. Perhaps they must, but some questions even we, may never answer.

Rrio feels himself overcome at last by an enormously heavy and relieving slumber, unlike anything he has felt before, as the Cherubs' last words move through him like waves: *We left clues. In your mother language, the word time is emit, backwards, didn't you ever notice that?*

And the ship shudders loose of its bonds at last, pulling up into space, leaving the Earth to freeze over like a closing eyelid dusted with sparkling frost: embracing its exquisite rest.

APPENDIX:

I.

The anthropologist Johanna Holferns survived for three years after being wounded and taken prisoner by the wolf tribe of the western Glasendorf Forest. During this time, she learned much of their language and developed the basis of a kind of pidgin Wolfish by which the human voice box could attempt to emulate wolf sounds and achieve a limited mutual communication. Tragically, she and about five hundred of the tribe died in the Fermancrough massacre, only after which were her notes and manuscript discovered. In these, she writes movingly of how she had come to appreciate the complex art, music and folklore of the wolves, and even came to forgive them for the death of Szceczin and so many of her other scientific colleagues. Today, after the centuries of rapprochement that followed, Johanna Holferns has come to be equally revered as a visionary and inspirational figure in human and wolf culture.

II.

The Madrid Conference, as they became known: steadily grew in number to become a one-hundred-and-forty-four component group-brain which met and interfaced with increasing intensity over the next four decades. They evolved to become a de facto European government in the chaotic aftermath of the Oberon Event, able to channel thoughts and anxieties from throughout the entire population within a five hundred mile radius. With the cooperation of the army and police, this led to a massive reduction in premeditated crime, but also to some surprise discoveries: most notably the detectable presence of an equivalent and potentially hostile group-consciousness somewhere in space above them. Later conjecture pointed to this being the overheard "thoughts" of the alien civilisation who would make contact with the frozen northern cities and become known there as "Cherubs". File records from the time of this psychic eavesdropping, point to the uncomfortable possibility that the Oberon Event may not have been the foolhardy human accident it had at first appeared, but rather a precipitated act of external sabotage to disable human civilisation and tip the terrestrial climate towards a new ice age.

III.

Historians still debate the final score of the interaction of human and alien civilisation. The Earth was covertly mined for vast quantities of natural resources required by the colonists, but in return: the genetic splicing of human genes with other species, in particular wolves, resulted in a more hardy set of descendants who were subsequently better suited to survive the ensuing "Snowball Earth" scenario.

IV.

Reports have been promising of late, and we await with interest the possibility of the evolution of a truly intelligent species on Earth, able to combine the previous traits of curiosity and resourcefulness, without the usual fatal side-effects of aggression and greed.

V.

Of all the worlds we have visited and studied, it might be said that Earth and the life it nurtures, is both the most appalling and the most beautiful. One suspects that this paradox is not an ironic accident, but a revelatory axiom, from which much, perhaps everything, might one day be gleaned about the ultimate meaning of the universe.

~

Acknowledgements

"Twenty Twenty" was first published in *New Writing Scotland* 26.

"Dogbot™" was first published in *Theaker's Quarterly* 41.

"Theonae" was first published in *Midnight Street Magazine* 16.

"Narcissi" was first published in *The British Fantasy Society Journal*, October 2013.

"Postcards from the Future" was first serialized on the *Elsewhen Press Millifiction* blog, 2012.

"Black Sun" was first published in *Theaker's Quarterly* 44.

"Multiplicity" was first published in *Impossible Spaces* anthology (Hic Dragones, 2013).

"Quasar Rise" was first published in *Theaker's Quarterly* 43.

"Gravity Wave" was first published in *Catastrophia Anthology* (PS Publishing, 2010).

The first chapter of "Volwys" was first published in *Albedo One* 42, 2012.

Thanks to Nina Allan, Allen Ashley, Peter Buck, Trevor Denyer, Hannah Kate, Chris Kelso Adam Lowe, Rona MacDonald Sarah Newton, Liz Niven, Johnathon Penton, David Rix, Stephen Theaker, Brian Whittingham.

ABOUT THE AUTHOR

Douglas Thompson has been a director of The Scottish Writers' Centre since 2011. His short stories have appeared in a wide range of magazines and anthologies. He won the Grolsch/Herald Question of Style Award in 1989 and second prize in the Neil Gunn Writing Competition in 2007.

His first book, *Ultrameta*, was published by Eibonvale Press in August 2009, nominated for the Edge Hill Prize, and shortlisted for the BFS Best Newcomer Award, and since then he has published six subsequent novels:

Sylvow (Eibonvale Press, 2010)
Apoidea (The Exaggerated Press, 2011)
Mechagnosis (Dog Horn Publishing, 2012)
Entanglement (Elsewhen Press, 2012)
The Rhymer (Elsewhen Press, 2014)
The Brahan Seer (Acair Books, 2014)

Thus *Volwys* is his eighth published book, a sequel of sorts to *Sylvow*, being set 200 years into a future and linked by the character of Vittorio Reinwald.

douglasthompson.wordpress.com

ND - #0469 - 270225 - C0 - 229/152/22 - PB - 9781907133886 - Matt Lamination